To Mel,

Aether:

The Fleur de Vie

with love,

Emmy

Raleigh

Aether: The Fleur de Vie

by
Emmy Riley

Cover design by Emily Riley. Editing by Gareth Riley
Printed in the United Kingdom
First Edition 2023

For more information, contact the author at
theentropiclibrary@gmail.com
or via the *Aether* page on Facebook

'To Sam McKenzie who has been my comfort buddy since the beginning of this journey.'

About the Author

Since leaving school Emily has left mathematics and science to others while she focuses her efforts on creating magical characters and imagining wonderful worlds for them to exist in. She projects her own autistic traits into her invented worlds, ones that value aesthetic qualities, with its independent and intuitive characters. When the distant Southern Island with its inclusive, eclectic inhabitants is threatened by the dark force of the Nether, she brings together the sensitive and emotional Sam and his sky-pirate friend Frank to its rescue. Long may their story continue.

Emily lives in North Yorkshire under the watchful supervision of Larry and Sparkplug, her two cats.

Aether

The richness of the Southern Island is founded on four traditional elements: the warmth of fire, the strength of earth, the wisdom of water, and the freedom of air. Elements that combine to establish a force greater than the sum of its individual components.

But the potential for imbalance and fear remains. For as dark as night, as cold as an arctic storm, comes a dark, menacing power, bristling in deep aubergine colours. A formidable force seeking to fragment and decay everything that stands in its way, and to claim it as its own.

Two guardians: Gaia and Techna, are tasked with bringing harmony to the worlds of nature and technology, forging them together as one. Once admired and celebrated, the guardians have faded into folk lore; relegated to the pages of storybooks. Today, human-beings are oblivious of the competing energies affecting the world they live in. Neglected, the guardians have grown weary; they stand abandoned, caught between the gathering storm and its tranquil eye.

But Gaia and Techna are not alone. There is a fifth element: something celestial; something fantastic and utterly beautiful. An element that brings balance and regeneration to lost worlds, an energy greater than the other four elements combined. This is the story of that fifth element and its calming astral force. This is the story of the Aether.

Map of the Southern Island

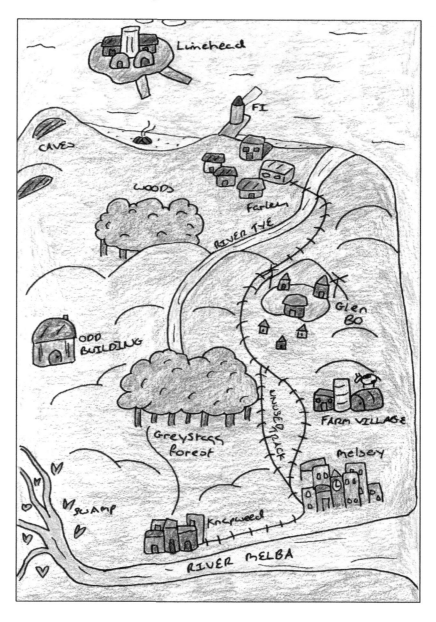

Chapters

An Airship in the Sky

W elcome to Melsey. A neat eclectic city that thrives on the distinctive architecture and cultural styles brought from other parts of the Southern Island. There is a cool autumnal morning light filtering over the buildings, transforming and animating the city. The sun rises slowly into the sky, shining brightly over the docks occupying both sides of the River Melba. A cormorant perched atop a floating buoy screeches loudly, disturbing another that twists in the air as it darts past. A long dark shape slips through the water; an otter twisting gently with the river current, its whiskered snout sniffs at the air.

In the heart of the city, streets fill with pedestrians and vehicles. People immersed in their daily routines march gently undulating streets and cobbled pavements. Tram carriages roll noisily up and down metal tracks; drivers ring their bells to greet the people they pass. Above, the sky is busy with frolicking birds: sparrows, finches and blackbirds, circling the large park at the centre of the city; keeping eager eyes open in search of grains or breadcrumbs or bugs.

Sandy Sanderson is a florist, diligently propping fresh flower bouquets into wooden casts laid out in stalls on the pavement outside his shop. He douses the plants with water, poured from a large pink plastic watering can. Elsewhere, on Carol Lane, Johnny and Mary are occupied, serving breakfast inside their cosy café and refilling their customers' large mugs with hot fresh tea or coffee. While on Hunters Road, sunlight streaming through a crack in the curtains falls on the face of Sam McKenzie, waking him. Sitting up groggily, he stretches. His right arm, his bionic arm, squeaks in protest from its hinge. Swinging his legs over the side of the bed, he trudges into the bathroom to start his morning routine. He stares intently into the mirror, at the deep scar running vertically through where his left eye had once been.

He touches the scar with his left hand. A constant reminder of that humid, rainy, fateful day. The day a strange fortune-teller had revealed her prophecy to Sam; one that would direct him to contain a violent blast inside a building. Now his life seems defined by that single, crazy moment when he valiantly held the doors shut to contain the blast from a terrifying gas explosion. His courageous actions had cost him his right arm and left eye. Melsey declared him a hero, an acclamation that continues to feel unnatural to him. He sees his actions that day as part of a greater destiny. A consequence of the mounting curiosity that had first driven him into the tarot shop to speak to its mysterious owner. Their conversation had determined his fate.

Following a revitalising shower, Sam dresses and steps out onto the balcony outside his bedroom. Leaning against the rail, he studies the pale streaks of translucent clouds trailing beneath a deep cerulean sky. The cold tingles his scar.

Something is missing.

Ah, of course!

Returning to his bedroom, Sam collects the long red and yellow striped scarf lying on his bed and carefully wraps it around his head, arranging the scarf so it covers the left side of his face. Heading downstairs, he passes the stillness of the living room and heads for the door into the kitchen and catches the lingering, earthy smell of brewed coffee. He finds two mugs, each coated with lines of thick viscous brown residue, discarded in the sink. They have been left by Johnny and Mary, part of a hasty breakfast before they left for work.

While rinsing the mugs, Sam is distracted by loud yapping, emanating from inside the living room. The sound gets louder. Turning around, he sees a small fluffy, black and white puppy, Bonnie, half-skipping, half-sliding towards him. It is time for her breakfast biscuits. Bonnie offers encouragement by pushing her red food bowl with her nose, sliding it across the floor, aiming for Sam's feet. Leaning down, he pats Bonnie gently on her head. He then fills the bowl with biscuits, before preparing his own breakfast: rolled-oats and a small mottle orange gala apple.

Preparing for his morning stroll, Sam places a harness around Bonnie and then takes his tattered, paint-stained sketchbook and stuffs it inside an old leather shoulder bag. Then leash in hand, he chases after Bonnie, out of the house and into Hunter's Road. From Hunter's Road they follow the main thoroughfare into the centre of the city. The street is busy: filled with commuter traffic creeping slowly forward; and pavements packed with people rushing to work, although some may have other purposes in mind. Few have time for casual conversations, or even a moment to exchange morning greetings.

A tram trundles past Sam and Bonnie, the driver urgently ringing the bell. Sam and Bonnie cross the road and turn from the main road into Cedar Avenue. Five minutes later and they are approaching a familiar building. This had once been the tarot shop. The one where Sam had met the mysterious stranger and discovered his fate. It now sits empty, its windows darkened and covered with old posters; their once vibrant colours faded with age, their edges frayed from the wind and rain. There was a time when the shop had been filled with brightly coloured dreamcatchers, when the door would swing back and forth in the breeze, repeatedly banging loudly against its frame. Now it is bordered shut. Sam stops outside the shop and is greeted by a sharp chill, colder than the morning breeze, that slides down his spine. Bonnie tugs against the leash, directing Sam to continue onto the park.

Ten minutes later and Sam strides through the giant wrought iron gates marking the entrance, stopping briefly to release Bonnie from the leash. Despite her newfound freedom, she stays reassuringly close to Sam. In contrast to the frantic bustle of the streets, it is peaceful inside the park. There are only a few people here: some sit relaxing on wooden benches; others stroll across the lush green lawns lazily kicking at the scattered fallen leaves. Sam heads towards a vacant bench facing the fountain at the centre of the park and sits down. Reaching inside his jacket pocket, he pulls out a small brown paper bag containing sunflower seeds. Groups of small birds approach the handful of seeds he has scattered liberally over the ground. They scramble greedily at the tiny morsels. Sam watches the feeding birds for several minutes before retrieving his sketchbook from inside his bag. Then, with his tiny pencil in his hand, he begins sketching a lighthouse. He concentrates hard, drawing on his memory to fill in the detail: carefully illustrating signs of wear on the body of the tower standing before a rocky cliff; sketching energetic waves crashing against the rocks forming the base of the lighthouse. Finally, he adds a thin crescent moon, set high on the sheet of paper.

Sam stops and rubs his nose. Holding his sketchbook at arm's length, he meticulously studies his completed drawing. Deep in contemplation, he remains oblivious to the well-rounded figure approaching from the main gate. It is Sandy, the florist, taking his mid-morning exercise. A casual stroll from his shop into the park.

Greeting Sam with a smile, Sandy says. 'Good morning Sam. How's things?' He sits on the bench, next to Sam. 'It's a wonderful day, isn't it?'

Closing his sketchbook, Sam glances at his friend. 'And a good morning to you, Sandy. Yes, it's beautiful isn't it. Can you smell that lovely fragrance?' He smiles at the florist. 'Are you taking a break?'

'Yeah! But I also wanted to catch up with you, and Bonnie too, of course.' Sandy replies, petting Bonnie's head. He stares at Sam's right hand. 'I thought you'd be here. How's your arm?'

'It's not too bad. I'm slowly getting used to it.' Sam replies, 'I think I'll always be getting used to it.' He sighs and shakes his head. 'At least people are beginning to lose interest in what happened. They're finally losing interest in me.'

'You can't blame people for wanting to meet the hero of the gas explosion. What you did that day, it was very courageous. Yet you don't want people knowing what you did?'

'Being in the spotlight just isn't for me Sandy. People are too pushy.' Sam groans. 'I prefer it when I'm left on my own.'

'Be patient, my friend. They'll soon tire of your story and move onto the next one.' Sandy pats Sam on the shoulder. 'But as a friend, let me tell you this. You should be proud of your selfless actions and the sacrifices you made for the sake of others.'

They gaze silently at the fountain: watching birds prune their wings and fluff their feathers in the water bath; listening to the water gently tumbling into the pond.

Sandy shuffles uncomfortably in his seat, pressing his hands against his knees. 'Do you ever get a feeling Sam, that no matter how wonderful and diverse Melsey appears, something might come and turn everything on its head.'

'Hm?' Sam frowns. 'What do you mean?'

'Oh, I don't know. Sometimes I get apprehensive and sense there's something terrible waiting out there; something that will shake up the good things here.' Sandy sighs sadly. 'It's like we can never see what lies in the corner of our eyes?'

Sam opens his mouth, but closes it again without speaking.

Sandy continues. 'Ah, listen to me blabbering. Perhaps it's just me overthinking things. After all, Melsey is thriving, isn't it? We're living in harmony. What can possibly come and spoil life here?' He checks his watch. 'I'd better get back to my shop. My customers will think I'm slacking.' Standing, he takes Sam's hand. 'Hey, why don't we meet up later for a drink?'

'Sure Sandy, I'm performing tonight.'

'Excellent! Then I'll see you later in *The Root*.'

Sam waves as his friend passes out through the park gates. 'It's certainly calm here, isn't it, Bon? Very peaceful. Though it makes you wonder what discord is worrying Sandy.'

Bonnie cocks her head and looks up at Sam. She offers him a concerned bark.

'But there's no time to think about that now. Let's get back home. I need to tune Angie ready for this evening.'

Sliding his sketchbook into the saddlebag, Sam strolls out of the park with Bonnie trotting close behind. The streets are even busier now and the bustling crowd forces Sam and Bonnie to stick close together as people bump and shove into them. Some carry with them a most unpleasant odour. *Yuk!* Sam pushes on, pausing when he finds space to breathe.

The world above him darkens, as if heavy clouds have suddenly rolled across and shielded the brilliant sunshine. Looking around, Sam is met by a cold breath of wind accompanied by a low, rumbling groan. Vehicles are brought to a halt and people on the pavement stand, gawping.

Is it thunder? A storm?

Staring up into the sky, Sam sees that the cause of the agitation is nothing natural. It is a flying ship cruising above the buildings, a huge contraption comprised of wood and metal. Its boat-shaped body has large mechanical wings fixed to both sides, while above the main deck sits a large, tan-coloured airbag, supported with fastened rope-locks. At the bow he spies a figurehead carved in the shape of a ram's head, complete with massive horns. The airship is being pushed forward by a large metal propeller rotating slowly at the rear of the craft. *What an imposing vehicle!*

Sam gasps. There is no-one captaining the craft. No-one is standing at the helm!

Watching on intently, Sam begins following the airship as it continues over the city landscape. Mesmerised he pushes on, ignoring the road in front of him. His foot slips into a large crack in the pavement, throwing him off balance. As he stumbles into the road he is met by a heavy gust of wind, which catches his red and yellow scarf and pulls it from around his face and up into the air. Sam chases after it, with Bonnie following close, skipping around bystanders, desperately reaching for his floating scarf.

A hand reaches out and grabs it. 'Gotcha!'

The hand belongs to a scruffy looking person wearing a distinctive wide-brimmed brown hat. Perhaps a traveller; certainly not someone local to Melsey. With a twist of the head, a long, untidy, reddish-coloured ponytail bounces across their shoulders. The man staggers towards Sam, limping. *Tap-Tap-Tap.* He is taller than Sam, and lanky, but Sam is immediately influenced by the broad welcoming smile, surrounded by rough stubble. It is a smile suggesting an easy attitude.

'Here you go.' The man says, handing the scarf to Sam.

Sam grabs his scarf and holds it against the left side of his face. 'Thank you.'

The traveller laughs and ruffles Sam's hair. 'You're cute.'

Sam blushes as his mouth gapes open in a failed attempt to respond.

The shadow of the floating airship looms over them, causing the traveller to stagger after it. Shaking a fist skywards, he hollers. 'Hey, wait up! I haven't got my land legs yet!' Then turning to Sam, he offers a friendly wave. 'Bye, for now!'

'Hey! Wait, I...' But Sam can only stand and watch as the stranger disappears into a crowd of people. As the sound of the airship gradually fades, the people on the street return to their daily routines. Sam wraps his scarf back around his head, tighter this time. Standing loyally by his feet, Bonnie cocks her head, as if asking: *who was that stranger?*

'Me too, Bon. I wonder where he came from.' Sam shrugs his shoulders. 'At least I've got my scarf back, thanks to him, huh?'

*

As the evening greets Melsey, the skies clear again. Shops close as pubs and restaurants open. Streetlights glare through a deepening dusk over Hollandaise Street, where pride of place shines the bright green argon lights blazing *The Root's* famous logo. The red-bricked walls are decorated with posters displaying the many artists who have performed here, punctuated with advertising posters displaying various everyday beauty products. The music venue is buried deep under the streets. Music reverberates up the spiralling cellar staircase threading down into the heart of the club. Inside consists of two separate lounges. The larger one contains several small round tables and stools arranged randomly on a stone-tiled floor. The cellar walls are covered in hand-written graffiti and framed photographs of musicians and bands. Both lounges contains a bar, serving drinks to music-loving patrons. A wisp of disinfectant lingers in the air.

Sam, with *Angie* his beloved electric-acoustic guitar hanging off one shoulder, stands on the small stage, accompanied by a half-filled glass of water balancing on a metal stand. As he finishes his performance the small, intimate crowd applaud enthusiastically.

Sam offers a low bow in gratitude. 'Thank you! I hope you all have a good evening.'

Unplugging his guitar, he heads for the adjacent lounge where a black, portly singer performs raspy vocal jazz, complemented by intermittent blows on his trumpet. Tonight is open mic night. Offering a supporting smile and a friendly wave to the artist, Sam returns to the main lounge. His friend Mandy is sitting at a table with a couple of her friends; several drinks lined up before them. Mocktails: a virgin piña colada, a soda float with a vanilla ice-cream scoop, and a non-alcoholic cranberry-apple cider. They appear preoccupied, talking and playing with their mobile phones.

Mandy sees Sam and waves, before resuming her conversation. 'Hey! Kelly! Fran! Did you hear about the strange ship in the sky?'

'You mean the dingy-looking pirate ship stuck under a big scruffy looking balloon, yeah!' Kelly replies. 'Did it have one of those old rustic steering wheels?'

'I don't know, I missed it.' Mandy sighs. 'I wish I hadn't though. I bet it looked cool!'

'Oh please Mandy, don't be so silly!'

'She's right,' Fran adds, slurping her soda float, 'you don't see real flying pirate ships in Melsey, do you?'

Mandy nods. 'Yeah, I guess you're right. It must have been some marketing gimmick.'

Sam continues to the bar where Sandy is sitting, sipping whiskey from a glass. The amber coloured liquid splashes against two large ice-cubes.

The bartender acknowledges Sam as he sits down. 'Want your usual tonight Sam?' He asks, wiping a glass tankard squeaky clean.

'Sure Ted.'

'One black forest milkshake with extra vanilla comin' right up!'

As Ted prepares Sam's drink, bringing a tall glass to the blender, Sam finds himself captivated by Mandy and her friends' conversation. He plays absentmindedly with a loose strand of his scarf.

'It seemed real,' he mutters to himself, 'and the traveller with the bad limp, I wonder if he has anything to do with the pirate-ship Mandy and her friends are blabbering about?'

Ted finishes the milkshake by dropping a black cherry on top of a thick layer of cream. He slides it across the bar towards Sam.

'Thanks, Ted.'

'No problem Sam, and it's on the house. It was a great gig tonight.'

They are interrupted by a customer standing at the other end of the bar. 'Hey Ted! Can you get us s'more drinks 'ere, please?'

'On my way!'

Sam sucks hard at the straw in his drink, an action met with sharp, stabbing pain: *ice-cold*. Pinching the bridge of his nose, he slowly recovers. He distracts himself by peeling the skin of the black cherry, and then eating the sweet flesh, taking care to avoid the hard stone inside. A deep, merry blast of a trumpet begins pouring from the adjoining lounge, causing Sam to start snapping his fingers with its melancholic melody.

'Louis can sure slay it.'

Oblivious to the music, Sandy sits, studying Sam's arm. 'Hey Sam,' he says, running his hand along the metal surface, 'I've this nagging question.'

'Yeah?'

'Your arm, I know it's synthetic, but it feels really warm and alive; as if there's a life force inside.'

Sam pulls his arm away, feeling only the sharp cold of its surface.

Embarrassed, Sandy chugs at his whiskey. 'Ah, don't mind me, with my strange cryptic musings. I better finish this and head home. I've another busy day tomorrow.'

'Good night, Sandy.'

Louis the jazz singer finishes singing and is met with a ripple of warm applause. His gruff, smokie voice rasps. 'You've been a wonderful audience. Thank you and goodnight!'

*

Leaving *The Root*, Sam rubs his tired eye and begins the walk home. From Hollandaise Street, he crosses the small channel running between the road and the main body of the pavement, softly humming a tune to himself. And it is truly a wonderful sensation, this solitude, having the pleasure of one's own company. It has been a while since he has felt this comfortable. The past few days he has not been accosted by reporters: the members of the intrusive media who have made the past couple of months unbearable. Perhaps, finally, they have lost interest in him.

Arriving at the doorstep outside his home, Sam lets himself in. Bonnie is waiting inside the hallway. Johnny and Mary are sitting in the living room listening to the radio. Pushing open the kitchen door, he takes a deep breath, filling his nostrils with the welcoming smell of supper: fresh pasta with marinara sauce and shredded cheese.

Just what he needs.

Lily, Sam's mother, had been close friends with Johnny and Mary. She trusted their love and generosity to meet any favour asked. Growing up, Johnny had been there to help her with the garden, or taste the products of her new baking recipes. She went to Mary with homework problems, and later, to learn how to drive. When Lily left Melsey, Johnny and Mary remained close in her heart, so when she became ill, it had made perfect sense to turn to her beloved friends to take care of Sam. And they did, without question; flattered when he still, occasionally, refers to them as his Gramps and his Nana.

Later that evening, feeling full and content, and wearing pink and purple nightclothes, Sam places Bonnie into her wicker basket and gently wraps her in her blanket. The pup wiggles her paws, wearing a sheepish doggie grin. Task complete, he walks out onto his bedroom balcony carrying a telescope. From the kitchen below comes the comforting sounds of clinking cups and plates. Johnny is finishing the washing up, accompanied by his deep baritone voice singing a familiar song. Gazing up at the moon, resting high in the sky, Sam attempts to count the brighter stars filling the sky. An impossible task.

Setting up the telescope, he is distracted by a gust of wind carrying a cloud of white and red flower petals, which twist and twirl past the balcony. Brushing away the petals sticking to his cheek, one slides across his nostrils, causing him to sneeze.

There is a knock on his bedroom door and Mary enters carrying a tray containing two glasses with white liquid slushing inside. 'I've brought you some oat-milk to help you sleep.'

'Thanks Nana.'

Carefully placing the glasses on the bedside table, Mary joins Sam on the balcony. The wind catches her hair. 'It's an incredibly beautiful night, isn't it Sam?'

'Yeah. The city looks wonderful. Sometimes, after night falls, I'll watch the pulsating night lights cast the buildings into silhouettes. And I love the cool breeze, blowing in from the countryside. It feels so calming. Sometimes I think it's drawing me away from here.'

Mary watches the breeze carrying more flower petals and scatter them over the balcony. 'I know Sam,' she sighs tiredly, 'it's a pity Johnny and I haven't been able to get out of the city and into the countryside. We're working all hours in the café and training novice baristas,' placing a comforting arm around Sam's waist, she adds, 'but it would be nice to go and walk in the fresh meadows and watch the river flowing through the mountain valley. Maybe we should think about taking a holiday and go and stay in one of the pretty little rural villages, like Farley.' She smiles. 'Yep! I know you'd like to do that too. It's such a big world and there are so many wonderful things to experience,' chuckling, she shakes her head, 'perhaps you should think about going on some great adventure?'

Sam puts his telescope down and scratches his head. 'Nana?' He pauses. 'Do you think there's something out there that might spoil things?'

Mary starts, pulling her arm away so she can stand in front of Sam. 'Why would you ask that, honey?'

'Oh nothing really. It's just something Sandy said in the park today.'

'Sandy is quirky, isn't he, heh? To be honest, me and Johnny don't usually get his silly little jests!' Mary suppresses a laugh. 'But regarding your question, I cannot say, not for sure. I wish I could. Melsey is a busy place and there's all sorts here. Most are good, but some, I guess, have their troubles. Some things we can't understand, some call it fate. But if there are things we have no control over, then I say: *don't worry about them.*' She gently strokes Sam's cheek. 'It's probably just Sandy blabbering, like he does.'

'I guess you're right.'

'Things never turn out as bad as some people fear.' Mary smiles. 'Now, let's swig down our oat-milk.'

Sam follows Mary into his bedroom where they drink their oat milk together, sitting on the edge of his bed. Wiping a thick white line marking his upper lip, he stretches his arms and yawns, before burying himself into his lavender scented bed.

'Night Nana.'

'Goodnight Sam.' Mary presses her lips onto Sam's brow. 'Goodnight Bonnie.' She says to the pup, who yaps in reply. Picking up the two empty glasses, she leaves Sam's bedroom, closing the door behind her.

Alone, Sam drifts into another world. It is a mystical place where the green countryside stretches away beneath blue skies and white clouds. He sees himself walking, his feet crunching on thick grass deep inside a mountain valley as a soft breeze carries dancing flower petals. He listens to the sound of bubbling water, a river running through the valley. Drawing closer, he spots three figures standing before him: the taller one is wearing a large brim hat, similar to the one worn by the mysterious traveller he had met earlier; another figure is dressed in a long poncho and has mid-length hair; the final figure appears shorter than the others and is carrying a quiver filled with arrows, flung over their shoulder.

The strangers in his dream gesture Sam, calling out to him. Two large bird-like shapes soar high across the sky, producing transparent white trails that paint circles above his head. As Sam approaches, the figures slowly fade away. Disappointed, he turns his head and catches a glimpse of a shadowy shape, an image of someone looming out from a cloud of white smoke. This figure appears to be moving in slow motion, with what looks like a giant fishbowl under one arm. The other arm is waving at Sam.

Another gust of wind carries flower petals that dance around Sam, catching him within a mini whirlwind. A voice enters his head; a voice he has heard before.

It whispers. 'Trust your senses Sam. Trust in its power.'

Its power, what power?

Sam wakes and bolts up in his bed, his cheeks clammy with sweat. The bedside clock reads: 2:02. Bonnie is still asleep in her basket, snoring softly. The gentle grumbling sound is soothing.

'What was all that about?' Sam asks himself, slipping down onto his pillow. 'What was that place? And those strange figures, the two strange birds; and who was it, carrying the giant fishbowl?'

A thought clarifies within his confused state. Perhaps his desire to see the world beyond Melsey has spilled over into his dream? And in that instant Sam realises he wants to see it all: the mountain valley, the river, the lush green meadows, everything.

He will go on a great adventure.

The Journey

Sam spends the next few days battling with the overwhelming consequences of the ideas swirling around inside his head. Does he follow through with his dramatic decision to leave the familiarity and comforts of Melsey; to go and explore the world beyond the city boundaries?

Eventually, and after much soul searching, he makes his decision.

One week after experiencing his strange dream, Sam is sitting in the backseat of Johnny and Mary's car, staring out of the window at the buildings and people scrolling past. People occupied in their usual morning routines, heading for work or partaking in daily recreation. He sighs. At least there are no troublesome reporters here to witness him leaving.

Johnny chuckles. 'You must be serious Sam, to be up and about so early,' he pauses to safely navigate the car into the adjacent lane of traffic before continuing, 'and all because you've got some crazy idea of seeing the countryside. Ah, kiddo! I don't think I'll ever get to understand what goes on inside your head.'

Sitting in the passenger seat, Mary turns to face Sam, a twinkle in her eye. 'You are sure you want to do this Sam? You know Bonnie's going to miss you.'

'I know she will,' Sam groans, 'she'll miss me badly.' He dare not admit it aloud, but it was he who suffered the most seeing the sad, expectant gaze on his pup's face as they made their farewells. 'But as you told me Nana, the world is vast and full of things to see; and it wouldn't be fair to drag Bonnie away from the comfort of her home.'

'Ah Sam, you remind me so much of Noah, and on what a good person he was. He too yearned for adventure,' she smiles, fondly, 'always wanting to seek out and explore the unknown. It was that incurable curiosity that made him to travel into space, just so he could look down and see everything below.'

Sam gazes silently through the car window, noting how less dense the city is here: the buildings are smaller and more spread out. The truth is he knows little about Noah, his father, apart from the stories his mother repeated fondly to him. She loved him as much as she loved her dear Sam. Yet his father remains a stranger to him. A man called Noah; an astronaut lost during a dangerous mission in space. Listening to Mary, Sam reflects on the shadowy image in his dream: the figure stepping through the strange white billowing cloud. *Had that been Noah?*

Travelling towards the city boundary they traverse progressively fewer and fewer intersections, until they finally reach the open road. They drive past a large billboard bearing the legend: "*Thank you for visiting Melsey. We hope to see you again*". At last, they are out of the city and in the countryside. Unwinding the car-window, Sam stares across the flat terrain stretching out towards the horizon. A fresh breeze blows against his face. In the distance he spots the tiny peaks of remote mountains, whilst the city trails further and further behind.

Johnny turns from the main highway and onto a quieter, meandering road. Within minutes they are lost amongst the surrounding fields and meadows. Pulling the car into a layby, Johnny brings the vehicle to a halt. Out through the car window Sam spots a pair of rooks perched on top of another billboard. The birds peer down at him with mild curiosity. One-by-one they climb out from the car, catching the cool westerly breeze sweeping over the adjacent fields.

'Well here we are, beyond the city limits.' Johnny declares, sniffing at the sweet air. He begins coughing, verging on spluttering. 'You can't beat this fresh air.' He wheezes.

The city landscape, with its eclectic collection of buildings of assorted styles and sizes, now appears as a row of simple two-dimensional blocks against the horizon. But Sam is more interested in what lies before him. He gazes out across the open green spaces, feeling the countryside beckoning him.

'Yeah!' He says, stepping forward. 'I can't wait to see what lies ahead: the mountains, the forests, the rivers... and yes, perhaps I shall find my way to Farley.' He stops short and turns coyly, facing Johnny and Mary, who are standing, waiting. Tears pool in their eyes. 'Nana, Gramps. I can't tell you how grateful I am: for looking after me, for taking me in and encouraging me.'

'Now don't you worry about that, Sammy. Perhaps you're right, this is the time for you to go and discover who you are.' Mary says softly, taking Sam's right hand in hers. 'Just you promise that you will stay safe and call us regularly. We want to know everything about your amazing adventures.'

'Mary's right.' Johnny adds, proudly punching Sam on the arm. 'We'll be just dandy, keeping busy dealing with demanding customers wanting their morning coffee.' He pulls Sam into a tight embrace. 'Remember what we say here in Melsey,' he whispers, 'the light that is shrouded, shines the brightest.'

Sam nods, confused. 'Right?'

Mary steps forward and they share a group hug. They feel their arms tighten, knowing that pulling away means an end, a final separation, for now.

Sam loosens his grip and steps away. Above his head, the rooks perched on the billboard scatter to the heavens. 'I love you both, and thank you again.' He takes another step, adding. 'I'll return, I promise. Give my regards to everyone in Melsey,' he brushes a tear away from his cheek, 'and give Bon a hug for me.'

'Of course we will.' Johnny and Mary chorus. 'Take care, Sam!'

'I will!'

Sam stands at the edge of the road, watchful of a car driving towards the city. There is another car, travelling in the opposite direction, its exhaust kicks out a trail of nostril-irritant fumes. He waits patiently as Johnny and Mary climb inside their car. Johnny turns the car around and heads, at a leisurely pace, back towards the city. Left alone in the layby, Sam waves after them one final time.

'Take care.' He whispers, as the car gradually disappears.

*

Step by step, starting slow and deliberate at first, but getting progressively quicker and quicker, Sam strides across an adjacent field, following a thin line of compressed grass where others have tread before him. One field leads to another and then another. The world appears to be opening up before him and he can barely contain his excitement. Walking alone in the countryside is not something he has done for a while, not since he moved to Melsey.

The previous evening, whilst safely tucked in his bed, Sam had copied out a map and plotted his route: a trail leading north. Standing in the middle of an open field, he studies the landscape, comparing it to the carefully drawn lines on his precious map. First he needs to find a disused railway track that will lead him deeper into the countryside. And there it is, marking the boundary of the field. Sliding down a small embankment, he finds himself standing next to the lost and forgotten route. He inspects the rusting iron rails, consumed by grass and clusters of wildflowers; the worn out, broken wooden sleepers and small stone ballast that are gradually being reabsorbed by the surrounding soil. Nature is reclaiming the land. It must have been many, many years since a train has rolled along these tracks.

Studying his map, tracing the track's route stretching northwards towards the distant snow-tipped mountains, he begins walking, following the neglected path. After a couple of hours he stops and turns to look behind him. Melsey has shrunken to an indistinct form, slipping beneath the edge of the world. For the first time Sam feels alone and he instinctively thinks about Bonnie, wishing that he might have found a way of bringing her with him. He is distracted by a gust of wind that plays with the loose strands of his scarf, causing them to dance about his head. Grabbing the ends of his scarf, he wraps them securely around his neck before continuing on his journey.

So long, Melsey.

After a few minutes, to raise his spirits, he begins singing, projecting the warm tones of his voice out over the landscape.

> *'It's just like the worlds we've heard and seen,*
> *With dragons and fairies,*
> *With gnomes in the woods, and creatures o' the sea.*
> *With my travel kit in my hand and my head held high*
> *I could find many things, from the meadows and across*
> *the sky!*
>
> *Where will this path ahead lead me to?*
> *Will it be waiting with open arms or evading eyes?*
> *I will not know until I get there.*
> *And when will I come back to the place I came from?*
> *I will not know until I'm there.'*

Sam makes steady progress through the day, content with passing by lush green meadows, following the worn dusty trail laid out by the railway track. Stretched across the northern horizon is his destination, but the distant mountains appear as far from him now as they did when he started. But despite this apparent lack of progress, he remains happy and continues humming and singing jovial tunes, at one with the world around him.

Finally, after several long miles, he decides to stop and rest. He has reached a small farming village alive with the sounds of braying animals and spluttering tractors. This rustic scene is graced with tired, worn-out buildings: some with draped greying thatched roofs; others topped with slanted slate stone tiles. Sam takes time to shout out greetings and wave at the villagers passing by.

'Ah, I wish I'd brought Angie along with me.' He mutters regretfully. 'I can think of nothing better to do than to sit here surrounded by all this nature and strum my guitar. No Bonnie. No Angie. It's a high price to pay to go on my adventure.'

Sitting atop a large boulder at the edge of an exhausted rock quarry, Sam rests his aching feet. Pulling open his bag, he takes out a sandwich and some apple slices from inside. Absentmindedly nibbling his food, he is transfixed by the everyday events happening around him: farmers busy at work, riding tractors and harvesting crops; in another field there is a shepherd with a pair of dogs, directing flocks of shaggy-coated sheep. Reflecting on his journey so far, he wonders if he might have found a faster mode of travel, a bicycle perhaps. Except, of course, he has never got around to learning how to ride one.

His late lunch eaten, Sam sets off, leaving the village and the farmers' fields behind him. This is really wonderful, he tells himself, having fallen in love with the sights and sounds of the countryside. Occasionally he stops and gazes skywards to pick out unfamiliar bird species: sparrow hawks, buzzards and red kites, hovering high above his head. Guesses made, he pushes on, his feet skipping through brightly coloured wildflowers dancing in the breeze.

Later, with the sun dipping dramatically towards the horizon and marking the onset of evening, Sam grows concerned about where he might find shelter, somewhere safe to sleep. The skies are darkening quickly, preparing to embrace the night. More worryingly still, there are dark clouds gathering from the horizon; thickening obstacles concealing the rising moon. He starts at a low rumbling sound, the warning signs of an approaching storm. With increasing urgency and fading light, he scrambles towards the edge of the field and the small group of trees beyond, desperate to find refuge.

The rain soon arrives, thundering down and soaking everything in its path, including Sam. Wrapping his scarf tighter across his face, he forces himself forward, frantic to find shelter and protection from the storm. He realises that he has not planned his journey very well at all, as this new, idyllic world quickly turns into a nightmare. He must find somewhere safe to sleep, somewhere out of the wind and rain. There are puddles, puddles everywhere, large threatening ones. Entering the small wood, he staggers between large trees, their branches dancing wildly in the wind. At least they offer some protection from the elements. The noise of the raging storm swirls about him, forcing him to clasp his hands against his ears to prevent the chilling force of the cold howling wind from banging against his eardrums.

A flash of lightning reveals the entrance to a small grotto, offering the potential for shelter. Sam hurries towards it, squeezing his sodden frame inside. Finally shielded from the rain, he stands shivering, gazing out into the dark and the ferocious storm. Why had he not accounted for this: the sense of cold isolation; his freezing body shaking inside his soaking clothes? His body feels numb, completely detached from his thoughts. All he can do now is wait.

Swaying inside the grotto, he hears a strange noise gathering over the natural sounds of the storm. Listening hard, he makes out a slow, rhythmic beat: the sound of a giant pair of wings. The deep reverberating sound gets closer and louder. *What could it be?* Sam trembles as his right arm tingles from the cold. And there it is, caught in another flash of lightning: a large dark shape looming out from the sky. Its long body glows with an electric azure that outlines the creature's frame against the night sky. It hovers above

Sam's eyeline and slowly turns to face him; a pair of glowing blue circles staring out through the dark.

Sam gasps and backs into the shadows, staring at the creature who remains perfectly still and is watching him intently. Minutes pass with each studying the other in a silent interaction. Finally, the strange creature offers a loud croak, before it turns and soars away into the night.

Clutching his jacket tightly, Sam gasps. 'What was that?'

He calls out, seeking help, but instead the world swirls about him. Worse still, his vision becomes blurry and the uncomfortable sensation in his arm gets stronger and stronger. Wobbling on his feet and feeling queasy, he collapses, sinking to the ground. Lying alone in the dark, drifting in and out of consciousness, he hears footsteps trampling over the wet grass. Footsteps that are getting closer and closer and closer…

*

Opening his eye, Sam wakes to find himself lying on a wooden bunk, wrapped tightly inside a heavy blanket. He is alone inside a homely, rustic-looking room; his nostrils fill with the scents of lavender and cedarwood. A single light shines from a small lamp swinging from the ceiling above his head. He realises that it is still raining outside, but the sound of the storm is muffled by thick sturdy insulating wooden walls. The bunk he is lying on is the size of a small double bed, complete with a brass frame, a red quilted blanket and thick white pillows. As he sits up, the blanket slides off his chest. Above a small wooden cabinet on the opposite wall there is a pair of drawn beige curtains, concealing a window and the roaring tempest outside. Sam thinks hard: is he inside a remote wooden cabin deep in the forest; or perhaps in a cabin aboard a ship ploughing through the ocean waves? *Where is he?*

'*Yip!*'

Distracted by a heavy thump, the sound of someone, or something, crashing against the door. Sam gapes nervously across the cabin. The door opens and he hears the sound of wood brushing against the floorboards as someone enters: *tap-tap-tap*. He is greeted a bright cheery voice.

'Hey! You're awake!'

Sam gazes at the familiar face peering down at him. It is the ponytailed person he had met in Melsey. The traveller who came to his rescue as the breeze threatened to steal his scarf.

'How're you feeling, buddy?'

'I'm…' Sam is overcome by a fast-approaching sneeze. 'I'm okay. It's just a sneeze. It must be from the cold and the rain.' He smiles. 'Wow! I didn't think I'd get the chance to see you again. Where am I? Did you bring me here?'

'Yeah, I sure did. When I found you I could see you were out on your feet and just about to pass out. So I landed and brought you inside, to get you warm and dry. I couldn't just leave you there, could I? Not in such heinous weather.' The ponytailed traveller reaches inside his deep baggy trouser pocket, and hands over a small crumbly pastry wrapped in brown paper. 'Here, have some of this. You must be hungry.'

Sam pulls the pastry in half and chews a piece. 'Thank you,' he mumbles, enjoying the soft, mild flavour, 'it tastes as good as one of Johnny's cakes.'

'I'm glad you like it. Now you need to rest and regain your strength. We've quite a journey ahead of us.' The traveller tousles Sam's curls and then heads for the door. Turning he smiles warmly. 'I'm Frank by the way.'

Alone again, Sam settles down on the bed and pulls the blanket over his body, right up to his chin. This cabin might be different to his own bedroom in Melsey, but it feels just as comforting. For now, he is grateful to be somewhere safe and out of the rain.

*

Several hours later and Sam wakes to the sounds of creaking wood. Sitting up on the bed, he leans against the wall, allowing the blanket to slide from his shoulders and drop onto the floor. *Is he still dreaming?* He feels weightless, vulnerable to the forces of nature. Sliding from the bed, he stands and heads for the door. Outside he is greeted by breezy clouds and bright sunshine that almost blinds him as he steps out onto a large spacious deck; with lines of wooden barrels secured by ropes on both sides of the craft. Squinting, he spots the shape of a sheep's head looking out over the bow. He leans over the side and gazes at the ground, at least a hundred feet below him as fields skip past beneath the cruising airship.

'Hey! Great morning we're having, eh?' Frank walks across the deck and stands beside Sam, resting his elbows against the railing. The wind tugs his ponytail. 'This breeze is really pushing us along.'

'Where are we?' Sam asks, unsure which of the many questions dancing about his head he wants to ask next. 'Is this your ship, Frank?'

'You saw it in Melsey, didn't you?' He says, patting Sam on his back. 'Well chum, welcome aboard the *Puppis*!'

Sam steps back in awe, wanting to take his time studying this amazing craft: from the deck he is standing on, to the large air-sac above his head. He listens with amazement to the mechanical whirl of the rear propeller, working in tandem with the rhythmic creak of the giant wings sweeping on either side. To gain a better viewpoint of the air-sac above, he steps towards the centre of the deck, spinning slowly in circles. Up close, it is a very imposing contraption indeed!

Frank chuckles. 'Hey, be careful you don't space out. I don't want anyone going overboard.'

'You man this ship alone?'

'Aye. The name's Captain Frank Joyce. I go behind the helm when it suits me, but it's a magical craft that can pilot itself. Well, sometimes,' he adds, ruefully, 'which is useful when you want to do your own thing. By the way, speaking of introductions, I didn't get your name.'

Sam coughs with embarrassment. 'Oh, it's Sam.'

They shake hands.

'Sam, huh! You're from the city, am I right? Which means you're a long way from home. What brings you out here?'

'Well, it's a strange story…' Sam's voice trails away.

Out of the corner of his eye he has spotted a large blunderbuss propped against the cabin door. Its dark highly polished wooden handle is scored with deep scratches, which combined with patches of decolourisation provide give-away signs of its age and frequent use. The shiny brass funnel is etched with thick grooves running along the inside.

Sam gasps, spotting something pink and lumpy hanging out of the funnel. 'Is that a blunderbuss?'

'That is indeed a blunderbuss, and my very own.' Frank smiles, grabbing the remarkable instrument and holding it out in both hands. 'Old Faithful, as I've lovingly dubbed her: robust, surprisingly good range, and brilliant for parties by shooting cake.'

'Wait. Did you just say it shoots cake?'

'Yep! Old Faithful makes an especially good cake mix and can fire it out in the blink of an eye. Just add ingredients and shake well. Observe.'

And to Sam's amazement, Frank stuffs flour, two eggs, a splash of milk, sugar, a bit of vanilla, and finally some lemon-curd into the funnel. Primed, the blunderbuss churns, its internal workings getting louder and louder.

Frank grins. 'One giant fondant fancy comin' right up!'

Pop!

'*AHH!*'

The blunderbuss shoots a blast of cake mix... straight into Sam's face.

Frank sits up from the floor where he has been dropped by the blunderbuss' recoil. 'Ah!' He winces. 'There's always room for improvement. Hey, are you okay Sam?'

Sam scoops a handful of the mix from his cheek and takes a mouthful. 'I agree, some improvement is definitely needed; but I do like lemon curd.'

'That's good.'

Removing the rest of the cake mix from around his face, Sam is drawn to Frank's wooden appendage. 'What happened to your leg?'

'Ah! That!' The sky-pirate replies thoughtfully. 'I lost my real leg after running into bandits on some distant, remote island.'

Reaching down with one hand, he begins rubbing the wooden peg where it connects to his knee. The sky-pirate winces, more from memory than the effects of any physical pain. He begins telling Sam his story, describing events on the island and how the bandits and their guns shocked the life out of him, severing his leg at the knee. With his cheeks paling in colour, he recalls how helplessly he had felt watching huge volumes of blood pour from his injured leg. The dramatic loss had caused him to pass out. Frank swiftly jumps to the story's conclusion, recounting how when he finally regained consciousness he had discovered that his damaged leg had been replaced with a wooden pegleg.

'It's a bit uncomfortable, and it's not as sturdy as it was when first fitted,' he sighs, 'but it does its job well enough. I'm fine walking around, despite the limp.' He pauses, thoughtfully. 'So that's my story on how I lost my limb; how about you telling me yours?'

'I lost my arm and eye in a huge explosion.' Sam stutters, gazing down at his feet. 'But would you mind if we keep my story for another time? It's a difficult tale to tell and I still get very emotional about what happened.' He looks sadly out towards the horizon. 'Where're we heading?'

'I'm heading home to Glen Bó, I haven't been back for a while.' Frank nods. 'When we get there, we'll make a stop to get our land legs back, yeah?'

'Sounds a great idea.' Sam staggers, grabbing the side of the craft as it shifts suddenly in the wind. 'And I don't know about land-legs,' he groans, 'it's my air-legs I've got problems with.'

Interlude - Hold the Door, Sam!

Several months after Sam had first moved to Melsey to live with Johnny and Mary, and long before departing on his great adventure, he sits on a wooden bench inside the park near the impressive stone fountain playing Angie, his guitar. Despite recent traumatic experiences that culminated with him leaving his home on the northern coast, he has settled into living in the city. It is a warm, humid day and he has to concentrate hard when applying his canary yellow pick, meticulously strumming through the chords of his favourite songs. A gentle breeze tickles his buttercream blonde hair, causing the ends to dance in the air. Reaching the end of a song, he gazes down at the legion of little finches hopping about his feet. Dipping his hand into a small paper bag, he tosses a handful of seeds across the neatly trimmed grass lawn. The birds peck eagerly at this welcome snack, while he resumes playing his guitar.

Sam has been playing for nearly an hour when he becomes aware of someone, a girl, watching him from the other side of the fountain. She is chatting with two friends, but Sam convinces himself that her attention is consistently switching towards him. Perhaps his music is distracting, or maybe she finds it appealing and pleasing to listen to. Her interest makes him more and more curious, until he is continually observing the girl from out of the corner of his eye. Looking towards Sam, she tugs at one of the plaits hanging over her shoulder. She then excuses herself from her friends and starts striding around the base of the fountain towards him. Her heavy tread sends the feeding finches high into the air in fright.

She yells. '*Yo! Hermit!*' Sam does not respond. 'Hey! I'm talking to you!'

As she approaches Sam stops playing and lifts his gaze, meeting her imposing glare with his gentle round brown eyes. 'Hm?'

'Finally! I've got your attention!' The girl grins, clearly pleased with her accomplishment. 'So! Hi!'

Sam replies, softly. 'Hello.'

Scowling she mutters. 'You sound different to what I expected: more high-pitched.'

'That's how I speak.'

There is an awkward pause.

The girl frowns. 'So what's that you're playing?'

'A guitar.'

'Yeah I get that, I'm not dumb. What *songs* are you playing?'

'I'm just practicing really,' Sam shrugs, 'jamming a few chords here and there; looking for something catchy to pop up.'

'*Right!* And you play with bands in *The Root*, don't you?'

Sam is surprised by the girl's question. *How does she know he plays there?* 'I do, but I prefer to perform alone. The regular bands tend to have packed schedules.'

'I suppose, *hermit*.'

'Um, I do have a name,' Sam stutters, wincing at the girl's second hermit reference, 'it's Sam, Sam McKenzie. And what about you, what's yours?'

The girl opens her mouth to reply, but is interrupted by her friends calling impatiently out to her. She bows her head and mutters quietly to herself. 'I have to get outta here. They're getting impatient with me talking to this oddball.' Glancing at Sam, she offers a friendly smile. 'Well it's been just dandy talking to you. Keep up that rhythm, Sammy-boy!'

'Wait!' Sam holds out a hand. 'You haven't told me...'

But the girl has already spun on her heels and is marching towards her friends, giving no indication of turning around and offering him a wave: *au revoir.*

'What a strange girl.' Sam mutters to himself, puckering his lips to form a sad pout.

Confrontation typically makes him feel uncomfortable, and despite his efforts to engage in conversation, this one has ended abruptly and awkwardly. It was her friends' fault, he reasons. They want her to leave, but the girl could have made a proper introduction. She could have told him her name.

No longer wanting to play, Sam puts Angie aside and sits in silence as the finches return one-by-one. Dipping his hand inside the paper bag, he throws the remaining seeds across the lawn and watches as more birds descend. Convinced his afternoon has been spoilt, he decides to leave the park. Beyond the park gates, he edges past people thronging the pavement. He needs his wits about him to avoid colliding into anyone. Pressing forward he pursues spaces in the crowd, gaps to make better headway, but the numbers are overwhelming. Eventually he decides to seek out quieter, sparser streets and turns into Cedar Avenue. With room to walk freely, Sam rubs his shoulder, feeling the weight of his guitar slipping across his back.

Sam reaches the far end of Cedar Avenue, a part of the city that is unfamiliar to him. Slowing his pace to an interested crawl, he becomes distracted by the sound of a door repeatedly swinging back and forth in the breeze and clattering against its frame. Crossing the road to investigate, he approaches the banging door. It is the access to a small, strangely decorated shop. Compelled to look inside, he pulls open the door and steps through. The interior is dark, and it takes several seconds for his eyes to grow accustomed to the dim light. The small shop is full of darkened shapes, streaked with vibrant purple fabrics. He hesitates to take a final look at the empty street behind him, before entering and allowing the door to slam shut behind him.

There is a small metal lamp sitting on a black robed counter; it is the only light inside. Sniffing at the air, Sam takes in the heavy incense and the rich scent of cedarwood tickles his nose. Above his head, colourful dream catchers hang from the ceiling, gently brushing the top of his head. In one corner sits a large poinsettia on an old wooden chair, its once glorious red and green foliage looks withered and yellow. Stepping further inside, he spots a small highly polished wooden table positioned towards the rear of the shop. It is draped with a vibrant dark-purple cloth with a large crystal ball sitting at its centre.

The place is quiet, perhaps too quiet. Sam shudders. It feels as if someone is inside watching him.

'Hello?' Looking around, he waits patiently for an answer, but there is nothing, just an eerie silence. He tries again. 'Hello?'

This time there is a reply. A voice emanating from out of the shadows. 'Good afternoon...'

The greeting is accompanied by a flash of rose-coloured light, which startles and momentarily blinds Sam. Instinctively he takes a step backwards, stumbling against the counter. As the bright light fades he sees there is now a woman sitting at the table. She is wearing a long dark-green robe with a lavender decorated headdress, pulled tightly over her thickly curled dark hair.

The woman's face looks wise and compassionate. '...and what a pleasant good afternoon it is too.'

'Is it?'

She beckons Sam to sit at the table. 'Come closer, my friend,' her voice is silky smooth and carries a heavy accent, 'you seem troubled. I can tell. Please sit. Perhaps I can ease what is troubling you.' She adds, smiling. 'I sense something strong inside you.'

Laying her hands over the crystal ball, she begins sliding them around the highly polished, mirror-like surface. Magically the lamp on the counter dims, casting the shop interior into near darkness. The only source of light radiates from inside the crystal ball, which fills the shop in swirling multicoloured patterns.

'How did you do that?' Sam asks, his voice trembling with anticipation. 'The lights?'

'Hush now!' The woman commands, staring deeply into the crystal ball. 'I'm sensing something coming through: I see you confronting a large dark cloud somewhere in the city.' Sam watches, transfixed, becoming more anxious as the expression on her face changes. She mutters, concerned. 'It's dense, the cloud. I cannot penetrate it, to see inside.' She pauses briefly, concentrating hard on the spiralling coloured-patterns inside the ball as they gradually darken and lose their distinct colours, merging into a deep, dark purple. She gasps. 'There is great devastation: a traumatic event driven by bright flashing colours.'

Sam shudders, glancing nervously towards the door, which is now securely shut. This is not what he expected. He would give anything to be safe outside; to have ignored the insistent curiosity that had pulled him inside. *Why had he come in here?*

The woman lifts her gaze from the crystal ball and the expression on her face relaxes. 'You can view what I've seen as a fanciful prediction,' she says, assuredly, 'or a future possible predicament?' She speaks in crisp, clear tones. 'But I stress that one day soon you will find yourself lost in this city. And know this too, you have a crucial task to perform: *you must hold the door fast, keep it sealed with all the strength you can muster.* To fail in this task will be catastrophic.' She smiles weakly; an effort to reassure him. 'I must leave now, Sam. I trust you to know what you must do when this moment arrives. But take this from me, when that moment comes, you shall discover the power you need inside you.'

'Power?' Sam starts. 'What power?'

'You will see. You will understand.' The woman pauses. 'One day I shall be able to explain more to you, but until then, trust in yourself.'

The room is filled with a bright rose-coloured light. Speechless, Sam stares in disbelief as the strange prophet is absorbed into the light. Jumping to his feet he crashes into the back wall. Clutching his chest, he feels his heart pounding inside. For a moment the world spirals out of control, but then, as the light recedes, it quietly resets into the dark, tranquil shop he had walked into. He stares at the dull and empty crystal ball as the small lamp on the counter bathes the interior in a warm light. The outside door slowly swings open, revealing the world beyond, before swinging shut and slamming against the door frame. *Bang!*

Grabbing Angie, Sam pushes open the door and escapes into the bright afternoon sunshine. 'What a rush!' He exclaims, crossing the road. Safely standing on the pavement opposite, he turns and gazes back at the strange shop. 'What just happened in there?'

For a minute or two he stands, staring across the empty road, his mind churning over everything the strange woman had said. And then it hits him. *Sam, she had called him Sam.*

Desperate to find company, he retraces his steps until he is again being jostled along a pavement on a busier street; comfortable with the security offered by the other people bustling past him. He decides to take a tram, one that follows a looping lazy route around the city until eventually, it brings him near to his new home. The home he shares with Johnny and Mary.

With the sun slipping slowly closer to the rooftops, Sam jumps from the tram and heads into a narrow street: one lined with tiny stoned-houses and small shops. He stops outside a brightly decorated display window, his attention grasped by a brilliant red and yellow striped scarf neatly coiled around other handcrafted items: carved wooden toys, pretty watercolours, and knitted hats and gloves. There is something special about this scarf. Unfortunately the shop is shut, closed for the day, and so he walks reluctantly away. He finally reaches the junction for Hunter's Road, the cobbled street where Johnny and Mary live in their small, detached red-brick house.

*

The following morning, Sam wakes to a murky day. Sliding out of bed he glances through a gap in the curtains and stares at the rolling grey clouds crowding the sky. They look heavy and filled with rain. Turning away, he commences his daily routine: shower, getting dressed, eating breakfast with Mary before she leaves for the café to join Johnny who is already hard at work.

But today Sam leaves before Mary, who kisses him fondly on the forehead as he heads out through the door. He has left Angie at home, preoccupied with the mysterious fortune-teller and with retracing his route home from the previous evening. Her words play continually through his head: *what did it all might mean; what if something traumatic does happen?* Distracted, he turns from the main thoroughfare and starts walking along a side street. After a few steps he realises that something is wrong. His nose is itching and there is a distinctive, lingering smell of gas. It has an acrid, heady smell. He continues, slowing his pace, walking towards a group of people gathering outside a large concrete building. Its entrance lies away from the street, through a large green double door. The smell of gas is even stronger here.

Sam asks. 'What's going on?'

He hears disturbing sounds emanating from inside the building: panicked voices, shouted warnings. The people outside are confused and frightened, unsure on what they can do. *'Help is coming!'* They cry, struggling to sound reassuring. *'Help will soon be here!'*

Sam spots a small gap between the green doors, large enough for someone to squeeze through. Instinctively he makes for the door. He hears someone cry. *'Come back! Don't go inside!'*

Gas pours through the gap, its pungent smell dominating his thoughts. He should run and escape the danger, just as others are doing. Sam hesitates, peering through the partially open green door.

The interior is filled with swirling orange-grey smoke, partly concealing a dull red-orange glow emanating from deeper inside the building. The dancing waves of red and yellow lights sweeping closer towards him are mesmerising. They appear bright and beautiful; and very frightening.

He slips through the gap between the green doors and steps inside. With the exit to the building behind him, he continues cautiously along a smoked filled corridor, heading towards distant, desperate voices. Their fragile calls ring in his ears: begging, crying, sounds too chaotic to decipher. He presses forward, the words of the fortune teller whispering resolutely inside his head: he must do something; he must keep the door shut. *But which door?* Reaching the far end of the corridor he discovers an entrance to a large room. Looking inside he can see intense lights and sounds, created with incredible energy. An energy that tries to force him away. *This door!*

Leaning hard against the door he manages to close it, but the pressure inside is too great and forces the door open again. With his back against the door, Sam, mustering all of his strength, uses the weight of his body to push it into its frame. Knowing that if he steps away or relaxes, even for a moment, the door will blow open; he stays and holds it fast. His valiant efforts appear to antagonise the interior. The noises inside rumble ever louder until they reach a dramatic, perpetual crescendo. The waves of lights gain intensity, becoming brighter and brighter and brighter...

Instinctively Sam draws his right arm across his face. The world, once solid and rigid now feels fluid and precarious. The weight of his body lightens as he is lifted and carried through the air and shaken like a rag doll caught in a strong wind. There is a loud relentless ringing in his ears and a sheering pain runs across his right arm and up into his left eye.

Exhausted, Sam watches as his world fades to darkness; mindful of a faint rose-coloured light glowing around his frame as it drops to the floor.

*

Sam wakes to the sound of voices: voices sounding much calmer than the ones that previously filled his head. There is music too, playing from a radio. Forcing his eyelid open, light filters through his senses: a bright white light. He is lying in a strange, narrow bed; the sterile antiseptic smell suggests he is in hospital. The sound of people bustling around him feels comforting. He waits patiently for his vision to sharpen. The blurred image gradually forms the detail of a stranger's face: he is looking up at a doctor standing over him.

'Hey! Rise and shine Sam.'

Confused, Sam stammers. 'What happened?'

'You got caught in a terrible blast, one that battered you badly.' The doctor smiles sadly. 'Do you remember anything about the explosion?'

Sam gasps as he tries, but fails, to sit up. Something does not feel right.

'Take it easy Sam,' the doctor continues, 'you've been severely injured.'

Sam lies back, waiting for his senses to fully return and the reality of his situation to reveal itself. His head is covered in bandages, and he can only see through his right eye. Gingerly he touches the left side of his face, which sends a stab of pain shooting through his head. Gazing down over the right side of his body, he sees the red stained, bandaged stump: what remains of his forearm. A single tear trickles down his right cheek.

Closing his eye the darkness reminds him of the people trapped inside the gas filled building. The building he ran into. A wave of panic forces him to open his eye again and he hastily scans the rest of the ward, taking in the occupants in the other beds: injured and heavily bandaged; wrists connected to long plastic tubes. These are some of the people who were also caught in the explosion.

'You did well.' The doctor rubs their hand gently across Sam's shoulder. 'Your actions shielded the full force of the blast; you've saved a lot of people Sam. You're a hero.'

The doctor steps away and Sam looks on at the anxious faces of Johnny and Mary. The strain of events is etched across their faces. Mary is holding a bouquet of peach-coloured peonies and a huge bag of sweets. When they see Sam is awake their expressions immediately lighten.

'Sam! Oh, thank goodness!' Mary cries, wrapping her arms around Sam's shoulders; her hands still full.

Sam tries to return the hug, but it proves impossible with only one arm. He pulls away. 'I'm sorry.' He mutters, looking down at his stump. 'It's going to be strange being like this, isn't it?'

'No doubt,' Johnny sighs. 'but we've got your back.' He offers a cheering smile. 'We're proud of you kiddo, doing what you did.'

Sam rubs the back of his neck. 'I guess.'

'We've been talking to the doctor,' Mary explains, excitedly, 'and they've told us about the wonderful new prosthetics available and how they help injured people have a normal life.'

Johnny interjects. 'I'd think of it as having a bionic arm, that sounds much more impressive.'

'A bionic arm? Hm, sounds interesting,' Sam sighs wearily, 'maybe I'll look into that.'

Mary adds. 'And they said you could even still play Angie, with a bit of practice.'

*

Months pass. Months Sam spends in recovery. When he finally leaves the hospital, it is with a white leather patch over his left side of his face, and a newly fitted bionic arm hanging inside a sling.

'Hey! Sam! Over here!'

Outside Sam is surprised by a group of reporters waiting by the hospital's main entrance, all eager for him to answer their questions. They thrust microphones and cameras towards him as he steps through the sliding doors.

'How are you feeling?'

'What made you go into that building?'

'What made you think you would contain the blast?'

'Have you tried using that arm of yours?'

'Why do you wear pink-coloured clothes? Is that your style?'

Johnny hurries to escort Sam through, politely protecting him from an increasingly intrusive barrage of questions. Quickening their step, they catch a tram and head home. But there is something Sam must do. He is desperate to return to the shop, the one with the scarf displayed in the window. It has been the thought of having that wonderful scarf that has helped keep his spirits up, especially when they have been at their lowest: that brilliant yellow and red fleece scarf.

Standing outside the shop, looking through its window, Sam is overjoyed. It is still there, neatly coiled around the handmade items.

Johnny frowns. 'What is it?'

'I don't know why, but see that scarf,' Sam explains, 'the one in the window. There is something special about the colours, the vibrancy, that I find reassuring. I've been thinking about it ever since I first woke up in hospital.'

'Do you want me to buy it for you?'

'Would you Gramps?'

Sam waits outside while Johnny goes into the small shop. A few minutes later the shopkeeper appears behind the display. She smiles at Sam before carefully gathering the long fleece scarf into a huge ball.

At last, he has it. He takes the scarf from Johnny and wraps it loosely around his neck, pulling the soft fleece fabric up and over the left side of his face.

'Is that better?' Johnny asks.

'Yeah. I think this will do marvellously.'

'Then let's get you home, Mary will be wondering where we've got to.'

They walk home the rest of the way. At the corner of Hunter's Road Sam spots a familiar figure approaching. It is the girl he had met in the park. He gasps, staring at her smirking face.

The girl stops in front of him. 'Hey, it's you Sammy!' She cries. 'Hey! Are you alright? Man! Look at you! It's me, Mandy. I've been reading about you in the newspaper and...' The girl stops, becoming conscious of Sam's discomfort. Her cheeks flush red. 'Oh I'm sorry, I shouldn't have said anything. Me bad!'

Sam composes himself. Taking a deep breath, he wipes a tear from his eye. 'That's okay.'

'I really am quite a natterer, aren't I? I guess I should tone it down. People keep telling me I should.' There is a short, awkward pause, while Mandy scans Sam's clothes. She mutters. 'Pastel today, huh!' But she quickly recovers and beams. 'Cute style! Really!'

Sam blushes and manages a faint smile. 'Oh thank you. It's cute, is it?'

Mandy grins. 'Hey! It looks cute to me. My friends might say something different, but I'll defend you Sammy-boy.'

'Mandy has been telling us how you met in the park.' Johnny explains. 'She's been to see us, wanting to know how you were doing? What a thoughtful gesture, huh!'

'And I'm sorry I made fun of you before.' Mandy frowns. 'I didn't mean to upset you Sammy. I didn't understand.'

'That's all right. I get like that, awkward, when I meet people. The more I try to make good conversation, the more awkward I get.' Sam sighs. 'And now, with all the attention I'm getting, it's not gonna be easy.'

'Hey, you're doing just fine.' Mandy chirps, and Sam nods. 'So I guess we're good?'

'Yeah, we're good.' They exchange smiles and shake hands.

Mandy laughs. 'Heh, that's a cool arm you've got there. The geeks are going to get a kick out of that when I tell them!'

Johnny grins. 'Well, I'm glad to see you two getting along!'

'Looks like we are, Mr. Johnny!' Mandy exclaims. She glances at her phone and gasps. 'Hey! I'd better get moving, I'm late for lunch. We should meet up later, tomorrow perhaps, in the park if you like.' She smirks. 'And don't worry about being bothered by those press guys. I'll be there as your bodyguard and shoo them away.'

'You don't have to do that,' Sam chuckles, 'but it's good to hear that you'll be looking out for me. Thanks Mandy.'

Aloft in Glen Bó

The Puppis slices through thick white clouds, its wings beating with strong deliberate sweeps. Bathed in the faint sunlight diffusing through the clouds, the impressive looking craft brushes aside the mist. A bird's caw echoes over the air-sac skin as gulls glide past the airship.

Frank's blunderbuss fashioned tasty lemon curd is no substitute for real food, and so Sam, famished from his travels, readily accepts Frank's invitation for breakfast. He follows the sky-pirate down a hatchway that connects to the galley, positioned deep inside the Puppis' wooden hull. Inside it is spacious with plenty of headroom. The counter is piled high with pots, pans and other crockery, waiting to be cleaned and stored away. On the far side is a stove where a large pot sits on a metal plate with slowly steaming porridge inside. The thick, bubbling meal wafts a sweet, oat aroma. Frank opens a cupboard to reveal shelves stocked with supplies of boxed foods and canned juices. He grabs a bottle of honey and places it on the long thin wooden table at the centre of the galley. With Sam's help he carefully spoons hearty helpings of porridge into two clay bowls and brings them to the table. Taking a tablespoon Frank dips it into the honey, twisting it slowly into the viscous golden liquid, before pulling it out and drizzling the sweet accompaniment on top of his oatmeal.

He nods at a pile of cutlery by the sink. 'Grab a spoon. I'm sure there's a clean one somewhere.'

Sitting at the galley table, they dig greedily into their breakfast, periodically returning to add more sweetness from the honeypot. After completing their meal, Frank clears away the breakfast bowls and mugs. Sam turns to face the pile of the dirty crockery. It is the least he can do to thank his new friend for his hospitality.

Task completed, he re-joins Frank up on the deck and for a couple of hours he sits, transfixed by the sights and sounds of ropes tightening and relaxing in time with the air-sac bouncing on the invisible forces acting against the craft. The sky-pirate stands at the helm, guiding the Puppis on its leisurely route.

Looking across the bow, Sam sees a small town sitting on the summit of a mountain topped with cloud circles. The rooftops of the tiny buildings glisten in the sunlight.

'Hey Frank!' He cries, against the bracing breeze. 'Is that Glen Bó?'

Frank squints his eyes. 'Ah-ha! Why yes, it is!' He steers the airship closer to the mountain. 'Okay, here we go!' As they descend, the wings fold into the main body of the craft.

Sam studies the ground approaching from below, spotting two women waiting on a small circular deck. The approaching craft's propeller blasts air through the taller woman's sandy-coloured long hair; her younger companion has shorter, dark brown hair. With the Puppis hovering steadily above the ground, Frank throws two ropes overboard. He stands watching as they slip and unfurl over the side. The women grab and tie the ropes around two heavy metal locks secured deep into the cobblestone surface. Completing their task they signal to Frank, who then swings his legs over the side of the Puppis and expertly slides down the first of the secured ropes.

The taller woman steps forward and grabs his hands. 'Captain Frank, home at last,' she smiles, 'and in good condition too. Yes, very good indeed.'

'Good morning, Ms Hummus.' Frank bows, holding his hat closely against his chest. He then turns to the younger woman and cries, cheerily. 'Hi Faye!' Taking her up into a bear hug, he lifts her feet off the ground and swings her around in a circle.

'Hey Frankie!' Faye replies, hugging Frank with deep affection. 'I'm glad to see my brother is safe and sound.' As they pull part, she glances up at the craft. 'And who's that atop the Puppis?'

'He's a friend, someone I picked up.' Frank waves at Sam. 'Hey Sam! Come on down!'

Sam gulps. 'I'll try.'

Cautiously pushing one leg out over the side, Sam silently urges his courage to stay with him before risking the other. Clutching the rope tightly he begins his descent, sliding slowly and painfully down the rope. His legs are trembling and his natural hand aches with an irritating itch. Halfway down, his right leg slips.

Concerned, Frank holds out his hands, hissing through his teeth. 'Whoa, careful! Take it nice and slow. Those last steps are a doozy.'

Re-establishing his grip, Sam continues until with some relief he reaches the ground. He stands, waiting for his knees to stop wobbling.

'I think I'm happier here, with my feet on solid ground.'

'Well, I'll be darned.' Ms Hummus chuckles. 'Isn't it nice having visitors!'

'Faye, Ms Hummus,' Frank gestures his friends towards Sam, 'I'd like you to meet Sam McKenzie.'

Sam offers a friendly wave.

'He's travelled here from Melsey.'

'So the stories are true. The hero of Melsey is here, in our little town.' Ms Hummus takes Sam's right hand and runs her hand over the smooth metal surface. 'Sam, it's nice to meet you in the flesh.'

'*From Melsey!*'

The air fills with voices. Everyone in Glen Bó wants to greet them; the townsfolk emerge like gnomes from toadstool homes. Sam is surrounded by strangers, all eager to meet the visitor from the distant city.

Someone shouts enthusiastically from behind Sam. 'Yes! Indeed it is!'

'Nice to see you!'

Another cries. 'We've heard everything about you!'

'Can we have your autograph?'

'Well, I…' Sam's face reddens as the habitants of Glen Bó shower further compliments his way. He rubs his neck, nervously biting his lower lip.

Frank places a hand on Ms Hummus' shoulder. 'Um, Ms Hummus,' he says, clearing his throat, 'perhaps we should find somewhere for our guest to stay.'

'Oh, right, right!' Ms Hummus replies. 'I do apologise Sam. Yes, we'll make you feel right at home here in Glen Bó.' Lifting her head, she addresses the crowd. 'Alright everyone! Let's give our visitor some space. We don't want to embarrass him, do we?' She declares, winking at Sam.

Sam sinks his flushed face deep into the fold of his scarf.

*

Glen Bó is built on the flattened summit of a mountain, where the high altitude makes the climate noticeably cooler. At each corner of the town stands a tall white windmill, built to utilise the constant wind driving across the mountaintop. The town is an ambitious construct, consisting of small, homely-looking buildings constructed at strange angles; designed to prevent the frequent snowfalls from accumulating heavily on the roofs.

Sam follows Frank and his friends into the centre of the town, which is marked by a flower-clustered park. Sleek ivory benches surround a large marble fountain. A carved, horned mountain sheep spews water from its mouth. They continue through the park, finally arriving at a tavern called *The Tipsy Lark*, selling ales and spirits. Next to the tavern is a friendly-looking café serving tea, coffee and assorted flavoured fondant fancies.

Sam immediately takes to the town and the kind hospitality of its residents. With evening approaching, Faye directs Sam and Frank into a café to order milky tea. Between sipping his hot drink, Frank tries again to coax Sam to share his experience of the events that led to losing his eye and arm.

Sam smiles resignedly, returning his cup to its saucer. 'Driven by curiosity, I entered a strange tarot shop I found amongst a parade of other tiny shops, on a side street in Melsey. Inside I met a mysterious fortune teller who stared into her crystal ball and foresaw my destiny. The part I would play caught up inside an horrendous explosion. She told me to rely on my instincts, and that irrespective of the events she'd predicted, I should trust the power I have inside me.' Staring blankly over the table, he sighs. 'Not that I understand what she meant by that.' He continues. 'The next day as I was walking through the city, I smelt smoke. It's strange, but I can't recall which building it was, nor which street it was on. There was a group of people staring at smoke pouring from the building; they were just standing there, doing nothing. I remember feeling this wave of anxiety rising up inside me, realising that there were people trapped inside. I approached the main entrance and entered the building, just like that. A few steps and I'm inside, surrounded by this terrible noise. It was dark and there was a terrible rancid smell of burning oil. People were staggering about blindly: coughing and shouting and weeping, desperate to escape. A few were congregated next to this open door; the door I instinctively knew I had to force shut to contain the blast; just as the fortune-teller had foretold. I grabbed the handles and pushed it shut, throwing my weight against the door. Everything went white, and then incredibly quiet. The world filled with white smoke and lots and lots of pain. It felt as if I'd absorbed the whole shock of the blast.'

Sam pauses and gazes at Frank, who stares back in astonishment. 'There was this strange rose-coloured light surrounding me. I remember seeing it, just as I lost consciousness.'

He holds up his right arm, its shiny metal surface gleaming in the sunlight. 'I don't remember anything after that. I woke up in the hospital, hoping that everybody else had escaped from the building safely.'

Faye leans back in her chair, her lips wet with tea. 'And they did, Sam, didn't they? Such a wonderful thing. They must be so thankful for your heroic deed.'

'Um! I prefer not to think of it as heroic.' Sam strokes his chin. 'I was hounded by the media who kept pushing me to embrace my heroic actions, just to enhance their own stories. And if I'm honest,' he adds, thoughtfully, 'it was foolish going inside the building. I…' His words trail away, and his shoulders start shaking. 'Sorry,' he whispers, pulling his scarf. 'I don't like talking about it.'

'Aw, it's an amazing story and I'd like to know much more,' Faye smiles at Sam and runs her finger tenderly along his scarred cheek, 'but I can see it's upsetting you. You're a good person Sam, someone who is full of compassion for others.'

Sam splutters, his cheeks reddening. Squeezing his fingers into his scarf he whispers. 'Thank you.' He glances at Frank who is sitting opposite and finishing off a large slice of chocolate cake.

Brushing cake crumbs off his chest, Frank stands. 'I'd better find Ms Hummus and see if she's organised somewhere for you to stay tonight.'

Sam watches his friend disappear in the direction of the main town square.

Faye starts, amused. 'You're fond of Frank, aren't you?'

Sam laughs nervously. 'Um, yeah. I think he's cool. And he was kind, taking me in from the storm and aboard his airship.' Holding up his bionic arm, he continues. 'Of course we've things in common, I guess, what with him losing his leg fighting off a band of bandits.'

Faye half closes her eyes. 'It happened during one of his adventures, as he was travelling over some distant island. The Puppis lost power and he was forced to land. On the island he met four self-proclaimed adventurers, who predicted he would get involved in some vicious conflict and that it was his destiny. Sometime later poor Frankie got caught in the crossfire between bandits. He was helping a young lad, someone he described as a "rambunctious, practical fellow".' She chuckles, sadly. 'Frank had got caught in a large net, one of the lad's traps. Yet despite the circumstances of that first meeting, they became friends. It seemed a strange island, by Frank's account. He told me stories of hanging figures: dolls strung up on tree branches, deep inside the forest on the island.' She frowns. 'You should know Sam; Frank typically turns and runs from anything mysterious or ghoul-like. He hates all kinds of conflict. Yet on this occasion, faced by terrifying dolls, ridiculous old codgers and cruel bandits, he decided to stand his ground. Returning home wearing that ridiculous dinky pegleg, and telling tales of bravery.' She sighs. 'But despite his bravado, there are times when I see real sorrow behind his eyes.'

'What an extraordinary tale. *Frank the pirate.*'

'You mean sky-pirate.' Faye smiles. 'He is though, in his own way: pillaging for food and giving it to those who need it; especially when he's the hungry one. But is he a proper pirate? I think he's too friendly, and regardless of his adventures on the mysterious island, Frank is more a flier than a fighter.' She leans across and whispers in Sam's ear. 'And he's not particularly fond of parrots either.'

'Why? What's he got against parrots?'

'They always taunt him!'

'Ah, I see.'

Faye and Sam drink their tea and then head for the sheep water statue in the park. They meet up with Frank at the edge of the stone pond, who greets them with a friendly cheer.

'Hey Sam, Ms Hummus has fixed up a spare bed, one with a nice soft mattress.'

'That's good news.' Sam replies, wincing from an ache running along the side of his body. A memento from his previous night's rest aboard the Puppis. He slips his scarf from his face and tightens the ends behind his neck.

Standing by the fountain, Frank says. 'You know Sam, you still haven't explained why you were wandering through the countryside by yourself?'

'Well it sounds silly when you say it like that, but I had this strange dream, after running into you in Melsey.' He smiles awkwardly. 'And in that dream there were three people: and one of them looked just like you.'

'Me?'

'I think the dream was urging me to go on an adventure of my own. To go and experience the world.' He stops short. His arm is tingling again.

Faye asks. 'Sam? Are you alright?'

'Yeah, I think so. It's my arm. It's having one of its moments.'

'Does this happen often?'

'Not really. It's uncomfortable having an artificial arm.' Sam winces, before carefully caresses the lump near the crook of his elbow. The point where the cold metal connects with his warm skin.

'Oh! Right!'

Frank and Faye exchange a glance. Then together they escort Sam to Ms Hummus, who is waiting outside *The Tipsy Lark*. A cool breeze accompanies them through the town.

Sam shivers. 'Golly! It's chilly here.'

'It's always cold in the mountains.' Ms Hummus replies, squeezing a damp cloth through her thick fingers. 'Shall we go inside? I have a lovely chicken stew ready, and there's fruit salad and some cottage cheese too.'

Sam feels his face turning green. 'Oh, cottage cheese.'

He gazes up at the greying heavens and clouds thickening with rain. There is an accompanying soft rumble of distant thunder, and he shivers again as another chilly breeze rolls against the back of his neck. Quickening his step, he follows Ms Hummus and the others into the tavern.

Inside the inn they are met by an impressive looking dining table, one covered in a bounty of food and drink. This is to be an evening to look forward to: tucking into the chicken stew and mountains of breads and fruits; providing he avoids the dreaded cottage cheese. Tonight is a night to savour with new friends, and he is determined to enjoy the evening. Tomorrow and the days that follow will bring fresh challenges. Sam knows his journey must continue, but there is a part of him that yearns for Frank to come with him.

Later that night, Sam wakes to the sound of heavy rain thundering on the roof. Sitting up, he watches water trickle down the window next to him. He starts. There in the corner of his eye, he spots something passing outside, a flash of gold in the sky. There is a strange white shape hovering in the air outside. It seems to be searching for someone, or something. Sam steps closer to the window and peers outside. He is met by a flash of lightning. As the darkness returns, he sees the shape twist and turn in the air, before disappearing into the night.

*

By morning it is calm again and Sam gets up early and quickly dresses. Tugging his scarf securely around his neck, he steps onto the puddle-covered cobblestone street outside. He is eager to find evidence of the mysterious night-time visitor. But there is nothing to suggest that anything has been here. So instead he stands watching workers skip around pools of water on their way to work. It all seems normal. Yet deep down, Sam senses that things are changing, and concealed within this apparent tranquillity lies something menacing.

It is perhaps not surprising that it proves easy for Sam to convince Frank to accompany him on the next stage of his journey. In fact, it takes the time for the sky-pirate to butter a croissant. Yet having convinced Frank to join him in his travels, Sam feels compelled to argue against his friend travelling with him.

'You don't have to join me, Frank. It's not like I'm desperate.' He argues, watching Frank stuff a warm, jam-smothered pastry into his mouth.

'Nah, I insist,' Frank counters, nonchalantly waving the croissant in his hand, 'besides, if the person you saw in your dream was me, then I've got to come, haven't I? We both know the importance of destiny, and having the Puppis means we will get about much quicker.' To emphasise his argument, he points towards the distant plains, stretching away from Glen Bó. 'Like getting down into the mountain valley, for example.'

Sam laughs. 'You do have a point.'

Once they have finished eating their breakfast, Sam and Frank head from the tavern to arrange supplies for the next stage of their journey. They spend time collecting food and other resources before loading everything onboard the Puppis. Ms Hummus and

Faye are on hand to help too. Sam is given the task of organising the cargo inside the Puppis' hold. He struggles to climb back onboard, but quickly regains his air-legs and is soon engaged in stocking different boxes and parcels inside the hold. Later Frank joins him on deck to tighten the numerous rope-locks connecting the main body of the craft with the giant air-sac.

As evening draws in, they finally complete the task of securely storing everything onboard the Puppis. They take a moment to descend onto the small landing-deck to make their farewells.

'I think coming all this way from Melsey would be far enough for me,' Ms Hummus laughs, 'and now you're planning to go even further. I don't know how you fellas do it. So where are you heading?'

'Where exactly, I'm not sure,' Sam replies, 'but I've seen different places in my dreams. There's a purpose, but I don't know exactly what it is yet.'

Mrs Hummus leans forward and studies Sam closely. 'You know, when I look at you: your hair, your features, even your mannerisms; you remind me of that astronaut. The one lost during the VEGA expedition.' She nods her head. 'Yes. Yes. You remind me of him, Sam. He was a likeable fellow too, just like you. He used to come here, you know, to Glen Bó. He liked drinking tea in our café.' Waving her hand dismissively, she continues. 'Ah well! Sam, Frank, I guess it's time for you to go and let the wind take you where it pleases.'

'Let there be calm winds, and good fortune when the winds are less forgiving.' Faye adds. 'There's a part of me that wishes I could come too, but I've a café here to run. Stay in touch, won't you.'

'Of course. And don't worry, Faye!' Frank replies, patting her on the shoulder. 'I don't go looking for trouble, not without a plan to fight or flight!'

Faye laughs and gives her sibling one final hug. 'Take care, Frankie.'

'I will.'

'You too, Sam!'

'See you soon, Faye!'

Sam and Frank climb back aboard the Puppis.

Pulling the rope ladder up and over the deck, they routinely undo each of the locks, one-by-one. Frank shouts out instructions and Sam follows his lead. Below, Faye and Ms Hummus disengage the securing ropes and step back to watch the Puppis rise slowly into the air. They stand holding white handkerchiefs in their hands. They keep on waving, even as the Puppis disappears into the clouds.

No-one, aboard or on the ground, have noticed that the windmill in the far corner of Glen Bó has stopped moving: its blades have ceased to a rust-grinding halt.

Greystagg Forest

The Puppis sails west, leaving Glen Bó to slip slowly beneath the skyline. Reddened sunlight valiantly peeks through ever-thickening clouds as the sun slinks closer to the horizon. Sam leans against the side of the airship and gazes at the expansive green landscape below; observing groups of trees as their branches dance in the wind. The playground for tiny white birds flittering excitedly between the canopies. Occasionally he glances up at the huge air-sac as the stiff breeze pushes the craft forward.

It feels peaceful. *Too peaceful.*

The Puppis rocks abruptly to one side and Frank grabs hold of the helm and steadies the airship. He glances across at Sam, a sheepish grin fixed across his face.

Sam is holding on to the side of the craft. 'What do you think is out there?'

'Who knows Sam. It's a big world, even for seasoned travellers like us.'

Their journey returns to a languid silence, until the airship again swings from side to side. The forces acting on the craft are more violent this time and Frank struggles with difficulty to regain control and steady the Puppis' course. Steering the craft towards the right air current is not for the queasy and Sam is beginning to feel nauseous.

'What's going on,' he cries, 'and what's that rumbling sound?'

'No idea!' Frank replies, grappling with the helm.

The Puppis experiences another ferocious shove, which causes the sky-pirate to lose his footing and topple across the top deck.

Steadying himself, Frank stares at the calm sky. 'That's weird,' he gasps, 'the weather seems fine and dandy, and ideal for the Puppis.'

Again the airship swings violently, this time sending them both tumbling across the deck. Sam manages to grab hold of one of the wooden barrels. Taking a deep breath he stares out towards the horizon. Something is causing this disturbance, something he cannot see.

'What's happening?' He cries. You don't think we're being…?'

The powerful invisible force causes the Puppis to swerve again, loosening Sam's grip on the barrel and throwing him sideways with such ferocity it causes him to overbalance and topple overboard.

'*Sam!*'

Slinging Old Faithful and his bag over his shoulders, Frank dives straight over the side of the airship. Falling he reaches towards Sam and grabs hold of his hand. Above their heads the world swirls about them as the air rushes past, pounding their ears.

Sam stares skywards, seeing the Puppis shrinking away. 'Frank! He yells, his voice battling against the rush of air. 'How high are we?'

'I'd say too high to fall out of the Puppis!' Frank yells back. 'Hold on tight! This is gonna be a rough landing.'

SMASH!

Sam thunders into the top of a thick canopy of evergreen trees.

CRASH! Rustle! THUD!

One canopy after another, he slides through layers of the prickly pine needles, until finally he lands with a THUMP!

On soft damp grass. 'Oof!'

Wheezing, trying to refill his lungs, Sam rolls over onto his back, half-buried inside piles of broken twigs and leaves.

Struggling to his feet, he discovers that he is inside the forest, deep within the shadows of its heavy canopy. He checks for broken bones, but apart from his aching arm he appears unscathed. His eye gradually grows accustomed to the poor light: faint streaks of sunlight diffusing through tiny cracks between the leaves, which bathe the forest in an eerie glow.

He staggers tentatively forward, brushing pine needles from his clothes. 'Frank!' He pleads as loudly as he can, but there is no reply. 'Frank? Where are you?'

Nothing.

Despite the apparent solitude, Sam senses that he is not alone. Pulling his jacket around his chest, he tightens his scarf.

'He can't be far,' Sam says to himself, reassuringly, 'he must have landed somewhere nearby. I just hope he's safe and sound.'

It is quiet inside the forest, perhaps too quiet. There are no sounds of birds or woodland fauna over the crunch of the grass beneath his feet. Sam continues walking, unsettled by the lack of noise, still convinced that someone, or something, is watching. He must find Frank and someplace safe to spend the night. He steps carefully through the undergrowth, mindful of tripping over a fallen branch or a concealed rabbit hole; wary of calling out in case he attracts the wrong attention, from whatever it is that is out there. Stopping briefly every two or three steps, he listens out.

Sam drops to his knees onto a deep pile of red leaves. There is something rustling beyond a line of thick dense bushes: the sound of creatures chomping down on something. It sounds unnatural; unlike any sound an animal might make. This is different, something mechanical. Cautiously he steps away, but the rustling grows louder. Something is following him.

Quickening his pace he trudges through bushes, trampling over crunchy grass and heather. His world explodes into a cloud of feathers, accompanied by a loud screeching cry as a bird flies for the skies and safety. Sam glances nervously over his shoulder, his ears straining at the repetitive sound of relentless munching emanating behind him. Whatever it is, it is getting closer.

'Whoa!'

Sam staggers over a hidden root, but quickly restores his balance.

CRUNCH! CRUNCH!

Crouching low behind thick ferns, he spots a group of strange, menacing looking creatures. They are plant-like, the size of large rabbits, and are covered in silvery-grey scales that reflect the perforating sunlight. Sam counts a total of six: half have short squat frames; the other are thinner and taller. Each of the creatures have sprouted leaf shaped arms, but he is unable to see if they are fixed into the ground. *Do they have legs, can they move around?* Their prominent feature is a large toucan-like beak, stained with moss and streaked with mud. Sam continues watching as the creatures munch relentlessly on limp, yellowing plants. He notices there are tiny metal screws fastening hinges on their ever-moving jaws; hinges that creak noisily as they chew. Perhaps they are rusty? He cannot see the creatures' eyes, but he senses they are fully aware of his presence. *They are studying him.*

One by one they finish chewing and stretch their heads, peering ominously in his direction.

'Um, whatever you are,' Sam gulps hard, 'you're curious fellows.' He stammers, desperately trying to keep his voice steady. 'I mean you no harm,' he adds, stepping to one side, 'and I'll be on my way.'

One of the taller creatures hurries towards him. *They are not anchored.* It stops in front of Sam and opens its jaw and hisses, bearing sharp metal teeth.

Sam, his forehead beaded with cold sweat, holds out his hands. 'Look you can't frighten me! I'm here by mistake. If you let me go, I won't bother you. I promise.' He says, backing away.

The metallic plant-like creatures begin circling him, edging nearer and nearer. They start humming, producing a low threatening, rasping drone.

Sam gasps. *They are chuckling at me.* 'This is bad. What can I do?'

One of the rounded-shaped creatures lunges, snapping at Sam's ankle and causing him to yelp and fall backwards. Lying on his back, he becomes aware of a warm sensation spreading out from his outstretched right hand. He watches the soft rose-coloured light emanating from his palm. The creatures can see it too and they balk in disbelief at the mysterious phenomenon unfolding before them. They respond by screeching shrilled screams. One of the creatures hisses loudly and charges. Helpless, Sam closes his eye and waits for the creature to land its attack. There is a crunching dull thud, the sound of two bodies coming together. Opening his eye, his vision is blurred by a mass of black and white fur. The plant-like creatures are fixating on the newcomer, who is growling valiantly at them, daring them to continue with their attack. Sam cautiously pushes himself to his feet and stares in disbelief at his welcome ally: hunched on all fours, readying to pounce. He is greeted by a triumphant bark.

Sam gasps. 'Bonnie!'

The light around his hand begins to fade as the creatures slowly regroup. They are scrutinising their new foe, formulising their next attack. Bonnie turns and pushes Sam, guiding him through the forest and into a clearing with a large pond. Free from the cover of trees, they are immersed in bright sunlight. Light glistens across still waters, illuminating several large floating lily pads. It is a restful scene, a direct contrast to the menacing rustling coming from the deep vegetation behind them.

Sam groans, stooping forward. 'My ankle.'

'*Hey you!*'

Glancing up, Sam sees a figure with long caramel brown hair draped into the shape of bunny-ears standing next to a large oak tree. The person is wearing a pink sleeved poncho patterned with lilac stripes and flowers, with deep green leggings and thick brown leather shoes. Strapped to the trunk of a large oak tree are a pair of burning torches. He steps closer, staring into the stranger's striking eyes: the colour of polished jade. It is one of the people he saw in his dream. The one wearing the poncho.

'Quick!' Sam and Bonnie are motioned towards an opening in the oak tree and a spacious brightly lit room within. 'Inside!'

Sam hesitates, but the approaching shrieks of the metallic creatures encourages him to enter. Bonnie follows. The poncho-wearing stranger slams the door of the oak treehouse behind them.

The interior is homely. *A treehouse! They are inside a tree!*

At the centre of the circular room is a large wooden table covered with a soft pink fabric that drapes down to the floor. The inner wall contains three small, round-framed windows, each with clay pots containing yellow cosmos flowers. There are several colourful cushions scattered around the tubular room. The interior smells warm and nutty; something is being brewed inside. Despite this most unlikely location for a house, there is more than enough room inside to accommodate them all. Their host gestures Sam towards the table and then disappears through a thin pillar of steam into an adjacent room.

Sam, still shaking from the attack outside, sits down on one of the cushions. Bonnie nuzzles her head reassuringly into his knees, a puppy-grin spread across her face.

'Thanks Bon,' Sam sighs, playfully petting Bonnie's floppy ears, 'I'm sure glad you're here... but... how did you find me?'

'I just did what any dog would do, Sam.' Bonnie grunts. 'Follow her nose and track her owner's scent.'

Sam's eye widens. 'Whoa! Wait a minute. You can talk?'

'Of course I can. Check this out.' Bonnie clears her throat, and putting on a more refined accent, speaks. 'I now declare this bridge open.' She reverts to her normal voice. 'I've kept things quiet up until now in case I'm overheard. Great, huh!' She wags her tail enthusiastically.

Puzzled, Sam scratches his head. The past few days have been strange; why should he be surprised hearing animals talk? He smiles and pets Bonnie's head. 'More than meets the eye. Who would've thought it?'

The poncho-wearing person returns carrying a steaming cup of tea and a slice of nutty cake on a small plate. 'I've brought you something to eat and drink. Pecan nut cake and tea. They're my favourites!' Reaching deep into their poncho's inner pocket, they retrieve a handful of biscuits and places them on the floor next to Bonnie. 'And these are for you, lil' one.'

'Thank you for rescuing us and bringing us here, where it's safe.'

'You're welcome. Here, let me look at your ankle.' Kneeling on the floor, their host rolls up Sam's trousers, revealing a swollen bruise above his ankle. 'Ah! It's not serious. It's not drawing blood, which is a good thing. You'll soon heal.' Pausing briefly to remove a couple of leaves stuck atop Sam's hair, their host stands. 'It looks like you've just dropped in. Ha-Ha! Sorry, just lightening the mood with a little joke; it's my way. Oh and before I completely forget the formalities, let me introduce myself. I'm Mallory Elise, but you can call me Mal.'

'I'm Sam McKenzie.'

'Pleased to meet you, Sam. You've a friendly face, that's for sure; one that reveals a *down-to-earth* nature. My kind of person.' She turns her attention to Bonnie, who is busy crunching down on the biscuits. 'I must say your pup has a beautiful, shiny coat.'

'Thanks. Her name is Bonnie.'

'Bonnie. That's a nice name: blithe and bonnie! *Ha-Ha!*'

Sam laughs too, before being reminded of events in the forest. He looks out of one of the small windows. 'What are those things out there?'

'I don't know, I've not seen them before today. They appeared out of nowhere, but whatever they are, they're not natural. No, I don't think they're natural at all.' Mal peers through the window. The creatures have slinked away, for now. 'They don't make cheery dinner companions.'

And speaking of companions. Sam gasps. 'Oh no! I've forgotten all about Frank!'

'Frank? Is he a friend of yours?'

'Yes, although we only met a few days ago. I was aboard his airship.'

'An airship?' Mal snorts. 'Here in Greystagg?'

Bonnie stops eating and lifts her head. She twitches her ears and sniffs at the air, her eyes narrow.

Sam asks. 'What is it, Bon?'

'I can smell something outside, something faint. Sam, I think I can find your friend! Quick, let's make haste!' She bounds out through the door, with Sam struggling to keep up.

Mal cries from the doorway. 'Hey, wait for me!'

The forest is darker than before and Sam, tripping through the bushes, follows Bonnie, keeping a watchful eye for the metallic creatures. He stumbles over a rock and grabs a nearby tree for support. Ahead, Bonnie has stopped by a large bush. She sniffs at the air again, her nose pointing high.

'Golly Bon, you sure run fast!' Sam pants, catching up with her.

Bonnie lowers her head, sniffing at the air and surrounding foliage, catching something in her nostrils. 'Sam! I can see something moving. *There!*'

Sam squints, relying on Bonnie's heightened senses. He makes out a darkened shape stooping between gorse bushes. Concentrating hard, the distant figure begins to take on a familiar form. It is someone struggling to stand; someone who keeps tumbling to the ground with an accompanying frustrated grunt.

Sam calls out. 'Hey, is that you Frank?'

Bonnie wags her tail and bounds towards the figure.

'Hey! That tickles!'

It is Frank. Bedraggled, the sky-pirate staggers through the gorse bushes. Shaken from his landing, he is having difficulty standing upright due to his missing pegleg. But for Frank, it is his missing round brim hat that is of greater concern. Clasping Old Faithful in one hand, he pets Bonnie's head with the other.

His eyes meet Sam's. 'Hey, fancy meeting you here... Whoa!'

Sam wraps his arms around his friend's shoulders. 'Frank, thank goodness you're here! I've been looking everywhere.' His voice is muffled in Frank's shoulder.

'You were?'

'Yeah, of course.' Sam pulls away and looks at the stub where Frank's pegleg once stood. 'What happened to your leg?'

'Huh, well what do you know! It must have broken free in the fall, but it's left for the termites now. I'll need to get it replaced.' Frank proclaims, trying to prop his unstable frame against a tree. He wobbles for a moment and then collapses to the ground. 'Hopefully there'll be someone here who can make me a better one. A stronger build.'

'You don't look able to walk by yourself. Here, allow me.' Sam hoists Frank up bridal style, swaying on his feet as he gets used to Frank's weight. 'Let me carry you.'

'Wait! I gotta get my hat! It has to be around here somewhere.'

'Are you looking for this?' Bonnie asks, holding his hat between her jaws.

'Ah, what luck! Thanks!' Frank retrieves his hat and presses it down onto over his thick hair. 'Wow! I didn't know your dog can talk, Sam. Heck! I didn't know any dog could talk!'

'Neither did I!'

Sam carries Frank through the forest with Bonnie by his side; step by step through the brambles and trees, crunching on the undergrowth leaves and twigs. Stumbling a couple of times, they keep moving.

Mal is at the edge of the clearing, waving frantically. 'Sam!'

Frank turns his head and tips his hat. 'Hello!' It a difficult manoeuvre, considering his current situation.

'Ah, so this is Frank, the person you mislaid.' Mal continues, studying the figure in Sam's arms. 'What happened to you?'

'I've lost my pegleg during the fall, so Sam did the honours and carried me.' He stops, aware that Mal is shaking with laughter. 'Hey, err, why are you giggling?'

'Sorry.' Mal composes herself. 'It's just looking at the two of you right now, what a picture.'

Frank groans, his face beet-red. 'Okay, now this is starting to get uncomfortable. You can put me down, Sam. I can take it from here.'

Sam lowers Frank to the ground. 'Ah, that's better!' He groans.

Mal asks. '*You lost a pegleg?*'

'Yep.' Frank replies nonchalantly, putting an arm around Sam's shoulders. 'And from a big fall too.'

'Should we go and look for it?'

'No point.' Frank shakes his head. 'It's been wobbly for a while; I must have worn it out. Now would be a good time to get a new one fitted. I don't suppose you can help me out. Do you know someone who might fix me up with a new leg?'

Mal cups a hand to her chin. 'Hm, I just might know someone who can. Dr Woodchuck! Yes. I'm sure he'll be able to help you.'

'Dr Woodchuck?'

'He's our doctor and sculptor. He does a lot of woodcraft, so I'm sure he'll be able to make a new pegleg. Come with me, he doesn't live far from here.'

Supporting Frank, Sam and Mal push through the clearing, passing Mal's tree-house and onto another large tree, sporting an impressively decorated front door. Above the door is a sign: *Dr Woodchuck's Home and Carving Shop*, in chiselled writing. Mal pushes the door open, revealing a spacious room inside; one that appears larger than when viewed outside. Bonnie sniffs at the damp air. The walls are covered in shelves, from floor to ceiling, each packed with different carved wooden pegs, walking canes and three-legged stools. Each object is beautifully fashioned with distinct shapes and designs. There are also assorted bags of dried herbs, with strings of acorns and hazelnuts hanging from the ceiling. On the far side of the room sits a large, brown furry shape, propped on a stool. It is an animal with a bushy tail. There is a candle burning brightly on an adjacent table.

'Hello!' Mal calls, stepping inside. 'Dr Woodchuck, it's me, Mal.'

The shape swivels around. This is Dr Woodchuck, who is literally a woodchuck. Thick tufts of light, brown-coloured whiskers resemble a groomed moustache, while propped on his round nose sits a pair of large, round spectacles. Large round, beady eyes, magnified by thick glass lenses, study his surprised houseguests.

'Ach!' He exclaims in a thick accent. 'This is quite a party you've brought in with you.' He carefully scrutinises each of Mal's companions in turn. 'I don't often get visitors from beyond the forest. What can I do for you?'

Mal steps forward. 'Dr Woodchuck, I hope you're not too busy, but we have a huge favour to ask. Can you help Frank?'

Dr Woodchuck peers over his spectacles. 'And which one is Frank?' He stares at Sam. 'Is it the buttercream one here?'

'It's me.' Frank raises a hand. 'I'm Frank.'

'Ah, yes!' Dr Woodchuck leaps from his stool and immediately starts examining Frank's stump. 'Hm, yes, yes. A missing pegleg. This is a not a common accident, of course,' he sniffs at the stump, 'and there's a lingering smell of old cedar too, yes, yes, a fascinating aroma. Despite being an evergreen, cedars are not as sturdy as I believe you need. For better endurance, I think a nice piece of teak would work best for you. Strong and durable, and it would look nice too! But enough of my little lecture. Come, lie down and I'll measure you up for a new wooden limb – *toot-sweet!*'

Dr Woodchuck directs Mal, Sam, Frank and Bonnie into his workshop, where there is a large, cushioned bed. Frank lies down and tries to relax.

He stares at the ceiling. 'It's not going to hurt, right?'

'No, not at all, my new friend!' Dr Woodchuck replies reassuringly, before climbing the shelves stacked with piles of assorted wood logs and planks, from ash to oak to teak. He finally grabs a large teak log and carries it down, slamming it hard onto his crafting bench. Peering through his glasses he stares at his watchful audience. 'Trust me, I'm the best sculpting woodchuck in Greystagg. Even my greatest rivals respect my work. Now, let me get prepared; my most excellent carvings requires freshly fashioned teeth!'

Reaching into a drawer he furiously brushes his razor-sharp incisors with a large toothbrush made of thick, coarse bristles. Aerated toothpaste bubbles over his whiskers. Once he has finished polishing his incisors, he begins gnawing down on the wood, sending sawdust flying everywhere: across the bench, over the floor and into everybody's hair.

Sam brushes wood-shavings from his shoulders. 'He's good.'

Mal chuckles. 'He did say he's the finest in the forest.'

Fascinated, they watch Dr Woodchuck busy on his new masterpiece, enveloped inside a large cloud of wood-shavings. Eventually he makes his final, precise gnaws on the large log of teak, now morphed into a shin-shaped pegleg. It is perfectly smooth, its refined surface reflecting the candlelight.

'Ah! A masterpiece if I say so myself!' Dr Woodchuck exclaims, before fixing the new pegleg onto Frank's stump with a mallet, humming a robust tune through his buckteeth. Frank flinches with each rough pound.

Mal asks. 'How is Cedric doing, Doctor?'

'Ack, that crusty fowl will be slumming in his tree. You know how he hates having his sleep interrupted. It's like having someone around who has gone too long without coffee, not that Cedric needs to drink the stuff.' Dr Woodchuck explains. 'His feathers are ruffled up at the moment, shrieking at the tawnies and the barn owls; screeching there's a *serpent* in the grass, day and night!' Dr Woodchuck whistles, the *serpent* exaggerated in falsetto. 'Serpent. Par! I bet you it was just a worm. I don't know why he keeps up his constant blabbering all the time;?'

Sam shares a confused glance with Mal, who shrugs and rolls her eyes.

With a final vigorous pound, Dr Woodchuck completes his task. The pegleg is fixed tightly onto Frank's stub. 'And done! Good as gone and ready to go.'

Frank, swinging his legs over and onto the floor, stands. His new pegleg wobbles at first as he gains his balance; Sam instinctively grabs his friend's shoulder to ensure he does not topple over.

'Thanks Sam. I think I can handle it from here.'

'Are you sure?'

'Yeah, I think so. I just need a bit of practice, that's all.'

Dr Woodchuck sets about clearing away the large piles of wood-shavings using an old brush, accumulating the smaller piles into a much larger, single pile. He then picks up the shavings and chucks them out through an open window. Pausing to nod in quiet satisfaction, he strides across to Sam and begins examining his right arm.

'I must say, um, the one with the buttercream locks...'

'It's Sam.'

'Ah! I apologise.' Dr Woodchuck reaches out and touches the shiny metal. 'But I'm quite fascinated by your prosthetic arm. I don't believe I've ever seen such a material, not one as strong as this.'

'This?' Sam removes his jacket, revealing his bionic arm in full. From the crook of his elbow to the five metal digits on his artificial hand.

'Ah yes, fascinating. Yes! Yes! I would like to research more into such prostheses,' Dr Woodchuck adds, chuckling. 'Although, I doubt I could shave down such strong steel without breaking my choppers, even after a thorough brushing!' He sniffs hard at the metal and then pulls away. 'And yet there is something else, something interesting inside...' The woodchuck's words trail away.

Sam asks. 'What is it?'

Dr Woodchuck tweaks his whiskers. 'This arm really intrigues me. Perhaps Sable should see it.'

'Who's Sable?'

'Sable is our shaman, the overseer of the forest if you like. She is also our friend.' Dr Woodchuck explains. 'But she is an elusive character who is always travelling to distant lands: such as the eclectic city to the south, with her fragrant herbs or oils. I believe she once had a shop there.'

'City?' Sam gasps. Dr Woodchuck must be referring to Melsey, his home.

Dr Woodchuck continues. 'And I believe she returns tomorrow.' He regards Sam, Frank and Bonnie. 'But for now friends, enjoy your time with us in our forest. Mal will escort you to her home.'

'Of course, Dr Woodchuck. And thank you for fixing Frank's leg.'

Mal leads Frank, Sam and Bonnie out of Dr Woodchuck's house and into the pitch-black forest. A tawny owl hoots and the sound echoes through the night.

The sound is interrupted by a sharp, curt screech from another, larger owl. *'Ach!'*

Without moonlight to guide them through the trees, Mal directs her new friends to walk close together, hand-in-hand. She is well practiced navigating the forest and quickly guides them safely through the darkness to her oak-tree-home. In time for more tea and pecan cakes.

While her visitors eat, Mal prepares the main room, spreading out extra cushions and blankets so her guests can rest comfortably.

Frank and Mal are first to drift into sleep, while Sam lies awake studying his hand. *What was the strange light he had seen earlier, what has awakened inside him?* Drawing a blanket over Bonnie, who is lying next to him, his mind drifts to Dr Woodchuck's mention of the shaman.

'And who is Sable,' he asks himself, 'I feel I know her.'

Finally he too is overwhelmed with tiredness, and after a short struggle to keep his eye open, he succumbs to the onset of sleep. His head slips heavily into the soft pillow.

Fate Comes Knocking

The morning breeze greets Greystagg forest as the sun bathes the clearing in pale sunlight, filtering through thick treetop canopies. Deep inside the forest, a world is bustling with urgent activity: rabbits pop their heads from sleepy warrens; and families of jays twitter excitedly above, flittering from branch to branch to branch.

This peaceful idyllic scene is abruptly interrupted by a long-shrilled screech.

'Alert! Alert! Alert! Intruder! Intruder!'

The cries induce an eruption of sound throughout the forest as alarmed animals head for safety. The sound rumbles into the clearing towards the sleepy interior of Mal's house and shakes it, as if hit by a small earthquake. Sam leaps from his makeshift bed. Half-awake, he ruffles his hand through his tousled hair and rubs his blurry eye.

'That sounds like an owl, but in daylight?'

The screeching continues. He glances down at Frank, who is still fast asleep on the floor beside him, smacking his lips noisily. Next to the sky-pirate a sleepy Bonnie calmly scratches the back of her ear.

Mal rises blearily to her feet and steps to a window. 'Really Cedric,' she groans, 'have you any idea what the time is?'

She staggers to the front door and opens it, and then steps out onto the early morning dew. Above her head there is a large, long-eared eagle-owl, frolicking in the air: frantically beating its wings, creating clouds of greying feathers that scatter and settle like snow about her feet. The owl halts, mid-air, exposing its diamond-shaped patterned chest.

'*Alert! Alert! Alert!*' The eagle-owl parrots aloud, raising the alarm to all fauna in earshot: concealed in the collective shadows of adjacent trees; or skulking nervously inside their burrowed homes.

Sam follows Mal outside and peers with astonishment at the bird. *A talking owl!*

'Ach, Cedric!' Dr Woodchuck exclaims, entering the clearing and striding purposely towards the others. The eagle-owl settles onto a large, exposed root beside Mal's house. 'What's got into your fuzzy brain this time?'

'Save your minty breath, Woody!'

'Cedric,' Mal pleads, 'tell us what's wrong?'

Finally awake, Frank makes his way outside. 'Yeah. Why have you woken me,' he complains, rubbing his eyes, 'I was having a lovely dream about narwhals made of candy-floss flavoured clouds.'

Despite being perched on the root, the eagle-owl continues flapping his wings in a vigorous rhythm. 'We're being attacked by a mad intruder! I've seen the crazy glint in their eyes as they rampage through the forest, like a *serpent* in the grass!' Cedric reports, exaggerating the serpent in a shrill falsetto.

An approaching Dr Woodchuck glances smugly at Sam and Frank. 'You see what I mean?'

Mal is patiently listening to Cedric's mad babbling. 'I see, so there's an intruder, or might they be an innocent traveller who is lost and probably freaking out.' She counters. 'They may need our help, or directions, or perhaps they want to know what's good for breakfast?'

'Dearest Mal, I understand your reasoning,' Cedric retorts, 'but this is definitely a dangerous intruder, with ill-ambition, for they carry a bow, and from my perspective, they have good aim.'

THHWUMP!

Their discussion is interrupted by an arrow zipping from out of the bushes. It strikes the top of Frank's hat.

'*Whoa!* Where'd that come from?' Frank gasps, grabbing hold of his hat and pulling the arrow from its crown. 'Hey! I just cleaned this.'

'Look out!' Sam cries, pulling Frank to the ground as another arrow hits the tree above their heads.

THWACK!

There is a cry from deep inside the foliage. 'Come out, come out wherever you are!'

A figure leaps into the clearing and races up towards Sam. It is the intruder. The one Cedric is relentlessly blabbering about, filling the clearing in panicked screeches. The eagle-owl's antagonist stops before the group, a large white bow in hand, standing as tall and as proud as its owner. They are dressed in green and brown clothing, wearing thick leather boots, and with a quiver bag filled with feathered arrows strapped across their back.

Sam is drawn to the strong, hazel-coloured eyes staring defiantly at him; highlighting the small, round and rather tattered-looking face topped with thick, dark auburn hair, tied back into a curled ponytail. He gasps. They match the image of the third person, the shorter figure he saw in his dream.

'Ah-ha! I'm ready for you, yah crazy nut-bolts!' The intruder yells, holding the white bow high. 'Come on down, you're the next contestant for Silverhair!'

Mal steps forward. 'Whoa my friend! There's no need to be so impulsive. Maybe we can help you find whatever it is you're looking for?'

But the intruder shoves Mal aside. 'Out of my way, bunny-ears! Can't yah see I'm a little busy here?'

'*Bunny-ears!*'

'I can smell those metal critters here and they'll make me a fine trophy!'

Sam blinks, recalling the metal creatures that ambushed him the previous evening. 'Metal critters? You've seen them?'

'You bet your buttermilk locks I've seen them, *scarfy!*'

'*Scarfy!*'

The intruder studies Sam's right arm with increasing interest. A grin materialises. '*Hah-ha!* And it looks like we have one right here. Let me at 'em! Silverhair has a taste for oil.'

Sam steps back, holding both hands out in front of him. 'Wait a minute!'

A bright light begins leaking from his palms, causing the intruder to yelp and release an arrow high into the trees, startling the birds hiding inside the foliage. There is a collective gasp of astonishment.

'Well tussle my ruffles,' Cedric exclaims, 'you can't possibly have the power!'

'Geeze, what kind of sorcery is that? You sure got me distracted.' The intruder quickly draws another arrow across Silverhair and readies an aim at Sam. 'I'll show you sorcery!' They freeze, aware that everyone else is staring at something behind them. 'What's wrong? Y'all look like you've seen a monster,' the colour is paling from their cheeks, 'and where is that little black and white runt?'

A dark shadow climbs steadily over the stranger's shoulder, accompanied by a deep rumbling voice that fills the clearing.

'*Ahem!*'

The intruder slowly turns around, until they're staring straight into the fierce golden-coloured eyes of a dire wolf: large as a horse and covered in thick black and white fur. The gigantic creature is wearing a familiar looking yellow neck-scarf. The ashen-faced intruder drops their bow.

'What's the matter?' The dire wolf asks, cocking its head. 'Haven't you ever seen a black and white pup before?'

'Ah! Well! Uh! I've just remembered.' The intruder stammers. 'I have a date. No wait, I've left the oven on. No wait! Ah! Forget it, I'm outta here!' They flee, running past the dire wolf and into the surrounding undergrowth.

'They sure move swiftly.' Dr Woodchuck chuckles, pulling out a rough looking brush. 'What do you think that was about?' He adds, before enthusiastically brushing his teeth.

'I don't know, and frankly, I don't care!' Cedric retorts. 'That chump needs to cease crashing about and shouting. I've lost over two hours of sleep!'

The woodchuck pulls the brush from out of his mouth. 'I still like to know what all that blabbering fuss was about before they skedaddled. Left the oven on? Having a date? Sounds like nonsense if you ask me. Yah know, nonsense, like anything you'd get from captured tawnies?' Dr Woodchuck breaks away, avoiding the wing swipe directed at him by the eagle-owl. 'I'm kidding. I'm kidding!'

The others are still staring up at the large dire wolf, standing proud, swishing its tail.

'Bonnie?' Sam gasps, stepping forward. 'Is that you?'

The dire wolf leans down and presents Sam with a long, slobbery lick. 'Sure it's me Sam!'

Pulling out his handkerchief, Sam wipes his cheek and chuckles. 'As I've said before. There's more to you than meets the eye. But Bon, a dire wolf! How?'

Bonnie shrugs her shoulders. 'Beats me.' She releases a loud belch, and her body starts shrinking, returning to her normal puppy form.

Sam looks towards the gap in the bushes where the intruder has disappeared. 'They must have come across those metallic creatures too,' he adds, half-smiling, 'although they were a little overzealous about wanting to hunt them down.'

'Zealous yes, but only to fail! Ha!' Cedric scoffs. 'If they return with one of the metal heads, then maybe I'll change my mind. Heh! But I doubt they will, considering their poor aim.' He sniggers, scanning the array of arrows left scattered on the ground, stuck to the trunk of a tree, or lost to the canopies above.

'But I for one am more interested in the bright light we saw coming from out of your arm, my friend.' Dr Woodchuck says, studying Sam's prosthetic arm. 'How is it possible to have that kind of power inside you?' He raises his head, twitching his nose. 'Maybe Sable can tell us more.' His ears prick up. 'Ah! Speaking of Sable, I sense she has returned.'

'As always, with great timing!' Cedric adds, knitting his brows. 'Quick, come with us. She'll be with the Flower of Knowledge. Chop-chop!'

'I'm finally going to meet Sable,' Sam gasps in anticipation, 'I wonder what she's like?'

The party walk from the clearing, oblivious of someone concealed in the bushes following their progress. After several minutes they reach another clearing, a smaller one, littered with boulders and decorated with colourful flowers. There is a pleasant, fresh-flowery smell here. Birds dance playfully through the trees, scattering insects into the air. It is brighter too with the sunlight beaming through a large break in the natural tree canopy. The prominent feature is a large oak tree at the centre of the clearing, which is covered in a crown of red and golden leaves that shimmer in the sunlight. Its trunk is draped with vines of different fruits, including bright green apples, pears and even exotic golden papayas.

There is a figure kneeling in front of the tree. A woman wearing a long, brown-tanned leather dress decorated with painted spots and trimmed with a furry beige hem. Her long dark hair is tied into a neat, round bun.

A deep enigmatic voice speaks from within the tree. 'Sable, we have visitors.'

The figure rises to her feet as she nods, acknowledging the tree. She turns to greet her visitors. Her face is covered with a large painted deer mask, complete with an impressive pair of antlers. It is decorated with tails of coloured beads that dangle on either side of the mask.

Taking three graceful steps forward, she addresses Dr Woodchuck and Cedric. 'Thank you for bringing him to see us.' Turning to Sam she adds. 'I feel the warm sentimental sense of the city deep inside you. The smell of the park is embedded deep in your jacket. It's been a while since we met, Sam.'

Sam gasps. 'How do you know my name?'

'You remember the tarot shop, don't you?' The woman removes her mask, revealing a mature, tan-skinned face. It is a face that reveals great wisdom. 'Greetings my friend, and welcome to Greystagg!'

'*It's you!*'

The shaman bows her head. 'I am Sable, and yes I was the fortune teller you met in the city. The person who foretold the steps you would take. It is I who foresaw the blast of red and yellow colours.' She adds softly. 'I'm saddened by what happened, but I only revealed to you your possible fate. It was your instincts, the actions you chose to contain the blast, that awakened your abilities and opened the portal to your true capabilities.' She pauses, staring at Sam. 'I believe we now share the same power. The power I told you to trust.'

'But what is this power,' Sam stares at his right hand, 'is it the light I saw pouring from my hands earlier?'

'It is the power that brings security and prosperity to this world. A power stronger than the four elements: earth, fire, water and air, combined. This power forms the Aether.'

'*The Aether?* I have that in me?'

'Hold my hands Sam.' Standing face-to-face, the shaman takes hold of Sam's hands and squeezes them tightly. 'Relax and let the Aether come. Feel the power grow inside…'

Sam feels the ground shudder beneath his feet, like a mini earthquake. The wind builds and encircles them as rays of bright rose-coloured light shimmers from their hands. Sam opens his eye and looks down at the soft, warm glow of the Aether enveloping him like a blanket. Flower petals are dancing in the air, caught in the swirling wind of white dust. The small grassy mound they are standing on appears lighter in colour as the sky above darkens. A meteor shower bursts, showering streams of multi-coloured lights across the heavens. These are accompanied by an echoing cry from creatures high above, taking the form of wispy dragon-shaped clouds, white and grey in colour, that trail in circles. The lights and clouds fade away and the ground stops shaking, as Sam and Sable are returned to the forest.

'Was that the Aether?'

'The Aether keeps your instincts close. It is what protected you when you were trapped inside the building.' Sable explains. 'Very few are chosen to carry its power, and Sam, the Aether has chosen you.'

Sam tries to grasp the whirlwind of revelations swirling through his mind. His dry lips crack open. '*The Aether has chosen me!*'

Sable chuckles. 'It's a lot to take in, but you shouldn't be troubled Sam. You carry your compassion on your sleeve, but you also have a calm mind. After the blast you were regarded as a hero, yet you were determined to keep your *down-to-earth* ways. It's a wonderful disposition to have. It is why the Aether believes in you; and why it believes that you can restore harmony from the Nethmites' cruel clinch. But you have much to learn.'

'Nethmites!' Yells a now familiar voice, as Cedric's intruder hurtles into the clearing.

The eagle-owl groans. 'Oh bother.'

'So these metallic monsters are called Nethmites? What a corny name for those clanking critters.'

'But what are Nethmites,' Sam asks, 'and where did they come from?'

'They have been created by a terrifying dark power called the Nether.' Sable explains, shaking her head. 'It is a power as great as the Aether, but contains pure darkness. I fear it shall do terrible things, if left to grow stronger.' She smiles at Sam, who stares back wide-eyed. 'It's okay to feel intimidated by the Nether, but you can take strength from your friends,' she says, gesturing towards the others, 'they will help you learn to use the Aether to overcome the Nether's ever-growing threat.'

'Oh please!' Cedric scoffs, realising Sable's arc has encompassed the intruder too. 'Does that crazy ranger squirt have to tag along too? Isn't Mal sufficient, what with the sky-pirate and the buttercream fellow?'

Dr Woodchuck retorts. 'They do have names Cedric.'

'They're the names I'll go by.'

'The first thing you must do, Sam, is find the guardians of the Aether. Seek them out and they will help you. But take care,' Sable warns, 'they are elusive creatures who are wary of dealing with human-beings.'

Sam asks. 'Why?'

'I suspect it could be because they have grown weary of the actions of human-beings, and their recklessness in things relating to the natural world.'

'How do we find them?'

Sable steps to one side, revealing the Flower of Knowledge. 'Tell them.'

The tree rustles, preparing to speak. 'There is a book located behind the Door of Fate,' his voice booming over the clearing, 'which lies in a deeper part of the forest. It will be difficult to find, but this will guide you.' There is a rustle of leaves and a yellow pear-shaped fruit drops from one of the vines. It lands on the grass by Sam's feet. 'This special fruit shall lead you to the Door of Fate. You must then use the power of the Aether to open the door and gain access to the portal inside.'

Sam picks up the fruit. 'I understand sir, I mean, Flower of Knowledge.'

The Flower of Knowledge hums thoughtfully. 'The wings stuck to your back.' All eyes fall on the embroidered wings decorating the back of Sam's jacket: one white wing, one black wing. 'They look familiar, as if…' The tree sighs. 'I grow tired, and I must rest. My sleep was disturbed earlier.'

His remark is directed at the eagle-owl. Cedric grins sheepishly.

He continues. 'Go to the Door of Fate and open the portal. That is my instruction.'

Sam turns to Sable. 'Thank you for explaining the Aether to me, although there's still much I have to understand. At least now I realise how your premonitions played out. And it is true I shied from the attention. I'm no hero, definitely not. I'm just Sam, plain Sam.'

Sable rests her hand on Sam's shoulder. 'There is nothing wrong with being humble Sam, as there is nothing wrong with wanting to help others. You should never doubt yourself, especially with what's facing you in your adventure. When you need me, I will be there to help. Trust in the Aether Sam, trust in yourself!' And with her soft words floating in his ears, she vanishes inside a gust of wind.

Sam gasps. 'She's gone!'

'Don't worry my friend,' Dr Woodchuck smiles, 'Sable is true to her word. But shamans don't tend to stick around one place for too long. They always have something to do, somewhere else.'

'That Sable,' Cedric chuckles, 'always going her own way!'

'Trust your senses and trust yourself, huh? Now that doesn't sound like bad advice.' Cedric's intruder begins humming. There is a broad smile stretched across their lips. 'And Sam, it seems I've misjudged you, especially since hearing the Shaman describe your sorcery power. That Aether power gave me quite a shock. It sounds like some deep, deep stuff. But you've seen off the metal critters, which makes you an ally.' Stepping forward they grab Sam's hand and begins shaking it. 'Allow me to be in your service. I might not be as tall as any of you, but I still pack a punch! Guess you would call me a ranger, yes that's what I am. The name's Addie Hawkeye, I'm sometimes called Adelaide, but that's not the name I like. So just call me Addie.'

'Sure.' Sam nods, rescuing his hand from Addie's tight grip.

'Wait! So you're saying you're,' Frank interjects. 'Um, you're a...'

'That I'm a girl? Well I would say that ponytail!' Addie scoffs, batting Frank on the side of his head with Silverhair and forcing the sky-pirate to take a step backwards and drop his hat. 'Technically I'm pretty in my own way, so you'd better get used to the idea.'

Cedric ruffles his feathers. 'Well!' He huffs indignantly. 'I'm not wasting my time here. You guys go and have your fun, I'm heading home to get me some shut eye.' Struggling to get fully airborne, the eagle-owl growls and flaps away towards the edge on the clearing.

Dr Woodchuck follows after him. 'Would you like me to tuck you in?'

Cedric sticks out his tongue and offers a sharp raspberry in response. 'Don't even try, bucko!'

Addie clicks her tongue and shakes her head. 'I don't like that bird-brain.'

Sam busily examines the yellow fruit in his hands. It feels soft to touch and has a waxy texture. His face wrinkles into a puzzled expression. 'So, how does this work? Do we open it up, or...?'

Frank interrupts, drooling. 'Can we eat it?' He reaches out with both hands. 'It looks like a tasty plump pear! And that tree didn't say not to eat it, did it?'

'Wait, Frank!'

Frank snatches at the fruit, causing it to slip from Sam's hands and splatter on the ground. Everyone stares at the resulting fleshy pile of mush in disbelief. 'Oops.'

'Well! That was a comedown ponytail,' Addie groans, 'and a total waste of a good fruit too!'

As they stare at the pulpy mess it starts to glow. The light gradually grows more intense until it is blazing brightly. It materialises into a small white orb with a rose-pink aura around its rim. Slowly it rises into the air and floats in front of the party. Then having gathered everyone's attention, it zips away, passing close to Sam's ears.

'Quick, after that light!' Addie declares, setting off before any of the others can react.

Sam watches, bemused. 'The fruit is a homing device. Now I've seen everything!'

*

Running through bushes, collecting scratches, they chase the orb deeper into the forest; relying on the thin streaks of sunlight filtering through the thick canopy to guide them. Finally the orb comes to a halt, floating in front of a giant stone slab partially concealed by thick vegetation. Bobbing up and down it waits for the party to arrive. Then it starts rotating, faster and faster, until *whoosh*, it flies directly into the solid rock. Sam and his friends catch their breath while they investigate the stone slab, which stands two whole head lengths above Frank. Pulling away the entangled vines and branches, they reveal the edge of the slab. It is engraved with patterns of flames and ivy vines. On each side of the stone door stand two carved dragons with bird-like wings. Above the door, a legend reads, *Das Schicksal klopft an die Tür.*

'Da-something, something, klo...' With difficulty Sam attempts to recite the phrase, he scratches his head. 'What does it mean? Is it a message?'

Mal peers closely at the words. 'Hm, I wonder. Ah!' She exclaims. 'I've got it! It means, *fate knocks at the door.*'

'It does?'

'This must be the Door of Fate, the place the Flower of Knowledge told us about.' Mal adds. 'No-one has ever described what lies on the other side. If anyone did find a way to get inside, then I doubt they returned. The truth of what lies within might be something wonderful, or disturbing of course.'

Sam gulps. 'That's not reassuring me.'

Mal continues. 'And if I remember correctly, the Flower of Knowledge told us that only the power of the Aether can open the door and reveal a way through the portal.'

'Hey, sounds like a job for Sammy!' Addie interjects, grinning. 'The Aether has made you the chosen one, right? So what are you waiting for? Go and show it what you're made of!'

'Alright.' Sam steps tentatively forward and stands before the Door of Fate. Holding up his right hand, he closes his eye. A stiff breeze brushes against him as the Aether sparkles over his palm. The mystical light glows against the stone door, revealing a tiny vertical crack running the length of the stone slab. The crack grows brighter, increasing in size until it traces out an opening. There is a dull creaking sound, like one made when a tired, rusty hinge is forced open. Open-mouthed, they peer into the portal: the bright swirling colours inside gives it the appearance of a giant rolling marble.

'Wow, what a show!' Addie gapes. 'Much better than I'd expected. So what now?'

'Remember the Flower of Knowledge told us that only someone who holds the power of the Aether can enter through the Door of Fate and seek out what's inside.' Mal says. 'Only they can retrieve the book we were asked to find.'

'Sounds like another job for you, Sam!' Addie adds, helpfully.

'But what if I can't find my way out?' Sam shakes his head, hesitantly. 'What if I get lost?'

'We're here to help you Sam.' Frank reaches into his backpack and draws out a long coil of strong rope. 'Here take this.

When you want to return, or if things get ugly inside, just give this a yank and we'll pull you straight out.'

'Okay.' Sam nods.

He carefully ties one end of the rope around his waist and then steps towards to the Door of Fate. Pausing at the entrance, transfixed by the marbled motion of the portal inside, he wonders what new dangers might be waiting for him inside. Holding out his right hand, he pushes his fingers through its gelatinous liquid texture.

'Are you sure this is a good idea? I don't know if I feel... ACH! '

Just as self-doubt threatens to paralyse him, Addie cuts him short, and with a brisk, sharp shove, pushes him through the portal.

'Good luck Sammy!' She cries.

Mal glares at the ranger. 'Um, don't you think that was bit rash, Addie?'

'Nah, he'll be alright.' Addie shrugs, confidently. 'Sometimes destiny requires a little encouragement.'

*

Sam falls forward and collapses onto a cold smooth floor.

'Ow!' He groans.

The air is cooler on the other side of the portal. *Wherever that might be.* Instinctively Sam lies still, hugging the ground, listening. He hears music emanating from somewhere nearby: the sound of a deep baritone choir singing. *How bizarre!*

Feeling more confident, he drags himself onto his knees. 'Where am I?'

Staring in astonishment at his hands, he holds out his soft and fleshy-tight right hand. Then he blinks, with both eyes!

'Wha? I can see properly again!'

Cautiously he reaches up and strokes the left side of his face. There is no rough surface, no scar-tissue. With growing excitement he runs both hands over his cheeks, caressing soft smooth skin.

Turning around, he searches anxiously for his red and yellow scarf. It has disappeared.

Questions. So many questions. 'What is this place, and why is it important?' Sam asks himself, setting about the task in hand. 'I'd better get started: check this place out and find the book so I can return to the forest.' He reaches down to check that the rope is still tied around his waist. 'If I can get back.'

His eyes are now accustomed to the soft diffused light inside; he steps cautiously forward into a large hall. The rope drags reassuringly behind him. The hall is empty apart from two large statues marking an access into another room: two giant dragon-bird hybrids, just like the ones carved outside. One is bordered with flowers; the other has carved rocks and chipped bowls surrounding the base. It clasps a telescope in its talons, pointing up towards a holographic sky. The dragons' eyes shimmer azure-blue.

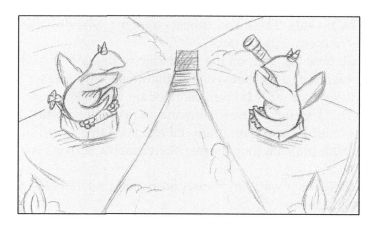

Touching the statues, Sam realises there is no dust, neither are there cobwebs hanging from the ceiling, nor dust bunnies sprawling across the floor. The hall is spotlessly clean. Passing between the two statues, he enters a room bathed in an eerie purple light with dancing violet flames projected onto the walls. He catches a faint fragrance. *Is it lavender or white musk?* Glancing behind, sensing that the dragon-bird statues are watching him, following his movements, he is reassured that they remain as they were. No-one else is in here: watching him, following him. He sees there is a giant stairway, on the far side of this second room. A spiralling staircase connecting to an upper floor.

'Nowhere to go but up and onwards.' Sam mutters, beginning to climb the stairs.

He is guided by a line of small candles spaced along the adjoining wall that mark his progress: step-by-step, flame-by-flame.

*

Meanwhile in Greystagg forest, Frank, Mal, Addie and Bonnie sit patiently outside the Door of Fate. They are watching their end of the rope, which Frank has tied securely around an adjacent tree trunk. To pass the time, Mal cuts out squares of pecan cake and Frank polishes the barrel of Old Faithful, with Bonnie sitting by his side. The forest appears tranquil, with only the sounds of birds twittering in the trees.

'So how big is it, on the other side of the door?' Addie asks, rolling blades of grass between her thumb and forefinger.

'I don't know.' Mal replies, handing a slice of pecan cake to the ranger. 'I've never known anyone go inside the portal, not even Sable. For all I know Sam might be inside a large mansion, or in a splendid temple with long marble staircases, or perhaps some giant library.'

'Well either way, he'd better hurry and find that blasted book. I'm already bored.'

*

Sam reaches the top of the stairs. The upper floor is smaller, and the light here fainter than below. Nevertheless, it is sufficient to see that he has entered a library: complete with giant wooden shelves running the length of the room. Long shelves stacked with thousands of books.

He reads out the sections as he passes them. 'History. Travel. Art…'

There is a strange shuffling sound, books sliding against the shelves. Sam stops.

CRUNCH!

Two books have mysteriously slid from an upper shelf and fallen, almost hitting him on the head.

'Oops. It wasn't me!'

Unperturbed, Sam continues walking alongside the bookshelves, listening to the sound of voices emanating from the other side of the library wall.

'It's a beautiful looking day. Temperatures are comfortable, and the astronauts are preparing to board the VEGA to commence this important expedition...' The commentary is abruptly drowned in static.

He follows the sound towards the door of an adjacent room. Pausing briefly outside, listening to a cheering crowd, he pushes open the door and looks inside. At the centre of the room is a marbled-coloured holographic projector. It is beaming the image of a large stationary rocket with steam pouring from its base. It looks ready to launch. Stencilled in black lettering along its side, descending from the nose, is the name of the rocket: 'VEGA'. The image on the screen switches to one showing two men and a woman in large white astronaut suits. They each carry a helmet under their arms. Sam watches on intently as the astronauts stride towards the rocket.

The crackling commentary continues. *'Mission control from VEGA, this is Noah speaking. We're preparing for launch, ready to meet the wonders of the universe with human technology.'*

Sam stares at the smiling holographic image on the screen. It looks just like him. He is gazing at the same soft brown eyes he sees every time he looks into a mirror.

He sinks to his knees. 'Is that…?'

Kneeling on the hard-polished wooden floor, he continues to watch as the astronauts disappear inside the rocket. The commentator's voice is heard describing a brief montage, a series of photographic stills of the astronauts' preparing for their journey into space. The image on the screen jumps to mission control, counting down to ignition. '*Preparing to launch: in ten, nine, eight, seven, six, five, four...*'

The rocket launches as hot steam pours from four huge rear exhausts and the VEGA lifts heavily from the white smoke billowing across the ground. As it soars higher and higher into the sky, stretching out towards the upper atmosphere, mission control cheers, celebrating a successful launch. Scientists and engineers embrace, planting high-fives, while outside a watching audience tosses confetti and jellybeans into the air.

Mesmerised, Sam watches a sequence of images detailing the VEGA passing up through the atmosphere and disappearing into space. There is one final image of the tiny capsule detaching itself from the giant rocket. The screen fades to darkness. Moments later light bursts from out of the projector, casting a picture of Noah sitting inside the spacecraft. He carries a sad, but immensely proud smile. He seems to be staring out beyond the camera and the screen, as if he is looking directly at Sam, crouched by the doorway. The ground below the rocket is shrinking away, captured as a reflection across his golden visor.

Noah speaks. 'If I don't come home, I want you to know this. I'm sorry I left you alone. Lily... Sam... Look for me here, with the stars ...'

The hologram image of Noah crackles and fizzles, and then fades to nothing. The hologram projector shuts down: light and sound extinguished. Sam scrubs at the tears escaping his eyes. *How long has he been here, alone inside the projection room?*

Slowly and surely, he forces himself to focus on his own task. Standing, he offers a final thankful glance at the inactive hologram machine and returns to the library. He scans the contents of the bookshelves, running his fingers along the spines of countless number of tomes.

He sighs. 'Now if I were a librarian, where would I put a particularly important book?'

As if in answer to his question, he hears the same shuffling sound he heard before. Glancing up he spots a burgundy-coloured book sliding off the shelf above his head. It misses him and falls onto the floor.

'And why do books keep falling off the bookshelves?' Sam retorts, picking up the book. The cover contains an illustration of the two dragon-bird hybrid statues in the main hall: the white one on the left, the black one on the right. They stand, back-to-back, facing away from each other. 'And why are there so many replicas of these two dragons?' Holding up the book, he reads the legend on the spine and smiles. 'What luck! My task is done, I can return to the others before any crazier stuff happens.'

As he starts for the staircase, Sam's nostrils begin tingling with the rancid smell of burning. It is a terrible smell, one that is awfully familiar. Quickening his pace he skips down the staircases, stopping abruptly on seeing a darkened shape at foot of the stairs. Approaching cautiously, he makes out a figure pinned beneath fallen debris: a body lying in a dark red puddle.

He steps closer.

'Is that…?' His words trail away as the fallen figure moves; his head turns and looks up at Sam. The left side of the face is covered in blood-caked hair. Sam's eyes widen and he lets out a coarse gasp. *'You're… ME!'*

The injured Sam sighs. 'Help me…' His head slumps towards the stained floor.

Frantically Sam begins clawing away the rubble as the injured Sam slowly fades away, disappearing in front of his eyes. 'Wha?'

The room starts to swirl around him, dominated by dark-purple colours that spark and fizz, like static. Staring at his right hand, Sam watches as it shifts between its fleshy and prosthetic forms. The sight from his left eye is beginning to fail and he feels his body weaken, crackling with electric discharges. He too is fading to nothing.

There is a sudden terrifying, deafening shriek: an eerie, chilling cry. Sam is overwhelmed by the fear that he is about to be overcome by an army of the metallic creatures. He wants to run, to get to safety, back to his friends. But he is disorientated. *Where is the portal?*

He sobs. 'Help me.'

*

'What's going on in there?' Addie exclaims, watching the portal swirling violently.

'I think the Door of Fate is collapsing,' Mal cries, 'from the inside!'

Frank jumps to his feet, tugging at the rope. 'Quick, pull Sam back!' Mal, Addie and Bonnie grab hold too. 'Okay, on the count of three.'

'One…'

*

Feeling a tug on the rope tied around his waist, Sam holds out his right hand, reaching towards two shadowy figures standing before him. The shapes tease his blurred sight, surrounding him in comforting colours of red, orange and yellow. He recognises the woman as gusts of wind snap into a whirlwind, accompanied by metallic screeching that threatens to burst his eardrums.

He presses his hands against his ears.

*

'Two…'

*

There is another tug. In that instant Sam remembers the book. The book he had come here to retrieve. The book is lying on the floor next to him. He wraps his arms around the tome, holding it tightly against his chest. The room he is in is becoming distorted, it is beginning to disintegrate. The images of the two people disappear. He squeezes his eye shut and releases a long heart-breaking scream.

*

'*THREE!*'

And with a final determined tug, Sam flies backwards out through the gelatinous portal and into Frank's arms. The book sails from his grasp and lands on the grass beside them. He is in Greystagg forest. Mal and Addie stare as the portal fades away and the Door of Fate slams shut. The vines bind together to form a secure lock. They turn to Sam.

'Sam!' Mal cries. 'Are you alright?'

'Damn! You look awful!' Addie gasps. 'Like, what happened in there?'

Frank cradles his friend in his arms. Sam's face is ashen, his frame a shuddering heap. Lifting his bionic hand, he grabs his red and yellow striped scarf and wraps it around his face. He feels his scar tingle and then mutters something incomprehensible.

'What was that Sam?' Frank asks, concerned.

Sam looks up at his friends, his vision blurred with tears.

'Have I?' He gasps, struggling to keep his voice steady.

He fails to complete his sentence. Exhausted, he buries his head into Frank's shoulder, who gently rocks him from side to side.

Interlude – Mandy and Sandy

Melsey has experienced several days of heavy rainfall and the city's traffic crawls slowly, splashing through giant puddles accumulating on the streets. Cars, vans, and the occasional motorbikes, take turns to spray water over the pavements, soaking unfortunate pedestrians. In the park there are hundreds of snails trekking lazily over the grass, beneath spiders hanging within webs decorated with fine water droplets. The wet air carries a distinct musky fragrance.

Stepping off a tram, Mandy walks along the puddled pavement running along the park, her hand clasping the hem of her cross-hatched skirt to prevent it from being caught in the wind. Her other hand clutches her near exhausted mobile phone. Its flashing red coloured LED battery light reflecting against her face.

'I can't believe Sam just left to go on his grand adventure,' she grumbles, 'leaving me behind and bored out of my mind.' She pauses to adjust her soggy plaited hair. 'Man, the city is so dull... and damp.'

Her phone chooses this moment to emit a final dull tone as its screen fades to black. With a despondent shrug, she continues on her way to see Sandy in his florist shop. She sees him standing busy watering a line of flower-filled buckets.

The florist glances up as she approaches. 'Mandy? How strange to see you out on your own. Can I help you with anything?'

'Huh? I've been thinking about Sam and wondering why he left so abruptly. Gee! It's been ages since he left: gone just like that,' she clicks her fingers, 'without a word.'

'You should have got up early to bid him well on his travels.' Sandy replies, chuckling mischievously. 'But there's no great mystery. He's out exploring the countryside. And I'm guessing you've never been outside the city, have you?' He teases. 'You're too much of a city dweller.'

'Cheek! Calling me a city dweller,' pouting, Mandy sighs, 'but maybe you're right. I just wish I knew how he's doing.' She plays absentmindedly with the petals of a flower in one of the brightly coloured buckets. 'Hey! Did you hear that Bonnie has run off too?'

'I did. She must have gone to find Sam. You can't underestimate the special bond between a dog and her human friend.' He nods thoughtfully. 'But she's a city pup and I'm worried she'll not cope on her own. I hope she's alright.'

Sandy steps inside the shop and Mandy follows him through the door. Picking up a watering-can he begins watering a small posy of pink lilies.

'He's strange, that Sam.' Mandy sighs. 'To be honest, I don't get the gist of him. He did something good, but he avoids the fame and refuses to give interviews with the media. I know they've hounded him, pointing mics and cameras into his face, but surely if he'd given them what they wanted they would have left him alone. What's with him? Does he like being a hermit sitting alone in the park?'

Sandy shakes his head. 'I think you're being too hard on Sam. He just wants to take the humble path and have his views respected. And there's nothing wrong with that. People shouldn't have to put up with the glare of publicity, not if they don't want it.'

'I guess,' Mandy shrugs, 'and I know he's a great musician, but why is he so different to my other friends? I mean he's so distant, not like normal city folk at all. He's like some sort of alien.' Feeling a prisoner of her own words, she grimaces. 'Not that I mean in an alien-alien sort of way, I mean, more like in an alien-human kind of way.'

Sandy smiles at Mandy's literal-mindedness. 'Then perhaps you don't know Sam that well. But in a way, you're right Mandy. Sam isn't from Melsey.'

'Wha! He's not?'

'No he's from Farley.' Sandy explains. 'He came to live with Johnny and Mary in Melsey, after his mother passed.'

'Farley?'

'It's a small town far away in the north of the Island. There are lots of people who have left Farley to make their homes here in Melsey. They are different to normal city dwellers, and like Sam they tend to be down-to-earth and not brag and put themselves forward. Sam... and Noah too.'

'Noah?'

'Yep! Noah McKenzie. Haven't you heard of him? He was one of the astronauts on the ill-fated VEGA mission, although it happened a long time ago.' Sandy glances at a now inquisitive Mandy. 'Noah was part of a team constructing a new satellite in space when there was a terrible accident and the spacecraft malfunctioned. Only two of the astronauts returned safely. No-one knows what happened to Noah.' His voice trails away. 'But he was just like Sam, a gentle fella with a friendly air to others.'

Mandy runs her hand over her plait, checking that her hair is in place. 'Huh, that's smart of you to know. I guess modesty runs in people from Farley.' She watches Sandy water bunches of red flowers with his watering can. 'Hey Mr Sanderson, there's something I've been wondering.'

'Shoot.'

'You spend all day tending flowers and selling them to customers, right?'

'Right.'

'And you know a lot about plants and flowers, yeah?'

'Yeah.'

'Well, I was walking through the park and noticed the plants are looking miserable and all droopy, as if they're gasping for water.' She pauses, deep in thought. 'But it's been raining for days, hasn't it? Which kinda bothered me. If they're getting watered, why are they looking so sad?'

Sandy starts. 'Really? That does sound odd. But don't worry Mandy, what with all this rain they're probably a little sodden, like the rest of us. Besides, I'm sure the park gardeners are looking after them.'

'Yeah, I suppose you're right.' She pulls out her phone, with its exhausted LED battery light and blank screen. 'Whereas my biggest problem Mr Sanderson, is I should have given my phone more R and R before leaving home this morning.'

Gaia and Techna

A clear cerulean sky stretches over the peaceful waters of the lake in Greystagg forest. Birds perched in the surrounding trees provide chorused songs to cheer the bright afternoon. A breeze blows through clumps of orange pansies and sends ripples across the surface of the lake. Cedric is sitting on a branch of an oak tree, his restless sleep interspersed with occasional grunts and utterances.

'Ooh, serpent! Ooh you little tawnies, I will get...'

Kneeling on the bank at the edge of the lake, Sam gazes at his reflection in the crystal-clear water. He strokes away a tear creeping down his cheek, but another drops into the water, distorting his reflection.

'Was it Noah, my Pa,' his soft voice cracks with emotion, 'that I saw inside the portal? Was it really him?'

He senses someone approaching from behind, hearing footsteps crunch the damp grass and leaves.

'Nice view of the forest clearing, isn't it?'

Sam glances up. 'Oh, hey Frank.'

'Howdy, Sam! You feeling any better?'

'A bit.' Sam replies, with a fragile smile. He gazes at his reflection. 'Though I still feel...' his words trail away. Distracted, he strokes his bionic arm, caressing the hard cold metal.

'I'm not surprised Sam. It's hard coming to terms with losing a part of yourself. My body is incomplete too, thanks to my dispute with those brutal bandits.' Frank sighs. 'And it's not just the physical pain that gets to you, it's the mental strain as well.' He runs a hand through Sam's curls. 'Hey! I've an idea. Why don't I

give your hair a brush? A good brush always makes me feel better.'
He laughs. 'And what with the wind and the dust, I reckon one's
overdue.'

'Yeah, maybe that would work.'

'Great! Make yourself comfortable.'

Sam removes his scarf and haunches his knees close to his
chest. Frank takes a large hairbrush from his shoulder bag and
begins pulling it through his friend's hair.

'Such wavy curls. Your hair is nice and soft; and so easy to
brush.' Frank continues. 'There's no troubling frizz or split ends.'

'Thank you Frank. You remind me of Ma when she brushed
my hair.'

Frank hums quietly, distracted by a fish popping its lips
through the surface of the lake. Behind him, bluebirds dance about
the trees as colourful butterflies dive in and out of wildflowers.
'Tell me about your Ma. Was she pretty?'

'She was.' Sam sighs. 'She was beautiful and honest; and she
always carried an open-mind and an open-heart. She was my best
friend. It broke my heart, finding out how much she was suffering.
Things got really tough, what with her inner struggles and rising
bills. But even so, she wanted me to do what I love most, playing
music.' He wipes away another tear. 'When she went away, I left
for Melsey to live with her friends, Johnny and Mary. It was her
idea. I think she felt living in the city would give me the
opportunity to play my music more.'

'What was her name?'

'Lily. Her name was Lily.'

'That's a lovely name.'

'Yeah. She made things as easy for me as she could, even
when she was ill. She used to make yummy cherry pies. We would
spent hours baking in the kitchen, learning her recipe so I can make
it again and again. Fresh morello cherry puree with halves of
leftover cherries, that's my favourite, served with a large dollop of
vanilla ice-cream.'

Frank hums, smacking his lips. 'That sounds amazing.'

'Yeah!' Sam chuckles. 'Her cherry pies were the best in Farley.'

Frank continues listening to his friend as he shares his heartache of being disconnected and his mixed feelings on leaving Farley. He desperately wants to cheer Sam up and do something more than just brushing his hair. The wind strengthens and plays with his ponytail. He drops the hairbrush, which lands with a soft pat on the grass.

'What's wrong?'

'Oh, it's nothing.' Frank picks up his hairbrush and stuffs it inside his rucksack. 'I think your hair is done.' He stands. 'Look Sam, I'm sorry if I've upset you asking about your mother. I was curious.'

Sam gets to his feet and places a hand on his friend's shoulder. 'I'm glad you wanted to hear about Lily. In fact it's really helped, after my experiences inside the portal.'

'So you're feeling better now?'

'Oh yeah, much better. Thanks Frank.'

'Then I'm happy to have been of assistance, buddy. And a good hair brushing always drives the cobweb blues away!'

Sam slips his scarf snugly around his scar. 'Where are the others?'

'They're reading the book you brought from inside the portal. It looks really promising, from what I've seen. Let's go and see how they're getting on.'

'Sure.'

Hearing something rustling in the bushes, Frank spins around and stares into the bushes.

Sam starts. 'Frank?'

'I thought I heard something over there.' Frank squints into the shadows and shakes his head. 'It must have been a bird or an animal, but I'm nervous with those metal critters about.'

'I get what you mean. One bit my ankle!'

The others are sitting by a large mulberry bush, a short distance from Mal's treehouse cabin. Addie is leafing slowly through the book, her back propped against a tree.

She glances up as Sam and Frank approach. 'Oy! Sammy this book is pure gold! It's got loads about magic sorcery, just as the shaman said: *Aether is a cosmic, spiritual energy, more powerful than any of the four elements.* Heh! Sounds neat, if a little corny!'

'Is there anything about the two guardians?' Frank asks.

'Ah, hold that thought.' Addie skims through the pages, flinching from a papercut. 'Here we go! *The two guardians of the Aether: Gaia is the guardian of nature; and Techna is the guardian of technology, from clay bowls to transport.* Hey, I wonder if they're a couple or something.' She gasps. 'Anyway... *The guardians ensure there is harmony with the Aether, and protects the world from creatures manipulated by the Nether.* It says here: *Gaia and Techna created and nurtured the Fleur de Vie.*'

'The Fleur de Vie?'

'It means, Flower of Life. Keep up! *It is a magical plant that harmonises the dynamic bond of nature and technology.*'

Mal sings. 'Ooh, that sounds pretty!'

Addie scoffs. 'A flower to bring harmony to nature and everyday man-made stuff? How cheesy! How can a flower stop those horrible metallic critters?'

Frank spins around. He has heard rustling behind him, but this time it sounds louder and is accompanied by a shower of leaves. Something is approaching from within the shadows.

Ignorant of its imminent arrival, Sam interjects. 'But those metallic creatures, the Nethmites, have risen from the Nether.' Studying the book, he reasons. 'Which means we've gotta find the two guardians and find out more about the Fleur de Vie and its purpose.'

'Uhm, I think we've got something more pressing Sam.' Frank gasps, quivering. 'Look over there!'

Creeping behind a line of trees, trudging through mulberry bushes, is something large. It bursts into the clearing, brushing away leaves and snapping back branches. Its appearance startles Sam and his friends. They stare open-mouthed at the creature, appearing larger than a horse. Its physical features resemble a dragon, except that its charcoal-coloured body is not covered in scales or feathers, but in fur. A pair of floppy ears bounce on the side of its head topped with two long moth feelers. There is a thick light-grey mane running from a fluffy collar around its neck along the length of its spine, ending at the creature's tail where it meets a large round tip that resembles a metal gear. The creature stops before the party and crouches, as if preparing to pounce. Its feathery wings glow an electric, bright azure. Its brilliant blue eyes stare down, a puzzled expression across its face.

'Wah!' Frank gasps, grabbing hold of Old Faithful. 'What is that?'

'More importantly,' Mal gulps, 'what does it want?'

'Beats me.'

'I bet it likes the taste of wood,' Addie grins, pulling an arrow across Silverhair, 'and I'm happy to oblige!'

The creature's eyes glow brighter as it stands tall, its fur bristling, and emits a deep droning sound.

Sam stares at the creature, recognising the same azure-blue glow emanating from the creature's eyes with those from the statues he saw inside the portal.

'Wait! Hold your fire!' Holding out his hand he steps forward and stands between the strange creature and his companions. 'I think it wants to speak to us.'

Frank cries. 'What are you doing, Sam?'

Sam does not respond. He is studying the aura surrounding the towering creature. 'I am Sam McKenzie, from Melsey, and these are my friends. We are here by word of Sable, to seek the guardians: Gaia and Techna. She told us they will teach us about the Aether.'

He holds out his bionic hand with soft rose-coloured wisps of the Aether glowing above his palm. It forms a small, rose-coloured flame. The creature relaxes its threatening posture and the ethereal blue-glow around its feathers fades. Its piercing azure eyes soften as it gazes down at Sam.

'You must be the hero of Melsey.' Its base tone resonates. 'I saw you before. When you were hiding in the grotto sheltering from the storm, but those were not ideal conditions for introductions.' The creature lowers its head and bows. 'I am Techna, and I am at your service.'

The party gasp in awe. This is one of the guardians: Techna, the Guardian of Technology. Yet despite its magnificent appearance, the creature displays a courteous manner.

The guardian chuckles, sending out a deep rumbling sound that fills the space between them. 'At ease everyone. There's no need to stand like *statues!*'

Sam clears his throat. 'So you're Tech…Tech…'

'It's pronounced *Tesh-a*, the "n" is silent.'

Addie mutters. 'That's not how I read it.'

'Fancy meeting one of the guardians.' Sam says, studying the creature. 'I thought you and Gaia were the stuff of stories! Stories I have read.'

'Perhaps we are, for most at least. Of course you humans are very curious creatures: ingenious, masters of practicality, but always curious.' Techna offers Mal a sly glance and adds. 'And I too enjoy the fruits of this world, especially when humans make them into something even tastier. Say for example, pecan cakes!'

'Absolutely!' Mal pulls out three pecan cakes from her bag and hands them to the Guardian. 'I'm flattered you've taken a liking to my pecan cakes.'

Techna closes his eyes and smells the warm cakes. 'Mm, lovely!'

Sam declares. 'You don't seem as intimidating as people say you are.'

'While I love listening to stories, the ones about me and Gaia aren't exactly accurate. Not at all.' Techna explains, his mouth full of pecan cake. 'Take my description of being dark, why should that be defined as something eerie? Look at me, I'm as chill as pills.' He pauses, furtively exploring the skies above, considering his words carefully. 'Although you should be wary of Gaia, he is quite opinionated.'

'Opinionated?'

'Well…'

But before Techna can explain he is interrupted by a dramatic rumble erupting from the clouds above. The sound is accompanied by a burst of brilliant white light. The party take a step back. *Is it a storm?* There is something approaching from the heavens, as quick as a lightning bolt zipping towards the ground.

BAM!

From out of a cloud of dust rises another creature, one as large as Techna; its body covered in ivory-white fur and feathers, complete with a creamy-coloured mane. It is Gaia. The guardian's coat glimmers with dew, from its impressive fluffy crown to its sharp bladed tail.

The creature shrieks, spreading their wings. 'Behold, Techna! The Guardian Gaia has arrived!' It has the same azure-blue crystal eyes as Techna.

'Hello Gaia.' Techna retorts impassively, unimpressed with Gaia's melodramatic entrance.

'The Aether's guardian of all things peaceful and vibrant is here! *Ha-Ha!*' The white guardian declares, his voice ringing through the air rouses birds perched in the adjacent tress. 'I am the guardian of wonder and joy, and of...' Gaia stops. Standing perfectly still, he glares at the humans with an intensity that causes them to shrink away. He offers a curt cough. 'Really, playing with humans? Honestly Techna, we have an important mission, and here you are, making friends with these petty creatures.'

'Gaia...'

Addie grimaces. 'Who's pushed his button?'

'Let's start on this puny one.' Gaia counters, scowling at Addie. 'This short-stuff carrying a tree branch fashioned into a weapon. Fortunately they appear none too strong, nor too bright, otherwise I might have been struck by one of their pesky arrows.'

'Oi!' Addie exclaims, her cheeks beet-red.

The white guardian turns to Sam. 'And what about this one. Let us see?'

He stops short and takes a step back. Sam is staring wide-eyed at the guardian, holding out his right arm. The guardian's eyes flash brightly, he has seen something: a faint trail of golden light flowing in the wind, and beyond Sam, there is an ethereal figure wearing a gentle smile.

'Ter...?' Gaia starts, but then shakes his head, dispelling the image. He reaches out and touches Sam's arm.

'As I was saying, *this* one has got a metal arm, which means they have acted foolhardily to lose the original.'

Sam gasps. 'Wha?'

Techna takes a step forward. 'Gaia...'

Spotting cake crumbs on the ground, Gaia turns on the other guardian. 'And what's this, Techna? Are these humans feeding you their filthy food? Seriously, look at your shape! I insist you go on a diet immediately,' he rants, shaking his head in disappointment, 'you know cakes go straight to your thighs.'

Techna silences Gaia by shoving a piece of pecan cake into the white guardian's mouth and then holding it shut. Turning to the humans he shares a sly, mischievous grin as Gaia mumbles loudly and beats his wings in protest. When Techna eventually releases his mouth, Gaia spits the remains of the cake out, spluttering and scraping his tongue.

'Easy Gaia.' Techna chuckles, calming the ivory guardian. 'Sable has sent us these humans for our guidance and protection. There's no need to insult them.'

'*Sable?! Wha? But... How?*'

Techna turns to Sam. 'Please pardon Gaia. As I've told you, he has strong opinions on humans.'

Sam smiles. 'That's okay.'

'*Peh!*' Addie mumbles. 'As if I'll ever pardon that white pearl jerk for calling me short-stuff!'

Ignoring Addie's complaint, Sam asks. 'Can you tell us more on the purpose of the Aether? Sable explained it is a force more powerful than the four elements, but how is it relevant to us?'

The two guardians face each other. 'Hmph! Don't look at me Techna,' Gaia scoffs, 'they're your friends.'

'It's complicated.' Techna sighs. 'Sable is correct when she describes the Aether is a power greater than the combined forces of earth, fire, wind and water. Gaia and I are tasked to guide its power to restore the world from disharmony created by the Nether.'

'But we know little about the Nether.' Sam adds.

Addie asks. 'And what exactly are Nethmites, those pesky creatures manipulated by the Nether?'

'I shall answer.' Gaia interjects. 'Nethmites are a parasitic horde who chew down and consume everything they find, whether it's natural or technological. The Nether feeds on ignorance, like you humans. It grows on negative vibes such as greed and fear, which increases its power and allows the Nethmites to multiply and prosper. Left unchallenged the Nethmites shall swarm as locusts and destroy everything in their path.'

Techna adds. 'And if the Nether and the Nethmites overpower the Aether, they will turn the world to darkness. The beautiful world you see around you will become a barren wasteland. Nethmites shall devour plants and drain lakes, turning the land and rivers toxic. It is our task to keep the Aether flourishing, so it never falls under the Nether's dark power.'

'And what about the Fleur de Vie?' Mal asks.

'Ah! The Fleur de Vie represents the circle of reawakening and growth that keeps the Nether at bay.' Techna explains. 'Regrettably, during the passage of time and our constant travels, Gaia and I have lost track of the Fleur de Vie's location. We fear that it might be lost for good. But we trust that we are wrong, and it has managed to secure a place of safety.'

A dramatic silence falls upon the forest, interspersed with gusts of wind rustling the tree canopy above.

'In that case, what can we do to help?' Sam asks. 'Perhaps we can help find the Fleur de Vie and help you fight the Nether?'

'You help us?' Gaia exclaims, with a sarcastic scoff. 'Ha! More like you'll make me collapse to the ground with laughter. How in all the Aether can you possibly fight the Nether?'

'Hm!' Techna hums, stroking his chin. 'Maybe you can help Sam, with your compassionate ways and your instincts; and the help of your friends.'

'We can help?' Addie exclaims. 'Yes!'

Gaia is dumbfounded. 'But Tech, they're *humans!* How can they stand up to the terrible dark forces of the Nether?'

'Aw, c'mon, Gaia! Isn't it wise to recognise that even the smallest of creatures can make a difference?'

Gaia glares down at the humans and huffs. 'Very well, if that's how you see it, but I really don't like, nor approve, on how this might work out.' He sighs. 'I'll be waiting for you Tech.' Then, accompanied by a flash of light and a clap of thunder, the white guardian disappears.

Sam rubs the back of his head. 'Golly, he seems put-off.'

'He is.' Techna nods. 'And now you can see what I meant about Gaia's thoughts on you humans. But let's not dwell on that for now. About the Aether Sam, I believe you can use it to help find the Fleur de Vie and bring an end to the rise in Nether's powers.'

'Yeah, we can do that!' Addie hollers, holding her hands above her head and grinning from ear to ear. 'We can stop the Nether! I bet those lil' Nethmite nut-bolts are already quaking in their roots. Ha-Ha!' She begins punching the air with her fists.

'Boy, she has an arrogant streak.' Techna leans towards Sam. 'I find her rather scary.'

'I know what you mean.' Sam smiles. He glances at the sun, already inching behind the trees. 'We should rest for the night. It's been a long day and we must plan for the next stage in our journey.'

'Then I shall bid you all adieu, for now. I'd better catch up with Gaia, I mustn't keep him waiting. He doesn't like me dawdling.' Techna moans. 'But if you need me, I shall be here: just seek out the raven.' The guardian winks at Sam and takes to the air, his wings glowing brightly as he climbs into the darkening sky.

'Bye Techna!' Addie puts her hands on her hips and beams. 'What a guy!'

Climbing towards the heavens, Techna follows Gaia's trail until he catches up with the white guardian, sulking inside the mountain valley. Gaia has puffed his body into a ball and is swishing his tail furiously from side to side.

He glances up as Techna approaches. 'So you've finally finished talking with the humans?'

'Yeah, I'm done.'

'Good!' Gaia pulls a face. 'I didn't like the way you shoved that unpleasant sweety mush into my mouth while I was trying to make my point. It was far too sticky and chewy.' The white guardian pauses and glares at Techna, who is snickering under his breath. '*What?*'

'C'mon Gaia. It wasn't as if it was made from some swamp creature.'

'Your point is?'

'My point is you could have created a better impression.' Techna smiles. 'Besides, I saw the look on your face when you were talking to Sam. He reminded you of her, didn't he?'

Gaia freezes, his wings taut and straight. 'Wait, what? Who?'

Techna rolls his eyes and struts past Gaia. 'You know exactly who.'

The black guardian swoops into the air, releasing a boisterous, ironic, guffaw.

Gaia puffs hard. He is still feeling sorry for himself, but he too leaps into the air to fly after Techna.

'Hey Tech! Wait for me.'

*

The party returns to Mal's house. It is a moonless night, and the darkness has quietly consumed the surrounding woodland. Birds and woodland animals have scurried home to their nests or burrows, except for those nocturnal creatures that embrace the night. Sam spots a cluster of moonflowers, revealed from their daytime hideaways in the thickets. Atop a birch tree, Cedric screeches, battering away a couple of smaller owls before they can get a chance to hoot.

The eagle-owl grumbles and shakes his tail-feathers. 'Pesky tawnies!'

Entering Mal's treehouse home, Sam and his friends settle around the table, wrapping their bodies inside heavy blankets. They are soon munching down on pecan cake and fruit salad, while drinking warm, sweet tea. Bonnie, sitting next to Sam, crunches down on her biscuits.

Addie, a mischievous grin stretched across her face, says. 'I don't usually enjoy nuts much, but these pecan cakes are rather good. My taste-buds are sure loving 'em and I'll give you two thumbs up for your cooking, bunny-ears.'

Mal sighs. 'It's Mal.'

'Right, right.' Addie's tone softens. 'Tell me Mal, why do you live on your own in the forest?'

'I haven't always lived here,' Mal explains, 'I used to live in a small town, to the south. But I used to get teased because I liked talking to animals, so I decided to leave and live in the forest, free from the taunting.'

'Aw, you should let me at 'em.'

'Thanks for your support Addie, but that isn't necessary.'

Frank watches Sam fiddling with the strands of his red and yellow striped scarf. 'Hey, what's bothering you?'

'Yeah Sammy,' Addie chimes, 'you can tell us anything.'

Sam replies. 'I think it was Noah.'

'Noah?' Mal starts. 'The astronaut?'

'Hey! What brought this up?' Addie asks.

'I saw someone inside the portal.' Sam's fingers twist and fold over the scarf strands. 'I think it was a hologram image of Noah.'

'Are you sure?'

Sam shrugs. 'I think so.'

'And you haven't seen him before the exhibition?' Mal asks.

Sam shakes his head.

Addie gasps. 'He dumped you and your Ma?'

'*What?!*' Mal and Frank shriek, stunned.

'Geeze… I was just asking a question.'

'Ma told me he was part of an important space expedition. She said he went away, up on that spaceship and never returned. We would spend evenings together out on the terrace, in Farley, looking up at the stars.' Sam sighs, a sad smile across his face. 'We had such a wonderful time together, despite it being so short. Even when I was living in Melsey I thought about Farley, with it being remote and rustic and different to living in the city. Farley is my home too.'

Addie's expression falls. 'Oh, I see. I didn't think about that.' She coughs and puts on a grin. 'Ah, whatever! We'd better rest up for tomorrow, if we're gonna find the Fleur de Vie, whatever that is. And I need my, what do they call it, beauty sleep. Heh! Like I would say that!' She pulls up the blanket and covers her head.

'Addie's right, and hopefully Cedric won't keep us awake tonight.' Mal nods. 'He means well, it's just he gets these strange and disturbing ideas.' She smiles. 'Night fellow chums!'

Frank removes his large brim hat and places it on the table beside him. He turns to Sam, who is watching Bonnie chasing her tail. She quickly tires and slumps into a round furry ball at the foot of Sam's blanket.

Frank asks. 'Are you going to be alright tonight?'

'I think so.'

'Remember if you're feeling down, then I'm right here. Just give me a nudge.'

'I'll be fine tonight,' Sam chuckles. 'but thanks Frank, I appreciate it.'

Within comforting shadows of the night, Sam lies awake, watching as one-by-one his friends drift off to sleep. He shivers from the cool night air and rising anxiety. Immediately he senses the Aether inside him, calming and warming his body, washing away his fears. Feeling at ease, he rolls his scarf into a makeshift pillow and reaches over the table to switch off the tiny lamp, casting the room into darkness.

Run Rabbit Run

C limbing into the sky the sun peeps over the top of the Flower of Knowledge's crown. It is a fine morning in Greystagg, without sight or sound of the fierce metallic creatures: the Nethmites. A family of squirrels dance around tree trunks, their bushy tails a blur; while a pair of finches tweet their songs perched on the branch of a dogberry tree. Sam is resting cross-legged against the Flower of Knowledge, busy reading the book and discovering more about the Fleur de Vie. Bonnie plays lazily with the butterflies fluttering by her head. Frank and Addie sit nearby, having an in-depth discussion.

'So you just wandered off on your own,' Addie says, 'with this lad called Marco Polo, to find hanging people?'

Frank interjects. 'They were dolls!'

'Right, dolls,' Addie sniggers, 'and despite him arguing against you going deeper into the forest, you rolled with it 'cause these old codgers, some so-called adventurers, thought it was your destiny. *Not theirs, yours!* Heck, that Marco's a darn sight smarter than you are. *You're so gullible!*'

'Hey! No I'm not!'

Addie chortles loudly. 'Whatever you say, ponytail!'

Frank's shoulders droop and he pulls his hat over his eyes. 'I might be a coward,' he mutters to himself, 'but I ain't gullible.'

The Flower of Knowledge hums: a sound resembling a low rhythmic chuckle. He is listening attentively. 'Silly, silly.' Clearing his throat, he turns his attention to Sam. 'The Fleur de Vie has not been observed, not for some time. I sense the Aether is weakening from its absence.'

Sam asks. 'Do you think it was the Aether that helped contain the blast, that day in Melsey?'

'Undoubtedly, but your act of selflessness has played its part too. The Aether recognises such sacrifices. It was with you then, as it is inside you now.'

'But I don't consider myself brave, not in my own mind. Surely it was more foolish than anything else.'

'I understand your interpretation, my friend, but you mustn't doubt yourself. Sable trusts you and knows you carry the Aether deep within you. I'll admit, I was sceptical at first, but now having spoken to you, I too believe in you.'

Sam gazes out into the clearing, listening to the birds singing in the trees. It is so peaceful here. How can anything as bad and as cruel as the Nether disturb such tranquillity.

'Flower of Knowledge, may I ask you something?'

'Of course.'

'Now I've met the two guardians, I don't understand their reactions: Techna is chummy and encourages our help; but Gaia's reaction is resentful and hostile. Why is he so aloof?'

'He met you with a rocky preamble.' The Flower of Knowledge rustles his crown of leaves, carefully considering his response. 'It might be that Gaia is focused on his task. But as the guardian of nature he has grown weary of humans mistreating the natural world. He treats humans with indifference, but there was a time when he behaved differently.'

'He did?'

'In fact...' The Flower of Knowledge stirs, distracted by a long loud cry. No, it is a squawk bursting through the clearing. The sound is getting louder and louder. The Flower of Knowledge groans. 'Oh dear!'

Standing, Sam asks. 'Is that Cedric?'

'Yes. What has that pest of an eagle-owl seen now?'

'*Alert! Alert!* Flower of Knowledge!' Cedric soars into the clearing, screeching. '*Alert! Alert!*' His cries spread-out far and wide, alarming birds perched high in the tree canopies and causing rabbits to dive for the safety of their warrens.

'Aw, what is it, beaky?' Addie teases, exaggerating Cedric's alarm call with a sarcastic falsetto. 'Is it another serpent, or is it a just a worm in the grass?'

'Spare your jests for later, cheek!' Cedric counters, gasping. 'But I'm serious, Flower. It's the Nethmites. They're coming!'

His announcement is met with a resounding shrill. '*What!*'

The sky darkens, casting the forest into deep shadow as an icy chill fills the air and an eerie silence descends. A silence quickly broken by the cries of birds chattering and parroting calls of danger.

'*The Nether is coming! The Nether is coming!*'

There is instant pandemonium. Squirrels scurry from trees, deer tramples over the grass; escaping birds and fauna flee, hooves, feet and wings thundering the air and earth, leaving the statue-like humans behind.

CRACK!

A bright deep-purple light flashes across the sky, followed by hordes of Nethmites sprouting one after another out from the ground. They shake their metal heads, scattering chunks of dark brown soil high into the air. Flapping their leaf-shaped arms as they stretch their metallic jaws, mimicking the actions of humans waking from a long night's sleep. They clamp the mouths shut in noisy unison, sending a metallic ringing vibration that shakes the ground.

Huddled in the centre of the clearing, the party look on as the Nethmites organise themselves.

'This looks bad.' Mal mutters, clinging tightly to her quarterstaff.

'Bad you say,' Addie grins, drawing Silverhair ready, 'but not for me. I'm prepared for this!' She cries. 'Hey! I came here to test Silverhair: to practice shooting at the trees, but you guys are much better targets.' She pauses, sheepishly glancing at a nearby yew tree, spotting one of her arrows stuck fast in its trunk. 'Sorry about that.'

The tree rustles its leaves.

TWANG!

Addie sends an arrow hurtling towards the metallic creatures. It strikes the open jaws of a Nethmite. A direct hit! But the creature sneers at her effects and chomps down on the arrow, crushing it into mushy pulp. It swallows the arrow with a noisy gulp.

'Blast!' Addie curses, firing more arrows, but with much the same effect.

As Nethmites chomp down on Addie's arrows, others are busy stripping leaves and berries from the bushes and ripping away tree bark. They appear determined to consume everything and transform the forest into a wasteland.

Addie cannot believe what is happening. Her arrows are treated with distain, as lunch. She cries. 'Why don't they just give up?'

Frank is occupied firing lumps of prepared cake-mix into the Nethmite horde. The sweet-tasting projectiles cause the Nethmites to snarl in disgust, desperate to shake the sticky mess from their beaks. They switch their attention to Frank.

'Uh-oh! Looks like desperate measures are needed.'
CRASH!

Swinging Old Faithful's barrel, Frank strikes the nearest Nethmite, sending it high into the air. Falling, it lands on a skinny Nethmite lurking in the undergrowth.

'Aw shoot, I forgot to shout *fore!*'

Mal grips her quarterstaff, watching the others fight the metallic scourge. She is shaking. The forest is being stripped away, right before her eyes.

'C'mon, bunny-ears!' Addie yells from the scuffle. 'Show these punks what you're made of!'

'But I don't want to fight!' She counters, turning towards two approaching thin Nethmites baring their grinning jaws. 'Would you like a pecan cake?' She asks, holding one out in her hands. One of the Nethmites swipes at her, grabbing the cake and drawing blood from her hand.

Munch, munch. It spits the mushy lump out.

'They don't like it.' Mal takes a step back. 'What can we do?'

Two short, plumper Nethmites, their jaws stained with green moss, are preparing to attack. But they are driven back, targeted by an invisible force projected from the Flower of Knowledge. It is a desperate attempt, one that drains his life-force. As the assault continues, his luscious green and gold crown slowly reddens, and then fades to grey.

Mal gasps. 'Flower! Your form…'

'The Nether's formidable force is overpowering.' The Flower of Knowledge gasps. 'I sense it taking over Greystagg. The Nether is too strong, their numbers too great. I must not let this world succumb to its terrifying power. There has to be another way… Sam!'

'Yes?'

'Head north and find the Fleur de Vie. Only it can overcome the power of the Nether. The forest is succumbing to its dark energy, and I have nothing left to combat it. You and your friends must escape: first head west from the clearing, it will be safer that way; then north for the coast. *Go. Now!*' The Flower of Knowledge begs. 'Locate the Fleur de Vie and use it to stop the Nether's power. And Mallory my dear loyal friend. Please forgive me. Goodbye!'

With a final exhausted breath, a fragile fragment of Aether seeps from the Flower's decaying frame, scattering dried dead leaves into the air.

Mal's eyes cloud with tears. 'Flower, I…'

KA-BOOM!

A bolt of purple lightning bursts from the heavy grey clouds, striking through the Flower of Knowledge and splitting the tree in half. As the light fades the party can only stand, watching in disbelief, as the final traces of living colour drains from the Flower of Knowledge.

'*Such noble nonsense!*' Retorts a cold, emotionless voice from above their heads.

'We've got to get out of here!' Cedric exclaims, his voice quivering.

Sam grabs Mal by the hand. 'C'mon Mal, we've gotta get away.'

They scurry out of the clearing and into broken brambles and stripped-away bushes. Following the devastating trail created by the Nethmites, they run as fast as they can in the wake of the terrified wildlife escaping the forest.

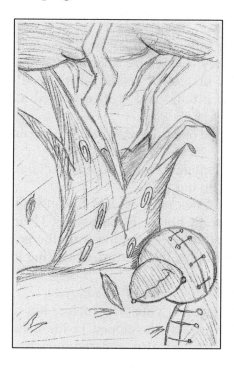

A deer crashes past, sending panicked birds high into the air.
'*The Nether is coming! The Nether is coming!*'
CRACK!
A dried broken branch crashes to the ground in front of Sam. It is followed by another branch, and then another.

Frank is losing ground, struggling with the imbalanced weight of his pegleg. The others are moving too quickly and there is a danger he might be left behind. This is not the landscape for a sky-pirate. His foot slips and he trips, crushing forcefully into the broken frame of a bush.
THUD!

Glancing up from the ground, he sees his friends disappearing into what remains of the forest. Behind he hears the advancing Nethmites chuckling menacingly.

'Hey, wait for me!' He cries, grasping at the remains of the vegetation around him. There is no response. He tries again, but sounds even weaker. 'Wait!'

There is a sudden rush of air. Frank shuts his eyes tight, hearing the heavy patter of approaching paws. The jaw of something grabs his collar, sending his world spinning as he is hoisted from the ground and is then carried at increasing speed through the forest.

Cautiously he opens his eyes. He is lying astride a huge black and white wolf.

'Set sail, Captain Frank!' Bonnie exclaims, racing between the trees. 'We're on our way!'

They make quick progress and catch the others as they reach the edge of Greystagg Forest. Bonnie stops. Their escape is blocked by a group of Nethmites, sprouting from the ground before them. A terrifying line of metallic sentries, chattering loudly; a solid wall of Nethmites.

How can they get through to safety?

Addie prepares to enter the melee, but as she is about to charge she finds herself enveloped inside a large rose-coloured bubble. The others are also encased inside. Sam's hands are glowing with the same-coloured light, that feeds into the skin of the bubble. Feeling their weight slip away, the bubble lifts them over the bewildered Nethmites. The metallic creatures strain their necks, reaching in vain for their adversaries; snapping at the bubble as it soars safely above their heads. Gathering speed, the bubble cruises effortlessly over the gently undulating terrain, clearing the last of the trees and leaving the Nethmites behind. When safely beyond the forest the bubble descends into a lush green meadow, dipping towards the grass. It disappears with a *pop*, and everyone lands on a carpet of soft grass.

Bonnie lowers Frank to the ground and hiccups. This signals her shrinking to her normal dog-sized shape.

Above their heads, thickening clouds begin spilling raindrops.

Cedric turns to Dr Woodchuck. 'Do we know how the forest creatures have fared?'

'I believe most have managed to escape,' His voice trails, 'but the plants...'

'We must send word to stay away from the forest.'

Mal gazes at the distant ashen grey tree trunks. Greystagg, the flourishing forest that is her home, has been reduced to wasteland. Silhouetted birch trees, stripped of bark, stand as frozen ivory white stalks. The animals have fled, and the plants destroyed. There is nothing but bare broken ground. She sinks to her knees, tears pouring down her face.

'My home. It's lost. All this desolation. The Flower's sacrifice is for nothing. What can I do?'

Sam says. 'You gotta stay with us, Mal.'

'I must stay positive. I must!' She shakes her head. 'It will get better again, right? Yeah! Let's remember butterflies dancing in the posies, birds singing, and squirrels playing in the trees. It will be the same again, won't it?'

The others look away.

Frank mutters. 'Sorry, Mal.'

Mal's forced smile is replaced by floods of bitter tears. 'Oh, what's the point! Look at what those creatures have done to the forest.' Grinding her teeth, she pounds her fist onto the hard ground. 'Curse them! Curse them! You metal pests!' She punches the soil in frustration, wincing from the impact of her hands hitting the ground. 'Why would they do something so mean? Why?' She buries her face in her battered hands; her body shaking as she sobs.

Sam places his hand gently on her shoulder. 'I'm so sorry.'

He removes his scarf and hands it to his friend, who holds it tightly in her hands.

Bonnie nudges her head against Mal's knee, whining sadly. 'This shouldn't have happened. It really shouldn't.'

Frank nods. 'All those pretty flowers and strong trees, transformed into mush.'

'Yeah! Nuts and bolts!' Addie exclaims, kicking the ground hard. 'I wish I had a better chance of taking down those Nethmite critters. I would have loved to show them what for.'

'Even if we could, we're still outnumbered.' Sam replies, his voice shaking. His eye is watering too. He dries it with the back of his hand. 'You saw how quickly the Flower of Knowledge succumbed to their power.'

'Wait…' Addie gasps, but she is cut short by Mal's sobbing.

Sam puts a comforting arm around Mal. 'Let's not jump to any conclusions, okay?'

Addie's lips purse as she rubs her shoulder. Before her stands the broken remains of the forest as the sickening sound of distant trees crashing to the ground report the Nethmites continued attack.

THUD!

She grabs hold of Silverhair and strides away. 'Let's just get outta here. This place is sickening me.'

*

The party travel north, away from Greystagg. Addie takes the lead, followed by Frank and Dr Woodchuck, then Bonnie, and finally Sam who walks arm in arm with Mal. Cedric flies overhead. He is abnormally quiet. All they can do for now is focus on the next part of their journey, mindful of how eerily serene the landscape appears under the cool rainy air.

They make steady progress, heading towards the mountain valley peeping through the mist.

Sam glances at Mal, cradling his scarf in her hands. She seems calmer than before. He smiles sadly and stuffs his hands deep into his pockets. High above his head, he watches two eagles circling slowly in the sky. They appear to be heading for the valley and the distant mountains beyond, perhaps trailing the party; tasked with ensuring they arrive safely at their destination.

Something catches Sam's eye. A distant figure is standing beside a gigantic boulder. It is the silhouette of a person wearing a large, dark hooded cloak that reaches to the ground. They are too distant for him to make out any characteristics, but the stranger appears to be studying their movement.

He stops, certain he has heard his name being called; a whisper carried on the breeze.

'Hey, can you see...?' But in that moment the figure fades away. 'Huh? Where did he go?'

Ahead, the others continue walking, oblivious to the stranger and Sam's cries. He quickens his step, anxious to catch up with his friends. There is someone watching but who they are, and why are they so interested in them?

*

As the party approaches the head of the valley, they are greeted by the reassuring rush of the fast-running waters of the River Tye.

'We should stop here and rest.' Frank says, stooping over the bank and scooping handfuls of water to drink. 'My legs need a break from all this walking.'

Mal, her face flushed and still clinging to Sam's scarf, asks. 'So what's next?'

'I'm not sure.' Frank replies. 'I mean, the Flower of Knowledge told us to head north and find the Fleur de Vie. It's just I'm not sure which way's north anymore.'

'Cripes!' Addie snorts, mimicking a parrot, strutting around Frank, *what a great pirate you make... what a great pirate you make...*'

'Please don't mention parrots.' Frank grimaces, as the ranger continues squawking at his expense.

Sam asks. 'Are you feeling better Mal?'

'I think so. Thank you.' She replies. 'I'm coming to terms with what happened in Greystagg, not that I'll ever accept it. But I'm feeling stronger, thanks to you guys.'

'That's good.'

There remains a distinct chill in the air, and the sky is filled with dark rolling clouds that perpetually rumble.

Addie groans. 'What is it with the weather today?'

'I don't think it's the weather,' replies Sam, 'look, over there.'

From out of the clouds, swooping low over the valley, comes a large, dark shape, carried on huge, deep purple bat-shaped wings. The creature's body looks similar to Gaia and Techna, except there is something immediately menacing about its appearance. Its body is covered with thick metallic scales that glint in the fading light; and there is a dark aura surrounding its frame. To emphasise its threatening behaviour, it emits a long drawn ominous drone. Then accompanied by a shrieking cry, the creature lunges towards the party. As everyone leaps for safety, the creature's giant talons pick out Sam, plucking him from the ground by the shoulders, and carrying him away.

There is a chorus of: *'Sam!'*

Having gracefully dodged the volley of arrows fired from Silverhair and a pound of cake-mix shot from Old Faithful, the creature calmly beats its wings, sending out rhythmic vibrations that beat heavily into Sam's eardrums.

THUMP-THUMP-THUMP!

They are flying high, heading for the distant hills. Sam stares at his feet dangling and swinging aimlessly in the air. He tries looking up at the beast that has taken him, but all he sees are the talons grasping his shoulders: sharp claws piercing his skin. Their grip is too powerful for him to pull away. A dart of bright rose-coloured light suddenly strikes the beast beneath its left wing. The creature shrieks with a mixture of surprise and pain, and releases Sam, who begins falling, spinning through the air, viewing his world in ever winding circles.

It is a long way down.

Falling helplessly, Sam grows aware of a warm sensation pulsing from deep inside his body. He feels his weight lessen as the action of gravity weakens. Cracking open his eye, he sees the ground approaching at a far more leisurely rate, as he descends slower and slower. Twisting around in mid-air, he spies a pair of feathery wings above his shoulders: a white wing on his left-side, a black wing on his right; their feathers fluttering against the rush of air. Sam discovers he can move them, altering their shape and angle, and through careful manoeuvring, he manages to glide safely towards the ground.

*

'*Hurry!*' Mal cries, as she and the others chase after Sam. 'He's heading deeper into the valley.'

They track Sam's progress: stopping abruptly when they witness the creature lose its grip, watching in desperate anticipation as their friend falls towards the ground; and then gasping with surprise on the appearance of Sam's wings, and saluting his measured descent with a rousing cheer. What with everything else that has happened, their friend sprouting wings seems a perfectly ordinary event. Relieved to see him spiral safely from his fall, they press on into the mountain pass.

They find him crouching on his hands and knees, staring at the ground. Standing between them is a large hairy mountain goat, who stares blankly as the party approaches. Pausing momentarily to offer a convivial bleat, it leisurely lowers its head to continue grazing.

Addie stoops, desperately trying to catch her breath. 'Holy flint 'n' steel, Sammy! You had us all panicking!' She gawps at his wings. '*Whoa!*'

Sam rises slowly to his feet, spinning clockwise, trying to get a better look at his wings.

'Cripes, Sammy! Where did you get those?' Addie cries excitedly. 'Although, I think your flying skills are clumsy at best.'

Sam swings around, his wings swiping Addie across her face. *BAP!*

Stunned, she mutters, 'Okay! Shutting up now.'

Sam lightly strokes his black wing. 'They sure feel real, just like bird feathers.' He gasps. 'Wow! This is fantastic! I've always wanted to fly, you know, like a bird.'

Mal touches his arm. 'You've certainly got over the fright of falling from such a height.'

'*Hao-he!* You're getting used to the power of the Aether my friend,' chuckles Techna as he glides towards the party, 'and one of each colour: black and white, to represent me and Gaia. That's a nice touch!'

'Sam grew wings because of the Aether?' Mal asks.

'Sam the flying human?' Addie adds. 'I must say, I'm feeling pretty jealous of you right now.'

'Remember, the Aether is bonded to Sam,' Techna explains, 'and it knows instinctively when it is most needed. But I admit, I was worried when the Nether beast lost hold of you, after I distracted it.'

'So it was you who attacked the beast, the one that carried me away?'

'You're not the only one full of surprises Sam, and there's no need to thank me. You're welcome.' Techna grins and tousles

Sam's hair. 'Now with your wings, you'll be able to observe the world as Gaia and I can. Believe me, it's incredible.'

'Wait!' Frank interjects. 'That flying monster was a Nethmite too, only bigger?'

'I'm afraid so. The Nether is able to create a variety of cruel creatures, ones I am sure we will meet soon.' Techna straightens. 'But now I'll take my leave. Gaia will think I'm hanging around with you again.'

Addie sticks out her tongue. 'Well you are!'

'I hope Gaia has a change of opinion about us humans.' Sam sighs. 'We could sure do with his help against the Nethmites.'

'Oh, I'm sure he'll come round, eventually.' Techna nods wearily. 'Gaia's a right old *stick-in-the-mud*, but he'll realise you're strong enough to stand up and face the Nether.' Then, with a single beat of his wings, he lifts up into the sky. 'I'll see you later, chums! It's alright to call you chums, right?'

The party stare skywards as the impressive Techna lifts towards the heavens, disappearing as a dot within a layer of high cloud.

'Sable always made the point that I should trust my instincts.' Sam mutters, watching his wings fold playfully around him. He grins. 'And I'd better polish my flying skills.'

Addie interjects. '*You think!*'

'Wait!' Mal steps forward to return Sam's scarf. 'You should have this back. It does belong to you after all.' She smiles, wrapping her arms around him. 'And thank you for comforting me.'

'It was nothing.' Sam returns the hug, his wings folding around her. 'I'm just happy to help a friend.' Mal steps away, giggling under her breath. 'What's the matter?'

'Your wings tickle!'

'Heh, is that so?' Sam watches his wings sway in the breeze. 'I can't believe this is happening. *I can fly! I can fly! I can fly!*' Twirling around, forcing everyone else to take a step away, he topples backwards and falls. 'Whoops!'

*

The party decide to stop and rest in the meadow. Sam finds a section in the book with instructions on how to fly and studiously flicks through the pages. A breeze picks up his wings, tickling its feathers, encouraging him to take to the sky. But he is not quite ready and his wings droop with disappointment. As the others partake on a snack of Mal's pecan cakes, Sam continues reading the chapter, back and forth, reading and rereading the contents thoroughly. Finally he snaps the book shut.

'Right!' He says jumping to his feet and carefully ruffling his newly formed wings. Pausing to wrap his scarf securely around his neck, he takes a deep breath. 'Here goes nothing…'

Running forward and flapping his wings in a slow, rhythmic beat, Sam leaps from the ground and up into the air, soaring higher and higher. Below him comes enthusiastic cheers from his companions, their tiny hands held high above their heads.

'Good luck, Sam!' Mal hollers after him.

Addie cries. 'You go, big birdie!'

Sam follows his shadow trailing on the ground as it dances across the terrain, listening to the beat of his wings slicing through the air. With his eye, he tracks the speeding treetops and changing landscapes. Ahead of him stand tall mountains, surrounded by thick grassy fields. Down in the valley, roaming wild beasts stop and lift their heads and stare in casual disbelief.

Feeling the accelerating wind slip through his fingers, he cries. 'This is really happening.'

He dares to climb up towards the mountaintop, shrouded in white wispy clouds; eagles circling the summit. They turn towards him, confused at the sight of a flying human. Spiralling away, Sam swoops into the valley, gliding past rock arches and over clumps of trees and bushes. As his confidence grows, he twists in the air, completing barrel rolls: clockwise, and then anticlockwise. His antics take him above a small farming village, where he surprises the farmers working in the fields. Goats and sheep bleat in mild protest as he waves reassuringly at the farmers, who scratch their heads and point back in puzzled amusement. Away from the village, he follows the River Tye, skimming his right hand over the cool water, his fingers rippling the surface. Finally, he hoists himself high, and with a single sharp beat of his wings, pushes himself up towards the peaks, gaping joyously at the sheer beauty of the world beneath him.

Sam's playful aerobatics are brought to an abrupt halt as he is captured inside a fiercely bright beam of light. Hovering in the air, shielding his face from the glare, he waits for the light to fade and shrink away. In the diffused light his sight recovers, and he is able to focus on the source of the light: a dark cylinder shape standing at the end of a long jetty. *It is a lighthouse.*

With rising excitement, he studies the surrounding landscape away from the jetty. Along the beach stands an isolated house with an open terrace looking out over a small grassy knoll. Tentatively he glides closer, picking out different neighbouring houses. It all looks so familiar. A quiet village by the sea. Waves of nostalgia spill over, tugging hard at Sam's heart. It is Farley.

He gasps. *'I'm home!'*

Lockjaw

Addie paces back and forth, hands on hips and gazing at the distant mountain peaks. 'Okay! It's been over an hour, where is he?' She mutters. 'He'd better be back soon, my fun's running empty.'

'Hey look, over there,' Mal cries excitedly, pointing skywards at a small, darkened shape bobbing on the air current, 'isn't that him?'

Frank chuckles. 'I hope he's practiced his landings.'

Sam is struggling to control his wings and is descending far quicker than planned. To his audience it appears as if his arms, legs and wings, all have different versions on what to do next. Pushing out his legs, he waits for impact.

'Incoming!' He screams.

THUD!

His feet slam onto the ground and he tumbles forward. Struggling to maintain his balance, he slides and skids and then rolls over the grass. Groaning, he struggles onto his hands and knees, shaking tiny clods of dirt from his hair.

'Okay, that didn't go too badly.'

Frank and Mal rush to help him to his feet.

'Welcome back to solid ground.' Frank laughs. 'How's flying?'

'It's fantastic, just as Techna said it would be. I flew as high as I dared, soaring up to the mountain tops, over the river, the valley, everything!' Sam's voice rings with joy. 'And then I saw it!'

'Saw what?' Addie demands. 'Don't leave me hanging, pal!'

'I saw Farley, my home! We're almost at Farley! I saw Fye! Dear Fye!'

'Okay, okay! Take it easy; and I thought I was the enthusiastic one.' Addie gasps. 'So how far away is this place?'

'Well judging by the distance I've covered, it will probably take at least a day by foot, longer if the river's difficult to cross.'

'That long,' Addie clicks her tongue, 'and we can't get carried there, even with bird-brain's help.'

Cedric sneers. 'I heard that!'

But then, right on cue, comes the sound of creaking wood. A familiar and welcoming sound to Frank the sky-pirate's ears. Gazing skywards, they watch the Puppis' slowly approach, cheering and shouting encouragement as the magnificent contraption emerges from white fluffy clouds, its propeller slicing through thin misty sheets. It comes to a halt high above their heads and a rope swings magically over the side of the craft and drops to their feet.

Frank presents a proud posture: hands on hips. 'Did you see that?' He grins at Sam. 'I told you. Old Puppis has a mind of its own!'

Smiling, Sam shakes his head. 'Now I've seen everything!'

Standing to one side, he waits as each of his friends climbs aboard.

'Hey!' Addie calls down from the Puppis. 'Are you coming up, or are you planning to make your own way?'

'It would be nice to relax on the Puppis,' Sam hollers over the whistling wind brushing against the air bag, 'but I think I should practice my flying skills.'

'Okay Sammy!' Addie yells, her bottomless pit of confidence spilling over. 'But you'd better lead the way!'

Sam sighs, shaking his head. 'Oh, Addie.'

With everyone apart from Sam and Cedric aboard, the Puppis rises further from the ground; its rear propeller-blade spinning ever faster. Sam leaps into the air and begins experimenting with his wings, gently easing the muscles in his shoulders and arms, until he achieves the same height as the airship. Cedric matches Sam's efforts, mindful of maintaining a safe distance from the novice flier and the swaying contraption. In his mind neither has any business being off the ground. At the helm, Frank steers the craft towards the distant mountains, listening to the comforting creak of the air-sac and happy to be back on board again. The rest of the party settle on deck, content with a few moments of rest and tranquillity.

'Wow! We're so high!' Mal gasps, looking over the side and watching the ground scrolling below. Turning to Frank, she asks. 'And this is what you do, Frank? The amazing adventures you must have!'

'Yep, just one of the perks of being a sky-pirate!'

Skipping along air currents, keeping close to the Puppis, Sam twists and turns, floating above fields, crossing streams and brooks that lead into the valley. Cedric flaps hard and twists away from the airships' swaying movement. He catches up with Sam.

'Ah-ha! It looks like you're taking to flying well, buddy;' he chuckles, 'I may be a crusty creature, but I can still keep up with you!'

Sam laughs. 'I've never doubted you, Cedric.'

'Hah! And nobody should ever doubt my spirit!'

Beyond the hills, through the cool thick mist hugging the valley, Farley eventually looms into view. *Welcome to Farley* is written across a large wooden arch spanning above the entrance of the parish. Sweeping into the village, Sam skims over red-slated roofs and towards the lighthouse at the end of the jetty. The Puppis follows behind, making its usual steady descent until it hovers above a small park beyond the wooden arch. Frank drops the anchor and the craft steadies to a halt.

Having circled the village, Sam returns and lands feet first onto the ground, his arms spread wide. Stumbling a few steps forward, he manages to keep his balance.

Cedric laughs, hovering expertly above Sam. 'A bit of a doozy landing, eh?'

Pouting, Sam glares at the eagle-owl. 'I thought it was rather good.'

*

Farley is a peaceful place. The party is greeted by clouds of colourful butterflies that dance around clusters of wildflowers. At the centre of the park, birds paddle inside a large stone bird-bath, indifferent to the new arrivals. A gentle breeze pushes the empty swings and a multi-coloured spinning globe, causing them to move, as if ridden by ghosts. The air is heavy with the smell of sea salt from the adjacent ocean.

Sam succumbs to the waves of longing that have threatened to engulf him since seeing his beloved home again. Closing his eye, he listens to the waves crashing against nearby rocks; the sound he used to listen to every night as he fell asleep.

'How long has it been?' He whispers gently. *It's good to be back.*

He is distracted by Mal's cry. 'Hey Sam! What about your wings?'

'Yeah!' Addie adds. 'You can't waltz around like that. You'll keep knocking things over.'

It is true. Sam's wings exaggerate every move he makes, and it is with increasing desperation that he waves his arms trying to find some way of folding them away. He has seen birds do it, so it must be possible for him too. Feathers fly everywhere as he tries first one position, and then another, and then another. Finally, having generated much mirth for his companions, he manages to fold the wings inside his jacket!

'Oh!' He gasps with relief.

Cedric guffaws. 'Well, that's one way to do it. Impressive, for a human.'

He stops short, conscious of the narrowed glances of the small audience that has accumulated inside the park since their arrival. The locals stand watching and listening, muttering inaudibly at the events unfolding before them. Their faces are etched in astonished disbelief at his sight of his wings; *but seeing and hearing a talking eagle-owl!*

In response, Cedric fluffs up his body and starts coughing out a series of unconvincing owl-like hoots, before hopping high into the sky where he circles before landing safely on the deck of the Puppis.

'Ahem, that'll do.' He exclaims, smoothing his feathers. 'I think it's best if I stay on the airship. I didn't like the odd way those humans were staring at me.'

Dr Woodchuck and Cedric watch on as the rest of the party decide to walk to the centre of the parish, merging with the locals and sharing friendly greetings.

'Have fun, my friends!' Dr Woodchuck cries, waving from his vantage point on deck. Scuttling over to Cedric, he adds with an amused smirk spread across his lips. 'Well! That was eventful!'

'Eventful, my crusty feathers! I almost got caught!'

Farley's inhabitants are moving cheerily between small rustic buildings. Many are carrying large wicker baskets loaded with fresh fruit or huge bustles of brightly coloured flowers. Music rings through the air, played by a small folk-styled band positioned on the edge of the village green. A family of cardinals flutter over their heads, escaping to the far side of the parish, where it is less busy.

'So this is Farley, eh Sam?' Addie scoffs, glancing around. '*Very run-of-the-mill.*'

Sam furrows his brow. 'Run-of-the-mill? What mill?'

'No, no! I mean it's ordinary in a sense, quaint in fact. It's a saying.'

'Oh.' Sam sighs. 'Well I like it. It's home to me. A place with many happy memories.'

Walking through the parish, they are greeted by people who recognise Sam and welcome him home with genuine affection. It feels like he has never left. There are flickers of concern, even alarm at the changes in his physical appearance: his lost eye, his synthetic arm. But they keep their questions to themselves. It is the Farley way.

Sam stops in his tracks and turns to the others. The breeze picks up and catches the strands of his scarf. 'Hey! We should go and check on Nina. She'll probably be at home with Greg. C'mon, they live near here.'

The party follows Sam away from the parish centre and along a short lane that leads to a row of neatly organised houses. He passes through an open gate and approaches the door of a small, red-bricked house surrounded by beds of colourful flowers. The house sits still and quiet. Peering through a gap in the curtains, he sees nothing moving inside. Tentatively, he walks around the side of the house, hoping to find the familiar faces he seeks. With rising disappointment he returns to the others, who are waiting patiently by the front door. As he opens his mouth to speak, a small voice bursts out from behind the garden wall.

'Who's there?'

They hear the patter of tiny feet. A small girl is running along the far side of the wall. Turning, she passes a small, open iron gate and stops, slightly out of breath, in front of Sam. She stares up at the others, her green eyes pooling with tears and her tiny doll-sized hands twiddling with the locks of her long blonde hair. She is wearing a yellow and white gingham dress that hangs over her knees; and a pair of light-brown buckled shoes on her feet.

'Nina!' Sam gasps, bending to his knees. But the small girl backs away. 'It's only me.'

Nina holds out her fists. 'W-W-Why're you here?' She stammers, putting on a brave face. 'Don't come near this house! Please! I'll scare you off! I... I mean it!'

'What's up with her?' Addie asks, cocking her head. 'Not to mention her attempts of defiance are embarrassing.'

Sam kneels. 'Nina, do you remember this?' He begins clapping his hands, to a familiar rhythm.

'Hello mister Postman
What've you got today?
Is there a letter,
To chase the blues away?'

Nina listens intently to the song and her sombre expression changes into a cheerful grin, as she claps her hands in time and sings along with Sam.

'Mister Postman, Mister Postman,
Is there a letter from your end?
Perhaps a card or a little pressie,
From my very special friend?'

They sing the final verse in complete synchronisation.

'Mister Postman, wait a minute,
Before you go away,
Please tell my special friend
I'll be seeing them today!'

The others watch in amazement.

As the song ends, Addie asks, deliberately enunciating every word. 'What. Was. That. All. About?'

Nina stares at Sam, her face beaming with excitement. 'Sammy!' She cries, wrapping her arms around his neck, her cheeks flushed with joy. 'It's you, Sammy! You're home!'

'Yeah it's me,' Sam chuckles, returning the hug, 'it's great seeing you Nina!'

Nina pulls away and begins studying the scar across Sam's left eye. 'You look different, Sammy.' She says, cautiously touching his scar. 'What happened to your eye?'

'It was something big and loud, and foolish. Something I walked into out of curiosity. Do you remember Greg's stories about cats and curiosity?' He winces with embarrassment. 'Some people say it was daring as there were people stuck inside a building, but I think it was plain stupid.' He brushes Nina's fringe with his left hand, his right arm securely wrapped around her tiny frame. 'Hey! I'm still the same Sam you know and love.'

Giggling, they press their foreheads together; until someone coughs, demanding their attention. It's Addie.

'Sorry to interrupt, but is this a little sister you haven't told us about?'

'No, not really, But we've known each other a long time. Nina's father, Greg, was a close friend of Ma.' Standing, Sam pulls Nina closer to him. 'Speaking of Greg, where is your father Nina?'

Nina's smile drains away. 'Papa. Sam, Papa isn't who he used to be.' She speaks quietly, but clear enough for Sam to hear the tremor of fear in her voice.

'What do you mean, he's not *who* he used to be?' He strokes her head. 'It's okay, you can tell me.'

'Yeah, lil' chum!' Addie chimes. 'You can tell us, we'll listen!'

'A couple of weeks ago, Papa went out of town looking for something, I don't know what. He left me behind with the neighbours.' Nina explains. 'But when he came back, he was like a stranger. He didn't want to speak to me, he wouldn't say hello, or even hug me like he always does. He just hid away inside his study and ignored me. Even at supper, he would stay away. He never came out.' She shrugs her shoulders. 'I thought he was sick, but I think I was wrong. And then... and then it happened.'

Nina shudders as tears roll down her cheeks. 'I could hear hissing sounds and funny scraping noises, like really big feet stomping on the floor. I thought somebody had broken into the house. I tried calling out for Papa, but all I heard was growling from his study. It sounded like a great, big, scary monster. I didn't know what to do, so I ran outside to fetch the neighbours. They came inside and I heard a lot of noise and I think they went down into the cellar. When they came back up, they all had big boo-boos. I think they'd been hurt by a big, mean animal. The neighbours took me outside and told me it wasn't safe for me to stay at home anymore and that I had to stay with them. It's nice of them to take care of me, but I just want my Papa back.'

Sam asks. 'Did you see what the *monster* looked like?'

'I didn't see its face, but it sounded deep and scary; and it kept repeating the same silly word, over and over again.' She stops, interrupted by a deep booming noise emanating from inside the house.

It sounds shrill and eerily mechanical. They listen to the random, repetitive noises, their ears growing accustomed to the jarring, recurring sound.

'*Lockjaw! Lockjaw!*'

The word is repeated again and again, getting louder and louder; accompanied by loud thudding sounds: ones made when one heavy object is bashing into another.

'*Lockjaw!*'

CRASH!

The front door reverberates from the sound reverberating inside the house.

'It's the monster!' Nina whimpers, burying her face into Sam's shoulder, her tiny hands grab hold of his jacket. 'Sammy, please get Papa!'

Sam hands Nina his scarf. 'There, there, Nina. You're in good hands now.' Standing, he turns to the others. 'Something feels very wrong here. That mechanical noise sounds familiar.'

'Yep and we're the ones to stop it, alright!' Addie adds, punching her hand. 'Nothing should ever scare a lil' kid like that. If anything, they're gonna be messin' with me!'

'She's right,' Mal nods, 'and we must keep her out of harm's way.'

'Yes Mal, and I have an idea.' Sam leads Nina from the house. 'Hey Nina, why don't you go and play with Bonnie?'

A smile spreads across Nina's face. 'Can I?'

'Of course. You need someone to cheer you up, and Bonnie here is the best there is.' Turning to Bonnie he says. 'I've got a job for you, Bon. Nina's pretty shaken, so keep her company while we deal with the monster, okay? I think the park might be the best place to go.'

'No problem Sam!' Bonnie replies, with a salute of her paw. 'You just leave it to yours truly!' She bounds over to Nina, yapping and dancing playfully.

'C'mon doggie!' Nina giggles, leading Bonnie towards the park.

A warm smile tugs at Sam's lips as he tightens his grip on his scarf. 'Yeah, they'll be just fine.' He looks back at the house. 'We should get going.'

'You betcha!' Addie replies. 'I see a power supply getting ready to be pulled right back down!'

Cautiously they push open the front door and enter the house. Their creaking footsteps resonate along the wooden floorboards as they step inside the lounge. It is in disarray with overturned furniture, collapsed shelves, books, photo frames and ornaments scattered across the floor. The wallpaper is covered in deep scratches, caused by the claws of some enormous animal, or perhaps a human with a serious nail problem. Sam sniffs at the acrid air, recognising the strong smell of paraffin.

Addie says. 'So how are we gonna to find this bad boy?'

'It's been a while since I've been here, but I remember it as a maze inside.' Sam replies. 'We should split up and search the whole house up and down.'

'Gotcha, bud!'

Separating, they begin searching room by room. Mal takes the nearest door and finds herself inside the kitchen. It is cleaner and tidier than the lounge. She opens each of the cupboards in turn, not knowing what she is looking for. There are several crayon-drawings mounted on the cupboard doors: Nina's artwork. There is a large picture portraying a large round, happy sun overlooking a green field covered in flowers; another consists of two stick-like figures, one taller than the other, caricatures of Greg and Nina smiling out from the paper. The drawings are all signed, *Nina*, scrawled in dark red crayon. Mal opens the fridge door, and the interior light illuminates the kitchen. She peers inside, the shelves are stacked full of fruit, vegetables and various dairy products. Closing the fridge door, she is distracted by water trickling from the tap, splashing into the metal basin, *tap-tap-tap*. Leaning over the sink, she turns the tap off.

Meanwhile Addie races upstairs and peers through each door she finds on the upper floor: Nina's bedroom, Greg's bedroom, the bathroom. *There are no monsters here.* Looking out of the bathroom window, she listens to the sounds emanating from somewhere below her. Sighing, she spins on her toes and bounds out of the bathroom, heading for the stairs.

Sam and Frank continue searching the living room, absentmindedly tidying the clutter and picking up fallen ornaments and books. Everything is covered in a fine, copper-brown dust. Very unusual. There is an eerie buzzing sound. The television lies on its side, emitting static. Sam steps across the room and removes the plug from the socket in the wall. The noise fades to nothing. He picks up the television and sets it on the table. Frank busies himself by picking up the books on the floor and arranging them on the coffee table. He peers down at one of the larger books lying open on one of the collapsed bookshelves. The double spread pages display the periodic table. Picking up the chemistry book, he skims through the pages.

'Gosh! This Greg fella sure likes his science.' He chuckles, slamming the book shut. 'But it's not for me, far too dangerous.'

Sam spots two broken photo frames. The first is lying faced down; the other displays a photograph of three smiling people: a man with thick auburn hair; a woman with longer and lighter brown coloured hair; and between them stands a smaller version of Sam.

Standing smaller than the other two figures, he is waving with his fleshy right hand. Bending down he picks up the photograph and gently runs a finger over the image of the woman.

'What you got there, Sam?' Frank asks, looking over Sam's shoulder.

'It's a photo of me, with Ma and Greg,' he holds up the image for Frank to look at, 'but the frame's bust.'

Frank gasps. 'So that's what Lily looked like. Wow-ee! She was really pretty.'

Sam's cheeks blush as he chuckles with embarrassment. 'You could say that.' Gazing at the picture of Lily, his smile drains away. Carefully he slides the photograph into the damaged frame and places it on the coffee table. 'It's just a photo of the three of us, when we were together.'

'Hey fellas!' Addie hollers from the hallway. 'Come and look at what I've found! Didn't little Nina mention a cellar?'

Sam's eye widens. 'She did.'

He and Frank stride out from the lounge and meet Mal and Addie by an open door towards the rear of the hallway. Through the door they can see a flight of stairs descending beneath the kitchen. Staring down into the poorly lit stairwell, they spot another door near the foot of the stairs. They hear a burst of muffled vibrations from beyond the far door, a signal that they are on the right path.

Addie grins. 'Looks like we've found what we're looking for!'

They descend slowly down the stone steps, Sam first, followed by Frank, Addie, with Mal bringing up the rear. Reaching the foot of the stairs, they huddle together by the door, listening to the weird hissing sounds emanating from the other side. Sam pauses, wondering if this is such a good idea.

Addie leans heavily against Sam's shoulders. 'C'mon Sammy! We can't stop now.'

Sam nods and turns the handle. Pushing open the door, they find themselves standing at one end of a short corridor. At the other end is another door, beyond which they suspect, lies the creature responsible for the eerie, nerve-tingling noises reverberating around them. This door appears damaged, perhaps from the neighbours' efforts to help Greg. *What will they find inside?* The party readies themselves: Frank primes Old Faithful, Mal holds out her quarterstaff, and Addie slides an arrow into Silverhair. Sam pauses, sensing a hollow pitiful ache, deep inside his chest. *There is something here that does not feel right at all.*

'This must be it,' he whispers, 'but I don't like it. Something is wrong.'

'You bet something's wrong,' Addie grins confidently, 'and we're ready for whatever is waiting inside. Let's give them what for!'

Sam nods. Together with his friends, they begin to pry open the door, tug-by-tug, until the door suddenly flies off its hinges and crashes to the floor, shattering into pieces. They freeze, staring through clouds of dust and wooden-splinters. Inside they can make out a dark lumbering shape, standing eight feet tall: a half human, half mechanical giant. As the dust settles and their eyes grow accustomed to the faint light inside, they begin to make out the creature in terrifying detail. Its frame consists of a complex combination of rusting pipes and bolts. The left side of the head is metallic, with a large, heavy metallic jaw that grinds consistently as the creature opens and shuts its saw-toothed square-shaped mouth. The right side shows what could be a human face, with tuffs of auburn hair. It swings towards the party, its long metal arms drooping, apelike, over the floorboards. Sam notices that on the right side of the monster's chest appears fabric remains of a white collared shirt, partly concealing more humanlike features. Its gigantic mechanical feet start shuffling heavily over the floorboards and the creature cautiously approaches, leering at its visitors with listless eyes.

One eye glows an eerily red. '*Lockjaw!*'

Frank shrieks. '*OH, MY CREAM CAKES!*'

'What a hideous creature!' Addie gasps, holding her hand over her mouth.

'This is the monster,' Mal adds, 'Nina's monster?'

Sam watches as the creature stoops, muttering in a low-bass tone: huffing and heaving.

'Perhaps?' He lifts his hand, signalling the others to hold back, especially Addie. 'Wait, don't attack.' He steps cautiously forward, trying to make eye contact with the strange, pitiful looking creature before him. 'I think this could be Greg,' he whispers, 'which means we have to find a way of saving him without hurting the creature.'

The monster stares back inquisitively and emits another low, mechanical groan.

'I know you're in there, Greg.' Sam smiles. 'We'll get you back.'

Frank yells. 'Sam, look out!'

Lockjaw lunges forward, swiping at Sam and sending him flying across the floor and into the wall. It then turns to the others, who instinctively ready their weapons. Mal yelps at the sight of Lockjaw's terrifying blood-red eye burning brightly. The creature attempts another step, but is stopped in its tracks. Holding its hands over its head, it stares down at its left leg, which is pinned to the floorboards, tangled in a rose-coloured rope. A rope of light formed by the Aether's energy. Sam yanks hard at the other end of the rope, preventing the creature from reaching his friends. Lockjaw growls and begins pulling at its leg with increasing desperation, trying to break free. Its efforts causes Sam to be dragged across the floor. He holds on tightly, gathering the constraints around the creature's leg, but Lockjaw keeps pulling too. Its giant arms snapping at the Aether until the light-rope eventually shatters and its tiny fragments evaporate into the air.

Sam seething through gritted teeth, sighs. 'Oh no!'

Free at last, Lockjaw resumes its attack. Clasping Sam's shoulders in its strong mechanical hands, it lifts him into the air. The creature drags Sam further into the room, away from his friends. His scarf unravels and drops to the floor.

'Greg, don't do this.' Sam gasps, kicking his feet, which flail harmlessly in the air. 'This isn't who you are. This isn't the Greg I know!'

'*Lockjaw!*' The monster hollers, pinning Sam against the rear wall.

Sam clasps his hands around one of the creature's wrist and tries to release its vicelike grasp. Gritting his teeth, he manages to repress a painful scream as the creature's grip tightens on his shoulder blade. His body glowing in the rose-colour of the Aether.

'We can't just stand here and watch!' Addie cries, running into the room. 'We've gotta help!'

'But we can't fight it.' Mal protests.

Frank pleads. 'C'mon, Mal!'

POP! SPLAT!

Old Faithful spurts out a ball of cake mixture over Lockjaw's head, causing the creature to shriek and paw at the sticky mess covering its head. Frank's direct hit succeeds and the metallic monster releases Sam. As the creature turns away, Mal dances around and swings her quarterstaff, striking its metal thigh:

CLANG!

Addie fires an arrow, striking Lockjaw's right arm. The monster flinches with pain as the arrow punches through the white linen shirt and the metal surface beneath.

'Ha! How do you like that, big boy?' Lockjaw emits a lowly growl and clasps the end of the arrow, yanking it out and then crushing it. Addie's eyes widen. 'Uh-oh!'

'*Lockjaw!*' The monster cries again.

It picks up Frank and throws him into Mal and Addie, sending all three sprawling across the floor. Addie crashes into a shelf and is buried under falling books, Mal tumbles over a broken table, whilst Frank slides across the floor through shattered glass and into a small, upturned desk. Sam jumps back onto his feet and retrieves his scarf, which he holds above his head. Staring hard into Lockjaw's left, boiling-red eye, he tries to locate the other eye concealed behind tuffs of human hair. The creature stops, confused. It is breathing heavily, its mind churning over the strange images it sees through its mind. It comes to a decision, and raising its arms, prepares to launch another attack.

'Greg! Stop!' Sam cries, targeting the Aether's light-rope and wrapping it around Lockjaw's feet.

Reaching up, he places his hands against the sides of Lockjaw's head and stares deeply into the creature's eyes, finding the soft light reflecting from the hazel iris of its right eye. Steam begins billowing from the creature's jaws and hot breath engulfs Sam's face.

'It's okay, Greg. It's me, Sam.' He whispers softly, trembling with emotion. 'Don't you recognise your Sam?'

The metallic monster stares at Sam and grunts, as if trying to speak. It sees an image, something vaguely familiar, yet distant: an image of a boy with two soft brown eyes, smiling cheerily. It senses something else. The memory of a beautiful woman. An image of Lily.

Lockjaw's eyes widen. 'Sam?'

The light inside its terrifying reddened eye dulls, as its other eye, the human eye, glistens with the approach of tears. The soft rose-coloured light covering Sam's hands extends around Lockjaw's bulky frame, penetrating the metal exterior and dismantling the terrors within. The creature takes a step back, clutching the sides of its head.

'Lockjaw…'

Its voice is shaking, contained within the competing cacophony of mechanical and organic sounds. Sam can do nothing more than watch as the monster lifts its head, pushing it up against the ceiling, before releasing a long, agonising scream. The creature's body is fully consumed within the rose-coloured light of the Aether that pulsates with bursts of light, sending waves of energy through its body. Sam holds his arm across his face, shielding himself from the brilliant light as Lockjaw stoops towards the ground. Thick steam billows out, filling the room.

CLONK!

Something heavy drops to the floor.

Slowly the steam and smoke disperses and the brilliant light-energy fades, revealing Greg, fully restored to his human form: just five feet eight inches tall, a fraction of the mechanical Lockjaw's bulk. There is blood oozing from a wound in his right shoulder, staining his ripped white lab coat red. His face is ashen, and his once soft, refined auburn hair stands on end, frizzled.

'Wha?' Greg starts, staring at his hands. 'What happened?'

He looks around, puzzled by everything he sees. At the damage he has caused. Finally his eyes come to rest with Sam, and they widen.

'Sam?'

'Yes. It's me.'

Greg gasps and staggers forward, arms held out, desperate to reach out and hug Sam. Stumbling, he clutches his arm and collapses, emitting a pitiful groan.

Tiny soft footsteps approach swiftly from behind. 'Papa?' Nina runs into the room and sees Greg; she gasps and her eyes pool with tears. 'Papa!' She cries, falling into his arms.

'Nina!' Greg sighs, staring in turn at the crumpled frames of Frank, Mal and Addie; the fallen books, the shattered glass. 'What have I done?'

'Nothing Papa. You haven't done anything bad. It's okay. You're here now.'

Greg relaxes and envelopes his arms around Nina, pulling her close. He tightens his damp eyes shut. 'Nina.'

Sam's shoulders are shaking with emotion as he rubs at the tears spilling from his eye. Forcing a cheering smile, he places a reassuring hand on Greg's shoulders. He spots a small black shard, the object that had fallen from Lockjaw's body, pinned to the floor. The jet-black-coloured material is smooth and highly polished. Leaning down, he studies the strange object, but as he stretches his hand towards the shard, his fingers tingle and sparks fly from the tips.

SNAP!

The shard cracks open and Sam takes a step back. Then, with everyone watching, it transforms into a black, ethereal essence, brimming with an unsettling darkness that slowly fades away.

Frank starts. 'Wha... What was all that about?'

'Nothing good, I bet.' Mal sighs.

With a mixture of astonishment and relief, they begin exploring the room that had been Lockjaw's prison cell. Rubbing aching heads and limbs, conscious of their blossoming bruises, they collect their thoughts.

Addie is the most confused. 'Aw, did we miss the monster?' Her face crumples into a disappointed frown. 'And I really wanted to get a piece of it as a souvenir!'

Frank steps over to Sam, who is caressing his collarbone. 'Are you alright, Sam?'

'Yeah! I think so. I'm just relieved it's all over.'

The party looks on at the reunited family, tied in their firm embrace.

Frank is fiddling nervously with the brim of his hat. 'So the monster was the girl's father, huh?' He shakes his head. 'Man that's cold, real cold if you ask me. But at least things turned out alright, thanks to you Sam.'

Sam nods, a sly grin spreading across his lips. 'Yeah! And before Addie got the chance to do any real damage.'

Frank laughs. 'Yep, that was fortunate.' He grabs Sam's arm as they step from the room. 'Hey, don't you want to spend time with your friends?'

'There'll be plenty of time for that later.' Sam replies, hearing Nina's whimpering, her face buried beneath Greg's shoulders. 'For now, I think it's best if we give Nina and Greg some space. They've had a rough time.'

He turns for the stairs, followed closely by the others. Climbing the stairs from the cellar, they stride through the hallway and outside into the waiting fresh air.

Addie takes a deep breath. 'Ah! Much better! I couldn't stand the stinky petrol smell, not for another minute.'

Bonnie is waiting patiently in the garden. She leaps towards the party as they emerge from the house. 'Hey, there you are! Is Nina alright? She heard her father's voice and ran inside.' Noting the exhausted faces on her companions, with their collection of abrasions and bruising, she adds. 'I take it the monster's been taken care of?'

'Yeah. Except the monster was really Greg.' Sam pets Bonnie's head. 'Another example of the Nether's power. Its dark essence controlling Greg and turning him into that creature.'

'The Nether did all this?'

'I afraid so.' Sam nods, sadly. 'To witness such a good person turned into a mechanical monster. For him to lose all will and conscience. The Nether is truly terrifying, to transpose such dreadful power to achieve its horrible ends. I don't understand it.'

*

Desperate to put some distance from their confrontation with Lockjaw, the party decide to take a stroll into the village. They welcome the contact of other human-beings, who greet them with friendly smiles. For Sam, happier memories surface with everyone and everything he passes. They stop to purchase a basket of apples from a greengrocer, and eat the delicious crunchy fruit as they circle Farley and then return to Greg and Nina's home.

Evening is drawing in as they return to the house. The atmosphere inside could not have been more different to when they left. The neighbours are rallying, working together to bring back some sort of normality. The furniture has been righted and the shelves fixed back in place against the walls. The picture frames are mended, and the books and ornaments neatly arranged. And the dreadful smell of petrol has been replaced by the lingering fragrancies of fresh flower petals.

They hear the excited voices of Greg and Nina, emanating from inside the kitchen.

'I know it'll sting,' Nina says, 'but please, don't flinch Papa.'

'Yeah! I'm sorry.'

Entering, they find Greg sitting on a wooden chair. His shirt has been removed and is now busy circling inside the washing machine. Nina is trying to fix his wounds, wrapping bandages around his chest. Mal leaps in to help her support Greg's arm with a sling and securing the ends together behind his neck.

Nina smiles. 'Thanks, miss!'

'Always happy to help.'

Greg looks up at Sam. 'Sam.' He tries standing, but instantly sits back down, feeling his limbs sting in protest.

Sam puts his arms around Greg. 'Hey. I was in the area, so I thought I'd pop by to say *Hi*.'

'And it's a good job you did.' Greg wraps his left arm around Sam's back. 'It's good to see you again.' Pulling away, he studies Sam's bionic arm and the scarf wrapped around his left eye. 'Oh, my dear friend! I've heard about the blast. I'm so sorry.'

'Don't be sorry. It was destiny. It was predicted to happen.'

'And then…' Greg cries. 'To attack you. How can you ever forgive me? All I can say is, my awful actions were made against my will.'

Sam rubs his shoulder, which is still aching from Lockjaw's ferocious grip. He leans over and pulls Greg's hand into his own.

'Greg, there's nothing to forgive. You were brainwashed by the Nether. I'm just glad you're back to normal.' He takes little Nina's hand. 'And poor Nina was struggling without you, but she's been so brave and strong. She never gave up.'

Greg chuckles, ruffling Nina's locks. 'Yep. She's amazing. The neighbours have told me how courageous she has been. I'm so proud of her.' Noticing the people congregating inside his kitchen, he starts. 'Oh my! We don't usually get so many visitors. It seems I've a lot of tea to make.'

'Let me do it,' Mal interjects, before Greg stands, 'you need to take it easy.'

'I'll help you, miss. I'll show you which tea-leaves to use.' Nina leads Mal to a cupboard and points out a couple of coloured tins on the middle shelf. Mal fills the kettle with water, whilst Nina finds some mugs to put on the table.

Sam asks. 'Can you tell us anything that you remember about being transformed, Greg?'

'Everything is pretty murky,' Greg confesses, stroking his dishevelled hair, 'but I do remember finding this strange black object in the surrounding woods. It was as black as the night and smooth like polished glass, but I felt this eeriness. It was mesmerising. I wondered if I should bring it home, so it would be safe to research its possible origins. Then as I caressed it, I cut my finger. I don't know how because the surface was so smooth.' He frowns. 'And then it vanished, just like that. I began feeling strange, distant. *I wasn't me anymore.* My mind kept pushing these dreadful thoughts, ideas I would never have normally. That's when it started, turning me into that dreadful creature. I remember coming home and seeing how afraid Nina was of me, knowing that I had to keep myself away from her. When the neighbours came and forced me inside the cellar, the tiny part of me left was so relieved.'

He glances away, listening to those same neighbours fixing his damaged home. 'I was this wild, terrible monster. I had pushed everything that was good away, but as the terrors continued to rage inside me, I knew I was contained in the cellar and the people I cared about were safe. When you and your friends arrived, I sensed something was helping my battle against the darkness.' He stops, staring at Sam's right hand. 'That strange light, I don't know how, but it reached that part of me buried deep inside that metal contraption. You'll never know how thankful I am to be myself again. For Nina to run and hug me like she did, instead of seeing the fear she had in her eyes before.'

Sam nods thoughtfully, thinking of the black shard that fell from Lockjaw. It must have been the same black object Greg found in the woods. *This is terrible!* The Nether can manipulate people and get them to act against their will.

'May I ask something Sam, what was that warm light I felt?'

Sam holds out his hand. 'You mean the Aether.'

There is a soft residual glow of the Aether's power covering his palm, which materialises into a small flower bud, surrounded by tiny sparkling seeds.

'The Aether? Oh my, I'd never thought it could be… real.'

Sam closes his hands around the flower bud, which collapses into tiny sparkles that dance between his fingers. 'Neither did I.'

Mal and Nina have finished preparing the tea and they begin handing out the hot drinks. Mal hands the first mug to Greg.

'Ah, it does feel good being normal again.' Greg sighs, taking a sip of tea. 'I'm so thankful to everyone for looking after Nina and fixing up the house for us.'

'They're just glad you're well, sir.' Mal says. 'They've been worried about you.'

'Oh dear. I should go outside and help them.'

'You stay here and rest up. We'll do what we can.' Sam stands, preparing to go outside. He feels someone tug at his jacket, stopping him in his tracks. It is Nina.

She looks up at him, smiling playfully. 'Are you going to stay with us, Sammy? You only just got here, and I'd love to hear about your adventures in the city. Please say yes! Please say you'll stay for a while!'

'What do you think, Greg?'

'It would be nice if you and your friends can stay, even for a day or two.' Greg replies. 'Little Nina has missed you, as have I.'

Sam chuckles. 'Well! How can I say no to that?' Picking Nina up, he adds cheerily. 'C'mon Nina! Let's go and have some fun. I'll tell you stories about the things I've got up to in Melsey.' They begin dancing around the kitchen, laughing merrily.

'This is really mushy,' Addie smiles, 'but there's something cute about it too. They do act like siblings together, don't they?'

This Old House

I t is a perfect day in Farley. Since rescuing Greg from his metallic incarnation things have gone smoothly. The party have been busy helping the neighbours fix-up Greg and Nina's house; and by the following afternoon they are completing the final touches. Greg stands proudly on the new welcome mat outside his front door and breathes in the fresh ocean air, a broad smile stretched across his bruised face. Nina pushes past and runs into the small garden, greeting Sam and his friends with warm affection. Greg steps into the garden and begins thanking his neighbours again for taking care of Nina while he had been holed inside his self-imposed prison.

The sun slips behind thick billowing white clouds as Sam suggests spending the remainder of the afternoon taking a leisurely stroll around the parish.

'Sammy, can I come with you?' Nina squeals. 'Can we go to the park?'

'Sure Nina, the park. That's a great idea.'

Sam and Nina lead the way and the others trail behind, with Greg bringing up the rear. They are welcomed into the park by a stiff breeze that slowly spins the play globe and pushes against the swings, causing them to rock back and forth. Their chains squeak in protest. Bluebirds perched on the wooden benches take to the sky, beating their wings; disturbing clouds of butterflies dancing over beds of wildflowers, aligned against the dark-green painted fence.

'Hey, I've got an idea! Let's go on the swings!' Addie yells, making for the play area. 'I'll race y'all to them!'

Mal laughs, chasing after her. 'That sounds like fun!'

'You go along,' Greg waves his hand, 'I'll watch you from over here.'

Greg makes for the nearest bench and sits, leaning back into his seat. Bonnie follows and lies by his feet, encouraging him to reach down and scratch her ears. She responds by thumping her tail against the ground in appreciation. Sam is standing on the edge of the play area watching Addie, Mal and Nina on the swings. Frank attempts to walk along the balancing beam forming part of a small obstacle course. After a couple of steps the sky-pirate teeters, overbalances, and drops to the ground. Glancing skywards, he spots several imaginary tiny canary-yellow-coloured birds circling around his head. After some effort, he manages to clamber back to his feet and returns to the starting point. Step by wobbly step he tries again, until again he teeters and falls.

Chuckling with amusement, Sam is distracted by a loud groaning caw. 'Hey Sam!'

High above his head, a large black, scruffy looking raven swoops down and perches on top of the nearby fence. The raven's beady eyes shine a familiar striking azure blue.

'Hey Techna! It's good to see you,' Sam says warmly, stroking Techna's feathered crown, 'and you're disguised as a raven?'

'Yep! Taking the shape of birds is a useful way of concealing our true forms.'

'But why?'

'Because humans are suspicious of things they do not understand.'

'I suppose you're right.'

'I told you to look out for a lone raven, when you wanted to speak to me.' Techna flits his raven head from side to side. 'Besides, it's cool being a raven. If only I had a writing desk to go with it.'

Sam glances around, wondering where the other guardian is hiding. 'Where's Gaia?'

But before Techna can answer, the air fills with a long, high-pitched scream. One that threatens to burst fragile eardrums. The sound is closely followed by a disturbing sequence of cat screeches. Turning, Sam spots a large white dove flapping through a flowerbed, its wings beating furiously as the bird attempts to fly. It manages to glide over the path, chased by a large, round ginger tabby. Both animals zoom past.

'Get away from me,' the dove cries, 'you filthy fur-ball!'

'Aw Gaia,' Techna scoffs, 'have you been chasing the kitty again?'

'Cheek! *It's chasing me!*' Gaia manages to reply, while performing a tight mid-air turn. 'And why isn't your friend helping me? I swear, humans are so lazy!'

Techna sighs. 'Gaia isn't so enthusiastic about his white dove form. It's his fault really, refusing to enter the spirit of nature and aggravating everyone he meets. He's as stubborn as a rock.'

Craning his head, Techna turns his attention to Nina, who is playing with Mal and Addie. Frank has given up walking the plank and is now pushing Nina on her swing. She kicks out her legs, screaming with excitement.

'It's good to see them having fun.'

Sam nods. 'Yep. We needed to take a break, after the Nethmites' last attack.'

Techna looks around the park, sniffing the salty air. 'Farley is your old home isn't it? It looks nice.'

'It sure is. I've a lot of happy memories living here.'

'Do people remember you?'

'Yeah. It's like I've never been away.'

Techna mutters, '*Never been away.*' He lowers his head.

Once again they are interrupted by Gaia's high-pitched dove caw, followed by another excited screech from his feline foe. The guardian zooms past, his wing brushing against Sam's cheek. The cat slides to a halt and adopts a crouched, primed position, swishes its tail vigorously from side to side. It is waiting for the dove to circle around. As Gaia approaches the cat leaps, pouncing like a stalking lion, causing the dove to twist in the air and safely clear the fence.

'Techna! Don't just stand there!' Gaia whines. '*HELP MEEEEEEE!*'

Techna shakes his head. 'I better go and calm him, before he becomes the cat's play toy.'

'Okay Techna,' Sam nods, 'I'll see you later.'

'Don't be a stranger! You know, I've always wanted to say that.'

Sam waves as the raven soars after the dove. He joins his friends by the swings, standing beside Mal.

Addie is counting loudly between swings, kicking her legs as hard as she can. '34…35…36…'

'What's she doing,' Sam asks, laughing, 'trying to get to one hundred?'

'You bet!' Mal replies. 'She's so focused.'

'Indeed she is.'

Gazing over the line of buildings tracing the park perimeter, Sam traces the coastal path, resting his eye on the familiar shape of the lighthouse standing at the end of the stone jetty. Strange shadows are cast across the sea; tricks of light caused by the clouds floating in the sky. For a moment it feels as if he is alone, focused on the strange shapes. A powerful gust of wind pulls against the strands of his scarf. His detachment from the others is broken by Nina and Frank's voices cutting through his dream world. Nina is talking to the sky-pirate, describing her relationship with Greg and how she was first accepted into the family.

A revelation that nearly causes the swing to smash into Frank's face. 'What? Wait!' He exclaims. 'So you're adopted?'

'Yeah! I think it's called adopted. I remember being on my own, with no other family at all. Then one day Papa came, with Sammy's Mama. They found me and brought me home. They told me they couldn't leave me there and that I was part of their family.'

'What was Sam's mother like?'

'She was so pretty, and she made really nice, yummy cherry pies.' Nina rubs her tummy, reminded of such pleasant memories.

'So you see mister-pirate, I've always known Papa isn't my real Papa; but he's the only Papa I have.'

'Now Nina,' Sam chuckles, 'you're making Greg blush.'

With rising pride, Greg pushes himself up off the bench and joins the others. He plants his hand on Sam's shoulder and smiles at Mal. 'Sam told me that you live in the forest?'

'Yes, Greystagg forest. At least I did, before it became a wasteland. Thanks to the Nether, it's all…'

Her words trail away as she is overcome by the feelings of hurt brought on by the hordes of Nethmites. The cruel metallic creatures that devoured every flower, every blade of grass and every slice of tree bark. How they stole every drop of cool, clear water from the lake. Trapped within this traumatic silence, she relives the moment they escaped, driven by the Flower of Knowledge's commands. *Oh! The Flower of Knowledge and his noble sacrifice.* The memory of him begging for her forgiveness as his power drained away, causes her eyes to sting with tears. Her shoulders shake as she recalls the tree's withered frame: standing alone, abandoned in the wasteland with the other lifeless plants.

'Um, hey?' Greg asks. 'Are you okay?'

'Uh?' Mal composes herself, wiping away the tears trickling down her cheeks. 'I'll be okay. Don't worry.'

Concerned, Frank asks. 'Are you sure, Mal?'

'Yeah, yeah. It's alright. I'll be alright Frank.'

Greg follows Sam's gaze, along the coast towards the jetty and lighthouse. 'I can tell how much you've missed Fye. She was always a great comfort to you. Especially when we were caring for your mother.' He smiles. 'I bet she'll love to see you again too, huh?'

Sam sighs. 'I'd love to see her again, up close.'

'Then why don't we take a stroll down there right now?'

'Yeah! That would be nice.' Sam calls to the others. 'Hey! Do you want to come and see Fye with me?'

Nina nods excitedly. She allows her swing to slow before jumping off and skipping towards the park's entrance. Mal and Frank follow.

Addie stops kicking out her legs, regretfully allowing her swing to slow to a halt. Her shoulders slump forward. 'Aw, but I haven't reached my one hundred swinging record.'

*

They exit the park and head for the centre of the parish. From there they walk along the coastal path towards the sandy beach and the jetty beyond. Nina is keen for Sam to display his newly acquired wings. They spread out from inside his jacket. Greg is amazed by how real they look and feel. Nina likes them because they tickle. They step cautiously along the uneven surface, listening to their feet crunching on the moss and weeds growing between the cracks on the stone path. Reaching the beach, they are welcomed by the sounds of waves periodically crashing against the wall of rocky boulders and the rhythmic ripple of water running across pebbles. Ahead the lighthouse looms larger as they approach. Its tall, limestone grey tower shimmers in the sunlight.

'Wait a minute.' Addie pipes, with a dubious lilt. 'This is Fye, the Fye Sam's been blabbering on about all this time. It's a lighthouse. Who gives a name to a lighthouse?'

'Who wouldn't name a lighthouse?' Frank counters. 'Besides, you've named your bow Silverhair, just as I've dubbed my blunderbuss, Old Faithful.'

Addie smirks. 'Touché.' She turns to Mal. 'Hey Mal, why haven't you given a name to your quarterstaff?'

'I don't know,' Mal mutters, 'I'm not someone who names inanimate objects. Besides, I don't think I could come up with a good name even if I wanted to.' She adds, more assuredly. 'My quarterstaff doesn't have to have a name, right? It's a part of me, and that's what matters.'

'*Riiiight.*' Addie nods, pursing her lips. 'Suit yourself, cause I was thinking of calling it *Unreliable.*' She feels a knock against her ankle as Bonnie cuts her sentence short. 'Hey!'

The pup blows a short, sharp raspberry, causing Frank and Mal to snigger.

Reaching the end of the jetty they stare up at the lighthouse, looming high above their heads. The ocean spray trickles continuously down the side of its stone-tiled structure. Fye looks a sorry sight, bearing the scars of being pummelled by nature. Two of the upper windows are bordered up with wooden planks, replacing the broken glass panes. The main tower glass remains in place. A testament to the still working lighthouse, despite the evidence of neglect. Sam spies several chipped tiles that urgently need replacing. They sit on the base of the lighthouse and look out over the ocean, mesmerised by the waves rolling up and down, over and over, before crashing into the jetty wall below. A flock of gulls soar overhead, cawing loudly.

Sam softly strokes the solid wall of the lighthouse, pressing his ear against the cold stone surface.

'It's been a while, hasn't it my friend?' He sniffs at the salty air and closes his eye. 'I've forgotten how nice and fresh the ocean breeze is. The city air cannot compare with this!'

Frank asks. 'Did you name the lighthouse, Sam?'

'Actually, I didn't. It was Ma who dubbed it Fye, just after she met Pa. She thought the name suited the lighthouse, and he liked it too. She told me they came here all the time. It was their peaceful repose.'

Mal gushes. 'How lovely!'

Addie snorts, but covers her instinctive riposte with her hand. Secretly she likes the sense of tranquillity here, not that she could ever admit to it. She watches as a couple of gulls skim across the ocean surface. One pecks at the water, hopeful of catching a fish swimming beneath the surface. It looks so peaceful here. The breeze catches her ponytail sending strands of hair playing across her ears. A small sad frown creases her face as she recalls long-held memories.

'I wonder if I might go there again?' She mutters to herself, shaking her head. 'Not today, nor tomorrow, for sure. But maybe one day?'

'Hm?' Mal asks. 'Did you say something, Addie?'

'Nothing. Nothing at all. I just got some salt in my mouth.'

Sam stands and heads back along the jetty, leaving his friends to admire the costal scenery. Climbing the stony incline, he makes for a small, bricked building positioned overlooking the beach. The surrounding greenery is overgrown, and the house appears covered in a shadowy shroud. It is his old house. The family home, complete with its swamp-green-coloured tiled roof. He tries pushing open the front door, but the squeaking rusted hinges protest loudly. Pushing harder, the door reluctantly opens. It is deathly quiet inside. Untouched. Unlived in. Stepping inside, he listens to the creaking floorboards under his feet. What was once his warm comforting home has been reduced to an empty deserted shack. There is a strong damp musky smell inside, which feels choking to breathe. Cautiously he climbs the stairs, his half-unfurled wings brush gently against the walls. He peers inside the first room at the top of the stairs, his childhood bedroom. Moving on and with emotions spilling over, he enters the next room, Lily's bedroom, and finally the bathroom. The rooms are empty, without furniture, picture frames, any reminders of his time growing up here. The wooden floors are covered in dust and spotted with pools of congealed water that have collected beneath holes in the roof. The windows are murky and smeared with grease, corrupting the sea views outside. *It is so sad.*

Returning downstairs, Sam heads into the kitchen. It appears empty inside here too. The once happy clutter he remembers while watching Lily make the best homemade cherry pies has been replaced by a deep, empty silence. Her cheery voice supplanted by sadness. Where is the little red radio that used to play the upbeat songs they used to sing and dance along to; and the bright green pinafore she wore that used to swish and twirl, making her the belle of the ball. He reaches out to touch the sunflower patterned wallpaper, now a sickly faded mustard-colour. Stepping through the damaged patio door, left hanging on its hinges, he stands on the small terrace. This had been Lily's favourite spot, where she used to sit and watch the majestic, eternal ocean roll away the hours. During long sunny days, with the sun set high, he would sit outside with her, drinking cold sweet tea and eating rosewater biscuits. Then during clear star-filled nights, they would set up the telescope and point it skywards to seek something, or someone. There is nothing left here now. The outdoor table and chairs have disappeared, along with the telescope and its stand. It is an empty house filled with ghostly memories. Feeling lost and sad, his eye stings as he wipes away a single tear. He should return to the others – *no, not just yet.*

Hearing footsteps treading the floorboards behind him, Sam starts. Turning around he sees Greg walking into the kitchen, who looks regretfully about the empty room.

'It sure looks sad, doesn't it?'

Sam steps inside the kitchen. 'Yeah. It feels as if there's nothing left, not since Ma went.'

Opening one of the cupboard doors, he finds the little red radio inside. The only object that remains. He begins tweaking its buttons, hoping for signs of electronic life. The radio remains silent.

He sighs. 'It's just a depleted house with nothing but memories.'

'I have endeavoured to look after the house, but I'm fighting a losing battle against the dust bunnies and the mould. At least I've managed to keep it structurally sound.' Greg explains resignedly. He rubs his chin. 'I hope one day you'll return. It will take some fixing-up.'

A smile flashes across Sam's lips. 'And maybe we could get Fye fixed-up too? That would be great! Perhaps when this is all over.'

*

The evening draws in and the sun casts long dark shadows over the landscape. Following a brief flight, Sam and Nina are sitting atop the tallest hill overlooking Farley. From their vantage point they watch villagers, each appearing as a small dark dot, move about the parish. Most are heading home after a long day at work. Some are preparing to journey further: a train is beginning its long trek through the surrounding countryside. Sam ruffles his wings, an exercise to counter the chilly air. Sitting beside him, Nina scrunches the hem of her dress. She is staring down at the quiet village, deep in thought.

'Sammy? Can I ask you something?'

'Sure, Nina.'

'I was wondering how you saved Papa from the monster, using that special power you have. Did you use it cause that was the only way, or was it something else?'

'I did it because I care about him as much as you do, but the Aether helped. I believed Greg was trapped inside the metal creature and his feverish reactions were due to his terrible confinement.'

'Oh.' Nina fiddles with her dress again, preparing to ask another question. 'And what about the blast, the one you kept from hurting all those people inside that building? Did you do that cause you cared for them too?'

'I didn't really think Nina. I acted on instinct and hoped it was the right thing to do. I knew that whatever happened, it was my destiny to hold the door shut.' He gazes at his bionic arm, flexing the mechanical digits. 'But if I'm honest, I wish I had both eyes and arms. They were a part of me and sometimes I wonder if I could go back, would I change what I did?' He sighs regretfully. 'I really don't know. There's a part of me that can't stop thinking that what I did was foolish, you know, running inside when I knew I'd get caught in the blast.'

Nina looks expectantly at Sam, her big round green eyes sparkling. 'Yet you did Sammy,' she says softly, 'despite everything that happened. You cared more about the people inside that building; more than your own safety.'

'I guess,' Sam chuckles, rubbing his head, 'and perhaps I do wear my heart on my sleeve!'

'*Wow!*' Nina gasps. 'I think you might be a superhero to some, cause of what you did in that blast; but to me, you'll always be my Sammy.'

Sam playfully nudges Nina's shoulder. 'You've grown much wiser since I last saw you kiddo.'

Above their heads the sky blushes in a glorious blend of red and orange colours as the sun caresses the ocean before slipping below the horizon. The houses in Farley are now brightly lit and smoke billows from ceramic chimney-tops. The final stragglers are making their way home as darkness creeps inland. Nina yawns, quickly covering her open mouth with one hand, while stretching tiredly with the other.

'It's getting late Nina. C'mon, let me take you home.' Sam picks Nina up and holds her in his arms. 'Your dad's waiting for us, as well as supper.'

Spreading his wings, they rise gently from the ground before following the contours of the hill, heading for the homely lights of the parish.

Nina stirs, her head nestled against Sam's shoulder. 'Sammy?'

'Yeah?'

'Can you tell me again what your Papa's name was?'

'Noah. His name was Noah. He was an astronaut, remember?'

'Oh yeah. I forget things,' she sighs, 'don't I?'

'That's okay Nina. You're tired.'

Landing beyond the garden wall they walk through the iron gate and into Greg's house. They are welcomed by the smell of supper being prepared: homegrown broccoli and cheese pasta-soup, seasoned with black peppercorn and served with rye bread. This evening's chef is Frank, under Mal's close supervision. After supper they sit together in the lounge sharing pleasant conversations until it is time for bed. Mal helps Greg collect cushions and blankets for makeshift beds while Sam collects Nina, tuckered out from the evening's company, and carries her upstairs. Her bedroom is decorated in pink and white flowers and is filled with the sweet scent of camomile. Spotting a fluffy rabbit toy lying on her bed, he tucks the sleeping child inside the pink coverlets with the rabbit wrapped inside her arms. Nina twists onto her side, a smile pressed on her lips.

Greg is standing, watching from the doorway.

Sam turns. 'Guess we've tired her out.'

'Me too.' Greg chuckles as they exit Nina's bedroom, closing the door behind them. 'Thank you for staying, Sam. Nina really enjoyed your company today.'

Sam smiles. 'And I've loved being back.'

He follows Greg downstairs where their friends are drifting into a peaceful reverie. The promising silence is interrupted by Addie's snoring.

'Hey Sam,' Greg whispers, 'do you fancy going outside?'

'Are you sure? It's rather cold.'

'Nah, the night chill doesn't bother me, not after being confined in the cellar. Come, just the two of us?'

'Well if you're sure. I doubt I can sleep right now, so a night stroll might help.'

Tucking his arm inside Greg's, they exit the house and step outside into the cool night air. The village sits peaceful and quiet under the moonlight; the dark sky filled with clusters of bright stars. There are spots of lights escaping through gaps in the window shutters of adjacent houses, although Sam suspects that most people are now tucked up in bed and fast asleep. They walk to the park, noting that some of the streetlamps flicker unexpectedly as they pass. Across the pond they watch swarms of glowing fireflies dance above the still waters, or deftly touching the tips of the petals of sleeping flowers. A large eagle-owl skips from fencepost to fencepost, hooting loudly as Sam and Greg approach. Sam offers the eagle-owl a friendly wave. It is Cedric.

As Greg and Sam move on, and with the coast clear, Cedric spits out an annoyed. '*Bleh!*'

A tiny tawny owl flees into the night sky, determined to avoid the cantankerous eagle-owl.

Circling the pond, Sam clings onto Greg's arm, sensing a chill under his jacket. A gust of wind picks up flower petals and deposits them gently over the pond, forming tiny ripples from their touch. From behind comes the sound of rustling feathers, which startles them. They turn and watch two birds, a dove and a raven, take to the sky.

'Would you look at that!' Greg laughs. 'Imagine seeing a dove and a raven together. They remind me of the stories about two bird-like dragons your Ma used to read to you.'

Sam catches a glimpse of the glare from the dove in the bright streetlamp. 'I remember it well. The bird-like guardians who seek out those who are sad, or afraid, or lost.'

'They were called Gaia and Techna, right?'

'Yeah. Gaia and Techna.'

Walking from the park and along the coastal path, they approach the jetty and Fye's rotating bulb; periodically projecting bursts of light that reflect off the ocean waters. Standing at the end of the jetty, they listen to the repetitive calming rolls of the waves. A shooting star soars across the night sky, before disappearing within Fye's brilliant illuminance. Sam rests his head against Greg's left shoulder, who places an affectionate hand on his head.

'It's a wonderful night, isn't it?'

'Yeah, it sure is.'

Greg shifts his gaze away, looking back over Farley. In the distance, hovering over the main gateway into the parish, a strange-looking craft is briefly illuminated by Fye's bright light.

'Is that how you got here from Melsey? On that amazing airship?'

'Part of the way; but don't ask me how it works.' Sam nods. 'Frank says the Puppis has a mind of its own.'

'And what's next for you and your friends?'

'We must find the Fleur de Vie.'

'The Fleur de Vie? What's that?'

'It's a special flower.'

Sam stops and gazes at Fye's bright light. Had there been a flicker, a brief break in its sequence, or is his tired imagination playing tricks on him?'

Shaking his head he continues. 'To be honest, when I first set off I only had plans to see the lands beyond the city. But since the start of my adventure, every step I take, every decision I make, leads me deeper into the mysteries of the Aether.' He smiles, resignedly. 'It's a path I'm destined to take, wherever it leads me.'

'I remember Noah when he became an astronaut. He was so excited.' He places his hand reassuringly under Sam's chin, lifting his gaze up to his eyes. 'And you share so many of his characteristics: his sense for adventure and purpose.' Greg's eyes soften. 'Even if you have Lily's eyes.'

Sam lowers his gaze. 'I have Ma's eyes.'

A thick cluster of flower petals begin circling around the solid frame of the Puppis, carried on swirling air currents they disappear into the night sky. Sam shivers.

'Let's head home Sam, you must be tired.'

Perched above the gate of Sam's old house, the dove and the raven grow larger, morphing into their true forms. Gaia and Techna lean against the fence they are standing by and gaze down at the scene below.

'Finally! The coast is clear!' Gaia huffs in relief, brushing cat fur from his breast. 'Look at all this fluff! I don't want to see another fur-ball again!'

Techna smirks. 'I think it wanted to be friends with you, Gaia.'

'Ah! Hold your tongue.' Gaia watches Sam and Greg walking from the jetty. His moth-feelers twitches. 'I didn't realise humans still think about us, you know, beyond our place in their fairy-tales.'

'Perhaps you'll see things differently now, having heard the human Greg recall our names!' Techna replies. 'I now feel we've acted cowardly by not showing them the truth and choosing to hide as our bird forms.'

'That's easy for you to say. You weren't chased by that horrible hairy cat. And yet,' Gaia shakes his head, 'what Sam did, recognising that creature for what it truly was, and not destroying it. *Pssh!* Might I have done so, in his position?' He pauses. 'Something made him aware that it was the Nether shard corrupting his friend. He saw through the Nether's power.'

'He might have destroyed that wretched creature,' Techna nods, 'yet his love was able to weaken the Nether and spare the man trapped inside and return him to his true form. I think Sam has found a better use of the Aether.'

'The shard may have been destroyed,' Gaia adds cautiously, 'but the damage it accomplished, manipulating the free thoughts of a human, makes me shudder. What dark potential has the Nether planned?'

'At least we know more now. But you are correct Gaia, we could be facing something vastly different from the Nether this time. Something harsher than before. And we cannot afford to underestimate those cunning Nethmites.' Techna ruffles his wings. 'It's essential we quickly secure the Fleur de Vie.'

'But Tech,' Gaia counters, concerned, 'do you believe the humans can find the Fleur de Vie?'

'I do, Gaia. As I believe in Sam, with or without the Aether.'

*

The following morning brings heavy grey clouds that threaten rain. The party rise early and after a brief breakfast, busy themselves with preparation to continue their journey. Sam, Frank and Addie hoist crates filled with supplies up onto the deck of the Puppis, before storing them inside the galley. Mal is away buying stationery supplies from the post office.

Nina and Greg arrive in time to watch the Puppis depart.

'So you're really leaving?' Nina asks, sadly.

'Yeah.' Sam replies, placing his hand on Nina's shoulder. 'But it's been lovely seeing you again, and I promise I'll be back soon. For now we have places we must go as events are moving fast, and it's important we face them. I'm gonna miss you Nina, and I bet you're gonna miss me too.'

'I will.' Nina's voice quivers, but she keeps smiling. 'I wish I could go with you, but I have Papa to look after, and I don't want to leave him. He'd be sad if I did go away, wouldn't he? It's been nice listening to your adventure stories and meeting your friends. I can't wait to hear more! I know you'll find the Fleur de Vie, Sammy. Is that what it's called? Yeah! I bet it'll look pretty too!'

Sam chuckles, tousling her hair. 'Cheers Nina.' Turning to Greg, he adds. 'I hope your fully recovered soon. Just take it easy with your arm.'

'I promise Sam. I'll keep myself out of trouble. No more picking up strange shards in the forest.' Greg smiles awkwardly. 'And we'll come and visit you in Melsey, once you've completed your adventure.'

'*You will!* I'll get Ted to give you free shakes when I take you to *The Root*.' Sam stops, unable to contain his emotions any longer. He swings his arms around Greg. 'Thank you again for offering to fix up my old house.'

They hold each other in reassuring silence, allowing the moment to stretch out for as long as they can. Eventually they separate.

'Take care, my friend.'

Sam nods, wiping away tears from his cheek. He steps towards his friends, who are waiting to board the Puppis.

'Are you ready Sam?' Addie asks. 'The adventure can't go on without you!'

'Yeah, I know,' Sam replies, 'and we've got a lot of travelling ahead for us.'

One-by-one they climb the rope ladder. Waiting on deck for Sam to climb aboard, they wave to Greg who is comforting a tearful Nina at his side. Sam smiles and begins climbing, rung-by-rung.

Stepping on deck he declares. 'Okay, I'm ready.'

'Full speed ahead!' Addie cries.

They feel the Puppis' rear propeller rev and the giant wings slowly flap, raising the craft higher into the air. Below, Greg and Nina stand waving as the airship drifts away, leaving Farley behind.

With tears running down her cheeks and her hands clinging into her father's side, Nina whispers. 'Bye Sammy. Bye-Bye.'

Oh Sable!

They leave Farley aboard the Puppis, driven easterly on strong ocean air currents and relying on the balmy breeze for a leisurely cruise. Their progress causes curious seabirds to scatter, swerving from the large air-sac as it sweeps past. By mid-afternoon the Puppis has left the Southern Island coast and slipped into the mountain valley, following the slow meandering River Tye. The airship is alive with activity: Frank dances around checking and tightening rope knots, while Mal attacks the deck with a dry broom, sweeping away debris and bird-droppings. In contrast, Addie is deep in thought, sitting alone on the wooden steps connecting the deck to the helm. Her eyes are drawn to Mal as she retrieves a large white feather from the wooden boards. She stands and walks to the side of the Puppis and peers overboard, staring into the valley passing below. Behind the Puppis, the distant ocean fades until it is lost beyond the horizon. Addie taps her fingers against the brass trim. There is something on her mind. Restless, she sighs and plonks down on the wooden steps. Dr Woodchuck comes and sits behind her, brushing at his whiskers, while perched above the helm, Cedric tries taking another afternoon nap.

Sam is sitting in the galley writing a letter to Johnny and Mary describing his time in Farley, deliberately skipping over the physical confrontation with Lockjaw. There is no need to worry them unnecessarily. Curled into a ball by his feet, Bonnie listens to the reassuring scratch of pen against paper. Putting the final touches to his letter, Sam drops his pen and gently scratches the pup's ears. His letters home mark mileposts on his journey: a measure of the time that has elapsed since leaving Melsey on his long and winding adventure.

A loud hefty creak sends a violent shudder along the body of the Puppis. Above deck, the air-sac grumbles and the airship begins swaying from side to side. Mal steadies her balance by planting the broomstick against the wooden deck.

'Oops! That doesn't sound good!' Frank groans, hurrying to the helm, almost toppling over his pegleg.

Sam rushes from the galley with Bonnie following closely behind. 'Frank! Frank! What's wrong?'

'Dunno! But we'd better land and check what's up.'

Frank grabs hold of the helm as the Puppis descends towards the river below, with its fresh sparkling water running from the cover of a small wood. Birds scatter from trees as the craft nears the ground, startled by the propeller grinding to a low, rough growl. With the anchor lowered and the Puppis secured, the party jumps down onto the soft grass, speckled with tiny flowers. Frank hobbles towards the rear of the airship and opens a small hatch. Then reaching deep into the void, his hand rummages for the blockage he suspects is there. His fingers wrap around something inside and he pulls out a thick round ball of tightly mashed twigs and clods of dry dirt. It smells strong and earthy, which causes him to sneeze.

Struggling on the tips of her toes, Addie leans over Frank's shoulders. 'What in the blazes is that?'

'It's just a clod of tumbleweed.' Frank explains, tossing it away. 'Nothing fancy. The Puppis can continue. Sorry about the delay.'

'No worries captain, but we don't have to make a move straight away, do we?' Mal asks, admiring the serene surroundings of the trees. 'It looks nice here.'

'Yeah, it's not half bad,' Addie agrees, nodding to the hedges and surrounding trees, 'and there's no sign of those nasty Nethmites either. So why don't we kick back and relax for a while? I'm sort of fed up with hanging in the air.'

'I guess that won't hurt,' Frank replies, closing the hatch door, 'resting our land-legs on terra-firma for a while.'

'Excellent! And I can carve more arrows for Silverhair.' Addie turns her gaze from the trees. 'I just need to find some feathers.'

'Oh no!' Cedric blows a curt raspberry. 'Don't you start plucking them from me!'

'Don't fret. I'd never use your moulting plumage, bird-breath.'

Addie and Cedric part, heading in opposite directions: Addie with Silverhair clasped in her hand, sets about looking for any stray straight branches lying on the grass under the trees; Cedric flies up into the tree-tops to find a strong branch to settle on, muttering something about bird-breath in a mocking tone. The others remain beside the river. Frank and Mal stroll together along the bank as Dr Woodchuck squats on all fours to sip the cool river waters. Bonnie lying beside him takes a drink too and they exchange observations on how refreshing the water tastes.

Sam pulls off his steel-toe capped boots and hangs his bare feet into the water. He spots trout swimming against the current; some pucker their lips through the surface, greedily eyeing the red dragonflies hovering over bustles of water reeds. It is peaceful here: the sights, the sounds, the smells.

WHOOSH!

Sam's quiet reflection is interrupted by an unexpected gust of wind that drives through a line of thick shrubs. Glancing up he spots a familiar figure approaching, surrounded by billowing clouds of white petals. She slides the deer mask from her face.

'Hey, Sable!'

'Sam, my friend!' Sable smiles and sits next to Sam on the riverbank. 'I'm glad to find you all safe and well. My animal friends have told me what happened in Greystagg, and the fate of the Flower of Knowledge. I sympathise with Mallory.'

Sam looks at Mal, who is now sitting on a large boulder talking with Dr Woodchuck. They are too far away to hear their conversation clearly, but it sounds cheery. Mal chuckles as the woodchuck flails his arms, trying to demonstrate some point of his.

'Yeah, Mal took everything pretty badly,' he sighs, 'but the Flower of Knowledge's sacrifice can't be in vain, can it?'

'Remember Sam, the Flower of Knowledge did all he could, by helping you escape Greystagg.'

'Mal loved the forest so much and it's hard seeing her with her heart broken.' Sam forces a smile. 'Yet since Farley she seems better. I think the pleasantness of my old home has helped her counter her sad thoughts.'

Another gust signals the approach of Techna, in his raven form. His arrival is marked by the nervous scatter of birds hiding in the trees. The black guardian lands on the grass, morphing into his dragon form. He shakes his furry body and ruffles his feathers.

Sam jumps to his feet. 'Hey Techna!'

Sable smiles. 'Nice to see you again, my good friend.'

Techna nods. 'Good day, Sable.' He turns to Sam, wearing a bemused expression across his face. 'Taking a break, huh?'

'Yeah!' Sam nods. 'There was a problem with the Puppis stalling on tumbleweed and we decided to take a break.'

Techna glances nervously around the landing site. 'Tumbleweed?'

'That's what Frank called it.' Sam pauses and stretches out his hands. 'Techna, can you tell me more about the Aether and why Sable and I have this power? Are we the only ones it has chosen?'

For a moment Techna seems agitated, perhaps annoyed with Sam's question, but his expression quickly softens.

'The Aether is a spiritual power and remains obscured to most humans. It chooses only those it sees as vessels of positive thoughts. In Sable, the Aether sees someone who understands the natural and spiritual world.' He continues. 'And with you Sam, it recognises your perpetual gentleness and belief in seeing the light when all else appears shrouded in darkness.'

Addie sneaks into the conversation. 'What's so important about the Aether?'

Smiling at the spirited audacity Addie brings into every interaction, Techna replies. 'The Aether brings the hope of calm, even during the fiercest of storms. It is more powerful than any device the Nether employs and it will stop it in its tracks.'

'So the Aether is the only thing that can stop the Nether?' Addie sighs. 'I've been shooting down Nethmites with my trusty bow and it has served me well.'

'Your bow is adequate, but it can only pause the Nethmites' attacks. The Nether sees your attempts as futile, as it does all individual efforts, even mine. We can only scratch the surface of the dark negative forces acting against us.'

'If you need the Aether so badly to stop the Nether, why don't you just extract it from Sam's body, wring it out of him, you know, like twisting a wet towel?' She wrings her fists, her face distorted into a mock grimace. 'And then you can combine it with your own powers to destroy the Nether.'

There is a resounding gasp.

'W-Whoa! A-Addie!' Sam stammers, waving his hands.

'I don't know exactly what you mean by wringing a wet towel,' Techna says, twitching his moth-feelers with unease, 'but if I assume correctly, then I can assure you that we would never extract the Aether from anyone else, by any method.'

'What? I'm only joking!' Addie laughs nervously. 'Can't you guys take one?'

Sitting unnoticed atop a grassy knoll, a white dove listens attentively to the discourse on the opposite side of the river. It morphs into Gaia, who ruffles his wings to shake away clouds of dust and moulting feathers. A single robin perches on a boulder beside him and glances anxiously at the white guardian, and then at the others on the other riverbank.

'Pathetic!' Gaia scoffs, swooping from the knoll and across the grassy bank.

The robin follows and settles onto Gaia's shoulder when the guardian sits down further along the riverbank. Gaia stares at his shimmering reflection captured in the fast-running water.

'Wanting to extract the Aether,' he starts, 'wringing it out like a wet towel,' he adds, 'how ludicrous!'

The robin offers Gaia a series of reassuring chirps and then begins pecking the white guardian's furry coat.

'Of course not, little guy. I would never consider extracting the Aether like that. Not ever. We guardians are beyond thinking that way. But Techna is right when he says only the Aether can stop the Nether, not petty bows and arrows.' He lowers his eyes. 'Huh! Such arrogance.'

The robin chirps and tilts its head.

'Yes. I had another human friend, but she went her own way. She left, after the battle, just as Sable will do. Just as every human will eventually go their own way.' He sighs heavily. 'I don't know if I can ever trust them again, no matter how much Techna tries to convince me otherwise.'

The robin chirps a long tweet followed with a short shrill, and then takes to the sky.

Gaia sighs again, waving at the departing bird. 'I know, but what would be the point in that?' He strolls leisurely along the bank, brushing against the bordering thicket. 'Trusting humans only leads to heartbreak. But Techna has grown fond of Sam, too fond.' He picks up a stone and skims it across the river, it bounces once, twice, three times. 'And what is it with him and those pecan cakes? He keeps on eating them, but they're far too stodgy for my taste.' He stops, realising that no-one is listening to his rant. 'But Techna may have a point. My views are tainted, especially when I think of Sam. It's just that he reminds me of her.'

Glancing sadly at the clouds billowing gently across the sky, he senses the soft trail of a breeze over his moth-feelers and sniffs at the faint flowery scent.

He shakes his head vigorously. 'Oh, what are you saying Gaia? You *are* thinking too much about her. Don't let her loss get to you. Perhaps Sam *is* different.'

*

Sam kicks his bare feet in the river, feeling the resistance of the water against his skin. His friends are scattered around the riverbank, busy with their own thoughts. Addie meanders in and out of the trees, battling with the embarrassment raised by her ill-conceived idea of extracting the Aether from Sam. She knows she meant no harm by it; she just says things without thinking. Mal is following her, trying to console her. They pass Frank, who is sitting atop a boulder and munching on the berries he has picked from a nearby bush. Sam studies a patch of dry grass next to where he is sitting. The blades are limp, and their once vibrant green colours have turned a sickly yellow. Kneeling behind him, Sable releases a small spark of Aether from her hand. As the rose-coloured light shimmers over the dry patch, it releases a burst of fresh growth of thick, lush green grass and strong looking flower seedlings.

'I wonder if I could do that.' Sam mutters, stroking another patch of dried grass.

The Aether responds, flashing from his hand and bathing the parched area with a mystical light. Fresh grass grows, green and straight, followed by clutches of daisies and yellow buttercups, bursting through the soil like popping bubbles. A bumblebee and a couple of red butterflies nestle on top of the newly formed flowers.

'Wow! The Aether sure knows its stuff.' He gasps. 'It's like magic!'

Sable watches the rose-coloured light dissolve from Sam's hand. 'It looks like you're getting used to the Aether.' She smiles. 'I'm impressed.'

'Thank you Sable.'

They are distracted by the arrival of a flock of geese that sprint across the surface of the river before soaring into the air. A sparrowhawk glides high above the treetops, keeping a keen eye for food. A trout puckers its lips through the surface of the water near Sam's foot, but disappears quickly, startled by Dr Woodchuck excitedly jumping to catch the flies hovering over his head. Oblivious to everything happening below him, Cedric fidgets restlessly, trying to find the right sleeping pose.

'I wonder how people are doing in Melsey? It's seems ages since I've been there, working in my little tarot shop with its smell of cedarwood.' Sable sighs. 'I miss my hanging dreamcatchers and how they'd entice customers inside to browse for gifts for their friends and family.' She smiles. 'Being a shopkeeper proved a humble and pleasurable experience: supplying my herbs and spices; providing an experience of distant lands for the city folk. You know Sam, I shouldn't admit this, but I liked having a steady income too.' She rests her hand on Sam's shoulder. 'Tell me Sam, are you planning to return?'

'Yes I will. It was nice meeting my friends in Farley, but much of my life is now in Melsey and I'm concerned that everything is okay there. How are Johnny and Mary, are they busy working in their café? And Sandy with his flower shop and Ted working in *The Root*; and Mandy who always finds time to talk with me, when she's not preoccupied with her friends or her mobile.' He smiles, sadly. 'I worry about the sparrows and finches in the park not having enough seeds, with me not being there. The city has a lot going for it, even for a Farley person like me!' He sighs heavily, glancing at Sable. 'You don't think the Nethmites have reached Melsey, do you?

But before Sable can answer, they are distracted by a loud rustling emanating from the bushes behind. His friends have heard it too and they stop what they are doing and turn towards sound. There is someone, or something, emerging through the leaves! They ready themselves. *Nethmites?*

It is not another attack. It is the hooded figure Sam spotted as the party had escaped Greystagg. The mysterious stranger is clambering over fallen branches and brushing the foliage from their body, muttering something about berries and leaves sticking to their clothing. The stranger comes to a halt directly before Sam. *Face-to-face.* Sam stares at the long thick strands of buttercream blonde hair cascading over the stranger's face.

Addie steps forward. 'Hey! Who the heck are you?' She demands, standing assuredly with hands on hips.

'I...' The stranger gazes on nervously, pondering on whether to make an introduction. 'I can't say, not at this time.' He glances apologetically at the ground. 'I'm sorry if that sounds rude, but I have my reasons.'

'I don't understand,' Sam frowns, 'why are you following us?'

'I've been observing your adventures.'

'You've been stalking us!' Addie snaps.

Mal winces. 'That does sound creepy.'

'Yep, just what bunny-ears said,' Addie steps closer to the stranger, 'and what business do you have with the Fleur de Vie? You better make your answer quick, or you can skedaddle bud. I don't mind which.'

The stranger takes a step backwards, unnerved by Addie's direct approach. His feet crunch heavily on the grass as he holds out his hands and waves them defensively. He looks at Sam and his posture relaxes.

'You're Sam?'

'Yeah.' Sam blinks, his mind racing. 'You know my name? How...?'

CRACK!

They are interrupted by a lightning bolt that strikes the ground between Sam and the stranger. Sam falls backwards, landing by Frank's feet.

Frank kneels. 'Sam!'

'Sam!' Mal gasps. 'Are you okay?'

The hooded person groans, stunned by the impact of the energy bolt.

TWONK!

An arrow lands between his feet. Glancing up, he watches Addie draw another arrow across Silverhair, a trigger-happy grin stretched across her face. Alarmed, the stranger turns and runs for the trees.

TWONK!

Another of Addie's arrows flies harmlessly over the stranger's head and with a final yelp, he quickens his pace and disappears into the foliage.

'Ha!' Addie roars with laughter. 'Go back and stalk someone else, buddy!'

Groaning, Sam struggles to gain purchase on his hands and knees. He looks over to where the hooded person has disappeared.

'Oh! He's gone.'

'Yep, I've sent 'em off with a proper warning, Sammy! He won't be bothering us again.' Addie grins. 'There's no need to thank me.'

'It was the hooded stranger, the one I saw as we left Greystagg. I wonder if he… Huh?'

Sam is interrupted by a chilling rumbling sound as thick threatening clouds gather over the cerulean-coloured sky. The wood is shrouded into shadow, accompanied by a series of short, sharp thunderclaps, which send birds flying from the treetops and animals scurrying for safety. The first black shards of rain fall, followed immediately by hordes of Nethmites sprouting up from the soil. They grow larger than those seen in Greystagg forest.

'More of you, eh?' Addie readies Silverhair, pulling back an arrow. 'Metal shish kebabs comin' right up!' Turning to the others she cries. 'What are we waiting for? Let's kick some Nethmite butt!'

The Nethmites ready their attack, streaming towards the party. They block a blow from Old Faithful, sending cake mixture flying over the grass and into the trees. One of the Nethmites leaps forward and bites the sky-pirate's on his arm. He yelps and releases the trigger. Old Faithful shoots another dollop of cake mixture, scoring a direct hit that sends the Nethmite sprawling across the ground.

Frank wipes the dregs of cake mixture from his face, muttering under his breath. 'Yep! I *definitely* need to work on my aim!'

Mal strides into the melee, swinging her staff hard across the head of a tall Nethmite as it attempts to bite her. Bringing her weapon round a second time, she whacks another, sending the Nethmite flying aside.

'Heh, not bad, bunny-ears!' Addie smirks, not seeing the approach of a round fat Nethmite, which crashes on top of her. 'Why, you varmint!' She cries, pushing the Nethmite away. Jumping to her feet, she chases it and then leaps, landing on top of the offending creature with all her weight. 'Trying to escape are you?' She picks up the creature and tosses it into the air. Brushing the soil from her hands, she grins. 'There, that's much better.'

Mal asks. 'Are you alright?'

'Heh! That was simple play.'

A lone skinny Nethmite slinks through the grass, targeting Sam. Its mouth bares sharp grinning metal teeth. Sam backs away until he reaches a tree trunk. The Aether glows around his hand, sending bursts of rose-coloured light that stops the approaching Nethmite in its tracks. The creature shrieks, shaking itself from the bright light. Too late, Sam hears a rustle of leaves behind him and is tackled by a shorter, fatter Nethmite who shoves him to the ground. The Aether's light flickers.

'Oh no!' Sam cries, covering his eye with his arm.

The Nethmites chuckle, celebrating their success. A growing horde begins circling him, skulking closer and closer. As they ready themselves to charge and sink their grubby teeth into flesh and bone, their attack is met full on by Bonnie, who has morphed into her black and white dire wolf form. Her surprise attack scatters the Nethmites far and wide.

'Don't worry Sam!' She cries, baring razor-sharp teeth. 'I'll take care of them!'

Biting the neck of a short, fat Nethmite, Bonnie tosses it aside. She grabs hold of another and throws into the river. She then sends a stout Nethmite high into a tree, and another into a thick thorny bush. But there are too many of them, sprouting incessantly from the ground. The chuckling Nethmites circle the tiring dire wolf. Panting, exhausted from her efforts, Bonnie crouches defensively as one of the stouter Nethmites pounces, biting fiercely down on her hind leg. A painful howl erupts, sending a chill through Sam. Back on his feet, He races towards the injured Bonnie, who starts shrinking into her vulnerable, feeble pup form. She rolls across the ground towards him.

'Bonnie!' He cries, picking her up. 'Are you alright?'

Bonnie manages a tired smile. 'I tried.'

The surrounding Nethmites emit a low rumbling laugh and with their confidence riding high, they pounce. But their attack strikes against the defensive shield of the Aether's rose-coloured light that has surrounded Sam and Bonnie inside a protective ball. Carrying Bonnie in his left hand, Sam stretches out his right hand, holding out the Aether's shield. He hears a triumphant howl, a call to arms, as an arrow strikes one of the chasing Nethmites. Another is instantly immersed in thick, gooey cake-mix as Frank, Mal, Addie, Cedric and Dr Woodchuck enter the melee.

A triumphant howl is heard from above. 'Have no fear, creatures!' Gaia declares, swooping into the battle, his white fur coat shimmering in the Aether's pale-rose coloured light. His splendent wings glisten brightly. 'The guardians are here!'

'Gaia! Techna!' Sam cries. His energy is draining away, which causes the Aether shield to weaken.

'We'll take it from here, Sam!' Techna shoves away the straggling band of Nethmites. 'Get Bonnie to safety.'

Wrapping Bonnie in his jacket, Sam hurries from the struggle as the battle continues. Gaia lifts an extremely fat Nethmite in his jaws, ripping the creature from the ground and tossing it away.

'Just like old times, Tech!' He cries as Sam and Bonnie disappear into the safety of the surrounding thick foliage. 'Sam you've done all that you could, but now find refuge and take care of Bonnie.'

Inside the sanctuary of the wood, Sam stops to catch his breath. Here they are safe, concealed by trees and bushes. Inside a small clearing he carefully sets Bonnie down on the grass next to a large boulder. He hurries into the bushes where he snags up a handful of leaves, dark green with reddish veins, from a cluster of peppermint plants he finds in a shallow drainage basin. Returning, he leans against the boulder and begins tending Bonnie's wounds.

'There's only a few scratches Bon, but you still need to rest. That's the ticket.' He drops the peppermint leaves and hugs Bonnie. 'I can't tell you how grateful I am that you found me on my adventure, but I'm sorry you've been exposed to all this danger.'

Bonnie manages another smile. 'A dog's loyalty to her friend is strong, Sam.' She glances over his shoulder. 'I hope the others are alright.'

'Yeah! Perhaps we should be getting back to them. Can you walk?'

Climbing from Sam's arms, Bonnie struggles to stand. Her legs wobble and her back hunches up. 'I think so.' She says, before swaying and collapsing. 'Okay, maybe not. I'm sorry Sam.'

Sam winces and tends to the gashes on her legs. 'We should wait here a little longer.'

There is a rustling of leaves. Someone is approaching.

'Sam!' It is Sable, pushing through berry bushes, holding out a leather bottle. The liquid slushes inside. 'Are you alright? How is Bonnie?'

'She's doing okay, despite the Nethmites' bites.' Sam replies. 'She's got amazing spirit.'

Sable opens the leather bottle and tilts it towards Bonnie. The sparkling clear liquid trickles out like a gentle waterfall. Bonnie lifts her head and laps up the water. She rolls her head, tapping her tail against the soft ground. Whilst Bonnie drinks, Sam and Sable take stock of the situation.

'Sable.' Sam begins, twiddling his scarf. 'The Nethmites are much stronger now, compared to when we met them in the forest.' His eye waters and his voice trembles. 'What are we going to do?'

'Shh! We can do this.' Sable whispers, a reassuring smile across her lips. She runs her hand over his fringe. 'Remember what I told you in the tarot shop. Trust your instincts.'

'I guess. And trust in the Aether too, right?'

'Always.'

A shadow looms over them, accompanied by a long, low rumble.

Startled by the noise, Sam gasps. 'What was that?'

'*The Nether!*'

'Here?'

Clouds thicken and the sky darkens to a deep dark purple-colour, sucking away the last of the natural light. Purple lightning bolts begin streaking from the clouds, sending the last of the animals and birds fleeing, screaming and screeching with fright.

'*The Nether is coming! The Nether is coming!*'

The rest of the party pour into the clearing and gather around Sam and Sable. Above their heads, thick billowing clouds descends below the tree canopies, shrouding the forest in hues of crimson red and deep purple. A gust of wind blows through bronzing leaves.

Mal cries. 'What's going on?'

'I'm not sure.' Addie replies, uneasily.

The guardians trample into the clearing, staring up at the dark clouds looming overhead. They huddle together, wrapping their protective wings around Sam and his friends.

'The Nether is strong,' Gaia mutters, 'I feel it vibrating along my moth-feelers!' The white guardian ruffles his wings. 'Sorry for the melodrama, but this is different. I've never seen the Nether with this much power before. I sense despair.'

Sam stares at the white guardian, bewildered. 'Gaia? What do you mean?'

The rumbling gets louder and louder, culminating in a burst of dark purple light that explodes from the centre of the cloud and targets the party. The guardians return fire, projecting a beam of the Aether's light that succeeds in shielding everyone from the blast. The gigantic clash of energy rings loudly in their ears as the ground beneath shakes violently, throwing Addie and Frank off their feet. In that moment the Nether breaks through the Aether's shield, shattering it like glass. A second bolt of purple lightning strikes the guardians.

'Gaia! Techna!' Sam cries, running to their aid.

The dark clouds continue rumbling as the Nether readies another attack.

A voice emanating from deep inside grumbles. 'Huh! The Doll of Melsey.'

It is met by a resounding cry. 'Watch out! Behind you!'

Sable pushes Sam out of the way, her mask drawn over her face. Holding out her hands towards the clouds, she releases a wave of Aether.

Gaia lifts his gaze towards Sable. 'What are you doing?'

The rose-coloured light flows towards the Nether as the forces of dark and light combine, locked together in a fierce battle. Energy surges back and forth: hot, steamy gust billows over Sable, messing her hair and nearly forcing her off her feet. She stands her ground. Her eyes glowing with an intense rose-white colour as she sends forth another wave of the Aether's energy. She succeeds in pushing the dark power away.

Sam cries. 'Sable!'

'Hang in there!' Mal chimes.

Addie yells. 'You can do it!'

The Aether forces the Nether to retreat, pushing it inside the dark purple cloud. Everyone cheers, but their optimism proves short lived. The Nether grumbles loudly and immediately commences another assault. This time its dark energy creeps closer and closer towards Sable.

Cedric gulps. 'She's losing control!'

A dull report marks the moment when the Nether envelopes the Aether and completely consumes it. Sable gasps and throws her hands out to try again, but in that fateful instant the Nether strikes hard and sends her high into the air. A chorus of choked voices calls out her name. Her broken mask falls to the ground; followed by her fragile figure that slumps gracefully onto the grass.

Above their heads the cold monotoned voice grumbles. 'A worthy opponent, shaman, to challenge the Nether. I compliment your bravery, your foolish feebleness, but understand it is time for the rise of a new era, one that celebrates the Nether.'

The sinister voice fades to an eerie silence and the clouds dissolve away, revealing a clear evening sky. The Nethmites have gone. The wood is empty. The party runs to where Sable has fallen, her back planted heavily on the ground. She struggles to move, her clothes and skin charred from the Nether's dark power. Sam gently lifts the shaman's head and holds her left hand. Her eyes open, meeting his. Blood trickles from her smiling lips.

'Why?' Sam asks, his voice cracking.

'I've done all I could.' Sable whispers, grasping his hand tightly. 'And now I must go. But Sam, I give you my part of the Aether, and my belief in you.'

'No Sable. I know I'm not strong enough, not now I've seen how powerful the Nether has become!'

Sable shakes her head. 'I was naïve, believing I might defeat it alone. But you are good and true. Believe in yourself Sam, and in your friends. All is not lost. Remember the Flower of Knowledge's command: find the Fleur de Vie and use it to defeat the Nether. I know in my heart you will succeed.' Her hand drops to her side, and she closes her eyes. 'The Aether will protect you Sam,' and with her final gasp, 'trust your instincts.'

'Sable, wait!' He clutches Sable tightly to him, as her body slowly fades away.

A gentle breeze sweeps through the clearing, carrying Sable with it; transforming her physical form into white flower petals that swirl up into the sky. Mal and Addie embrace each other, while a sobbing Frank removes his hat and places it across his chest. Bonnie whines sadly; Dr Woodchuck and Cedric are overcome with emotion. Standing behind the grieving party, the two guardians struggle to hold back their tears. Gaia silently watches the final petals disappear into the heavens.

Sam stands, his head hanging low over his chest. He rubs his eye with his sleeve. Turning away, he focuses on the ground by his feet. 'We should return to the Puppis.'

One-by-one they board the airship. The guardians, having morphed into their bird forms, perch above the deck.

Sam is the last to step aboard. He pauses. The air feels heavy and suffocating.

Clutching his chest, he sighs. 'Sable, you've given me all you have, yet I'm sure I want none of this.'

*

An hour later and the Puppis is cruising through wisps of clouds, its sheep masthead staring blankly towards the setting sun on a distant horizon. The craft creaks and groans as air currents rock it gently on a north-westerly route, back towards the ocean. On deck, everything is quiet. Curled up against a barrel, Bonnie cleans her wounds, whimpering sadly. The others sit, sharing a solemn silence. On the upper deck Dr Woodchuck is treating the guardians' wounds, carefully mixing a selection of herbs in warm water before applying the medicating pulp onto Techna's wing with a peppermint leaf.

Gaia gazes down at the downcast crew, his tail feathers twitching. 'I feel ashamed. This should never have happened!'

'I'm ashamed too, Gaia.' Techna replies, wincing between stings. 'Our attempts to defeat the Nether have proved useless. The scale of its attack has come as a complete surprise!'

'But Sable, her selfless bravery; she reminded me of her.' Gaia sighs regretfully. 'We could have, we should have done more!'

Dr Woodchuck shakes his head, dabbing Gaia's wounds with a damp leaf. 'It's a noble thought Gaia, but what is done, cannot then be undone.'

'Yep!' Cedric retorts. 'Besides, what could you have done if you had taken Sable's place?'

Gaia opens his mouth, prepared to argue, but shuts it, wincing at the burning sensation from his injuries.

'Perhaps...' He mumbles under his breath.

'Can we stop talking about this!'

It is Sam, who is hunched against the wall of the captain's cabin. His voice is strained and is barely audible. He runs his hand along his bionic arm, his cheeks flushed from the tears streaming down his face.

'Sable told us to trust our instincts. We should cling to that thought and stop pushing our misery onto others. Please, I just don't want to hear any more. Not right now.'

Gaia plays with his wings, running one slowly over the other before bringing them together across his breast.

'You're right Sam. We're sorry.' He winces again, as Dr Woodchuck treats a gash on his tail. 'Dr Woodchuck? Do be gentle.'

'I'm sorry Gaia, but I did say this was going to sting.'

*

The Puppis skims low over the ocean, sending spray high into the air. Its helm creaks as the breeze rocks the craft from side to side. Dr Woodchuck has finished tending everyone's wounds and sits exhausted on the helm. Beside him is Cedric. The eagle-owl stares vacantly out over the depressing scene. On the deck the others are sitting thoughtfully, reflecting on the day's sad events.

Addie lifts her head. 'Hey!' All eyes turn towards her. 'I've been thinking about our adventures, about how I've headbutted my way into trouble, and then out again.'

Frank starts. 'What do you mean, Addie?'

'It's my impulsive nature, I know,' the ranger sighs, 'but there are times when I just want to, you know, be more thoughtful and explore a more creative side. To be Adelaide again.' She glances shyly at Frank and Mal. 'I want to learn how to bake stuff and make cakes like you.' Nodding towards Sam, she adds. 'And I want to enjoy artistic things, like you do Sam. You know, writing poetry, singing songs, taking in the sights a bit more.' She chuckles, sadly. 'Yeah! Sounds silly, doesn't it? A ranger wanting to be *sensitive*. Hah! That's just moonshine talk! I guess sensitivity ain't for me, cos other people just laugh and ridicule me: pointing out my not so shapely posture.' She sighs, squeezing her hand into her hair. 'I'm just Addie, and I ain't pretty enough!'

'I think you look amazing.' Mal counters under her breath, sensing the trail of red-flushes across her cheeks.

Addie continues. 'Sure, I've self-taught myself practical skills, so I'm ready to take up Silverhair and seek out adventures. It's the only way I can feel good about myself. But despite being nearly big enough to be a proper ranger, and a good ranger in my humble opinion, I'm still not happy. Firing arrows at things isn't creative enough.' Her voice is trembling with emotion. 'What's the point of wanting to be *gung-ho* all the time? And I hear them muttering that I'm like a bull in a china shop. Yeah, that's why I keep hiding my sensitive side, cause I want to feel like I'm someone.' A tear trickles down her cheek. 'Oh look! Here come the tears. Shameful, ain't it?'

'No it isn't. Not at all.' Sam walks over and sits next to Addie, resting a consoling arm around her shoulder. 'You shouldn't feel ashamed of who you are, Addie. And I understand how you are feeling. We all do. There's gonna be people who will judge us on how we look, on what we believe, even how we speak.'

On the helm, Dr Woodchuck playfully shoves Cedric. 'Like how your voice is so high-pitched!'

The eagle-owl aimlessly swipes at the woodchuck in retaliation.

Ignoring the interruption, Sam continues. 'Standing out from the crowd and showing your sensitive side is lonely at times, but it doesn't always have to be that way.' He chuckles coyly. 'Do you want to know, at home, I wear pastel-coloured nightclothes patterned with pink and yellow stars, with white clouds.'

Addie cracks an amused smile. 'You do?'

'Yep! I love them, as much as I love the grunge style too, because they're comfortable, and that's what counts. And I love cooking too, it keeps me connected with Ma. It is part of who I am.' He squeezes Addie's hand. 'What I'm trying to say Addie, is I think you're great, and so's the archery. Be the outgoing cavalier ranger, but embrace your sensitive side too. No one here will think anything less of you. We all think you're wonderful, because despite everything we've faced, you've always responded with something courageous and encouraging. Am I right?'

'Adelaide,' Mal chimes, 'we've got your back. I'm glad you're with us. You're a brilliant companion, and invaluable fighting the Nethmites.'

'I've got to admit,' Frank adds. 'You were really cool taking them on today.'

'Frank's right! We wouldn't have you any other way. We love you Addie.'

'*We love you!*' They chorus, embracing Addie in a group hug.

Addie's eyes widen. 'Oi! You're so mushy,' she blushes, gripping tightly onto Sam and Mal's sleeves, 'but thanks anyway.'

Standing at the helm, Dr Woodchuck and Cedric smile, observing the caring moment unfolding below.

Dr Woodchuck says. 'Gee, I've never thought of the ranger that way.'

'Me too.' Cedric sighs, knitting his brows. 'I've always thought her a reckless squirt. Guess I shouldn't have settled on first impressions.'

'And Sam's so kind. The way he let her know how much she's appreciated. My wish is that there are others who show that same level of sensitivity.'

'Mm-hmm.'

Dr Woodchuck turns and playfully wraps his arms around Cedric. 'We should hug too!'

'Ack! Get your paws off me!'

'Nope.'

'Well I hope you're not going to break into a corny song, about friendship and being there for one another.'

'Don't tempt me. I can easily sing a verse or two.'

'Oh bother!'

Meanwhile, on the main deck, Addie extracts herself from the group hug.

'Well, I needed to let all that out!' She says, twiddling with her fringe. 'Hey, shouldn't we get something to eat? My stomach's growling like a wild boar!'

Frank says. 'As it happens, I have some *boar* sandwiches down in the galley.'

They descend through the hatch and into the galley. There are cheese sandwiches too, which Mal had made in Farley. Working together they arrange the sandwiches and the remaining pecan cakes, along with a bowl of apples and pears on the galley table. The plates of food are quickly joined by mugs of steaming hot tea. Despite the overlying grief, eating hearty food with good company helps to combat the underlining heartache.

As the sky darkens and tiredness draws in, they head for the captain's cabin for the night. Sam and Mal lays out bedding to ensure everyone will be comfortable. Frank draws the curtains over the windows, but leaves a small crack so he can observe the moonlight.

'It's at times like this that Ma would sing my favourite lullaby.' Sam says, turning to the others. 'She used to sing me to sleep, whenever I was sad.'

Frank asks. 'Can you sing the lullaby for us?'

Mal and Addie chime together. 'Yeah, please sing for us Sam!'

Sam chuckles. 'Well, if I can remember the words. Here goes nothing...' He taps the rhythm with his fingers against his knees.

'Rest now, rest your head against mine,
And listen to the rain or snow that falls.
Look back on the gentle moments we have together,
Till the sun comes to see us again.'

Feeling his voice strengthen, Sam fills the cabin with a soft, warm melody. The others huddle together, listening attentively. Outside on the deck, the guardians are listening too, taking comfort from Sam's voice. In contrast, Cedric blocks his ears with his wings, fearful that Dr Woodchuck might decide to open his mouth and sing along with his tone-deaf vocal chords.

'Come rain, come snow,
Come gentle moments, come and flow.
Let us listen, let us listen,
To your beauty within the winds that blow.'

Sam finishes singing, trailing the final verse into a soft hum. His friends have settled into a peaceful reverie, reflecting on the words of Sam's lullaby. Smiling, he leans back against a pillow, listening to the reassuring creak of the Puppis' mechanical wings brushing the tops of the ocean waves below. Staring at the wooden ceiling, he recalls happy memories of Melsey: Mary bringing him a glass of oat milk, closing his eye as she kissed him goodnight. Inside the cabin, there is no Mary, no fresh glass of oat milk, no cosy bedroom in Melsey. Yet despite the distance between them, he feels close to Mary and Johnny. Lying in the Captain's cabin, his precious Melsey feels far away, a misty blur fills his thoughts. How far-reaching is the Nether's dark powers? Have they already spread across the whole of the Southern Island? His reflections on happier times turn to icy apprehension as he prays that Johnny and Mary are safe and well. *Have the Nether and the Nethmites reached Melsey?*

His anxious melancholy is interrupted by the sound of Addie's snoring, accompanied by the sniggering of the others. With this reassurance playing in his ears, Sam snuggles into the bedding and drifts into a peaceful sleep.

Interlude – I Love you Lily

In his dreams Sam is reminded of Lily: her gentle smile, her easy nature; her green pinafore dress twisting and twirling in rhythm with the breeze. The memory of watching her bake homemade cherry pies in the oven, as she danced to cheery music playing from their little red radio. What a dancer she was. She would persuade him to join her, and their feet would glide lightly around the kitchen. Cherry pies were a favourite in Farley, richly flavoured with puréed fruit, the thick top crust shaped in a lattice and liberally sprinkled with tiny, glazed crystals of brown sugar. Lily would always serve the pie with a large dollop of vanilla bean ice-cream on the side.

Sam is transported back to when Lily used to sit behind her telescope on the outdoor terrace and gaze up at the sky. Wearing a resigned expression she would focus on the stars, waiting for something to happen. Whenever she turned to face him her expression burst into rays of bright sunshine. He yearns to return to those long peaceful evenings when they would watch the night sky together until tiredness drove them inside. His dreams carry him to a beautiful spring afternoon in Farley. Wispy clouds pattern a deep cerulean sky, and there are plum and cherry trees, all loaded with blossom, lining the park's perimeter. Their branches dance in the breeze, sprinkling clouds of petals over the neatly trimmed lawn. A man pushing a lawnmower comes to a halt and gazes at the petals swirling around the spinning globe. With each revolution they are scattered further, out beyond the parish. The grass is sprinkled with clusters of daffodils and crocuses; bumblebees hover over flower heads, dusted with yellow pollen, as bluebirds sing atop the playground fence. The parish is thriving. There are people carrying wicker baskets filled with groceries, topped with chocolate eggs wrapped in colourful paper. He hears the distant sound of a high-pitched whistle that breaks through the ambient sounds of the parish, as a train follows the winding trail towards the distant hills.

His dream shifts.

He is sitting at the foot of the knoll near the house, playing the patty cake song on Angie, his guitar. Nina is with him, singing and dancing. She spins in circles, her pink flowery dress billowing in the breeze as her tightly plaited hair bounces on her shoulders.

> '...Mister Postman, wait a minute.
> Before you go away,
> Please, please tell my special friend.
> That I'll be seeing them today!'

They finish the final line together and cheer loudly, clapping their hands together.

Nina laughs. 'We did it!'

'We sure did.' Sam smiles, tousling Nina's golden hair. 'You're getting much better Nina!'

'Yay, I did good! I love singing with you Sammy!'

'Ha-ha! We should do this more often!'

Greg sits at the wooden table on the open terrace, nibbling at a single rosewater biscuit. Its sugar dust pastes his upper lip. Standing, he reaches for the teapot containing rice tea. Lily is sitting opposite, dressed in her green flower-patterned pinafore dress. Her auburn hair looks lighter, thinner than usual, and her skin is pale. She smiles and her complexion immediately warms, matching for a moment at least, her positive attitude. Brushing a loose curl of hair over the top of her ear, she watches Nina chasing Sam. The little girl's arms outstretched like a bird extending its wings. Their laughter is music to her ears.

'Nina loves playing with Sam, doesn't she?'

Greg chuckles, pouring tea into two cups. 'Yeah! Do you remember how shy she was when we first brought her home? She was shakin' like a lil' rabbit. But she's settled well, with Sam's help. I can't help thinkin' of them as family, rather than friends.'

'Oh, is that so?'

'Sure. Don't you think the bond between them is thicker than water, if you know what I mean? Like siblings?'

'Siblings?' Lily chuckles. 'Yeah. Why not!'

Laughing louder, she leans into her chair, until a hoarse cough reaches out from her throat. Greg leaps from his chair and gently pats her back. She starts coughing again, but this time there is no respite. Finally she composes herself, rubbing her painful chest with one hand. She reaches out and wraps the fingers of her other hand around her teacup.

'Sorry about that. I got carried away.'

'That's okay. It's good to hear you laugh, even if it's at my silly little jokes.'

'I don't find your jokes silly at all, Greg. They make me smile.'

Greg bites into another rosewater biscuit, sprinkling more crumbs over his face and sleeve. 'When is your next appointment?'

'I'll find out in a day or two.' She shivers and fiddles with a strand of hair running across her cheekbone. 'I've been feeling the cold lately, despite this lovely weather. The doctor keeps telling me to wrap up warm.'

With a furrowed brow, Greg strokes the rim of his mug, watching ripples flow over the surface of his rice tea. 'Lily, I'm worried. I understand your diagnosis isn't good, and it pains me to see you like this. I will help, do the best I can, but there's Nina and...' His words trail away, and he glances across to the knoll to where Sam is giving Nina a piggyback ride. 'Sam concerns me too. Do you think he'll be okay?'

Lily's sight blurs as she gazes at Sam, 'I'm worried too. I know how desperate he wants to visit Melsey,' she smiles sadly, 'ever since I told him about *The Root*. He wants to perform there one day, with Angie.' She is tired and her failing body aches and aches. 'I've been feeling so exhausted lately. I can see that it's breaking his heart.' She pauses, wiping away the onset of tears with her sleeve. 'I just hope he keeps that carefree air. He's so sweet, just like Noah.'

'Lily...'

'I'm okay. I'll be okay.' She reaches for a biscuit. 'Let's not talk about this anymore; it's too painful.' Nibbling at her biscuit, she adds. 'Let's think happier thoughts. Tell me Greg, about your plans for this afternoon.'

'Well okay.' Greg forces a smile. 'I thought we could go for a walk along the beach: look for crabs in the rock pools; tickle our toes in the waves; and then go and get some ice-cream. If that's okay with you?'

'That's sounds wonderful! I've a craving for mint leaf ice-cream.'

'Ha-Ha! Your candy cravings don't cease, huh?'

'What?' Lily grins. 'You can't beat a double scoop of mint leaf ice-cream, can you?'

Meanwhile on the knoll, Sam stops running and carefully places Nina down. He takes a couple of deep breaths and slumps onto the grass next to her.

He grins. 'That was fun!'

'Yeah!' Nina gazes thoughtfully at Lily and Greg. 'Hey Sammy. Papa told me about your Ma. Will she be okay?'

'Well, I,' Sam stammers, looking at Lily. 'I don't really know, Nina. She's been so quiet lately, more so in the evenings. She just sits outside and stares listlessly up at the stars. It's like she is looking for something.'

'Does that mean she will leave you, one-day?' There are tiny tears welling in her eyes. 'If so, I'll be sad.'

'I know. I'll be sad too,' Sam places his hand over his chest, 'but Ma will always be right here, just like your Pa will always be with you. I think that's what family is about.'

His words float gently into Nina's mind, as a soft breeze picks up her blonde locks. She nods her head, forcing a smile across her tiny lips. 'Okay, I guess that's good.'

They watch Greg and Lily leaving the terrace, taking the teapot and the remaining biscuits inside the house. Greg stops by the door and waves at Sam and Nina, signalling that he and Lily are coming down to join them.

Sam stands and picks Angie up by the neck. 'I think they're getting ready to go to the beach.' He tousles Nina's hair. 'C'mon, let's go and get some ice-cream!'

'Yeh! I'm having double chocolate, with lots of sprinkles!'

'And loads of sprinkles it shall be!'

They wait patiently for Greg and Lily to leave the house and walk slowly across to the knoll. From there, they walk together towards the beach. Sam glances at Lily, who is staring out across the sea, a soft smile across her face. Progress is slow as they stop frequently to chat with friends and neighbours.

As they step onto the beach, Lily edges closer to Sam, until they're walking side by side. 'Are you okay, Sam?'

'Yeah. I'm just worried about you.'

Lily nods and takes Sam's hand. 'I know, but I'll be okay; and you'll be okay too. That's all that matters to me, remember that.'

'Yeah. I will'. Sam smiles. 'Thanks Ma.'

'Atta kid!' She grins. 'Now, let's go and check out those rock pools.'

Lily's words continue to resonate with him, even after he moved away to live with Johnny and Mary in Melsey. Her voice still comforts him during the lonely nights, when he stands on the balcony and gazes up at the stars. He imagines Lily staring up at the night sky next to him. When there are heavy clouds covering the night sky, he still uses the telescope for its connection with her. And they stand together and stare up at the sky, until it is time to go to bed.

The Leviathan

A gentle nudge from the Puppis stirs Sam from his sleep. Cracking open his crusty eye, he looks around the captain's cabin. He is alone. The floorboards are covered in dishevelled bedding, making the cabin look untidy. Listening to muffled voices outside, he sighs and then smiles. *Early birds, waking up before him.* Sliding from the bed, he navigates the pillows and blankets and then opens the cabin door; stepping out onto the main deck to greet a dull, breezy morning. The sun is concealed behind thick, dirty white clouds. The Puppis continues its leisurely flight over the ocean. The sound of gulls echoes through the air, in concert with the heavy rolling of the waves below. His friends are sitting around a picnic table, tucking hungrily into leftover sandwiches. The wooden deck creaks beneath Sam's footsteps as he approaches. Techna and Gaia are still onboard, huddled together, asleep on top of the steps by the helm. Sleeping above, Cedric and Dr Woodchuck shift and fall, landing on the deck with a dull thud. They gently roll onto their sides and continue snoring.

'Morning Sam!' Frank cries in a cheery voice. 'Thought we'd have breakfast, whilst we're on the go.'

'And we have rice-tea, which I got in Farley.' Mal glances at the sleeping animals. 'They're still asleep, best not to disturb them.'

Sam sits down and helps himself to a sandwich. 'You got it.'

The cheese inside the stale bread is dry. Fortunately there are pieces of ripe fruit to follow. He slowly chews his breakfast. The rice tea is served from the kettle boiling on a camping stove. Steam begins whistling from its spout, causing the sleeping animals to stir, but not wake. Mal picks up the kettle and pours hot water into each cup. The tealeaves float and swirl in the water. They prove mesmerising, as the liquid slowly darkens.

'*Woof!* I sure slept well last night!' Addie exclaims, leaning back into her seat, both hands behind her head. 'Your song soothed all my troubles Sammy, like a gentle waterfall. My lids felt so heavy, but now I'm fully refreshed. I've got to tell you how good your voice is.'

Sam's face reddens. 'I'm flattered Addie. I'm glad you liked the song. I hoped it would cheer us.' He blows through the steam of his tea and gingerly takes a sip. 'It's a shame I didn't bring Angie along.'

'Angie? Who's Angie?'

'Angie's my acoustic guitar. Ma gave it to me. But I left her in Melsey. Carrying a guitar on my adventures didn't seem a good idea. Good job too, especially with the Nethmites ripping up and eating anything made of wood. *Made of anything!*' He taps his fingertips against his mug. 'Maybe when we return to Melsey I'll take you all to *The Root*, on a gig night. Ted will serve you his marvellous floats and malt milkshakes, with whipped cream and a black cherry on top, if you like.'

'Wow! That sounds great!' Addie beams. 'You gotta promise, 'kay?'

Sam smiles. 'You have my word.'

After breakfast and with everyone relaxing on deck, Frank makes his rounds: tugging at rope-locks, ensuring that they are held fast. Gaia and Techna finally rouse from their sleep, shaking their feathers while looking sheepishly around the deck. Dr Woodchuck is also awake and is busy munching a large red carrot. Sam and Mal are standing on the side of the Puppis, watching energetic waves lap below. They watch a school of whales cruising in the distance, blowing air and fine water spray from their blowholes. With his tasks complete, Frank steps across the deck and picks up the leftover sandwiches from the table. Addie grabs the cooling kettle and they both head for the hatch and the galley below. Gaia turns his head and looks out over the edge of the craft. He has heard something, something soft and distant. His body stiffens and his feathers fluff up.

Techna tilts his head. 'What is it Gaia?'

'I thought I heard something,' Gaia shakes his head, 'but perhaps it's me being on edge. I'm always expecting something dreadful to pop out from nowhere... *Whoa!*'

The Puppis swings about violently, twisting at right angles as if it has collided with something large and heavy.

CLUNK!

The jolt wakens Cedric, who bolts frantically to his feet. 'Hm? Wha-what now?'

There is chaos on deck. The picnic table topples over and slides towards the side of the craft. Addie slips and falls. The kettle flies from her grasp, spilling water from its spout. It falls with a crash before rattling and rolling through the open hatch door.

CLANG!

Another jolt causes the airship to swing violently in the opposite direction, sending the remaining sandwiches flying overboard.

Mal gasps. 'What's happening?'

'I dunno, but there goes the last of the sandwiches.' Frank sighs sadly, watching the ravenous seagulls picking up mid-air snacks.

Sam makes for the starboard side and stares at the calm ocean below. He turns to the others. 'I don't see anything that might have caused the disturbance.' With a grin, he adds. 'Hey! This reminds me of the time I fell overboard in Greystagg...'

Right on cue comes another invisible impact, slamming against the Puppis and shoving the craft sideways. Sam makes a valiant attempt to grab hold of the side, but misses, and grabbing at the air, he topples overboard, again. His striped scarf sliding from his face falls safely onto the deck.

'Sam!'

His friends rush to look over the side and discover Sam lying on his back, having landed relatively safely on the giant mechanical wing. He groans loudly.

Frank cries. 'Hang in there buddy!'

As he frantically lowers the rope ladder, his hat flies from his head and skips across the deck. There is no way he can go and retrieve it now. Rung-after-rung he clambers down onto the wing, managing to maintain his balance, despite the uneven leathery surface and the jerky motions of the Puppis. Glancing below his feet, saltwater sprays over his face. The waves lapping over one another are much closer and larger, and bluer than before. They crash against the hull of the Puppis: splashing and showering water over him. Frank pushes forward: *tap-tap-tap*; reaching Sam he carefully lifts him onto his feet.

They are met by a loud mechanical-grinding shriek, accompanied by a violent gust of wind that nearly blows them off the wing. Gripping Sam's jacket with one hand, Frank pulls at the rope ladder with the other. He freezes, staring in disbelief at a large serpent-like shape shimmering under the surface of the water. On deck, Mal and Addie can see it too. They yelp in horror as the waters rise, revealing a huge mechanical, charcoal-grey-coloured creature. Its long flexible body is covered in metallic-scales, with metallic-like fins on its head. It cranes its neck, pivoting around huge hinges, as its head rises above the surface of the water and releases a terrifying prolonged howl.

'*Aieeee!*' Frank shrieks, as the creature dives back into the water. '*What is that?*'

There is no respite as the creature turns and leaps from the water towards them. It swings its gigantic frame and thrusts its head towards the side of the ship, sending those onboard sprawling across the deck.

Cedric grumbles loudly. It is bad enough having his nap interrupted, but to be awoken by such an aggressive, nightmarish creature is beyond the pale. Taking to the sky, he confronts the leviathan, squawking and shrieking in its face, courageously slapping his talons against the leviathan's metal head, *rat-tap-tap-tap-tap*.

He squawks. 'Be gone, you annoying, pestering… *leviathan!*'

The creature lunges towards the eagle-owl.

'*YEEK!* I'm not doing that again!' Cedric cries, swerving to one side and then making a beeline for the relative safety of the Puppis' cabin.

'That was brave of you, Cedric,' Dr Woodchuck retorts, 'too brave, perhaps.'

'Oh, don't patronise me!' The eagle-owl whines through the open cabin door.

Meanwhile, Addie fires arrows at the leviathan, but her efforts prove futile against its metallic skin. Annoyed by her interference, the leviathan's head swings around and crashes against the airship's frame. It drops back into the water. Relieved, Mal and Addie stare over the side, watching the creature's dark shadow meandering gracefully underwater. The shape slowly turns and heads towards Frank and Sam, who are struggling to stand upright on the wing. Frank staggers to the side of the Puppis, just as the leviathan launches out of the ocean. They meet face-to-face. The leviathan: beautiful, blind, and frightening, opens its mouth wide and releases a long, low drone through its raspy throat. Water sprays Frank's face, the breeze snapping his ponytail. He has never met anything as large and as menacing as this creature before. Sam's head shifts against his shoulder.

'Don't worry Sam, I'll get you back.' Frank cries, reaching inside his jacket. 'There's just one thing I need to do...'

Again the leviathan lunges out from the ocean. This time the creature is greeted by a large lump of pink coloured pastry, which lands directly into its open mouth. It recoils, spluttering at the mushy foodstuff. As its body coils, the water swells like a boiling cauldron. This time as the creature drops, a huge spray of water is sent skywards, drenching everyone onboard. Frank watches the leviathan's body slithering in and out of the water, shaking its head from side to side, disgusted by the sugary contents stuck inside its metal mouth.

Addie lets out a bellowing laugh. 'Hey! Someone's hasn't got a sweet tooth, Captain!'

Distracted by the strange tasting mixture in its mouth, the creature is now vulnerable to the guardians' attack. Diving, they aim for the centre of its gliding frame, snatching it in their jaws and managing to partially lift it above the surface. The leviathan wriggles in their grasp, shaking the guardians like manic ragdolls. Out of the water the creature proves far too heavy, and it twists free of their grasp. Techna and Gaia watch as the leviathan falls back into the ocean with a large splash. Onboard, the party watching with growing anticipation, gasp in disappointment. Bubbles emerge on the surface, a prelude to the leviathan turning and lunging out of the water. The white guardian manages to dance out of reach of the mechanical serpent, and twisting in the air, begins leading it away from the Puppis. Standing on the mechanical wing, Frank takes full advantage of the distraction. He grabs hold of the rope ladder and pulls Sam towards him. With his free hand he tugs hard at the rope ladder, signalling the others to pull him and Sam up on deck.

They cry in unison. 'Heave! Heave! Heave!'

And with one final effort, Sam and Frank are pulled over the side. They collapse, exhausted, on the deck.

'Frank, Sam!' Mal gasps. 'Are you alright?'

'Yeah!' Frank splutters, composing himself. 'That thing was just plain ridiculous!'

Panting hard, he pushes himself up onto his feet. He lifts Sam's shirt, revealing a huge round blossoming bruise on his torso.

Lying on his back, Sam's eye flickers open. 'What happened?' He gasps as Mal reaches out and grabs his hand. 'What was all that noise?'

The others are watching events unfold on the ocean waters as Techna and Gaia take turns attacking the leviathan. Finally, after mustering one final attack, the metallic creature climbs wearily out of the water and emits a long mournful cry. Its tail slashes at the ocean, before its giant body sinks slowly beneath the boiling waters: a dark shadow fading into the deep.

Addie asks. 'What the blazes was that thing?'

'It's a sea leviathan, one created by the Nether.' Cedric explains. 'Thank my crusty feathers the guardians took care of it. That thing didn't look pretty!'

'And with your help Cedric.' Dr Woodchuck's words are cut short, courtesy of a brisk slap from Cedric's wing.

'I tried, okay?'

The party hear Techna's rhythmic low croaks above their heads. The black guardian is hovering over the air-sac. They watch as he transforms into his raven form and perches on the helm next to Gaia, where he begins preening his shedding feathers.

'That'll teach the creature to disturb the peace! What a rousing battle!' Techna proclaims, staring at the now calm ocean. 'But I admit it's worrying, seeing the Nether resort to marine

Nethmites. They usually rely on the sky and land as mediums of attack.'

'The Nether has too many tricks up its sleeve,' Gaia adds, 'and I fear we should expect something even bigger.'

'Yeh. But not too soon, I hope.'

*

Dr Woodchuck treats Sam's bruise with a soothing cream; there is no need for a bandage. Sam takes sips of lukewarm water as Mal mops puddles of water covering the deck. Frank is standing at the helm, guiding the Puppis onwards. Addie stands studying the expansive ocean below, once again appearing dull and mundane after all the excitement. Turning, she watches Sam stagger into the captain's cabin to rest, his left hand clutching his sore torso. Bonnie follows him inside. Addie decides to leave the two of them alone, preferring to quietly observe activities on deck. Dr Woodchuck is tending his aching back, from where he received another playful swipe from Cedric. The eagle-owl heads for the upper deck for a private grumble. The guardians are resting on the steps to the helm, following their triumphant tussle with the sea leviathan.

As the morning spills into the afternoon the Puppis continues cruising north-westerly. Addie senses the breeze strengthen as it snaps against her ponytail and gazes towards the horizon. A dark shape gradually creeps over the horizon.

'Hey!' She cries, straining on the tips of her toes. 'Look, over there!'

Everyone rushes to the bow and sighs in relief, realising the object Addie has spotted is only a small island, and not another looming Nether attack. As the Puppis drifts nearer they pick out defined shapes on the island. There are two wooden jetties stretching out into the water; and inland, distinct buildings emerge, one-by-one. At the centre of the island stands a tall stone chimney that towers over a market square, puffing out perfect smoke rings. Closer still, and they make out tiny, coloured spots surrounding the island: sailing boats bobbing on the water.

Sam and Bonnie join the others on deck. 'What island is that?' Bonnie queries.

'Goodness! I'd never seen one looking so,' Gaia twitches his moth-feelers, 'technological.'

'That's my home, Limehead!' Addie hollers excitedly, her voice ringing loud and clear. 'I've never seen it like this, you know, from up high. But yes, I see it now. We should land and take a look around.' She adds, bouncing eagerly from one foot to the other. 'Gee! It's been a while since I've been home. I'd sure like to see how things are, and perhaps look up my old friends too.' Looking pleadingly at the others, her face creases into a suspicious frown. 'And I can check on Doris to make sure she's looking after my house, and all my stuff. *Hey Captain Frank, man the helm!*'

'Aye-aye, Addie!'

The Puppis dips towards Limehead, fully revealing the small fishing village below, complete with its busy market stalls set inside the main square. Merchants stop what they are doing to stare up at the strange looking craft drifting slowly above their heads. Passing the tall chimney, the Puppis, under Addie's direction, heads towards the harbour on the far side of the island. Cormorants and other seabirds scatter before the sweeping airship. It finally staggers to a halt over the quay. Frank lowers the anchor, which drops onto the sandy beach. One-by-one they use the rope ladder to descend onto the ground, leaving Cedric and the two guardians to glide freely above their heads. *Show-offs.*

Sam is last to disembark.

Frank guides him with each wobbly step. 'Are you sure you're okay, Sam?' He asks.

'I think so,' Sam replies, fixing his foot, 'apart from my legs. They don't feel stable at all.'

'I'm not surprised. You've had quite a fall, another one. The sea leviathan's attack caught us all by surprise, but at least we got through it in one piece.'

'Yeah,' Sam chuckles, 'and that was clever of you to distract it using your pastry missile.'

'You saw that? *Ach!* It was nothing!'

Strolling from the docking area through the thriving market, the party reach the market square, decorated in prominent cobalt-blues and steel-greys. Dark smoke puffs out from metal chimneys, obscuring the afternoon sky. Peeking through the mist, they spot flashes of reds, oranges and yellows.

As they approach the square, they are met by locals who holler greetings to Addie: 'Morning Addie,' and, 'good to see you, Addie!'

Addie smiles and returns their waves. It is like she has never been away. She spots a large ginger tabby-cat sitting on a roof, lazily studying the bustling crowd below. Its tail stands upright, swishing back and forth. The calls of the market traders ring out loud and clear over the square, advertising their wares from different foodstuffs to embroidered carpets. They lazily circle the busy shops and stalls, admiring the assorted foodstuffs: fruit and vegetables; meats and fish, all artfully arranged in trays.

'It's thriving here.' Mal says, politely refusing the fresh fish being shoved towards her.

'It's always like this.' Addie explains, tossing a few coins to a fruit trader in exchange for a paper bag full of red apples. She hands the fruit to her friends. 'It's not the busiest of places, but the market still makes a good trade. In fact, we're famous for our fish. The waters around the island are well stocked with the fanciest looking fish, especially the *Limehead Sword*.'

'Is it like tuna?'

'Oh. It's much better than tuna.'

Frank is already salivating. 'They sound delicious! I can taste it right now!'

'Yah better keep droolin' Captain.' Addie cheers. 'Welcome to Limehead, my friends!'

They continue browsing the market square, stopping briefly outside a tavern called *The Duck's Head*. Above their heads the signage: the head of a quacking mallard, swings lazily on its hinges. Beneath their feet tiny shoots of grass and weeds grow through gaps in the cobblestones.

'We should stop here for supper later; they serve the best food on the island.' Addie smirks, adding. 'It'll sure make a change from eating stale boar sandwiches.'

'Aw! Come on!' Frank protests.

They walk from the square, returning to the small quay with the two jetties. There is a welcoming, fresh sea breeze, carrying the smell of salt inland. The predominant sounds come from the creaking rusty windmills occupying the end of each jetty; accompanied by the waves lapping against the many small, moored boats, their sails flapping against the breeze. Fishermen stand along each jetty, clad in waterproof coats and thick rubber boots; casting lures over the water, watching and waiting for signs of a catch. Watchful too are the seabirds, circling high above the harbour, casting their greedy eyes on the fishermen's catch. There is a boat returning from the ocean. It lines up against one of the jetties. They stand watching fishermen unload huge crates filled with giant cod, silver herring, and the impressive Limehead Sword, a large silvery marlin with fresh pink meat. Others are busy sharpening knives, preparing to gut and fillet the fish into smaller steaks for their customers. It is a messy, bloody business and onlookers quickly turn their pale faces away. But not Frank, who is transfixed with the fishermen at work. He is finally dragged from the fishermen's wonderous wares by Mal. They pass someone who is busy brushing hard at the cobblestones, sweeping away the trash and scattering fish cuts dropped by villainous seabirds.

'What an amazing place, Addie. A little fishing island in the middle of the ocean.' Frank says, in admiration. 'What I don't understand, is why would you run away from here?'

'I wouldn't say I ran away, exactly. It was more like I wanted to get away and have my own adventures. To visit places different from the constant bustle of the market.'

'I understand that.' Sam interjects, his mind drifting to the busy city he left behind. 'In fact, it sounds a perfectly reasonable idea.'

'Yeah, you would know how busy it gets around the market: the sights, the sounds, the smells. *Bleh!* I tell you, some of those smells are not to everyone's taste.' Addie beams. 'Hey, I've got a great idea! Why don't we go swimming?'

'Yeah! Let's do that.' Frank replies, removing his hat and jacket. 'I could do with cooling down, especially after that blasted sea-creature messed up my airship. I'll go and grab some towels from the Puppis.'

'And I know where I can borrow some bathing costumes,' Addie adds, 'I won't be long.'

'Ready? Break!' Frank and Addie yell together, before heading from the harbour: Frank hobbling towards the Puppis, and Addie skipping back towards the market square.

Frank returns first. He removes towels from the bag he is carrying and throws them to the others. Addie arrives shortly afterwards, handing out a selection of tattered looking bathing costumes with striped patterns and bleached colours. Stripping off their clothes and pulling on their borrowed bathing costumes, they pile their dirty clothes high; planning to wash them after swimming. Skipping and diving into the cold ocean water, they cheer excitedly, skimming over the foaming surface. They keep to the shallow water, content with feeling the rocky seabed under their feet. After changing into his chosen bathing costume, Sam removes his black t-shirt, revealing his prosthetic arm. He gently runs his fingers over the pink scars, craning his arm: contracting and flexing the joint. Removing his scarf, he drops it on the ground and runs his hand across his face. His fingers touch the rough scar-tissue over his eye. It tingles as the breeze brushes across his face. It is chilly out in the ocean air.

'Come on in, Sam!' Frank calls, wadding out into deeper waters.

Bonnie prances up and down in the shallows. 'Yeah! The water's great!'

Sam cannot resist smiling. He pulls on the rest of his bathing costume. 'You'd better watch out, because here I come!' Running, he dives from the end of the jetty and into the water.

SPLASH!

Rising to the surface, Sam's hair is drenched and sleeked back. It glistens in the sunlight.

Addie smirks. 'You're full of surprises Sammy!'

The animals settle on the jetty to watch their human friends playing in the water: splashing water everywhere. Mal and Addie take turns battling the other, on who can create the largest and fastest wave. Bubbles foam over the surface, created by their frantic, happy activities.

'Watch out Cedric! Here comes a big one!' Mal cries, splashing water towards the eagle-owl.

Cedric laughs as the spray of water misses him. 'Ah-ha! You didn't get me, Mal!' He blows a raspberry, which is then met by another wave that scores a direct hit, covering the eagle-owl from head to talons.

'Bull's eye!' Addie cheers victoriously.

Mal covers a laugh with her hands.

Cedric shakes his damp head, muttering, 'Except for that one.'

Dr Woodchuck rolls onto his back, laughing. Cedric retaliates by slapping his friend, a swipe strong enough to push the woodchuck into the water. It is Cedric's turn to laugh, as he watches the woodchuck paddle to shore.

The two guardians are watching their play, perched on the branch of a nearby tree. A safe distance from the water.

'Too bad for you,' Techna chuckles, 'we're nice and safe up here!'

Gaia smiles, but his sense of joviality falls as he drifts deeper into thought. Something is bothering him. It is as if someone is whispering to him, trying to remind him of something important. He takes to the sky, leaving Techna behind, preoccupied with the fun activities below.

The afternoon slips past and the sun dips leisurely towards the horizon, producing a red-orange tinted sky. The majority of the fishermen have completed their long daily routine and are packing their precious tackle away into the wooden crates they have used as seats throughout the day. There are a few who plan to stay longer, hopeful of a better catch as the light fails. Out in the water the splashing games have calmed, and the friends have gathered in shallower waters. Their discussion returns to their great adventure.

'I wonder where we'll find the Fleur de Vie?' Mal asks. 'Does anyone know where it grew before?'

'I dunno,' Frank replies, 'but let's hope it's not far from here.'

'Yes. I'm sure it is close by, and we shall find it soon.' Dr Woodchuck nods. 'Remember, the Flower of Knowledge told us to head north, that's where he believed it would be. Only then can our journey be completed.' With a gentle sigh, he continues. 'There's a part of me that thinks it will be a shame. Despite encountering the Nether and the Nethmite hordes, being a part of this marvellous party of adventurers has been thrilling.'

'I concur,' Cedric adds, 'despite all the ruffling and tousling I receive. The spirit of adventure is, well, exhilarating indeed. Although it will be nice to rest my eyes properly again, and sit on my beloved tree branch.'

'Yeah! To be back inside a lush and bountiful Greystagg.' Mal shifts her attention to the early evening sky. 'That would be truly wonderful.'

Sam stares silently into the distance, seeking out the higher hills on the Southern Island. They are far away, appearing as nothing more than a faint grey line on the horizon. Wrapping his arms around his shoulders, he reflects on his long journey from Melsey and the incredible places he has visited. The days he has spent with his new friends; the encounters with the Nethmites. They have all come a long way, and in such a short time. Gazing down at the water surrounding him, he studies his distorted reflection staring back.

'Hey Sam,' Frank says, 'if you're worrying about us separating, once our adventure is done,' he grins, 'great friends standing side-by-side together, forever.'

Sam forces a smile. 'Yeah, you're right. Having best friends, that's what really counts.'

'You've got that right, Sammy. We make a great team!' Addie pipes, and the others nod in agreement. 'Now, who wants a final game of Marco Polo before we get dry and climb into our night clothes?'

*

Dragging themselves from the sea, they wrap Frank's towels around their shivering bodies before pulling on the clean dry clothes Addie has borrowed for them. The baggy, loose-fitting clothing feels soft and warm against their cold skin. Walking from the harbour towards the market square, they pause to observe the busy market winding down as merchants close their shops and stalls for the day. Folding away the striped blinds used to separate individual stalls, the traders pick up crates of unsold merchandise, or heave heavy bags over their shoulders, and head for home. Cedric, Dr Woodchuck and the guardians retreat to the Puppis. They feel more comfortable staying onboard and safe from meeting more curious residents.

The rest of the party head for *The Duck's Head* for supper. Inside they are served with dishes piled high with Limehead Sword steaks and roasted potatoes. There are also varieties of soups and breads, and the island's own cottage cheese, which Sam steers clear of. Not for him the crumbling texture of cottage cheese. *Yuk!*

'Don't you like cottage cheese Sam?' Addie asks, her lips smacking noisily over the cheese in her mouth.

'I'm not a fan.' He explains, waving his hand defensively at the plate of cottage cheese.

'You like cream cheese though?'

'Yeah, I don't mind cream cheese. I think it's the texture of the curds that puts me off cottage cheese.' He gazes thoughtfully over the heaped contents on their dining table, adding wistfully. 'Yet I do like rice pudding.'

'You like the texture of rice pudding, but not of cottage cheese. You're weird.'

Sam smiles. 'Maybe I am.'

Whilst feasting, Frank, who is already halfway through his second plate, announces that he will go out and buy a plentiful supply of swordfish steaks and stock them aboard the Puppis. This fantastic meal temporarily distracts everyone from their task and the sad events they have witnessed. It is late when they finally leave *The Duck's Head*; and outside the market square feels eerily empty. It is a beautiful clear night. Above the moon appears small and faint, accompanying the multitude of stars scattered across the deep indigo sky. There is nothing but the rhythmic click of their footsteps on the cobblestones to keep them company as they follow Addie to her house, which lies on the south-west part of the island. It proves to be a small, cosy abode.

As they approach the building they are greeted by Addie's friend, Doris. Addie has explained that Doris is an old friend and neighbour, who has been tasked with looking after Addie's home while she went away of her adventures. She nervously brushes a lock of her ebony-coloured hair over the rim of her ear as introductions are made.

'It's nice to see you home, Addie.' She says, clutching a broom in her hand. 'You'll see I've kept the house all *spick-and-span* for you.'

'Thanks Doris. I'm sure you've done a swell job.' Addie replies. Leaning forward, she adds in a softer tone. 'I hope you haven't been too nosy while I've been away.'

'Me? Nosy? Oh no!' Doris replies, in a mildly mocking tone. 'And no. I haven't been peeking through your written poetry again. *Not me!* I would never do such a thing.' She giggles. 'No. I haven't read a single word.' Stepping aside to allow Addie and her friends to pass her, she adds cheerfully. 'Now, nice as it is to meet you all, it's late and I must be getting home. Have a good night, y'all!'

Addie shakes her head as Doris heads home. Her mischievous laughter echoing from the shadows.

'She's always looking over my shoulder, whenever I'm writing.'

'Heh! She sounds like Mandy,' Sam muses, 'she's just as curious, especially when I'm strumming Angie.'

They enter Addie's house, stumbling over cluttered floorboards inside the dark hallway.

'Wait here,' Addie instructs, while rummaging inside a cupboard and pulling out a collection of small lanterns, 'we can light these.'

With the lanterns lit, they begin exploring the rest of the house. It does seem well cared for. It is clean and homey. The perfect place to spend the night. *Thank-you Doris.* Inside the small living-room there are soft and comfy chairs to sit on, and on a wooden table sits a beautifully engraved silver tray. After the excitement of the past few days, and with the large supper sitting heavily inside their stomachs, tiredness quickly settles in. They decide to huddle together, wrapped inside the heavy blankets Addie has retrieved from another cupboard. They are warm and fit for purpose, even if they carry a faint musky smell. With Mal's help, Addie arranges mugs of rich hot chocolate with a dash of hot milk.

With her guests organised, Addie removes the band tied around her head, letting her hair fall over her shoulders. Sam notices her collecting small pieces of crumpled paper from under placemats and small metal ornament boxes on the windowsill. As everyone settles down ready for sleep, Addie opens one of the pieces of paper she holds in her hands. There are words scribbled on one side. She begins reciting:

'Tumble – tumble, through and through
Goes the wild wolverine over the avenue,'

The poem is written as a limerick, and Addie reads it aloud in a clear, silver-tongued voice.

'Hunting for his meal:
Is it rabbit or veal?
While awaiting to come the morning's dew.'

As she concludes the final line of her verse, she places the sheet of paper on the table and precedes to neatly fold it in half, and then in half again.

Glancing nervously at her friends, she asks. 'What do you think?'

'That was great Addie!' Sam claps his hands. 'You show inquisitive imagery and rhythm. If I had Angie with me, I could have easily played a melody to accompany it.'

'You should write more poetry,' Mal chimes, 'and maybe join a poetry club.'

Addie smiles solemnly. 'You fellas are too much, but thanks. That really means a lot.'

'Why do you think Doris is nosy, or should I say interested, in your poetry?' Sam asks.

Addie laughs. 'Beats me. Maybe she's interested in writing poems too. Perhaps I'm a role model, who knows.' She looks out through the window before pulling the curtains together. 'C'mon, we should get some rest. We've got the rest of our journey ahead of us.'

After bidding each other goodnight, Addie extinguishes the lanterns and pulls one of the blankets up around her. Despite his tiredness, Sam struggles to sleep and finds himself staring aimlessly at the ceiling, wondering about the hooded stranger he had seen in the woods. Addie's warning shot must have given him a shock, along with the violent lightning blast that had preceded her attack. *It is no good.* His mind is too active for sleep. He carefully slips from under his blanket and tiptoes past his restless friends, stalling briefly as Addie turns on her side; but a loud snort indicates that she at least is in the world of dreams. Stepping over her, he manages to reach the front door and open it without protest from his friends.

Sneaking out into the cool night air, he softly closes the door behind him. He trudges towards the harbour. It is chilly and the cold air tingles his scar. He has left his precious striped scarf inside Addie's house, but no matter, it is peaceful outside. Reaching the harbour wall he listens to the waves crashing against the pier's supports. Cautiously, he walks along the metal pinned, cold wooden planks. He is not wearing shoes and the wood feels worn and soft against his feet. Below him, boats bob up and down as the waves splash against their hulls. Leaning over the railing, he gazes at a faint pinpoint of light gleaming from the edge of the world. *Could that be Fye?* Surely the lighthouse is too far away. Yet somehow, he knows it is her comforting light.

Someone calls out his name. 'Sam?'

The soft-toned voice is familiar. He looks up and spots the white dove perched on a metal railing on the jetty.

The bird's soft azure eyes are comforting. 'What are you doing out here?'

'Hey Gaia,' Sam greets warmly, 'where's Techna?'

'He's asleep on the Puppis, with Cedric and Dr Woodchuck for company. That cranky owl insisted we needed to rest, following our altercation with the leviathan earlier. But his constant blubbering keeps me awake. What about you? Are you unable to sleep?'

'Not really. The bruise on my chest is stinging, but what's worse is that I keep thinking about everything that has happened: going over and over things, again and again.' He steps to the railing Gaia is perched on and gazes across the harbour, shrouded in a faintly diffused light. 'Nice night, huh?'

'Yes. It's lovely indeed. The sound of the sea, the smell of the sea-air, and the gentle ocean breeze. It's magical.'

Sam notices that Gaia is bearing a concerned frown.

The dove offers him a fleeting glance, rubbing one wing against the other. 'I-uh, I hope you can forgive me about our first meeting in Greystagg. I know the things I said were cold, but I find it difficult believing that humans recognise and appreciate our true forms.'

'That's okay, Gaia. And I find it strange, knowing for sure that you are real. I remember you and Techna as part of my favourite stories, the ones Ma used to read to me. Grand tales describing heroic guardians, who championed those who are lost.'

'Fascinating.'

'Then suddenly, there you were, in Greystagg. The genuine articles. In the flesh, or perhaps I should say, *in fur and feathers!*' Sam smiles. 'A part of me thought I might be dreaming, that you were just an extension of my imagination that had escaped the confines of a storybook. But I think I knew deep down that you were real; and what an amazing feeling to see the world I've only ever imagined, existing right in front of me.'

'That's good to hear.'

They continue gazing out across the harbour and the ocean beyond, watching distant lights blink away and listening to the rhythmic sound of bobbing boats. Across the sky, a shooting star flies over their heads.

'Which brings me to my next question, Gaia. Why is it that you distrust humans when you used to help us?' Sam pauses, conscious he might not want to hear Gaia's reasons. 'Is it because we make you feel lonely and scared?'

The guardian opens his beak to reply, but quickly snaps it shut. He is thinking hard, considering on whether he should give his real reasons. *Perhaps it is time.*

'I don't want to conceal things any longer, not from you Sam. Yes, it difficult to trust humans, but not because of your naïve *obliviousness.* The reason for maintaining my distance is that I'm afraid humans will once again get caught in the Nether's crossfire. It doesn't matter that you want to help, and I am grateful for that at least. But you've witnessed what happened to Sable?' He swallows hard. 'Her gallantry when holding back the Nether. It reminded me of Terra.'

'Terra?'

'Yes, Terra. Like Sable she was a shaman, and a good friend.' Gaia laughs tersely. 'Yeah, it's true. I once had human friends, before this cold impression of Gaia you see before you. Terra was my friend: she was a bright ray of sunshine, a brilliant shaman and practitioner of natural magic. She helped Techna and me...' His voice trails away.

Sam tries to be reassuring. 'You don't have to explain anything to me.'

But Gaia continues, his voice filled with sadness and regret. 'And like Sable, Terra got caught up in the Nether's onslaught, despite our efforts to stop its dark power. She stood up to the Nether, brave and full of compassion. Our battle proved a gigantic struggle, but together we succeeded in driving the dark forces away. It was following that conflict that we planted the Fleur de Vie. Terra recovered briefly, but the time soon came when she moved on. She went away.' He sighs, adding. 'We didn't want her to go, Techna and I, we really didn't. She explained how she'd be okay and thanked us for placing our trust in her, and that we should do the same with other humans too. Techna understood that, but I bottled my grief instead and created an aloof mask to keep all humans distant. I left it to Techna's open-minded and generous nature to engage with you, while I hid away. That is until history was repeated. This time it was Sable who stood defiant, offering an act of futile bravery that allowed the Nether to overwhelm her. It was then I realised how wasteful and pointless my façade was.'

'Oh Gaia!'

'You humans are curious, but you are also delicate. Yet despite your obvious weaknesses, you still want to help.' Gaia manages a smile. 'I wish you could have met Terra; she would have liked you in a click.'

Another shooting star crosses the sky as the white dove lowers his head and runs his wings over each other.

Concerned, Sam asks. 'Gaia? Are you alright?'

'Yes, I'm fine. It's just…' His eyes sting. 'I'm sorry, Sam. You should go and rest. We must leave in the morning and continue our search for the Fleur di Vie. Who knows what the Nether is planning next.' And with a frantic beat of his wings, Gaia heads high into the night sky. 'See you in the morning, Sam.'

Alone on the jetty, Sam watches the dove turns into a small white dot against the night sky. A gust of wind picks up his curls.

'Oh Gaia. You shouldn't be sorry. Not about Sable, nor Terra. And I know, if they were here, they would tell you that themselves.'

Interlude: Night falls in Melsey

Meanwhile in Melsey, the evening is greeted by threatening thick indigo-coloured clouds looming over the city. There are no stars, nor moon on view tonight. The sense of tranquillity is interrupted by the sounds of rumbling vehicles and whining trams. One stops at Cherry Avenue, heading north. A group of passengers disembark, leaving a handful of stragglers remaining on board, eager to get home. Birds swoop across the sky, dancing in repeated circles before heading for a place to roost for the night. An eeriness descends upon an empty Central Park as the fountain tirelessly recycles water into its stone basin; water trickling from statue's mouth. Lights flicker occasionally through the windows of surrounding buildings. Most have their curtains drawn, or shutters bordered shut. Streetlamps cast a cool white glow over pavements, while inside pubs and restaurants, people are deep in conversation, finishing drinks with their evening meals. *The Melsey Clock*, sitting aloft in its tower, strikes the tenth hour.

Mary is walking home, carrying a large paper shopping bag. Her progress is unhurried as she follows the narrow channel of water flowing alongside the pavement. She feels comforted by the gentle trickling sound. Reaching a junction she stops and glances nervously at the streetlight above her head. It flickers, discharging a soft drone as tiny moths dance beneath its warm glow. She thinks about Sam, wondering where he is and what he might be doing. Reaching inside her coat pocket, she takes a cursory glance at the letter he has sent her. The letter describes his visit to Farley. Mary ponders on when she might get to visit there. To step beyond the city boundary and follow his footsteps. Clutching the paper bag across her chest, nestled tightly below her chin to prevent any of the loose apples from spilling, she walks on. Behind the streetlight continues flickering, sending out a series of rapid electrical clicks. Then it blacks out completely, casting a long dark shadow. Oblivious, Mary pushes on. Johnny is waiting for her at home; hopefully preparing a mug of hot rice tea.

Elsewhere in Melsey, *The Root's* neon sign struggles to stay illuminated. Typically on nights like tonight, the club below Hollandaise Street is filled with loud music and the sound of patrons singing and dancing to live performances. But tonight it is quiet. Deep beneath the spiral steps, within its walls, there are just a handful of people sitting on stools or couches, accompanied by half-empty drinks and bowls of peanuts. Ted has provided candles for each table, but most sit extinguished, their wicks blackened and exhausted. There is someone performing on the tiny stage. The poignant sounds of the portly jazz singer standing alone on the stage; his trumpet pressed against his lips as he blows a slow melancholic tune. Then, as the intense brassy sound fades, he begins to sing.

> *'These lights…*
> *These lights will go out when the night has come.*
> *(Mm-hm-hmm…)*
> *Underneath that sparkling moonlight,*
> *All through the night,*
> *Will you wait for me?*
> *And here, I'll take you swiftly into these longing arms,*
> *Oh, my moonlit blues.'*

A customer sitting at the bar swigs down the last of her whiskey. The ice clicks against the side of the glass. Swallowing the remaining liquid, she feels it warm the back of her throat. Coins are spilled across the counter. The woman slings her handbag over her shoulder and slips down from the stool.

'Have a good evening, ma'am.'

Ted collects the dirty glass and begins cleaning it with a damp cloth: *squeak-squeak-squeak*. Glancing across the sparsely filled lounge, he nods as another patron rises from their seat and makes for the spiral staircase.

'Ah, Sam, you've been gone too long.' Ted mutters to himself. 'This place feels so bleak without you playing. I hope you return soon. I miss you, my friend.'

Placing the clean glass on the shelf he steps from behind the bar, heading for the front of the stage. He sits on a stool. Only he and the jazz singer remains. Everyone else has slipped away into the night. A single candle remains alight on the table between them. *The Root* presents a sombre sight.

Ted smiles thinly at the jazz singer. 'Keep it comin', Louis.'

'The Melba makes its way for the sea,
And all through the night, could it be?
(Wait for me...)
I'll take you swiftly into my longing arms,
My moonlit blues.'

Louis the jazz singer mumbles something inaudible into the microphone and lifts his trumpet to his lips. It is a haunting instrumental. Ted nods his head to the slow rhythm of the music. The slow reverberating tone carries across the lounge, bouncing off walls and diffusing up the stairwell into Hollandaise Street.

*

Sandy stares out through his florist shop window, preparing to close his shop. He sets down his watering can onto the counter and begins a series of spot-checks; his final chores before leaving for home. He sweeps the floor with his trusty, sturdy broom. The sound of water dripping onto a hard, smooth surface accompanies the scrape of tough bristles on the wooden floor. Leaning against a wall, phone in hand, Mandy fiddles with the plait across her left shoulder. Turning down the main light, Sandy places the broom inside the storage cupboard.

'It looks like we're set for another damp evening.' He runs his hand through his hair. 'I hope we don't get soaked on our way home.'

'I sure hope not. This place has seen enough flooding already!' Mandy grumbles, glancing at the numerous puddles of water on the floor from where Sandy has watered the plants. 'I've got to say Sandy, the city feels pretty glum.' She looks up from her mobile, revealing dark circles under her eyes. 'People don't seem interested anymore. They're disappearing like, *ugh*, magic. Has everyone given up or something? I dunno. Even my friends ain't returning my calls, or my texts!'

'Maybe they're taking a break?'

'Why'd you think that?' She exclaims, indigently. 'They would *never* take a break from me! *The nerve!*'

Sandy chuckles, ignoring Mandy's pout. 'Whatever you say.' He stares through the open door and scratches his chin with a work-roughened hand. He glances at Mandy, who is staring at her phone. 'Mandy, I've been thinking on what you told me the other day, about the flowers in the park.'

'What do you mean?'

'Nah, I shouldn't bother. You wouldn't believe my blabbering anyway.'

'Spill it Sandy, I won't mess with you.' She grins. 'No promises though.'

'Okay. Here goes.' Sandy begins. 'Have you heard of Gaia and Techna?'

'Nope. Absolute zippo. Who'd have silly names like that?'

'They're characters in storybooks I used to read, as a child. They were guardians that looked like dragons, creatures with wings, if I recall.' Sandy explains. 'They would stand against terrifying beasts, mystical creatures who disrupted the natural order. Monsters that terrified animals and destroyed plants. It's difficult remembering details, but the way things are shaping up here reflect some of those stories. It's got me thinking,' he sighs, 'there could be discord in Melsey.'

Mandy scratches the top of her head and puckers her lips. 'Does that mean you believe in crazy, nonsensical kids' stories; that the guardians are actually real?' She glances for answers on her phone. *'Argh! Its dead!'*

Frustrated, she stuffs her exhausted phone into her jeans pocket and glares out of the window. Without her phone to occupy her, perhaps she can give Sandy's crazy ideas her consideration.

Sandy sighs. 'I don't know if trouble is brewing, but isn't it best to hope that there are guardians out there? To believe in their protection and the regenerating powers of the Fleur de Vie...'

'Fleur de-what now?' Mandy interjects. 'You're making less and less sense.'

'The stories described the Fleur de Vie as a natural entity, one able to restore anything that has been lost. The guardians are responsible for the Fleur de Vie too. Doesn't that sound intriguing, to believe in something that can bring splendid expectations?'

'But that's childish nonsense Sandy! And I bet if my friends were here they'd agree.' Mandy pauses awkwardly, her cheeks flushed. 'I did say I might mock your blabbering.'

'Maybe you're right. It might be just pollen up my nose.' Sandy sighs, long and hard. 'I did say it came from stories.'

He wipes a small smudge from the shop window with a cloth, his final task. He watches Mandy tiredly rub her eyes with one hand. Her other is caressing a concealed object in her coat pocket: her drained mobile phone.

'It's late Mandy, why don't I take you home?'

'But I'm not tired.' Her words trail away as she stifles a yawn, clamping her mouth shut.

'Sounds like it, little miss stubborn. Come, let me take you home. I'll tell you more about the guardians another time if you're interested?'

Sandy leads Mandy out of the shop door. They head for the parking lot and Sandy's large red pickup truck; complete with stencilled clusters of pink flowers running along each side.

Unlocking the truck's doors, he glances suspiciously at the public house opposite. It is called *The Wooden Bridge*. The windows are darkened. The pub appears empty. The sign hanging above the bolted door swings noisily in the wind: a bridge overlooking a stream. *Perhaps the publicans are on holiday?*

'Ted's says *The Root* has been much quieter.' Sandy murmurs. 'Where is everyone?' The streetlamp adjacent to the pub flickers and begins to hum. Its power decreases gradually until it is barely luminous. 'And what is it about the streetlamps?' He shakes his head. 'Taking everything into consideration, things are looking rather wretched.'

'What are you blabbering about now?' Mandy asks, rubbing her eyes again.

'Oh nothing.'

She opens the front passenger door of Sandy's truck. 'Whatever.'

They climb into the front of the trunk and simultaneously slam the doors shut. Turning on the ignition, the dashboard radio fires into life: first crackling with static, then music starts playing. Mandy reaches over and softens the volume as Sandy reverses his truck from the parking space. He manoeuvres the truck out of the carpark and cruises slowly along the street. As they pass successive streetlamps, the lights extinguish, one-by-one, accompanied by a series of powered-down clicks. A long shadow stretches across the street behind them.

Deep within the encroaching darkness something moves, a shape that grows larger and larger. It creeps along the bricked wall of *The Wooden Bridge*, its form momentarily captured in the residual red glow of the streetlights. The outline of a creature with a large craning beak. It stops beneath the doorway of the pub and looks on, releasing an ominous snigger that shakes the silence.

Cave Expedition

Another morning. Another day.

It is early and the inhabitants are preparing for another busy market day. There are already fishermen out: some on the water in boats; others are lined up along the jetty, their rods primed with lines stretched out over the water that gently ping in the breeze. At the far end two fishermen sit eating breakfast of buttered croissants and jam; prepared to fend off the hungry sea birds circling above. Having rested for two days in Limehead, it is time for the party to embark on the next stage in their journey. Sam and his friends have spent the extra day on the island recuperating and ensuring their clean dry laundry is folded away. They have restocked the Puppis' hold, including a large box of salted swordfish steaks, bushels of fruit, and caddies full of herbal teas.

As they climb apprehensively aboard the Puppis, their collective thoughts shift to where the day's adventures will take them. Addie helps Frank draws up the anchor and then heads for the helm. The propeller begins spinning, but then promptly stalls. A second attempt is successful, and the airship lifts higher into the sky. Standing on the quay is Doris, Addie's loyal friend.

'Come back soon. Good-bye!' She cries, waving furiously, as the airship cruises over the harbour, completing a slow turn before heading for the Southern Island coast.

With the islet waning behind, the Puppis hugs the ocean, the tips of its mechanical wings dip occasionally into the still waters, leaving ripples across the surface. On the bow, Frank holds the helm firmly, steering the Puppis on course. Mal is busy in the galley below, fixing up batches of pecan cakes made with the fresh pecans and other cake ingredients bought at the market. Dr Woodchuck sits on the steps inside the deck hatch, furiously brushing his incisors with a thick layer of toothpaste. Bonnie and Cedric watch on intently. Foam splashes from the bristles, splattering toothpaste over Cedric, who has strayed too near. Bonnie chuckles in amusement as the eagle-owl grunts in protest and ruffles his feathers.

Addie is standing at the rear of the craft, gazing out across the ocean as the final traces of Limehead dip below the horizon. She looks on as smoke rings emanating from the tall chimney diffuse away.

'Hope to see you again,' she mutters sadly, waving goodbye, 'it was fun while it lasted.'

Sam is sitting on the floor inside the captain's cabin, brushing dust and dirt from his precious striped scarf. Smacking his beak, Techna, in his raven form, skips along the bed and perches on Sam's knee. Despite the extra day's rest, Sam looks exhausted.

'Did you manage to get some sleep, Sam? You've been nodding off ever since we got on board.' Techna continues. 'There was a moment this morning when I thought we might leave you behind on the island.' The black guardian chuckles, noting Sam's cheeks redden. 'It's a good job Frank went looking for you, and practically carried you to the Puppis. He's a good friend.'

'He is.' Sam sighs, slipping his striped scarf over his left eye. 'I had another restless night, hence my bleary eye.' Deep in thought, he stares at his hands resting on his knees. *There is something he wants to ask the raven.* 'Hey, Techna?'

'Hm? Is there something on your mind?'

'Yeah, you could say that. There's quite a few things running through my mind at the moment, but most of all, I would like to know what happened to Terra?'

Techna opens his beak, but then snaps it shut. He looks away. A sad look drawn over his azure eyes.

Sam tilts his head. 'Techna?'

'It's a sad and challenging memory,' Techna replies, eventually, 'but an important one, nonetheless. Terra has not been a part of our story for some time, not since the Fleur de Vie first bloomed. She is walking a different path, one that is made for all of us by the Aether: to travel between worlds, to meet, and then depart.'

'And what will happen to the Aether when the Nether is defeated?'

'No-one can comprehend the purpose of the Aether, we can only trust in its fortune and destiny, and hope it stays true.'

Sam pulls on his jacket. 'And what about you and Gaia? What will happen to you when this is over?'

'Don't worry about us, my friend. We always have someplace to go once our purpose is complete.'

'But where?'

'Somewhere beyond the clouds, maybe somewhere we'll be able to kick up our feet. Even guardians need to take a holiday.'

'*A holiday!*' Sam gasps. 'Yeah. I suppose you do.'

He falls silent, taking solace in the peaceful ambiance inside the captain's cabin. It reminds him of his bedroom back in Melsey, with its faint warm smell of camomile. He lowers his gaze to his knees. Techna hops closer and peaks at the sleeve of Sam's jacket.

'We should check out what the others are doing.'

Stepping out onto the main deck, they are greeted by the cool ocean breeze. Sam rushes to help Mal climb up through hatch. She is carrying a batch of pecan cakes, artfully arranged on a tray. They meet Addie and offer her the sweet baked goods. Grinning mischievously, she grabs two, much to Mal's amusement. Sam takes one of the pecan cakes and joins Addie leaning over the side of the Puppis, watching the ocean below. They munch down heartily on their snacks and Sam shares crumb sized potions with Techna, perched on his shoulder.

They are distracted by a loud squawk. 'Ach! Ach!'

It is Cedric, who flies energetically out from the hatch, large soapy bubbles stuck to his tail feathers. Dr Woodchuck pops out his head, foam covering his whiskers, and with a sly shrug of his shoulders, drops back inside.

Techna flits from Sam's shoulders and lands beside Frank, who is still standing at the helm. 'How's the navigating, Captain Frank?'

'It's going swimmingly, or perhaps I should say *flightingly.*' Frank laughs, rubbing the back of his head in an embarrassed acknowledgement of his terrible pun. 'We should be back over the Southern Island soon.' Squinting over the sheep's head, he points at the giant mountains peeking over the horizon. '*There!*'

As the Puppis nears the coastline, the party watch the approaching features looming larger and larger, until they can make out details of the terrain. Reaching the coast, the airship turns westerly, and ambles slowly alongside sandy beaches punctuated by jagged headlands.

Sam asks. 'Where should we land?'.

Frank points along the line of a beach, with its mixture of greens, beiges and browns. 'How about down there, by those caves?'

The beach emerges from the edge of the ocean: a band of fine-grained white sand that rises gently towards a small grassy knoll. Beyond the knoll sits a rocky outline containing a series of arched caves.

Techna turns to Sam. 'What do you think, Sam?'

Sam nods. *It feels right.* 'Sounds good to me.'

Frank grins. 'Okay, let's do it.'

Steering the airship towards the beach, Frank brings the Puppis to a halt, hovering directly above the grassy knoll. The deck becomes animated as everyone prepares to disembark. Now considering herself to be an expert, Addie prepares the anchor and drops it over the side. It hits the sand with a loud thud. Mal unfurls the rope ladder, and one-by-one, they clamber down onto the beach, sinking their feet into the soft white sand. Along the beach, thick tufts of grass and rusty-red weed grow healthily, evidence that the Nethmites have not yet visited here. With the sound of the ocean breeze and the rippling of the waves playing in their ears, the party commence on a brief exploration of the immediate area. They discover a patch of black ash and charred wood, surrounded by a circle of large pebbles. The remains of a beach fire set before the rocky caves. The dark gloomy entrances into the caves amplify the whispering breeze, transferring the sound into something eerie and unsettling. They hear a single cry from an eagle, performing repeating circular patterns high above their heads.

'So here we are.' Addie starts, with controlled excitement. Turning to Gaia, she asks, 'Do ya think we'll find the Fleur de Vie, along this coastline?'

'I believe so. I can feel it in my ivory horns, err, I mean my moth-feelers.' The white guardian replies, twitching his moth-feelers. He sniffs at the salty air, adding. 'Yes definitely, it's somewhere close by.'

'Yeah I got that, but exactly whereabouts is it? It could take hours, even days, without a better idea of where we should start looking?' Addie stamps the ground impatiently. 'In fact, it could be way underground!'

'You make a fair point, Addie. Perhaps we should stop and think about our options.' Gaia nods, glancing anxiously towards the first of the caves.

Sitting on a collection of boulders decorating the knoll, the party debate their next move. Dr Woodchuck mischievously suggests that Cedric should check out the caves by himself and report back, only to receive a retaliative swipe across his back from the eagle-owl. Addie sits away from the group playing with a long stick she found on the beach. She draws over a patch of sand, sketching a cave with a series of arrows pointing towards its entrance. Then, with her sand drawing complete and ringed with a circle, she grunts, and starts scraping the stick through her doodles, returning them to the sand.

'Useless.' She sighs, tossing the stick aside.

They reach a consensus to explore the caves, but which one should they enter first? They have no idea how far and how deep the caves continue into the rocky ground. The caverns beneath might form a gigantic underground maze, which means they might easily get lost inside. Addie is right. It could take days to find the Fleur de Vie, assuming that it is actually here. Sam studies his disheartened friends and considers reminding them that they must rely on each other. They must trust that the Aether will take them to the Fleur de Vie. Shuffling with growing anticipation, he gazes at the relative calm of the ocean and takes solace from listening to the roll of the waves, juxtaposing the jovial squeaked and squawked banter between Cedric and Dr Woodchuck.

'Uh!' He starts, reacting to a wisp of rose-coloured light shimmering in the palm of his hand. The Aether is reacting with something. The light spreads across his body, glowing with positive energy. Sam sits rigid as a statue, as his friends leap to their feet.

'Sam?' Frank gasps. 'Are you alright?'

But Sam is dumbstruck, immersed within the eruption of the Aether. Gasping, he staggers to his feet as a burst of rose-coloured light releases a shockwave that throws everyone off their feet, causing them to tumble across the knoll. There is a flash of light that splits the beam of light into two, then into four, and then into eight. Long lines of light spiral above Sam's head, before converging and then zipping towards the entrance of one of the caves.

Sam relaxes and stumbles backward. 'Whoa!'

Composing himself, he stares at the cloud of the Aether's energy congregated around the mouth of the cave. His friends pick themselves up, brushing sand and seeds from their clothing. Addie steps slowly around Sam, studying him with increased suspicion. Then she turns towards the mouth of the cave.

'What was that about?' She asks.

'It appears the Aether in Sam's body has reacted to something inside that cave.' Techna explains, studying the entrance the Aether's light has centred on. His azure eyes glow brightly. 'Maybe, just maybe...' his voice rings with excitement, 'it's here!'

Gaia gasps. 'Tech, the Fleur de Vie is in inside this cave.'

'It must be! It must be!' Techna agrees, animatedly bouncing up and down, causing the ground to shake and throw everyone off their feet again.

Techna transforms into his raven form and glides into the mouth of the cave. Gaia shrugs and changes into his dove form, following the black guardian inside the cave.

Techna's voice hollers from deep inside the darkness. 'I think we've found what we're looking for!'

The others rush towards the cave entrance, stopping briefly to examine the inner walls. They are coated in thick, slippery green moss. There is a sharp rocky ceiling above their heads. Towards the rear of the cave they spot a pile of dry willow branches, concealing an object. It is something large and white, consisting of weathered marble. There is a distinct pattern covering its surface, an interconnecting emblem of black and white wings, embracing a blue circle. Evidence the guardians have been here before. Rounding the marble object, they peer anxiously into the darkness beyond. Cold air pulsates around them. It feels as if the cave is breathing, calling to them and enticing them deeper inside. With a final glance at the bright sunshine glistening outside, at the sandy beach and the beautiful blue-green ocean, they cautiously step deeper into the cave.

With Sam leading, they creep into a pitch-black corridor that stretches underground. The Aether glows above his right hand, shining brightly, adopting the shape of a lit torch; just like the ones he read about in adventure stories. *Fancy that!* They walk on, listening to the sound of their own breathing and the *tap-tap-tap* of Frank's pegleg on the rocky ground. The air around them feels colder. Pausing, the party is enveloped in an eerie silence.

Mal whispers. 'I hope the guardians haven't forgotten us.'

'Me too,' Cedric replies, hoarsely, 'this place is way too dark for my liking.'

'Why are we whispering?' Dr Woodchuck demands, his voice echoing off the walls. Startled, the others hush him. 'Sorry.' He whispers.

There are no signs of the guardians, who have pushed on far ahead. The party continue, hoping that they will rendezvous with them soon. The cave reaches out further: on, and on, and on.

'Woah!' Sam stops abruptly, causing his friends behind him to walk into each other.

Addie whispers. 'What's up, Sam?'

They hear another set of footprints, approaching from the rear. Heavier steps resonating along the dark, dank walls. There is a loud retort, a cry from the dark.

'*Ahoy!*'

Startled, Frank jumps and hits his head on the low ceiling. He yelps, sending a high-pitched sound that bounces off the surrounding walls, raising the fear level further. *But how more dangerous is it to run blindly through the cave?* They turn around, prepared to meet the someone, or something, following them.

And there he is. The hooded figure standing alone, staring out from the shadows.

Sam exclaims. 'Hey, it's you!'

'Is this the same fella who's been stalking us?' Addie mutters. 'If you ask me, that's plain creepy. I thought my warning shot might be enough, but apparently not. *Tish!* Persistent weirdo.'

Bonnie counters. 'And I thought you were the persistent one, Addie.'

'*Bah!*' Addie retorts loudly, her exclamation reverberates off the walls, causing them to jump.

The stranger takes a step forward. 'Are you heading into the caves by yourselves?' A stiff breeze snaps at the long fringe covering his eyes, which he sweeps aside with the back of his hand. The stranger gazes over Sam's shoulder, staring into the blackness beyond. 'It looks pretty dark in there.'

'I think we'll be okay, sir.' Mal replies politely. 'The guardians will look after us, they know where to go.'

'Even if they've gone on without us.' Frank retorts. '*Hey!* Cedric and Dr Woodchuck have gone on ahead too.'

But the others are too engaged with the stranger to listen.

'*Wait-a-minute.*' Addie starts, stretching out her words as she stares at the hooded figure. 'Are you telling us that you want to find the Fleur de Vie?'

The stranger glances down at the stone floor, twiddling his thumbs. 'Well, since I've got to know about your task: finding this mysterious object called the Fleur de Vie, I'd like to help, if I can.'

'I dunno.'

'Don't drag behind, you guys!' Dr Woodchuck calls out from the dark. 'We've lost Gaia and Techna!'

'Yeah! This place is like a maze,' Cedric adds, 'and we're bored of you talking to that stranger. *So chop-chop.* Whatever it is you're planning with him, we've more pressing things on claw, or talon, or whatever.'

'As you've made it this far,' Sam turns towards the stranger, 'you'd better come with us. But make sure you stick close, okay?'

The stranger appears to smile from inside their hood. 'Okay!'

With a new number added to its ranks, the party continues along the dank, rocky corridor, twisting and turning. The walls are gradually narrowing, squeezing them in from both sides, and from above and below.

'Are yah sure we can trust this fella, Sammy?' Addie hisses, casting a concerned glance at the stranger walking behind them.

'I'm sure Addie. He doesn't seem bad, even if he has been stalking us all this time.' Sam feels the stranger's hand brush briefly against his own. 'You should know Addie, there's something I find familiar about him.'

'Wow!' Addie replies. 'You sure like warming up to others, don't you Sam?'

'I've gotta try, at least.'

Deeper and deeper they pass into the cave. They finally catch up with Dr Woodchuck and Cedric, who are waiting impatiently for them at a rocky junction.

'You took your sweet time.' Cedric mutters, tapping his talons impatiently against the small boulder he has perched on. 'You'd better get used to being squashed, cause this alcove isn't size-friendly and I'm claustrophobic.'

The eagle-owl is right. The ceiling is scraping the crown of Frank's hat and the walls have narrowed sufficiently to force the party into walking single file. The ceiling drops even further, meaning they have to walk stooped, with their necks craning forward. Weaving around hanging stalactites, they are splashed with water dripping onto stalagmites reaching up from the ground. Progress is slow.

'Echo!' Addie yells suddenly, bored of the unrelenting rocky passage.

The cave walls reply. '*Echo! Echo. Echo.*'

'Wow! The caves answer to your voice. Amazing!'

And the cave walls dutifully repeats. '*Amazing. Amazing...*'

Reaching a wider access marking a junction, the party relies on the Aether's light to select the next corridor to enter. The rose-coloured light diffuses into a passage that winds steeper and deeper into the cave. They stick close to the rocky wall and their steps are taken with increased caution as the stony floor is wet and slippery. The sound of rushing water fills their ears, which gets louder with every step. Raising his hand, Sam holds the glowing Aether torch reassuringly over his head. Ahead is a waterfall, its waters flow from a dark void high above and crashes into a deep pool. A cool mist sprays their faces. Hidden above are bats, their wings fluttering frantically. The Aether's light reflects on the body of bats, giving the impression that the ceiling is moving. They squeak, fearful of the strange visitors inside their cave. It is very disorienting.

The stranger mumbles, reminiscing on cleaning out lumpy splotches of caramel pudding from inside a giant spinning vehicle: a centrifuge. *What a curious topic to bring to mind?* The stranger's shoulders shudder as he describes the sticky mess between his fingers whilst cleaning the vehicle, and how it stretched every time his fingers parted. *Very peculiar.*

'Centrifuge?' Sam asks, stopping in his tracks. 'You mean the big, spinning thing used by astronauts?'

The stranger's frame stiffens.

He chuckles nervously. 'Oh, it's just something I once saw that put me off eating caramel puddings. The sickly smell was just awful!'

'Okay?' Sam nods, trying to piece together this cryptic message.

The stranger sighs and clutches his stomach. 'And those caramel puddings were very filling, especially when you eat more than one.'

Sam listens carefully, trying to push the sound of the waterfall from his ears. Stuck here in this subterranean world, he studies the jagged ceiling with its rugged patterns and shadows cast by the Aether's rose-coloured light circling around his head. They push on until reaching a sharp bend. Sam stops abruptly, and once again his friends bump together like a sequence of primed dominoes.

Mal asks. 'What is it now, Sam?'

'Nethmites!' Sam mutters, recognising the familiar sound of crunching metal and squealing hinges.

Peering around the bend, they see an open area through a small alcove. Sitting inside, in soft, muddy soil, is a small round Nethmite, munching the remains of a long green plant held between its metal jaws. The soft diffused light is sufficient for them to see dark green stains around its mouth. The remains of the plant and thick moss it has devoured. Sam spots the remnants of mushed up red petals too. *Except this Nethmite is alone.* Swallowing the last of the plant, the creature cranes its head and emits a long rasping cry. It glances at the party, causing them to stiffen in anticipation for what might happen next. *How will they defend against another attack inside this cramped, dark space?* The metallic creature slowly opens its jaws and emits a longer, more piecing shriek. *A call to arms?* There are no signs of reinforcements, and instead the Nethmite begins backing away, its leafy arms held high above its head. It turns and scurries away, before burrowing into the ground.

'Hey, it didn't attack us!' Addie gasps, showing her disappointment. 'Aww, and we let it get away too. What a coward!'

'Maybe they don't attack when alone and isolated.' Sam suggests, shaking his head. 'It's sad really. Not having the assurance of its comrades.'

'Sad! Huh!' Addie snorts. 'You're even mushier than I thought, Sammy!'

Sam smirks. 'It's what I do best.'

*

They continue, persevering with their demanding trek into the depths of the cave, until they eventually reunite with Gaia and Techna. The guardians are waiting patiently inside a large dome, having resumed their dragon forms. Their wings emit a radiance of blue and gold colours, as their moth-feelers gently brush the rocky ceiling. The dome is sparse. There are no fungi growing here, nor grass, but neither are there signs of the Nethmites. All that remains are damp brown residue streaks where plants had once grown and prospered. Glancing to the far side, through a faintly diffused light, Sam spots a slight depression in the ground, suggesting that a small pool once sat there.

'Geeze! We've come all this way, just to find a sodden draught, huh?' Addie bleats, her teeth chattering. She swings her arms about her chest. 'And these are my warmest clothes!'

'Yeah! My poncho isn't enough to keep me warm either!' Mal stutters. 'Oh, I wish I'd bought some hot cocoa with us.'

The two guardians face the shivering party, their soft azure eyes staring sympathetically. They fold their wings together, wrapping the feathered insulation around the party, like a thick blanket.

Gaia asks. 'Is this better?'

'A bit,' Addie sighs, 'thanks pal.'

Techna frowns. 'I'm sorry for making you come all this way, into the depths of this cave.' His voice trembles and he appears to be on the verge of tears. 'I honestly believed the Fleur de Vie would be here, indeed, at this very spot. But there is nothing, except for dirt and rock. No plants. No water. Perhaps, if Sable were here...' His voice trails away.

'I felt confident too, Tech.' Gaia rearranges his wing around the black guardian. 'I wish Sable and Terra were here.' Turning to the others, with their bewildered expressions. 'We've relied so much on them. *Humans!* With your curiosity and your bravery, ready to stand against the Nether's power. It astonishes me.' Closing his eyes, his moth-feelers droop. 'We should have done more.'

Sam reaches out his hand and squeezes the white guardian's giant arm. Gaia stares at him with sad eyes, nodding his head, acknowledging the human's compassion.

'Now don't you get mushy, pal!' Addie counters. 'We can still help, can't we? We must be close to the Fleur de Vie, right? Sam's magic tells us that much. So we can't just drop things like that, not now. Not when we've come so far. That's silly!' She smirks, patting Gaia forcefully on the back. 'C'mon, treat yourself to a smile! For Addie.'

Gaia's azure eyes glisten and a smile spreads across his lips. 'Thank you, Addie. I needed to hear those heartfelt words.'

'Hey. I do what I can.'

'But are you certain the Fleur de Vie isn't here?' Mal asks. 'Might it not be hidden somewhere, perhaps beneath the dirt and rocks?'

'Yeah.' Cedric agrees. 'It's like you two haven't checked properly!'

As the eagle-owl speaks, the atmosphere inside the dome begins to change. The air feels warmer and the cave walls glow, displaying a range of different tones: from rose-white to ochre. Lights pulsate in a subtle rhythm, spreading across the walls and ceiling of the dome. Stepping from the guardians' protective wings, the party stare, entranced by the display. They feel their hearts lift, bubbling with delight, watching the patterns flash as the illuminated figures dance about them. Silhouettes lift partners up from their feet, whilst others twirl around each other in ever-repeating spins. Mal reaches out, causing tiny sparks to appear on the wall in front of her.

'Well!' Cedric mutters, with an amused lilt, as a tiny stream of blue light passes through his feathers. 'I've made my point,' he puffs out his chest feathers, smirking, 'and you're welcome.'

Intrigued, Sam steps towards the wall where the dancing figures morph together, forming the recognisable shapes of Gaia and Techna. The images of the guardians soar, crossing from one side of the dome to the other, projecting the rocky ceiling in strange green and blue hues. A spiralling aurora of the Aether glimmers above Sam's head, morphing into the shape of a person standing next to a tall, egg-shaped craft: with four wings on its side. It is a spaceship preparing for take-off. The figure shrinks into the spaceship. Moments later the craft darts over their heads and bursts into clouds of red, orange and yellow lights, radiating out from the ship's rockets. As the spacecraft reaches the top of the dome it transforms into streams of stardust that swirl like a celestial nebula: a five petalled flower with alternating blue, violet and rose colours.

Stretching out his right hand, Sam strokes the stone wall. Upon contact, lights burst from the wall, spraying into the air, before pouring, as a concentrated beam of light, onto a small dried-up patch on the soil covered ground. The lights fade.

Dr Woodchuck gasps. 'Well that just happened. A colourful show to lift our spirits. Although, I thought it finished rather anti-climactically, if you want my critique.'

Addie nods. 'Yeah. It did finish abruptly.'

'Hey!' Cedric counters, with a point of his beak. 'But hardly anti-climactic, I would argue. *Look! There's something there.*'

They step towards the patch of soil, staring closely at the darker brown mush mixed within the dirt. The faint hue of a deep blue light blinks steadily from its centre.

'Could this be the Fleur de Vie?' Frank asks.

'Maybe.' Gaia replies. 'Sam, help us unearth it.'

Sam kneels next to the patch of dried earth and carefully picks up handfuls of soil, one scoop at a time. Tiny specks of dust scatter into the air.

He gasps. 'Ah!'

There is something nestled beneath the soil: a small, smooth orb. It looks like a child's marble, tinted with the colours of the ocean. He examines the thin silver-coloured band around the edge of the orb, speckled with tiny green fragments. The band is slowly rotating inside the globe, its light reacts with the Aether causing it to emit a pulsating burst of light that illuminates Sam's face.

'Is this what we've been looking for after all this time?' Addie's shoulders slumped. 'The Fleur de Vie is a glass ball? Huh! I thought it would be something much more spectacular. I thought it would be a flower, at least. *I feel cheated!*'

Techna is peering closely at the orb. The green flakes move to the edge of the glass, interacting with the black guardian. 'Actually, we may not be cheated. This looks like a seedling of the Fleur de Vie. Maybe it needs something to help it work.'

'If you're sure...' Sam's words trail away as he lowers the orb, resting it on the ground.

A tiny white petal instantly sprouts out through the glass surface, followed by another, and then another. More petals emerge and swirl around Sam's head, darting back and forth. They drop slowly to the ground and sink into the soil. Moments later, green shoots rise through cracks in the rocky surface, sprouting clusters of small yellow flowers. There is a bright flash beneath their feet, which sends out waves of rose-coloured Aether, casting shadows against the rocky interior of the dome. Each pulse is brighter than the one before. Fresh green grass and flowers cover the rocky floor. The light reaches the depression in the corner of the dome, causing it to fill with water, replenishing the pool. Lily pads sprout and drift across the water's surface, beneath the dome's shimmering light.

'Incredible!' Mal exclaims. 'The Fleur de Vie's powers have restored vegetation and brought back water too.' She adds, defiantly. 'I don't think we have anything more to fear from the Nether, not anymore.'

'Hopefully,' Sam says, picking up the glass orb, 'with this seedling and its power, we can restore everything lost to the Nether.'

'Like Greystagg Forest?'

'I bet it can!'

The voice of the stranger adds. 'And I bet it will.'

They spin around and stare at the stranger. His long cloth cloak has been replaced by a bulky silver-white suit with tiny patterns of blue, red and yellow on its sleeves and collar. *Fit for an astronaut.* For the first time they can properly see the stranger's face, with his head topped with a mop of buttercream blonde hair that cascades over his shoulders.

'Hey!' Mal exclaims. 'Wasn't he wearing a large cloak before?'

'Yeah, he was,' Addie nods, 'where is it now?'

The man is smiling. 'You know Sam, your calming optimism reminds me so much of Lily.'

The party gasp in astonishment and they turn towards Sam.

Addie raises an eyebrow. 'Did he just say Lily?'

Sam starts, his eye misting in a pool of tears. 'How do you know Ma's name? Does this mean?' He swallows hard. '*Pa?*'

Noah

It is a slow and uneventful trek back to the world outside. Despite feeling exhausted, everyone is in a jubilant mood, having completed their expedition inside the cave and locating the Fleur de Vie: protected inside the glass orb. Finally they have the means to restore everything that has been destroyed by the Nether. Walking with a bounce in her step, Mal imagines Greystagg Forest restored to its former glory: the tallest of trees topped with thick canopies; bushes blooming with flowers and fruit; the lake once again filled with clean cool water. The fauna will return too. The Flower of Knowledge shall be complete again: covered in strong bark and wearing a healthy, leafy green crown. Cedric is happy too, managing to blabber incessantly about returning to his tree, and grumbling on being forced out of the forest and on this adventure.

With each step the cold subterranean air becomes warmer, until they finally reach the mouth of the cave. They step out into the fresh evening air and stand by the knoll and watch, open-mouthed, as the sun sinks slowly beneath the horizon. The world is incredibly beautiful. The sky reaches a deep shade of indigo, speckled with wispy dark blue-grey clouds. Reflecting the skies, the ocean has a purple hue across the gently rolling waves. Stars twinkle through an almost transparent sky, blinking in harmony.

Addie gulps at the fresh air. 'Ah! At last. We're back in the open! I don't want to go in there again: never, ever! The darkness really creeped me out. Also,' she adds, rubbing her belly, 'all that cave trekking has made me peckish.'

'You said it Addie!' Frank nods. 'I could go for some snacks. C'mon, we've still got some marshmallows!'

'Yeah! You go and get them, and I'll get a beach fire going.'

The rest of the party continue to the top of the grassy knoll, eager to take a well-deserved rest. Mal helps Addie prepare a beach fire by collecting the driftwood scattered across the beach and piling it high inside the centre of the pebbled circle. Addie bashes two stones together, hoping to create a spark, but to no avail. She then tries rubbing two sticks together, but despite her frantic efforts, there is no flame. Mal strikes a match.

WHOOSH!

The flame catches on dried shavings and quickly establishes itself within the stacked wood. Addie shrugs, musing that perhaps using a match was the better option. Frank returns from the Puppis carrying bags of fluffy pink and white marshmallows, together with packets of nuts and a wicker basket of fruit. They take turns poking twigs into the marshmallows and lightly toasting them over the tips of the crackling flames. Frank's efforts, despite closely observing the skilled Mal and Addie, turn tarred and sooty. With increasing frustration he tosses each attempt aside, onto a growing pile of failed, tarry mush. Away from the fire, Cedric and Dr Woodchuck peck on some nuts and an apple, whilst Bonnie curls up beside them, munching her favourite biscuits. Gaia and Techna are sitting away from the fire, feigning disinterest in grabbing and toasting marshmallows. But Techna's curiosity rises until he decides to stride across the knoll towards the beach fire. Tentatively, he reaches for a marshmallow, much to Gaia's wry amusement.

Meanwhile, Sam and Noah McKenzie stroll from the beach fire and towards the edge of the knoll. They sit on the soft grass and stare out at the distant glittering lights of Limehead. Immersed in the soft rumbling sound of the waves, they watch the water lap over the sand: back and forth, with foaming bubbles. Sam turns to Noah, who is staring vacantly at the sky. The cool breeze picks up his long buttercream hair, brushing his fringe across his face. His brown eyes twinkle as they meet the stars.

'I never thought I'd get to see you,' Sam starts, exhaling a sigh that trails from his lips, 'the idea of being together seemed impossible. It's wonderful, getting this opportunity.'

'Really?'

'Yeah.' Sam looks up at the stars, closing his eye. He chuckles. 'Ma told me a lot about you. How you inspired others to follow you into space.' He turns to Noah. 'And now you're here, I know she was right.'

Noah smiles, relieved to hear such fine words. 'Sam you are sincere and compassionate, without reservation. That's definitely Lily's influence.'

Sitting around the beach fire, the others watch Sam and Noah continue their conversation: one sprinkled with laughter. Whenever Noah ruffled Sam's hair, the latter would fix it in place, brushing the fringe from his face.

'Now that's gushy, but sweet.' Addie chuckles, a difficult task when chewing a large spongy roasted marshmallow. 'To think the hooded stranger was Noah, the lost astronaut from the VEGA spaceflight. I kinda regret shooting arrows at him.'

'You've got to admit, looking at them side-by-side,' Mal says, 'they are so alike, especially their buttercream blonde hair.'

'Oh! I'll scoff down another marshmallow to celebrate that!' Addie cheers. 'Not to mention they're both ridiculously syrupy in nature. Hey Frank! Pass me another one.'

'Hang on.' Frank splutters, sniffing cautiously at the charcoal-coloured marshmallow he has been roasting over the fire. He throws it away and reaches inside the open bag, throwing a marshmallow to Addie. 'You know what Addie. I think I'll eat mine raw.'

'Aww, c'mon Frankie! You are getting better!'

'You just need to keep it further from the flames, like this.'

Mal grabs Frank's hand and raises the twig so the marshmallow is positioned just above the flame. A faint brown spot grows on the surface of the sweet.

'See? It's hot around the flame, just the right temperature. No! Don't thrust it inside.' She pulls at his hand. 'Perfect. It's just the right colour. Now you can eat it.'

Frank blows over his toasted marshmallow before biting gingerly into it. He laughs. 'I guess I learnt from the master!'

Addie counters. 'You mean the masters?'

Gaia approaches Techna, who is greedily munching down on a paw full of marshmallows. His eyes narrow as he watches Techna chew the mushy contents.

'You do like those Tech,' he declares, with an amused lilt, 'but I bet they wrap themselves around your thighs.'

'Heh! I don't care. I could eat hundreds of these little blighters.' Techna retorts, smacking his lips together. 'Are you sure you don't want one?'

'Very sure. I prefer eating peppermint candies on the occasions I crave tasting something sweet. Peppermint leaves a nice fresh aftertaste, but alas, I didn't bring any with me.'

'Augh! We should have asked Sam to get some while we were in Farley.'

'Never mind. It's not a big deal.'

Oblivious to the conversations behind them, Noah and Sam gaze skywards, scanning the wisps of cloud and the glistening stars beyond. A shooting star darts over their heads, soaring across the deep indigo sky. It blinks once before vanishing. They spot a larger light, twinkling in different colours as it moves at a leisurely pace across the night sky.

'Hey!' Sam starts, turning to Noah. 'You know, aside from Ma, there were others who spoke to me about you. Telling me how special you were.'

'Really? I never thought I was so popular,' Noah laughs, 'I guess I haven't thought about it in that way.'

Sam nods, recalling on what Ms. Hummus had said to him in Glen Bó, when she had described meeting Noah. Listening to the rolling ocean waves, he studies the silhouette of a single seabird as it soars across the sky. It caws forlornly on its long seaward journey. Sam switches his attention back to the rolling waves. He twiddles his thumbs; there is something he desperately wants to ask Noah.

'What was it like in space?'

'It's quite large,' Noah begins, stating the obvious, 'and it's very dark, much darker than the night. But it is extraordinarily beautiful too, especially when you look back home. Imagine for a moment looking at a vast painting, one made up of glorious, rich colours that constantly change before you. You never get to see the same pattern twice.' He pauses. 'But it was also very lonely, being away from Lily and not seeing you. After the incident, I was alone. My colleagues were gone. I assumed they managed to escape and returned home. I was desperate to see someone, to hear a familiar voice. How long was I up there on my own, I don't know. Isolation plays tricks with time. Things suddenly changed and I was here, and I could see you and your friends.'

'Tell me about the centrifuge, the one you told me about inside the cave?'

'Yep! That really happened, but what I forget to say was… it was me who ate the caramel pudding before taking a ride.' Noah laughs nervously. 'Boy, it was a harrowing experience, and what a mess I made inside. *Silly me!*'

Sam glances at his friends sitting on the beach, roasting snacks over the fire. They raise their hands and wave. He responds with a warm smile, amused by their chirpy shouts. His adventure would have been harder without them.

'They're good friends, aren't they?' Noah smiles.

'Yeah. The best!'

Noah stands and looks down at Sam. 'Hey! How about we dance, you and I?'

Sam smiles. 'I love to.'

'Well, c'mon then!'

Standing with their feet planted in the sand and their hands clasped together, they begin rocking from side to side, in rhythm to the rolling waves. Listening to nature's accompaniment, they imagine coming together for a simple waltz. They dance, making circles in the sand, and then Noah lifts Sam off the ground and swings him in a half-circle, just as he used to do with Lily. Sam laughs with surprise as he is lifted from the ground, feeling the cold air brushing against his cheeks.

Sitting on the knoll, the others watch attentively. Even Addie is enthralled by this tender scene: *marshmallows, snacks and a show*. Techna hurries towards the fire, eager for another handful of marshmallows. Gaia remains seated, intently watching Noah and Sam dancing across the beach. He is reminded of the warm sensation genuine affection brings. A smile spreads across the guardian's lips. It is a feeling he has not experienced for a long time. He begins humming a familiar tune. It is a song he has not sung since Terra went away.

'It was one small step - and then there's two.
And here they are, coming into view,

Tis a pleasant sight in my eyes.

Here they swing, here they dance.
Here they laugh, here they shout,
And here they prance!

Caught up in the moment, he composes a new verse:

He is good. He is kind.
He was like her!
With a heart worth more than gold,
Yes… he is kind.'

The white guardian pauses. A tight frown stretches across his face and his moth-feelers droop. In a softer, more demure tone, he continues:

'Oh Gaia, you fool!
Why'd you tread in water?
How could you stay hidden from this?
When this… Sam… is just like… her.'

Noah and Sam are spinning around at arm's length, completing full circles. Sam feels the air flow around his frame, dragging the strands of his scarf off his face and across his shoulders. After the fourth spin they stop. Their feet push into the sand, burying their toes.

Noah bends over, clutching his chest. 'Sorry. All that spinning around is making me dizzy, reminding me of... *Ugh!* That damn caramel pudding. I think we should stop.'

'Uh! We have stopped.' Sam replies.

'Oh, right.'

BOOM!

'Hey!' Jumping to her feet, Mal steps across the knoll. *'What's that?'*

Above their heads is a brightly lit object. It is gliding down towards them. All eyes are transfixed on the approaching oval-shape, which settles onto the sand, a short distance from the knoll. Its high-pitched engines wind down, until there is silence. The light fades around the shape, revealing a spacecraft: a large, smooth, silvery egg-shaped vehicle. Its black-tipped nose is shaped like a dolphin. It has a single round window framed in shiny brass, but it is too high for them to see through. White wings slide slowly out from its side; painted in royal blue stripes. Along the side of the craft, printed vertically in big bold letters is the legend: 'VEGA'.

'What's that?' Addie gasps. 'Is it a spaceship?'

'It's the spacecraft I saw in the library.' Sam explains. 'The VEGA, but is this the genuine thing or a replica?'

'But more importantly,' Mal interjects, 'what is it doing here?'

Noah steps towards the spacecraft and slides his hand over the smooth surface. Scanning the body of the craft carefully, he says, sorrow choking his words. 'I think I understand.' A long, thin sigh passes from his lips as his body glows in a faint, golden light.

The others crowd forward, converging around Noah. 'Sir?' Frank asks. 'Does this mean…?'

'I'm afraid so.'

Sam grabs Noah's hands. 'You're leaving?' His voice cracks with emotion. 'But I've only just met you! You can't go. *Not now!*'

'I'm sorry Sam, there's something I have to do. The satellite, the one we were meant to install, I must complete my mission.' Noah rests a hand on Sam's shoulder and smiles. 'Don't worry about me, I'll be okay. I have my mission, just as you and your friends have yours: the Fleur de Vie. You've found it, it's in good hands.'

Sam rubs his hand across his shoulder and digs his feet deeper into the fine sand. 'Yeah, I suppose.'

Noah turns full circle, acknowledging the concerned expressions worn by Sam's friends. 'You have all proved loyal to Sam, through everything that has happened. He's fortunate to have you as his companions, his friends.'

Faces blush a range of pinks and reds.

Mal chuckles. 'Oh, it's nothing.'

'Yeah!' Addie grins sheepishly. 'And sorry about the arrows.'

They are interrupted by a hissing sound, which signals the door of the spaceship sliding open, sending clouds of vapour pouring over the sand. There is a musky smell lingering inside, which tickles everyone's nostrils. From inside the spacecraft, they hear *beeping* and *blipping*. There is an impressive control panel with rows and rows of flashing multicoloured lights.

'Ah! My mission is about to resume.' Noah turns and holds Sam close. 'We're heading for the next part of our journeys. We both have challenges ahead of us, and the next one is going to be a doozy, that's for sure.' Parting, they hold each other by the hand. 'We don't know what's going to happen, not for sure, but I know in my heart that you'll succeed Sam. You will succeed in making the Fleur de Vie bloom again.'

The party choruses. 'For sure, sir!'

'Please, it's Noah; being called *"sir"* isn't my thing. And Sam?'

'Yes?'

'Do it with a smile on your face.'

'I will, Pa.'

Noah steps forward to embrace Sam one final time. Sam is shaking, but relaxes as Noah gently rubs his back. It is a reassuring gesture that says everything is going to be fine. Burying his face deeper into Noah's shoulder, he digs his fingers into the soft insulated suit.

The others watch on quietly. Removing his hat, Frank holds it tightly in his hands. Mal and Addie hold hands, managing to maintain their composure. Watching intently, Bonnie's ears and tail droop as she offers a soft comforting whine. Cedric and Dr Woodchuck are struggling to control their emotions as tears pool inside the woodchuck's glasses.

'There, there.' Cedric mutters, gingerly patting the woodchuck's back.

Stepping away, Noah punches Sam lightly on the shoulder. He then picks up his space helmet and squeezes it over his head, securing the fastenings.

Turning to Sam and his friends, he says. 'You'll be fine Sam! With your gentle and compassionate nature, all's going to be swell.' Then he winks and offers everyone a thumbs up. 'See you later!'

They stand as statues as Noah steps into the spaceship, watching the VEGA's door slide shut: *HIIIISSSS! SNAP!*

Strapping himself into his chair, Noah sets about working on the array of levers and buttons. Outside, Sam and the others pace a safe distance from the steaming spacecraft. Finally, with his tasks completed, Noah leans back into his chair and stares skyward through the thick glass, gazing up at the stars.

'Mission control. This is Noah McKenzie of the VEGA. I am ready for ignition.'

He waits a few seconds, counting down from ten in his head... before pulling a long, red lever. Blast-off!

WHOOSH!

Steam billows out from the VEGA, carpeting the sand and sending the spacecraft into the evening sky. It is a majestic object, rising from the ground. A bird reaching for the stars. Below the audience watch in awe, lifting their hands to their forehead and saluting the astronaut on his final mission. Mal waves her handkerchief, whilst Frank presses his large brim hat to his chest.

Addie hollers, fiercely waving her hands at the sky. 'So long, rocket man!'

They observe the spacecraft surging towards the upper atmosphere, snipping through thin sheets of cloud, reaching closer and closer to the heavens.

Noah stares at the array of stars blinking back at him. What a beautiful background to fly your vessel into. The sky grows darker as the VEGA draws higher. He glances over his shoulder at the world falling away; at Sam disappearing as a hue of rose-coloured light. Below he knows that Sam is smiling proudly at him, just as Lily had when he first departed on his mission. His eyes sting and he turns away to study the astral screen.

'I love you Sam.'

Back on the knoll, watching the light of the VEGA flicker in the twilight sky, Sam stands perfectly still as the wind plays with the strands of his scarf. As the final trace of the spacecraft disappears into the black void, he holds his right hand over his chest and pulls his scarf across his shoulder. His fingers squeeze the fleecy texture as he lowers his gaze and stares out over the ocean with its soothing rolling waves.

'Take care, Pa.'

He feels a consoling hand rest on his shoulder. It belongs to his good friend, Frank.

'You did good partner.'

'Yeah! You've earned yourself a pat on the back!' Addie chimes. 'You've showed a lotta courage, watching your pop leave like that.'

Mal adds. 'And with such dignity, too!'

Sam smiles, feeling his spirits lift. 'Thanks guys.'

His friends bundle around in an affectionate group tackle, which makes him laugh. As they separate, he remembers the glass orb inside his jacket pocket and his own mission.

'We should make our way to the Puppis. We have our own journey to complete.'

'Yeah! Absolutely,' Addie starts. 'Where are we going?'

'To Melsey. I think that would be best.'

'Alright then! Onwards we go! Anchor's away! Full-speed ahead!'

The party make their preparations to board the Puppis. The slow soft purr of its propeller spinning greets them as they climb aboard. The craft is ready to leave.

Techna grabs the last of the marshmallows before catching up with Gaia, who is making his own way to the airship.

'Hey, have I missed anything?'

*

A waning crescent moon hangs low in the night sky, accompanying the Puppis as it sails eastwardly. The sky is clear and there is a following cool breeze that carries a sweet lavender fragrance. Glowing white flower petals flutter through the air, shimmering in the moonlight. Swirling around the sheep masthead, they dance in front of the airship, before slipping along its sides and trail behind the air-sac. The reassuring sound of the rope-locks twang in response to the Puppis gently rocking in the air currents. It is peaceful and quiet.

The party settle on the main deck, seated around a table. Rice tea is to be served from the kettle, brewing on the small stove in the galley below. Dr Woodchuck and Cedric sit on the upper part of the deck, watching the helm spin from side to side. Its hinges squeaking with every swing.

Dr Woodchuck mutters. 'Tis a quiet night.'

'Aye.' Cedric replies.

'No black clouds. No signs of the Nether creatures.'

'Aye.'

'Anything else to say?'

'Nah!'

The kettle whistles, signalling that tea is ready. Carrying the kettle onto the deck, Mal pours hot water into each mug, handing the first to Sam.

'Does anyone know what the Fleur de Vie looks like in full bloom?' She asks, gazing at the glass orb held in Sam's palm.

'Gaia? Techna?' Addie hollers. 'Any thoughts?'

'The Fleur de Vie is a mysterious plant. It's a bohemian,' Gaia explains, 'but this is a seedling, so we can't tell which flower will bloom. It might be a rose, an iris, or some other type of exotic looking flower. Who knows? I can't remember what it bloomed into the last time. It was such a long time ago. It is up to the Aether to show us its new form.'

Addie chimes. 'That sounds like something you can do, Sammy.'

All heads turn towards Sam.

'Me? But how do I decide what the Fleur de Vie will bloom into?'

'There's no need to overthink this, Sam.' Techna offers a reassuring smile. 'The seedling is with us, and once bloomed, the Fleur de Vie will calm the storms. Its rejuvenating powers will overcome the Nether and put an end to its negative schemes.'

As the others nod with enthused agreement, Gaia turns away and folds one wing over the other. He glances down at the floorboards. 'I hope that's true.' He mutters quietly to himself.

When they finish their rice tea, Mal collects the dirty mugs and kettle and carries them down the hatch and into the galley. Sam folds the table and stores it in the main hatch. Meanwhile, Frank completes his routine of checking the rope-locks while the others relax on deck. Above their heads, glowing flower petals zip and sway over the air-sac, making mesmerising dancing circles and tiny pattering sounds as they bounce gently against the leather fabric.

'Hey, so I was thinking,' Addie starts, hands held behind her head, watching the petals floating above. A few land on her nose and she brushes them away. 'You and Gaia will be leaving, once the Nether has been taken care of.'

'Wha? How do you know about that?' Gaia demands.

'I heard Techna and Sam talking about it this morning. What can I say, I have sharp ears.'

'Yes we will. We've been here too long.' The white guardian continues. 'It's difficult remembering what things were like before the Nether came. But once it's defeated, I think we will leave.'

'I know this sounds sentimental,' Addie's voice softens, 'but I'll miss you fellas. You've been great guides, even if our first meeting was awkward.'

'Your reaction was understandable, and I should apologise for my attitude towards you.'

'No need. We were both rude.'

'Heh! It's a small world, you might say.'

*

Their journey brings them back to Farley, where the Puppis edges slowly over the parish. The coastal town is shrouded in darkness: all lights inside houses and shops are extinguished. The exception is Fye's. The lighthouse peers over the ocean, swinging its narrow beam of light over land and sea. Sam is awake, leaning over the side of the airship. He tries catching a glimpse of Greg's house below, but it proves impossible to see anything in the dark. Instead he imagines Greg and Nina below him, perhaps watching the airship as it passes overhead. But it is late, and the reality is they are tucked away in bed and oblivious of them passing overhead. Turning his attention to the stars, he listens to the comforting sound of the airship's propeller rumbling behind.

He sighs. 'The Aether must stop the Nether, even if I'm the person who must confront it. There's a good enough chance we'll prevail, right?'

'Yes Sam,' Gaia replies, 'but we must wait for the right time.' He looks up at the sky and a smile crosses his lips. 'My! Just look at how peaceful it is, with the flower petals carried in the wind. It's hard to accept that something dreadful is happening.'

*

The Puppis turns southwards at daybreak. But it will take another day and night before they reach the entrance to the mountain valley and Glen Bó. When they finally approach the town, Frank peers through the gathering gloom, thinking of Faye and Ms. Hummus and hoping they might be thinking of him. He is distracted by a high-pitched metallic grinding sound. Gazing towards the square, he notices that each of the four cornered windmills are motionless. Their huge blades stand rigid. Surprised he takes a step back, mindful that in his short life he has never seen the powerful windmills stationary. Perhaps they are undergoing maintenance, he reasons. *Not all four at the same time!* He distracts himself with his task of checking the rope-locks.

*

On and on they push, over the mountains. By morning they approach a series of giant white windmills looking over the pastures. The air smells sweet here. The windmills here are working, their giant blades propelled by the wind, chasing trails of flower petals and scattering them high into the air. It is an impressive sight. But as the Puppis nears the first windmill, it screeches to a rusty halt, showering electrical sparks from the blades. Frank looks on as the white structure slowly morphs to a charcoal grey.

'That's odd.' Mal gasps. 'Did you see that has windmill stopped rotating?'

'Yeah! Yeah it did!' Addie frowns. 'But why?'

'I don't know,' replies Techna, concerned, 'but it's happening to the others too!'

One-by-one the windmills cease turning and their white frames blacken from their hinges. They spot familiar wisps of a dark purple vapour erupting from the blades, evidence that the Nether's dark power is at work. Above their heads, thick grey clouds begin covering the sky, threatening rain. Within moments they are caught in a thunderous storm that splashes hard on the deck. Puddles form quickly. Everyone retreats into the captain's cabin, grabbing blankets and feather pillows to wrap around their bodies. They huddle together as the storm's ferocity increases.

Cedric slams the door shut. 'Not again!' He moans, fluffing up his feathers and showering everyone in a fine spray. 'Ooh! What a soggy mess!'

'You're telling me.' Dr Woodchuck scoffs, shaking water droplets from his fur, which has puffed up, making the woodchuck appear much rounder than normal. 'I couldn't stay out in this. I'm a woodchuck, not an otter.'

'Nor a sitting duck!'

Techna glances at the ceiling, listening to the rain pattering outside. 'My word, what a change in the weather!' He exclaims, with a curious lilt. 'It was nice and clear when we were passing the mountains. Huh, shoddy weather forecast I'd say.'

'And what's caused the windmills to stop so abruptly?' Sam queries, 'Was it the storm?'

'I don't know. But the sudden loss of energy is a concern, as well as the windmills changing colour to that dull shade of dark grey.' Techna's eyes glow briefly. 'Something's happening here. Something bad.'

Addie rolls her eyes. 'You don't think?'

Frank dives into his bed. 'Let's just stick inside until the storm passes. The Puppis will take care of us.'

The airship battles forcefully through the storm, twisting and bending in the wind, swaying from side to side and dipping precariously over the pastures below. The continuous force of the driving winds begins loosening the rope-locks securing the air-sac, which causes the airship to judder violently. Frank is first to react. Pulling on his raincoat he leads the others onto the deck. Even Cedric is keen to help and battles valiantly against the wind, until it proves too much, and he is blown back inside the cabin. Reaching the top deck, Frank grabs the helm as Sam and Mal struggle to tighten the rope-locks.

A ferocious gust shoves Frank to one side. Desperately, he tries pulling the helm about. 'We've got to keep the Puppis on course.' He yells. 'Mal! Sam!'

'We're doing all we can here!' Mal cries, straining against the forceful winds. Her grasp on the rope loosens and she topples across the deck. 'Addie! Have you a free hand?'

Addie rushes to help, followed by Cedric, who has managed to extract himself from inside the cabin.

'I'm barely keeping up, what with this wind, bunny-ears!' Cedric squawks, grabbing the rope in his beak and pulling hard. He feels his grip slip and topples backwards, sliding through puddles accumulating on the deck and back into the captain's cabin. His soaked feathers spray water over the startled occupants. 'By my feathers, my friends! This gale's a devil!'

Meanwhile, Sam pulls hard on the rope he is holding, forming a knot with the rope lock and fixing it in place.

'*Whoa!*'

A fierce gust forces him off his feet and he too slides across the drenched deck.

Frank groans. 'It's at times like this that I wish the Puppis had seat belts!'

The humans continue struggling against nature, fighting for control. The Puppis, caught in the height of the storm, tilts to one side. One of the rope-locks has broken loose causing the vital securing rope to break free. Mal is first to react. She climbs over the edge of the craft and reaches out with her free arm for the flaying rope. With the rain spraying over her, she glances over the wing and the ground below. It looks an awfully long way down. But for once the wind is assisting, pushing against her body and preventing her from falling overboard. Focusing on the loose rope swaying before her, she grabs it and in one deft movement, leaps back on deck to thread the rope through the lock. With Addie's help, she pulls hard, securing the lock before twisting the rope securely around the metal loop. She tightens the knot. The Puppis rights itself and Sam hurries across to congratulate Mal on her efforts.

She gasps. 'That was a real rush.'

The moment is interrupted by a loud rumble from within the thick, dark clouds hovering menacingly above the air-sac. The noise startles everyone standing on deck, causing them to drop to their knees. On the top deck Frank's hands are torn from the helm, causing the wheel to spin rapidly. The Puppis spins, caught in the relentless air currents swirling about the airship. There are screams of panic as the world flails around as their fragile frames bounce against the sides of the craft and everything in-between. At any moment they may be thrown overboard. But then, unexpectedly, the wind calms and the rain eases. The Puppis regains its course. There is a communicable sigh as everyone realises the danger is over, for now. They pick themselves up and head for the captain's cabin to recover.

*

The rest of the day and the following night passes uneventfully. The party is greeted by another bleak morning with heavy clouds forming a dark leaden sky. The Puppis begins descending, heading towards a small farming village. It is the same village Sam had walked past at the beginning of his adventure. The village appears abandoned. There are no signs of the farmers Sam had watched working in the fields. Fields that are now devoid of crops. Where are the villagers and their livestock? They can see no-one. The small houses have blackened windows, the tiny chimneys are cold and there is no trace of smoke. Despite feeling exhausted from the previous storm, the party decide to reveille and recover the remaining food from the galley. The storm has succeeded in tipping the large soup pot and spilling its contents over the galley floor. Collecting broken chucks of pecan cakes and handfuls of sorry-looking fruit, they return to the captain's cabin with their meagre findings.

'Man, what a journey!' Addie mutters, running her fingers through her messy hair. 'I hope we find ourselves a food court soon.'

'Yeah. If anything, I would go for a pizza.' Frank shivers, despite the thick blanket he has wrapped around himself.

Sam looks out through the porthole, watching the mountains shrink from view. 'I think we must be nearing Melsey.'

'I hope so.' Mal offers a pitiful whine. 'I want my land legs back.'

'I do too, Mal. I do too.'

CLANG!

The Puppis is brought to an abrupt halt. It has collided with something solid.

Mal lifts her head. 'What was that?'

'Maybe we've hit a food court?' Addie replies, hopefully.

Sam stands and walks from the captain's cabin. 'I'll go and check.'

Splashing through puddles in his steel-toe boots, he sprays water over the deck. The air is still and cold. He stops in his tracks, a reaction to the strong, pungent smell that has greeted him. Wrapping his scarf tightly around his face, he climbs onto the top deck. Beyond the bow, he finds the top of a large billboard. The tiny lights around its giant frame are glowing a dull amber colour. Looking over the sheep masthead, he catches sight of emerging black clouds, billowing towards them. Beneath the clouds he spots faint lights blinking from shadowy, depressed-looking buildings. The lights surrounding the billboard sign continue to flicker, struggling to maintain power; flashing and fizzing as the energy inside them fluctuates.

POP!

CRACK!

HISS!

The amber lights turn a menacing red and momentarily burns brightly, accompanied by an electrical fizzing sound. Then, as their energy is exhausted, they dim to nothing. The road below the Puppis lies empty. Its surface is cracked and severely corroded. Feeling anxious, Sam gazes out towards the horizon and the swirling thick black clouds patterned with flashes of purple lightning, accompanied by rumbling thunderclaps.

A gasp trails from his lips as he stumbles over the helm. *What has happened to Melsey?*

A City Laid to Waste

The once thriving city of Melsey has been reduced to a shattered, crumbling ruin. The atmosphere is eerie and quiet, a striking contrast to its previous vibrancy. Buildings stand consumed inside thick grey clouds as rain floods the city. The streets are pitted with cracks and potholes, littered with a myriad of dirty grey puddles and strewn with abandoned vehicles. A single empty tram carriage sits stuck, rusted to the tracks. A solitary rook, perched on a railing adjacent to one of the blackened building, observes this solemn scene. Sporadically it caws, hopeful of hearing a reply, but nothing comes. The stillness is burst by the high-pitched screech of a Nethmite. The rook frantically beats its wings and escapes to the skies.

Central Park lies bereft of healthy plants. The trees are shorn, their branches stripped bare, leaving only paled pillared frames. The fountain is bone-dry, its once proud statue stands damaged and abandoned. The luscious plants that decorated the park have long since been consumed by greedy Nethmites. These relentless creatures now roam the city as rulers of their newly plundered kingdom. A lone red rosebud stands beside the gravel path, the target of the short plump Nethmite slinking towards it. The tiny flower twitches, reflecting the vibrations created by the approaching creature. Stretching its greedy grinning beak the Nethmite offers the flower the briefest of sniffs, before snatching it up from its roots and snapping the fragile stem into pieces. The plant slides down its jaws as the creature gulps down its prize. Another Nethmite staggers forward, scavenging the ground for any remaining fragments. It sniffs at a fallen petal, craning its cruel jaws, but the first Nethmite turns and hisses viciously and drives the interloper away.

The city's buildings are fractured and covered in soot-black patches. Most have sharp edged metal girders growing out of them, appearing as mutated fungi burrowing through a carcass. The once tall and impressive constructions appear shrunken. Windows sit darkened with curtains or blinds drawn tightly shut. There are no lights or signs of movement from inside. The few remaining streetlights offer a dull red light and discharge a low electronic drone. The narrow streets funnel cold wet gusts of wind, intermittently accompanied by bursts of hailstones that cascade from the thick purple-black clouds looming overhead.

The Puppis creeps cautiously over the city, its wings folding inwards as it rises to clear the taller buildings. The craft creaks with every stealthy adjustment, its air-sac groaning as the ropes strain against the rope-locks. Standing by the helm Sam stares into the city, ignoring the stiff gust that dislodges his scarf from his shoulders. The craft begins to vibrate violently beneath his feet, causing him to stumble and fall onto his hands and knees. The helm starts spinning anticlockwise, its hinges screaming in protest. *Perhaps the Puppis has decided to turn around and flee.* Unperturbed, Sam picks himself up and refocuses on the broken city. The wind begins howling in protest, pounding his ears. How has this city, his beloved Melsey, been transformed into a dark shadow? His shoulders shake as he tries to control the simmering anger. Standing beside him are his friends who share his despondency, struck silent by the city laid to waste.

Gaia's azure eyes widen and flash. 'By the Aether!'

'So this is Melsey, eh?' Addie declares, hands on her hips. 'Sure looks pretty salty around the edges.'

Mal nods. 'Not to mention gloomy.'

'Dark.'

'And quiet.'

Frank climbs up to the helm and grabs the wheel, correcting the Puppis' course. As the airship passes over sunken buildings he stares at the devastation below, mindful on how bright and noisy the city had been on his previous visit.

A gust picks up his untidy ponytail. 'Gosh! This ain't the Melsey I remember,' he mutters to himself, 'it was bright and noisy and full of colour. It's terrible seeing it go so sour!' He turns to Sam. 'How long do you think it's been like this?'

But Sam does not reply. He is mesmerized by the level of devastation. Tears trickle down his cheek.

Frank glances at the guardians. 'Gaia, Techna?'

'Not long.' Techna replies. 'The Nether's power is growing more quickly than we imagined.'

'You're telling me,' Dr Woodchuck retorts, 'and this damn smog is irritating my nose!'

Bonnie gazes up at Sam. 'Things have sure changed since we left, hasn't it Sam.'

'Yeah!' Sam replies, his voice cracking as he scrubs the tears from his face. 'And we haven't been away *that* long. How can somewhere so vibrant and exciting have its essence destroyed so quickly?'

'The Nether has sure done a number here. *Wow!* They are fast travellers to have got here before us.' Addie declares, stepping across the top deck. 'But these lil' blighters will soon be quaking in their roots, now we have the Fleur de Vie.' She pats Sam's arm, adding. 'Whatever happens Sam, we're all in this together.'

'Thanks Addie.' Sam smiles, looking over the city. 'Now we must prepare for the coming storm.'

Frank carefully navigates the Puppis over the city, passing over buildings that now look part of an alien world: darkly coloured, monstrous shapes sticking up from the ground. They travel southerly and hover briefly above a line of shops, which Sam recognises as Hainsworth Road. Gazing down at the broken scene, he picks out the individual shops that were once so familiar to him. This had been the place where the gas-blast had rendered his horrific injuries. It is hard to believe that despite the events of that traumatic day, Hainsworth Road presents as even more horrendous, bleak and unwelcoming. With its rope-locks protesting, the Puppis slips on, until it reaches Cedar Avenue and grinds to a halt above the abandoned tarot shop. Frank signals Addie to drop the anchor, which crashes with a loud thud onto the stone pavement below. Sam and Mal help toss over the landing ropes, and then descend, one-by-one, onto the gravel covered road. At street level, the barren city appears even more intimidating. It is dark and cold here. *It is unnerving.* The corroding buildings loom over them, their broken windows casting ominous, pitiful expressions that seem to follow the party as they move across the street.

BANG!

The door of the tarot shop slams against its frame and as Sam approaches the wind blows open the door, which then slams shut again. It is a cycle that keeps repeating. He peers into the blackened windows, but the glass proves too dark to see through. There are tiny fragments of paper stuck onto the glass, the remnants of posters. His chest tightens, a reaction to this oppressive scene. What he needs is some of Sable's wisdom: *but she is no longer here.* Sighing with quiet resignation, he turns from the shop and hurries after the others. They are striding purposely into the surrounding gloom, alert for any movement within the black smog. Violent gusts of cold air rattle trashcans and sends cardboard boxes cascading along the narrow side-street.

From Cedar Avenue they follow the now bone-dry canal. Sam scans the buildings, searching in vain for signs of the people hiding inside. He hopes that Johnny and Mary are somewhere safe, and that Sandy and Mandy are safe too. His thoughts are interrupted by a heavy rumbling sound as the ground begins shaking. It is an all too familiar signal to run for cover. The vibrations are followed by shrilled shrieks as the road cracks open before them. Hordes of Nethmites emerge through the splintered road and adjacent pavements. They begin scavenging, pulling up and munching down on any tiny green shoots creeping through the stone.

'Just as I suspected,' Gaia mutters, 'they've been building their strength, feeding on the contents of the city, both natural and technological. They are getting stronger, which means even with the Fleur de Vie, our task is not going to be easy.'

'Not gonna be easy, is that what you think Gaia-boy!' Addie counters, grinning. 'We'll see about that! C'mon, let's get them!'

Frank primes and then shoots thick, pink cake mixture from Old Faithful at a couple of skinny Nethmites. But this only stops them temporarily, as they fling chunks of the cake mix caught in their gaping mouths. Frank takes the opportunity to step forward and bats them away with a smooth swing of Old Faithful. Addie fires a quick succession of arrows as Mal strikes one of the Nethmites on its head with her quarterstaff. Bonnie bites down on another's neck, chucking it high into the air. Sam readies his rose-coloured Aether shield, easily blocking the attack of a skinny Nethmite. Cedric too enters the melee, squawking as he charges, airborne, grabbing a short fat Nethmite and carrying it skywards, before dropping it into the dried-up canal. Dr Woodchuck swipes at another with his tail, knocking it to the ground.

'It's a good thing I've brushed my teeth this morning!' He exclaims, chomping down on the attacker and tossing it away.

'That you did, although I'm thinking you should have given them a dose of halitosis!' Cedric retorts, grabbing another Nethmite with his talons.

'Halitosis, my tail!'

WHOOSH!

The battle is interrupted by the thunderous roar of water as clouds of mist and dust balloon into the air above the Nethmites. Everyone stops in astonishment at the jet of water aimed at the attacking Nethmites, flinging them across the street. They recover quickly and reform as a group, raising their heads and chorusing a chilling screech that pierces the air. More Nethmites sprout from the ground. Shaking their heads they prepare to attack, banding together they creep closer, grinning manically. A collective deep chuckle emanates from their throats: shrilling, hissing. The party retreat, their backs pressed against the wall of a broken building...

WHOOSH!

Another powerful jet of water crashes into the Nethmites, sending them sprawling across the pavement. *What do you know!* Sandy stands opposite, holding a fire hose. Turning off the water, he blows dramatically across the tip of the hose, as if it were a smoking barrel.

'I thought you could do with some help, my friends.'

'Sandy!' Sam exclaims.

The sodden Nethmites are already regrouping. They hiss menacingly at the florist; indignantly flapping their leaf-shaped arms and spraying water everywhere.

'Uh-oh! This is getting ugly.' Sandy cries, holding open the door to his shop. 'Quick, come inside, post haste!'

Everyone charges inside and slams the door behind them. Sandy secures it using two substantial looking padlocks. Congregating by the window, they look anxiously outside. The Nethmites are lining up, preparing to slam their frames against the door.

'Brace yourselves!' Frank cries.

Taking turns, the Nethmites crash against the door, sending vibrations through the wooden frame. Each impact is accompanied by screechy frustration. Finally, following another futile effort, the Nethmites give up and shuffle away, muttering. One stops and turns, appearing to raise its leafy arm in a rude gesture.

'That should do it.' Sandy grins, clapping his hands.

It is dark inside the florist shop. The only light comes from a single ceiling lamp that swings over their heads. Sam looks around. The shop stands sad and quiet; the air inside feels humid and stuffy. On a long wooden bench there are several healthy-looking lilies and roses; the first blooms Sam has seen since returning to Melsey. No wonder the Nethmites are interested in getting inside Sandy's shop. Water trickles from a tap, where it is fixed to the hose. Sandy turns the faucet and the water drips to a stop.

CRASH!

A burst of hailstones hammer onto the rooftop. This horrendous weather appears a permanent fixture.

'Are we all here?' Sam asks, glancing around. He is met with a variety of *yeses*, but notes that the two guardians have made a discretionary retreat. 'That's good. Thanks for your help Sandy.'

'No problem. I'm so glad to see you, Sam.' Sandy says, trying to maintain a cheerful tone. 'But things are bad. Everything that was pleasant, or fun here, has been destroyed by those strange creatures, who roam freely and decimated the city.'

'How long have they been here?'

'The creatures? A few days. They appeared from nowhere, like magic, well, some dark kind of magic. Shooting up through the ground they plundered the city and have been stripping it bare ever since. They have terrified everyone. Those who haven't fled are now holed up inside the remains of buildings, despite them becoming more unstable. They have chewed electric pylons, ripped up flowers and stripped the bark from the trees! They are very greedy critters, let me tell you that!'

'Sam!'

Mandy steps out from the rear of the shop. She looks dishevelled, her usually neatly plaited hair looks frazzled. Gripping her pink jacket tightly across her chest with one hand, she holds her precious mobile phone in the other. Tired, weary eyes suggests she has not been sleeping well.

'You're back, that's awesome! Although you could have come back sooner.' She clicks her tongue impatiently. 'And what do you know about all these blighters? I mean, what are they and what have they done?' She pauses, aware of everyone staring at her. 'You know, I can't even text my friends anymore. They're really messing with my mind.'

'Whoa! Whoa missy!' Addie interjects, standing between Sam and Mandy. 'No need to bite more than you can chew! It's not Sammy's fault he's late for the party.'

Mandy scowls defiantly. 'Oh good, someone is finally going to get rid of those things. Best get cracking then, shorty.'

Addie puffs up her cheeks and steps towards Mandy.

But Sam plants a hand on her shoulder. 'Easy Addie. Mandy's a friend of mine.' He chuckles, switching his gaze between the two. 'And from where I'm standing, you appear as two peas in a pod.'

'What!' Mandy exclaims.

'Sammy!' Addie demands. 'What do you mean by that?'

Sam ignores their protests and turns to Sandy. 'You said the Nethmites arrived a few days ago?'

'We began noticing weird changes in the park.' Sandy explains, wincing as Mandy clears her throat. 'Well Mandy did, originally. It was as if the lifeforce of everything inside the city was being drained.' He frowns. 'Then these creatures appeared and began stripping the trees and plants. And the fountains and canal dried-up, despite this endless rain.'

'What about the people?'

'Many escaped, jumping into vehicles and fleeing at the first sight of the creatures. But the creatures then attacked the trams and trains, consuming the energy from the city.' Sandy peers through the window, staring at the empty street outside. 'So they're called *Nethmites*, these creatures? They could have come straight from a fairy-tale: the stuff of nightmares.'

'Believe me sir, we've run into Nethmites on many, many occasions,' Mal counters, 'and despite their size and appearance, they mean business. True to their name, they are parasitic in nature. They've taken my home in Greystagg forest, and now they have mastered Melsey. The creatures are able to blight both nature and all things technological too. Nothing is safe from their advances.'

Sandy whistles. 'Yeh! I've seen them munching down on just about anything. That's weird, uneasy stuff. Like termites, huh? Metal munching termites!' He sighs sadly.

Sam asks. 'Do you know if Johnny and Mary okay?'

Sandy bows his head. 'I'm sorry Sam. I haven't heard from them since the first attacks. And I dare not leave the shop with the creatures circling. I guess everything is bordered shut now, including their coffee shop. But I'm sure they're fine.'

'I hope you're right.'

'I'm sure they are, Sam!' Mandy smiles reassuringly. 'There are still people here, hiding inside buildings and maintaining a low profile, waiting for those damn blighters to move on.'

'Do you know how many people are trapped inside?'

'No idea. Some who couldn't leave stayed like Sandy and me, despite the city collapsing into a wasteland.' Mandy explains. 'I didn't know what to do, or where to go, apart from to stay here with Mr Sanderson. At least I'm not alone, and it's nice and sound here. There's no way those creepy critters can get inside.'

Sam eyes the row of plants sitting proudly on shelves, their petals and leaves flittering from a light cool draught. These plants are too tempting for hungry Nethmites to give up on. And right on cue.

BANG!

'Uh! I think something's knocking on the door.' Frank gasps.

They stare at the door as it is hit, again and again, with tremendous force. The top hinge has loosened, and screws start dropping to the floor.

BANG! BANG! BANG!

The floor of the florist shop buckles, sending chips of wood flying into the air. The metallic hissing of the Nethmites sound much closer than previously. They continue their assault on Sandy's florist shop, except they are now more organised and are targeting identified weaknesses in its defences: the hinges on the door are one; and having created cracks in the concrete foundation, the wooden floorboards are another.

CRASH!

The whole shop shudders as several heavier Nethmites crash against the door, ripping it from its frame. The door slams to the floor, accompanied by a resounding cry.

'RUN!'

Bolting out through the rear door and into the alley outside, they leave the Nethmites bursting through the broken doorway behind them. Others emerge through the floorboards and clamber eagerly for their feast. Fights break out between Nethmites desperate to munch down on the fresh roses and lilies inside the shop. Others are distracted by electrical cables, preferring to chew on the wiring, stripping away the plastic insulation. The lighting dims before fizzing to darkness. In the resulting chaos, the party continue to make their escape.

Sandy whimpers, finally defeated by the Nethmites. 'My flowers! My flowers!'

But he knows he has no other option but to flee and leave his precious plants to their fate. He follows Sam and his friends, running along the side alley and into the empty street. They head for the park, feet trampling and splashing through numerous puddles. The smog is getting thicker, shrouding the buildings in shadow. As they approach the towering park gates, Sam halts abruptly at the entrance, causing the others to stop behind him. They are met by a mechanical droning that sends chills through the air. The threatening sound gets louder and louder. Concealed behind a corroding statue adjacent to the park gates, Sam peers towards the central fountain. Hovering above the fountain's dry-stone bowl is a large, winged serpent creature, its body covered in thick metal scales and pulsating finlike wings that stretch across its head and shoulders. The creature's head turns slowly, patrolling the park with its single piercing eye.

Mandy gasps. 'What is that thing?'

'I don't know.' Sam replies. 'It has to be another Nether creature, but not one we've come across before. It's like a serpent, but with wings.'

'Just what we need,' Addie snorts, 'a flying Nethmite.'

'Nether creature, another one?' Mandy exclaims. 'The tone of her voice rising anxiously, causing the others to gesture urgently in an attempt to quieten her. 'That can't be right. It's way bigger than those critters in the shop. But what I wanna know is this: what is this ugly-looking monster doing here?'

The beast turns its head, spotting them hiding behind the statue. Its eye glows crimson red and its body starts shaking, sending out an agitated rattling sound that reverberates through the air.

'Oops...' Mandy yelps, ducking her head.

Techna cries. 'Take cover!'

'Who said that?' Sandy asks, perplexed. 'Was it that raven?'

'Just duck Sandy!' Sam drags the florist to the ground, just as the beast lunges forward.

CRASH!

It strikes hard, but fortunately it misses Sandy and slams into the statue instead, smashing it into pieces. The serpentine Nethmite swoops high, its long body swirling like a ribbon in the air; its scale swathed in a deep-red glowing light. They retreat to take cover behind a stone wall, mesmerised by the giant beast patrolling the park. Eventually it slips away, gliding through a gap between two buildings. Relieved, they watch as the deep red-light fades into the distance, and then step out from behind their hiding place.

'Wow!' Mal gasps. 'What a rush.'

'You're telling me. The creature reminds me of the sea leviathan.' Addie says, brushing rubble from her clothing. 'Just thinking about it makes me shake in my boots. There's no way Silverhair will strike it down!'

There is a murmur of acknowledgement before Frank declares, anxiously. 'Let's get out of here, before it decides to return.'

*

Leaving the park, they maintain a cautious lookout for the Nethmites; pacing quietly through empty streets, paraded by vacant soulless buildings. They reach a line of small shops and stop outside the remains of a greengrocer, with its ripped green and white striped canopy. The shop sits dark and forgotten. The pavement is littered with empty trays and boxes that have been turned upside down and inside out, and chumped into tiny pieces. Addie sighs, rubbing her stomach. The fruit and vegetables they once contained have long since been gobbled up by the Nethmites. All that remains are the faintest smears of rotting skins spread across the pavement. They push on, passing more desolated shops: a butcher, a bakery, and even a candlestick maker. Everywhere the shops stand empty, their interiors ripped apart.

Addie stops in her tracks; she has spotted something. 'Hey, what's that over there?'

The others look towards where she is pointing. Sitting behind the road they can see an access to a small grove that lies dark and abandoned. The small wooden gate at the entrance has been hacked to pieces and lies scattered over the ground: wooden chunks covered tattletale bitemarks. A handful of cawing crows stand atop the broken stone wall, scraping their beaks against the rocky fragments. At least these birds are brave enough to remain inside the city.

Sam mutters something inaudible. *He knows this place well.* Witnessing the broken gate causes an uneasy fear to creep through his body as he hastens towards a gap in the wall. As he passes through the entrance the watching crows scatter. Sam stops just inside the bordered grove and stands alone on the exposed ground, between trees that stands as white skeletons. They peer accusingly at him, their fragile branches groaning as the wind brushes overhead. A silvery-shaded branch breaks and falls, landing beside his feet. *How can this small peaceful sanctuary be transformed into something so bleak and depressing?* He is joined by his friends who carefully step over fallen branches and broken stone, consumed by the oppressive atmosphere. Encouraged by the silence, the crows return and perch on branches overlooking the party huddled below.

Walking towards an arch-shaped stone, Sam stumbles over the broken path and falls headlong onto the parched earth. Resting on his knees, he stares in mounting disbelief at the marble stone before him. Its once smooth polished surface, bordered with etched lilies, is chipped and broken with a deep crack running through it. At its base lies the stripped remains of a bouquet, surrounded by scattered strips of cellophane. His friends stand behind Sam, staring solemnly over his shoulders.

'Whoa Sam! What's up now?' Addie gasps, gazing down at the headstone; her face frozen in realisation. 'Aren't those flowers… Wait. No!'

'No way!' Mal and Frank cry.

Sam leans forward and presses his forehead against the cold broken marble. Fighting back tears, he grabs at the gravel with his fingers.

'What have they done?' He whispers, his voice cracking with emotion.

No-one knows what to say. There are no words that can offer their friend any comfort. Mandy grunts and shakes her head, wanting to gesture to the others that she understands how terrible wanton vandalism is. Mal, Frank and Addie exchange desperate glances. The others can only look on dumbfounded. It is Sandy who steps forward and places a consoling hand on Sam's shoulder.

'Sam, I'm so sorry,' he starts, his voice cracking with remorse, 'I should have warned you. I can't believe they've done this to Lily. I just...' His words fade away.

The Nethmites have done a massive number on the grove, as they have everywhere else. And they continue to roam supreme throughout the Southern Island. Sam caresses the marble as Sandy helps him to his feet.

'Hey Addie,' He says, his voice barely audible, 'wanna hunt some Nethmite?'

Sam's words sink deep into Addie's psyche, forging a fierce grin across her face. She begins dancing giddily on the spot.

'*Aw, YIPEE!*' She cheers, raising her fists skywards. 'That's what I wanna hear! Look out everyone, cause here comes Addie Hawkeye!'

Brushing the dirt and gravel from his clothes, Sam turns to Sandy and Mandy. 'You two head for the Puppis. It's located above the tarot shop. You'll be safe there.'

Mandy tilts her head. 'The Puppis? What's that?'

'It's my airship,' Frank explains, 'and she'll look after you.'

'You mean, *the airship?* But why'd you...'

'Good thinking, Captain Frank!' Techna interjects from his vantage, in his raven form perched on the branch of an adjacent tree. 'That would be the best place for these two. Cedric, Dr Woodchuck, escort them to the Puppis straight away.'

'Right!' Cedric and Dr Woodchuck reply.

They direct the confused Sandy and Mandy back through the broken gate and onto the street as Techna swoops through the air, surveying the immediate vicinity.

He mutters. 'Let's hope you can get there without any trouble.'

Dr Woodchuck trots quickly along the pavement while Cedric glides just above his head.

'Keep your eyes peeled Cedric! And I hope my feet don't get chafed from all this running!'

'Ah-ha! Flying is such an advantage, landlubber!'

'Oh, shut up!'

Bewildered, Mandy follows obediently, listening in disbelief at the two animals' conversation. 'Those animals are talking, Mr Sanderson! Can you believe it?'

'Talking animals.' Sandy chuckles. 'Now I've heard everything!'

'And there's me hoping that I wasn't hearing things.'

*

Mal offers a forlorn wave as they exit the access and disappear into the street. She sighs. 'We better make our move too!'

As his friends head out beyond the broken gate, Sam lingers behind to take a final look at the broken headstone. He stokes his hand over the fragmented lily decoration.

WHOOSH!

His reflections on everything that has happened inside the grove are interrupted by metal girders shooting out from the ground around his feet. Startled, he steps back as the earth beneath him loosens and more metal spikes sprout, twisting and turning through the air. They are forming a steel wall that threatens to block his escape.

'*RUN!!*' The others cry frantically from the gate. '*RUN! SAM! RUN!*'

Once again the crows flock to the sky, as Sam bolts across the gravel; forced to weave around the sprouting metal girders and falling branches. Leaping over a menacing metal pillar, he makes it out of the grotto, just as the metal shards seals the exit. The attack of the girders gives the party greater impetus as they hurry through the streets, trampling through puddled strewn streets. They reach a junction where a café stands half-buried in rubble, covered in metal wires interconnected into a web-like pattern that has grown across the doors and windows.

Frank leans down, resting his hands on his knees. 'So what's the plan?'

A white dove descends from the heavens and settles on an adjacent wall. 'We have to get to the centre of the storm for the Fleur de Vie to bloom.' Gaia explains. 'Sam, is the seedling safe?'

Sam feels the glass orb rolling inside his jacket. 'Yeah. I have it in my pocket.'

They are joined by Techna, who perches next to Gaia.

'Then we're good to go.' The black guardian says. 'What we seek cannot be far from here.'

CRASH!

Mal cries. 'Watch out!

The large serpentine Nethmite they had met in the park has returned, emerging from the partly buried buildings. Its scaled-body slithers through the air and stops, hovering before the party with its wings spread. It glares towards them, its red eye glowing as it emits the same dull relentless drone as before. It twists its head and releases a loud piecing shriek. From near and far Nethmites respond to its call, sending out their own terrifying chorus across the city.

'I wish they wouldn't do that!' Frank winces, covering his ears. 'It's really annoying.'

Sam replies. 'I don't think they're listening.'

The creature lunges at a nearby lamppost and rips it out of the ground, sending huge clods of debris into the air. It tosses the remains at the party, but Sam responds by holding up his rose-coloured shield and deflects it safely away. Addie blows a triumphant raspberry towards the clearly irritated creature.

Techna is busy studying the surrounding buildings, thinking hard for a plan to distract the creature. His tail twitches hesitantly as his wings glow with a bright blue hue. 'People are watching and viewing our actions with suspicion,' he turns to Gaia, 'but I don't think we have a choice.'

'I know Tech. It is time to reveal the truth to those hiding behind the curtains.'

The guardians' new resolve is met by a brilliant flash of light as they transform into their dragon-bird hybrids. Several curtains move revealing faint lights diffusing from inside the surrounding buildings; revealing silhouettes, darkened figures who stop and stare out into the street. The unexpected sight of the mysterious guardians only adds to the series of astonishing events the inhabitants inside have experienced. The guardians muster a fierce attack on the mechanical serpentine Nethmite, smashing the terrifying creature into the side of a building with a thunderous crash. The creature retaliates, lunging forward it sends Gaia hurtling into a nearby pylon. The wires tangle around the white guardian's wings, singeing his feathers. Gaia scrambles to his feet, his moth-feelers twitching.

'Go on!' Techna cries to Sam and his friends, extracting the white guardian from the coils of cable wrapped around him. 'We've got this.'

Once Gaia is free the guardians launch another attack on the Nethmite, firing bolts of rose-coloured Aether. The creature snarls and charges towards the guardians. The engaged combatants are captured inside thick clouds of dust and debris.

'C'mon, you heard Techna.' Bonnie cries, morphing into her dire wolf form. 'Hop on my back!'

Mal and Frank climb onto her back, pausing to glance at the large dusty ball containing the heads and tails of fighting creatures which periodically emerge from out of the chaotic melee. The guardians battle fiercely with the metallic beast to buy time for Sam and his friends to locate the centre of the storm. Bonnie leaps down the street with Sam and Addie running alongside, skimming past metal girders spurting out from the walls of buildings. One scratches Bonnie's shoulder and draws a cut, but the dire wolf keeps running. They hear hordes of Nethmites chasing them, their metallic shrieks getting louder and louder. Bonnie swerves to avoid the snapping at her heels, a manoeuvre that nearly succeeds in throwing Frank and Mal off her back. But the gaining Nethmites are able to attack in numbers, forcing the party to stop and stand their ground. Bonnie grabs a Nethmite by the neck and tosses it away. Addie manages to release several arrows and Frank fires his cake-mix into a crowd of metallic attackers, but there are too many. The Nethmites advance, demonstrating the full force of the Nether's power, firing its dark aubergine-coloured energy into the brave party and sending them sprawling across the ground.

Bonnie howls. 'Sam! Above you!'

A single Nethmite leaps through the air, aiming for Sam, who counters by hitting the attacking Nethmite hard with his rose-coloured shield. Stunned and with its beak agape, the creature slides down onto the pavement.

A short fat Nethmite crashes into Addie, pinning her to the ground. 'Hey, not fair! I didn't see you!' She whines, staring up at the grinning Nethmite. She tries pushing it away, but it is too heavy. '*Fore!*'

WHACK!

With a strong swing from her quarterstaff Mal sends the Nethmite high into the air. It crashes into a broken lamppost. A group of Nethmites musters before them and Mal steps forward and twirls her quarterstaff above her head.

'Stand aside, Addie! Mallory wants to show off her moves.'

The Nethmites snarl and charge. Two are struck by Mal's spinning quarterstaff, sending them high into the air. Two more leap forward, but these too are wacked away with such force that they roll along the ground, reaching the opposite pavement. With four of their number despatched, the other Nethmites stop in their tracks. They emit a scratchy, dumfounded cry, craning their heads to one side.

'Driving you all nuts, am I?' Mal jokes, reaching into her poncho pocket. She holds out a lump of broken pecan cake in her palm. 'I just thought I'd ask.'

She throws the cake pieces into the Nethmites' open jaws. The creatures cough and splutter, and with her foes suitably distracted, she sends them high and far with a mighty swing of her quarterstaff.

'*FORE!*'

Watching with her mouth gaping, Addie gasps. 'Whoa!'

Mal offers a few more spins before bringing the end of her quarterstaff to rest by her side. 'That's better.' She turns to Addie. 'How're you doing?'

'Aside from that grinning critter, I'm swell.' Addie replies, smirking. She gets to her feet, with Mal's helping hand. 'Looks like I've misjudged your weapon, Mal. *Unreliable* should mean, *Reliable!*'

Their moment of mutual admiration is interrupted by a heart-breaking howl.

'Bonnie!'

They race towards the dire wolf, who is surrounded by a pack of Nethmites. Already outnumbered and with her energy draining away, a large Nethmite swoops through Bonnie's defences and snags her in its jaws. Exhausted, Bonnie reverts to her pup form and manages to wriggle free. With Frank's help, Mal and Addie attack the Nethmites and force them to retreat, allowing Sam to rescue his beloved pet.

'Bonnie!' Mal cries. 'Are you alright?'

Bonnie can barely raise her gaze as the screeching Nethmites encircle the party. Their chanting sounds more and more intimidating, but they hold their attack, preferring instead to snicker and shriek a victory song. Above the battle the clouds thicken, and it begins to rain. The cries of the Nethmites, beaks open and leafy arms swaying, are joined by a low-pitched rumbling sound. The ground shudders as the party huddle close together.

'These blighters sure like to brag about their successes, huh.' Addie mutters.

A cold ominous voice reverberates through the clouds. 'They do, and there's no use running. Your journey has reached its endgame, and it's not going to be jolly.'

Sam retorts. 'What do you mean?'

'If I were you. I'd stay put: down and out!'

The wind strengthens, building into a gale that forces everyone to seek for something secure they can grab hold to as the

Nether creates a powerful vortex. Gravel and dirt is captured inside, the debris swirling skywards forming a dark, foreboding tunnel. Watching in gleeful celebration, the Nethmites double-up their revelries. Wrapping his arms around a fallen lamppost, Sam tightens his grip and glances anxiously at the others. Frank and Mal desperately cling to some railings, whilst Addie arches her back against a post-box. Without anything to purchase against, Bonnie is in trouble. She bites frantically at the ground as she is dragged helplessly across the rough road surface. Stretching out his hand, Sam makes a hopeless grab at she slides past him. He is targeted by a severe gust that snatches his hand from the lamppost, drawing him inside the swirling vortex that carries him high into the air.

His friends gasp. 'Sam!'

'Frank!'

As Sam is dragged into the air his striped scarf slips from his face, but he manages to grab it before it falls. Frank tumbles forward, and with one hand clasping the railings, reaches out and grabs Sam's foot.

'I've got you, Sam!'

But Frank is battling the terrifying force of the Nether and his attempts to stomp his pegleg into the gravel as an anchor appear futile.

'Hold on!' Mal cries, as she and Addie grab hold of Frank.

Even Bonnie musters her remaining strength to tug at Addie's trouser leg. Together they pull, and they pull, and they pull. But it is to no avail. A vicious gust snatches Frank's fingers away from Sam's foot and they fall backwards. Helpless, they watch as Sam is sucked into the sky.

'NO!' Frank cries.

As Sam disappears into thick clouds the gale weakens, and the scene below slips to an eerie silence. Frank rests on his knees, with Mal and Addie by his side, gazing up at the densely leaden sky. Bonnie nuzzles Frank's hand, offering a sorrowful whimper. Watching nearby, the Nethmites expressions twist with gloating pleasure. They slowly slip away, their task complete, leaving Frank to stare at the leaden sky. He fights hard to control the tears.

'Sam. Wherever you are, do what you can to stop the Nether! You can do it! I know you can.'

*

Strong air currents carry Sam deeper and deeper inside the clouds. Surrounded by thick mist and separated from the rest of the world, he feels the strength of the force weaken. Swallowing hard in fearful apprehension, he prepares for what comes next. He begins falling, slowly at first, but then faster and faster, spinning through the mist until he lands with a thump. On top of a rotting flower bed.

'Ow!'

Lifting his battered frame, Sam rests on his knees. He pushes his hands firmly into the soil, his fingers digging into the grit and gravel. With a deep breath, he finds the strength to stand and brush dust and debris from his clothes. Shaking his curls, he arranges his striped scarf over his scar. It is quiet here, wherever *here* is. There are distant creaking metallic sounds that are carried through air that is filled with heavy, petroleum odours. He walks towards the sound, heading for a large shape looming from out of the surrounding shadows. As he approaches he makes out broken pipes sticking out from the sides of debris piled high. There are sparks of electricity fizzing from broken wires. The rubble is the remains of a collapsed building. Sniffing the air, he grimaces. It is the same caustic stench he remembers from inside the Door of Fate.

Holding his hand over his face, Sam gasps. 'That awful smell, but why is it so much stronger here?'

He begins examining the broken building: blocks of charred and sooty concrete; the shattered windows, the door smashed into pieces. A thin column of black smoke billows through a hole in the roof. He listens to the sounds playing in his mind: hearing people panicking. This is the vision he saw inside the Door of Fate.

'Oh no!' He cries. '*That smell*. This has to be...'

'Indeed.' Interjects the soulless voice of the Nether; the clouds flashing in time with the Nether's cold words. 'I welcome you back, back to the place where you experienced that wild, wild ride.'

Sam stands motionless, recalling everything that had happened to him during the blast. When he was pinned against the door as flashes of red and yellow lights burst through him. The images of people scurrying about him, frantically seeking escape. *The loss of his right arm and his left eye.* Glancing at the swirling storm above his head, he realises that the Nether is looking down on him: gloating, taunting.

'Ha! How foolish you are, plodding into places you shouldn't.' The cloud pulsates with a deep purple glow: an ominous, scornful sight!

Sam reaches inside this jacket pocket, feeling for the glass orb. There is something he can do. *Right now!* Grasping the glass orb, he pulls it out of his pocket and lifts it above his head.

'Come on, Fleur de Vie. Do your stuff!' He cries, his body shimmering faintly with the Aether.

The orb glows brightly, its life-force strengthened by the Aether's power. It shoots a beam of energy that is met by a blast of Nether, fired from deep within the clouds. With a thundering crash, the two great energies collide, ebbing back and forth. Bright light bursts and scatters in all directions. The air is filled with a deep droning sound, which builds quickly towards a crescendo. Still holding the glass orb, Sam feels the forces acting on him as his feet slide across the uneven terrain. His hair flails about his face. With his free hand he reforms his Aether shield, and pushing his feet deeper into the gravel, he manages to hold firm. Closing his eye he mutters something under his breath. He musters a short fierce pulse, sensing that the Aether is overcoming the Nether's energy. But in that moment of hope, there is an almighty blast as the Nether delivers a powerful burst of dark purple lightning that shatters Sam's shield and throws him off his feet. The glass-orb is ripped from his grasp.

The Nether scoffs mercilessly. 'Are you seriously trying to defeat the mighty Nether with that pathetic glass-orb? My, how droll!'

Helpless, Sam watches as another bolt of dark purple lightning strikes... *CRACK!* ...shattering the glass-orb into a thousand fragments that shower splinters over Sam, lying prostrate on the ground.

'No!' He cries, staring at the tiny broken shards.

'It is done. Your pathetic Fleur de Vie is proved useless against the Nether's awesome power!'

The tiny blue-green fragments fade to a dull, lifeless grey. *There is nothing that can defeat the Nether's negative energy.* Sam's right arm stings: a sharp pain emanating from the crook of the stump. Crushed, he buries his head in his hands, coiled on the rough gravel: lost and alone.

'No... No... No...'

'Hah!' The voice booms, gleefully. 'Just as I thought, you're nothing but a feeble doll. To think that snooty Gaia was right: how petty and pathetic you humans are. And now, without your precious friends to help you, all you can do is coil up and spill tears. Poor, pitiful creature.'

'You're wrong.'

Sam struggles to get onto his feet, his legs wobbling as he tries to find the inner strength to hold himself upright. He glances wearily at the skies above.

'They know I'm here,' he says resolutely, 'and as for Gaia, he felt troubled, after what happened to Terra. But I know he believes in me too.'

Staring at the broken rubble, Sam recalls Sable's words, spoken the day they met inside her treasured tarot shop. Her words of reassurance and belief resonate with him as he pictures himself back beneath the rubble inside the Door, having trusted his instincts and acted with such selflessness. He winces, his nose wrinkling from the smell.

'Stepping inside that building, knowing the danger, but knowing too that there was a purpose: to hold the door and contain the blast. Sable believed I could do it. She knew I had something in me: the Aether.'

He steps towards the broken doorway and stares resolutely at the storm clouds. A sly grin spreads across his face. 'I may not be able to take you down, not by myself. But I know the guardians will defeat you; and I know that deep down you fear them, don't you?'

The storm clouds rumbles as the Nether contemplates Sam's words, exhibiting signs of frustration. The skies darken and a single bolt of the Nether is fired at Sam.

CRASH!

The explosion throws him across the ground. The force of impact pulls the scarf from his face.

'Hmph! Such petty drivel, doll!'

Once again Sam picks himself up, muttering under his breath, complaining at the damage suffered by his cherished scarf. Spreading out his arms, the Aether's soft rose-coloured light builds around his frame, and then in a defiant gesture, it bursts in a brilliant white flash that drives deep into the Nether cloud. His attack is greeted with a howling cry, ringing through the air. Large lumps of debris are thrown from the collapsed building rubble, revealing Gaia and Techna, who trample out looking tattered and battle weary.

Sam leaps forward, joyous at seeing the guardians again. He collapses.

Gaia gasps. 'Sam!'

Techna's bright azure eyes blaze brightly as he gazes at Sam. 'My word.'

The white guardian lifts the human gently into his arms. 'Sam, are you alright? Wait! How many claws do you see?' He lifts his paw in front of Sam, switching numbers from five to two, and back again.

Sam squints his eye and mumbles. 'Four?'

'Close enough.'

The white guardian glares up at the clouds, which is brewing into a more powerful storm. It is laughing at them, taunting them. Gaia sighs and closes his eyes, pushing the guilt still festering inside him.

'This is all our fault, for allowing our human friends to get in the way of the Nether. Just as we did with Terra.'

In his mind he sees his dear shaman friend, Terra: spiritual and energetic. Her long golden locks flowing in the wind as she dances through sunny thickets. Her joyous laughter trickles through his mind.

'This world is precious to you, as it is for us, but we've let it fall to the Nether. I'm sorry, Terra. I'm sorry, Sam.' Gaia opens his eyes, his paw lying reassuringly on Sam's shoulder. 'But we won't let this happen.' Turning to Techna, he extends his wings. 'This will be our finest hour, Tech.'

Techna's moth-feelers stand erect. 'Gaia?'

'The Nether must be stopped, no matter the cost. Let's tear it down with all the Aether we can muster.'

Techna grins as he takes Gaia's paw. 'How can I refuse? Let's show this malevolent wanna-be what we're truly made of.'

Sam watches the two guardians as an electric blue and golden hue encompasses their bodies. Their wings glow, shimmering brightly against the Nether's dark clouds.

He cries. 'Gaia! Techna!'

'Let's go!'

Gaia and Techna leap forward, spinning in circles as they drill up through the clouds, their bodies dazzling with a brilliant light. The heavens rumble as the guardians fire beams of Aether into the centre of the clouds, opening a tunnel. Sam spots a faint patch of green in the depth of the storm. *What could that be?* His curiosity into this anomalous reassuring patch of colour at the far end of the tunnel is interrupted by a huge flash of light that fills the sky. A signal that the guardians have reached the centre of the cloud, and are plunging deep into the void.

The Eye of the Storm

Sam cries in despair. 'Gaia! Techna!'

He stumbles across the rubble, watching the final traces of the guardians' golden-blue hue as it is absorbed into the heavily veiled skies; desperately seeking a change in the patterns of the clouds that might signal their return. His shoulders droop. He is completely alone.

'Gaia! Techna!' He whispers to himself.

Switching his attention onto his immediate surroundings, he realises that he is standing inside one of the broken buildings in Melsey. The hallucination created by the Nether appears to have morphed into reality: the stacked debris, the broken pipes, the awful petrochemical stench. Lying by his feet are the shattered glass fragments of the orb. The precious prize he had carried with the hope of recreating the Fleur de Vie. *The Fleur de Vie?* Its vibrant green-blue colours now reduced to dull, lifeless grey fragments. The orb has been rendered redundant, defeated by the Nether's powerful attack. Its powers lost for good. Sam gently pokes at the glass fragments with his tip of his boots, burying them into the gravel. Rubbing his eye with his sleeve, he pushes down on a long shard of glass.

CRASH!

He is distracted by the sound of debris falling nearby. The surrounding metal structures creak loudly, groaning from every stress points.

SNAP!

An adjacent streetlamp twists and bends, before toppling to the ground. There is a series of long, drawn-out metallic groans, accompanying dancing dark shadows. *The girders!* Sam springs, mustering all his energy to leap aside the collapsing structure. He is forced to skip around black metal girders slicing through the broken landscape, he runs hard, veering between fallen streetlamps and dry naked trees. Tripping over a concrete slab he stumbles forward, landing heavily on rough gravel. He rolls over and picks himself up. The thick smog swirls around him, generating a close, claustrophobic world.

He cries in desperation. 'Frank!' But there is no reply. 'Mal! Addie! Bonnie!'

All he hears is the harrowing howls of Nethmites crowing triumphantly over the landscape. Distraught, Sam trudges deeper into the broken city, scraping his steel toe-capped boots through the gravel as he passes unfamiliar streets lined with anonymous buildings. Their dark hollowed windows stare out accusingly at him. If people are still inside then they remain concealed, too terrified to reveal themselves. He remains preoccupied by the now too familiar metallic-sounding sneers of the Nethmites, conscious that they might emerge from the shadows and attack him at any moment. Peering cautiously over a wall, he spots a gang of the metallic creatures patrolling the street. Their bellies are full, yet still they crane their jaws for another meal of nuts and bolts and broken wires. He watches one crunch down on an empty can, its jaw slicing it in half. The creature chews on the part of the can clasped inside its maw, as the other half falls onto the ground. A second Nethmite hurries to snap it up, chuckling greedily. From his vantage point, Sam watches the Nethmites continue on their search for another prize, their tiny feet etching long scratches in the concrete slabs as they creep relentlessly along the pavement.

A gust of wind carries a soft flurry of snow that settles as a dusting of white powder over the gravel. Snowflakes caress Sam's skin, settling momentarily on his face. Their soft touch makes a pleasant change from the thundering hailstones that had greeted the Puppis' arrival into the city. As the last of the Nethmites disappears into the shadow he emerges from his hiding place. He waits patiently, feeling a stiff breeze push against his back, staring in the direction of the Nethmites in case they might return. He sighs. The coast, for now at least, appears clear. Allowing instinct to direct him, Sam trudges forward, heading for the High Street, walking past stranded vehicles. They are all badly damaged with ripped roofs and flattered tyres: the rubber patterned with chewed edges. There are pools of dark oily liquid that has dripped from broken exhaust pipes. Sam walks briskly, deviating from the High Street, following rusted tram tracks overlain by broken cables that have been ripped from overhead pylons.

Reaching the junction with Hunter's Road, he stops. The smog is thicker here. His thoughts are now trained on finding Johnny and Mary, perhaps they are hiding safely inside their home. He stares in despair at the debris piled high along the entrance to their street. Further progress into Hunter's Road is impossible. Sam calls out and listens keenly for a reassuring reply: a friendly voice, perhaps even Johnny or Mary's. His efforts are met with silence. With a resigned sigh, he turns away and walks back towards the High Street. He starts to sing, to raise his flagging spirits: *From dragons to faeries*. The song he sang when he began his adventure. The sound of groaning metal vibrating around him offers an accompaniment to the melody. He sings quietly.

'From dragons to fairies,
The gnomes and creatures of the sea.
Where they would sing,
Where they would dance,
And where they would feast and watch the stars,

Where they would be singing and dancing,
Where they would be singing,
Where they would be.'

From dragons to fairies...'

Sam stops, his heart pounding with expectation. He has reached the curved cobblestones of Hollandaise Street! The street that means more to him than any other. A place that typically thrives in light and colour; with crowds of people milling around the petite niche shops, listening to music. As he stares into the deep mist his eye widens and his mouth gapes open. Hollandaise Street is an exciting and vibrant place to visit. But today it is just like everywhere else in Melsey: empty and swathed in dank grey smog. Another magical place consumed by the Nether's destructive energy. Trampling over the cobblestones, he passes bordered shops and bars that stand dark and unoccupied. The street is strewn with fragments of boxes that have been chewed and ripped apart. Sam approaches *The Root*. A short sharp tingling pain shoots inside his arm, forcing him to caress the muscles to ease the discomfort. *The Root* is locked tight. Above the doors the bright green light that normally bares its name hangs limply from its frame, extinguished. The posters that decorated the entrance have been ripped away, leaving the exposed, red-bricked walls smudged with soot. Leaning against the door, his ear pressed against the solid surface, Sam is desperate to hear the familiar beat of music spiralling up from below. Anything that might suggest there are people inside, taking refuge. He is met with silence.

'Ted?' Sam pounds his fists against the door. 'Ted, are you in there?'

Nothing.

'TED!' His eye fills with tears as he beats the doors again and again with his fists. 'TED!'

Sinking to his knees, Sam leans against the cold brick wall and stares at the snow-covered stone pavement. *This is hopeless.* Standing, he steps from the entrance and gazes along the length of this once colourful and vibrant street. He spreads out his wings, enveloping the insulating feathers around his body to use them as a blanket to cloak his slumped shoulders.

CRASH!

The sound of debris falling from a nearby building, followed by the unyielding groan of broken metal pylons twisting under stress. Sam is lost deep inside a landscape of buildings stabbed by black girders, each of the spiny structures are covered in a glowing deep-purple aura.

'Oh Melsey!' He croaks. 'What has happened? Was this caused by me leaving: to seek adventure, to see other places and experience other cultures? Is this my destiny, to encounter the Nether and then witness everything collapsing into its evil grasp. *Did it have to be like this?*' He takes a deep breath. '*But what can I do?* The glass orb, the Fleur de Vie, the hope we searched far and wide for, lies shattered. The guardians are lost inside the storm; and where are my friends: Frank, Mal, Addie, Bon?'

He is distracted by the flutter of tiny wings that sound soft and gentle against the heavy industrial noises screeching around him. A small finch drops from the sky. It is an unexpected, but comforting sight. With a frantic beat of its golden-brown wings, the little bird lands on Sam's shoulder, tweeting and chirping excitedly.

'Hey little guy.' Sam forces a smile. 'But I don't have anything for you, I'm sorry. Not today. I don't think there's anything left here to scavenge.'

The finch chirps and pecks at his jacket. It tilts its head towards the sky. Puzzled, Sam cranes his head and stares at the clouds. The little bird is studying him closely, and then, with a single shrilled chirp, it flies away, heading up through the smog.

'Yeah you're right, little guy,' Sam sighs, 'we can't just sit here moping.'

The adjacent lamppost still offers a residue of light: a faint orange-red colour emanating from inside the glass bulb. The light is sufficient to cast a weak comforting glow over Sam's face as snowflakes settle, caking his scalp and wings. Holding out his right hand, snowflakes land on his palm and he watches the tiny white crystals melt away. His thoughts return to the fate of the Flower of Knowledge, to the events surrounding Greg and little Nina in Farley, and then finally to Sable. *Dear Sable!* He reflects on how her path had become interconnected with his: their fates entwined. Closing his eye, he pictures Sable bravely standing her ground and resisting the Nether's vicious assault; hearing her reassuring words as she gave him her part of the Aether...

Wait!

Her part of the Aether!

Sam's eye opens and a sly smile creeps across his lips. Lost inside the broken city he can finally see a glimmer of hope. Grabbing hold of the strands of his scarf, he lifts his head and peers through the surrounding gloom.

'Thank you Sable.'

Brushing gravel and snow from his clothes, Sam stretches out his wings, rustling their feathers, which glow from the warming power of the Aether. Shimmering with rose-coloured energy, the Aether envelopes his body. He steps determinedly away from the pavement. The light above his head brightens, diffusing into the dank grey smog. Other lights flicker through windows of the buildings that line Hollandaise Street, creating ethereal silhouettes of the people hiding inside. The shutters of one window move, revealing the pale round face of someone braver, more curious, as they dare to peek outside into the street.

Sam plants his hands on his hips and casts a confident pose. He smiles. 'I shan't be long folks! There's something I have to do.'

Stretching his legs he staggers forward, bounding gawkily like an albatross learning how to fly for the first time. He increases his pace, running past broken streetlights and rotting rubbish, feeling the wind beneath his wings.

'Up, up and away!'

He leaps forward and with a single beat of his wings takes to the air, sensing the weight of the ground slip from his feet. Swaying in between buildings he glides above the streets, picking out several groups of Nethmites patrolling below. The metallic creatures crane their heads, curious of the flying shape twisting and circling in an acrobatic dance. They listen to Sam's buoyant shouts, watching every brisk beat of his wings take him spiralling skywards, up towards the swirling storm clouds above the city. The world within the storm rumbles ferociously, accompanied by shards of purple light erupting from the clouds. The howling wind snaps at Sam's face, as sharp tipped metal girders sprout through the clouds and reach out towards him.

BAM!

The girders shatter on contact with the Aether's glowing shield. Laughing, Sam watches as more and more materialise, only to dissolve away as they touch the rose-coloured light. Twisting and turning in the currents of air, he approaches a bright white light shining from deep within a tunnel that burrows deeply through the clouds. As he stretches out his hand, his red and yellow striped scarf gets caught in the strong gusts, causing their strands to snap wildly. The scarf slips from his face and falls away. Distraught, he watches his cherished scarf falling, like a feather, towards the ground. It vanishes inside the dark void below.

Resigned to its loss, Sam turns and beating his wings harder, pushes towards the glowing white core of the storm. It is so bright he is forced to squeeze his eye shut as he moves closer. The strong forces acting on him disappear. Cautiously he opens his eye. He is drifting gently through thin wispy sheets of cloud. Below him is a lush green landscape, which he drops towards before landing softly inside a large meadow. His feet plant securely on the thick carpet of green grass carpet, but his momentum carries him forward, and he tumbles and rolls over the ground.

'Oof!'

Standing, he gazes over the vast meadow. Above his head is a clear evening sky containing complex hues of pink and purple that stretch away towards the horizon. The rich green carpet is speckled with sleeping peach-coloured peonies. The budding flowers are grouped into tight bushes. Taking a deep breath he spins around slowly. It is so calm and tranquil here: a peaceful Eden, an oasis inside the centre of the terrifying storm. The air smells sweet, reminding him of a slice of warm morello cherry pie, with a dollop of vanilla ice-cream on the side. Picking a direction he tramples through the grass, listening to the rhythmic crunch his steps make. He wants to prance across the meadow, to run freely over the field of pretty peonies, but he still has a job to do. The meadow stretches endlessly in all directions and after walking for several minutes he appears no closer to a destination, nor indeed any further from his starting point. Perplexed, he sits and begins running his fingers through the long grass and over the delicate petals of the sleeping peonies. Perhaps this is the sanctuary he had seen as Gaia and Techna flew into the clouds. Who would have thought such a heavenly place might be here, within the dark and terrible storm? But the meadow is empty. There are no signs of the guardians. *What is he expected to do?* He leans back onto the grass, absorbed by the silence, watching white doves and ravens glide high in the sky.

'Sam! Sam!' Someone is calling out to him.

He gazes at the swirling candy-coloured clouds floating above his head, gliding towards a strange shape in the distance. Jumping to his feet, he realises it is a large tree standing on a distant knoll. He begins running towards it. Reaching the knoll he stares at the tree's lush green leaf crown covered in ripening acorns and vines. Sam brushes his hand against its strong bark and traces the stiff wooden wrinkles with his fingers. It is an oak tree, and a remarkably familiar one too.

He starts. Someone is approaching from behind. He hears the sound of someone clearing their throat. Preparing to speak.

'It's lovely here, don't you think Sam?'

Peering around the trunk of the oak tree, he sees a figure standing on the far side of the knoll. *It is Sable.* She is gazing out over the meadow. A stiff breeze catches the hem of her dress as she turns towards him and smiles.

'Sable?' Sam gasps. 'You're here, inside this… this place?'

'You should know the Aether makes anything possible.' She chuckles. 'Although, having been on the receiving end of the Nether's attack, I'm more content here in this beautiful meadow. It's better than fighting Nethmites.'

Sam walks around the tree; with the backdrop of the meadow and multi-coloured sky. He follows the breeze trailing over the grass, the green blades shimmering in the diffused light. Peony buds bob in the breeze as ravens croak in chorus as they circle the skies, trailed by a dule of doves.

'We're inside the eye of the Nether storm, and for now we can take solace from this oasis.' Sable holds out her hands. 'It feels good to be part of the image of what is needed. It's reassuring.'

Sam clasps Sable's hands. It does feel reassuring, but the events in Melsey remain too close. And now after the destruction of the orb containing the Fleur de Vie, the task he faces appears immense.

'What can I do Sable?' He whispers. 'The Nether destroyed the sapling, and with it our only hope for the Fleur de Vie to bloom.'

'My dear Sam, your doubts are misplaced.' Sable places her hand on Sam's shoulder. 'The Fleur de Vie shall bloom again.'

'It will?'

'Sable is correct.' A familiar voice booms from within the tree. *It is the Flower of Knowledge!* 'The Fleur de Vie brings hope through the Aether's positive energy.' A gust of wind rustles his leafy crown as he continues. 'It has the power to restore everything destroyed by the Nether. Yes Sam, hero of Melsey, you have the power to bring forth the Fleur de Vie. It lies within you.'

Sam turns away, his cheeks flushed. He glances skywards and stares at the circling birds, wishing he might see the guardians again. *Where are they?* What has happened since they disappeared inside the storm clouds? He sits on the ground and crosses his legs. Sable stands close behind as they stare at the peonies filling the meadow. Holding out his hands, the rose-coloured light of the Aether fizzes over the palms of his hands. As he watches, the light-force forms a flower-bulb that dances over his hands.

'Having the Aether inside me is really something,' he smiles, tossing the flower-bulb from one hand to the other, 'and it was the Aether that contained the gas-blast through me. It enabled me to act to help me then, and it keeps helping me.' He sighs. 'But we still have things to do, to help the places we visited, the people, my friends.' Closing his eye, Sam thinks hard, picturing all his friends in turn: Captain Frank, Mal, Addie, Bonnie, Dr Woodchuck, Cedric. 'They're all out there, waiting for me, depending on the Aether.'

The wind brushes over the Flower of Knowledge's leafy crown. 'Do you know what you're going to do?'

Caressing the rose-coloured flower-bulb, Sam rolls his hands together, causing the bulb to split into a multitude of particles. Flying through the air, the tiny particles of light circle around his head. He stares at the sleeping peony buds bobbing in the breeze and takes a deep breath, taking in the faint sweet fragrance of the meadow.

A smile draws across his face. 'I know exactly what I'm gonna do. There's a reason I have this incredible power and I can get the Aether to resurrect the Fleur de Vie. I'll recreate the Fleur de Vie myself!'

Sable and the Flower of Knowledge chuckle, a sound that gradually builds into joyous laughter. The Flower of Knowledge's leafy crown sways in rhythm.

'Sam, your words are gentle and true.' Sable says, tears pooling in her eyes. She wipes them away before they can fall. 'The

Aether will serve you well, and because of your compassion, you will succeed.'

Sam beams. 'Thank you Sable, for helping me understand the power of the Aether.' He stands and takes her hand. 'And thank you for believing in me.'

'Now you are ready,' the Flower of Knowledge adds, 'go and release the power of the Aether Sam. Bring forth calm to the storm!'

'I will!'

Sam steps towards the edge of the knoll and stares out over the meadow. Stretching his arms, he holds up his hands. The Aether glows, covering him in waves of brilliant rose-coloured light. The ground by his feet rumbles as the breeze stiffens and forms a vortex around his frame. Across the meadow peony buds stir and shimmer. Sable steps away and joins the Flower of Knowledge, to observe this momentous event with pride.

The Aether's rose-coloured light sprouts from Sam's hands, unfolding different shapes that morph into a flower. Its petals unfurl. There is a dazzling flash of light and in the palms of his hands is a red and yellow lily!

Sam gasps.

The Fleur de Vie has bloomed. Its eight open petals ripple in waves of the Aether's energy. He hears Noah's words inside his head, his final words to him before returning to space. *Do it with a smile on your face!* His lips curl as he stares intently at the lily in his hands.

'Okay Fleur de Vie, do your stuff!'

He blows gently over the flower, causing its petals to burst and fly out from his palms. As the petals are carried away the peony buds in the meadow unfold. Their petals are snatched away and carried by strong air currents, forming a long glowing stream that dances across the meadow. They circle Sam, Sable and the Flower of Knowledge, who watch the trail of petals swirling under the evening sky. The birds sing in harmony as the petals concentrate above the knoll, before trailing towards the horizon. At the edge of

the meadow the petals shower from the clouds, falling into the
raging Nether storm.
    WHOOSH!

An earth-shuddering blast of the Aether directs a healing
wave that reaches out far and wide. Across the Southern Island,
alarmed Nethmites crane their heads as waves of rose-coloured
light pulsate towards them. Falling petals settle on the ground and
turn the harsh gravel into a carpet of fresh green grass. The metal
girders planted in the ground implode as the Aether hits them.
Witnessing the transformation of their dark kingdom the Nethmites
scurry away, desperate to escape the Aether's power. The air is
filled with shrieks from the retreating hordes, but their efforts prove
futile as they are consumed inside the Aether's magnificent light.

*

In Glen Bó a stream of pink light diffuses from the shadows. The windmills lighten in colour as their creaking gears begin to move as flying flower petals lubricate the giant blades. Standing on the landing deck, Faye and Ms. Hummus watch clouds of colourful petals pour over the countryside. Faye stumbles over her words, trying to make sense of the world reblooming. Ms Hummus simply scratches her head with a bemused smile.

*

In Greystagg, the forest is transformed back into its array of diverse natural colours. Grass sprouts through the gravel covering the barren wasteland. Trees regain thick canopies and healthy bark; evergreens sprout rich green pines. Birds and woodland animals step cautiously into the now fertile environment, overjoyed at seeing their homes restored. Deer and rabbits prance, as birds flutter playfully high inside the luscious forest canopy. The lake inside the forest floods with fresh water and the River Tye once more flows freely, filled with fish and other aquatic life. The refilling of the river extends into the valley, following waves of Aether. Flocks of sheep and cattle bray, watching newly bloomed flowers sway on the meandering riverbanks. Farmers step from their hiding places, inside houses and barns, to stand and watch this fantastic metamorphism of the landscape.

*

The dark storm clouds that had suffocated Melsey are vanquished, dispersed by the Aether's showering light. In their place flower petals gentle swirl through the air before settling and painting the city in vibrant colours. The broken buildings are transformed: standing upright, their newly restored glass windows reflecting the bright sunshine. On the streets vehicles are repaired: sporting new parts, with inflated tyres. The smell of fresh paint fills the air, and the River Melba flows with clean sparkling water. The population of Melsey open their doors and windows and watch in wonder as the last of the monstrous metallic girders corrode into white dust. High above their heads the sky returns to a cerulean blue, and inside Sam's beloved park, grass and flowers thrive once again. Birds frolic, chirping melodious songs as they dance between the branches of heavily blossomed trees.

*

Sam opens his eye and gazes at a purple evening sky, woken by a calming melodic lullaby playing from somewhere within the swirling wind. He is still in the meadow, lying on the grass. Running his fingers through their soft blades, he stares out over a meadow devoid of flowers: the peonies are gone. And so have Sable and the Flower of Knowledge. He is alone, once again. Struggling to his feet, he realises that the meadow is fading, diluting in colour and sound. It is gradually dissolving, piece by piece, leaving nothing but a void. All that remains is an echo of Sable's final words. '*We must leave Sam. A shaman's path runs far and long.*'

He hears someone calling out his name. Looking around he spots two darkened shapes approaching. *The guardians!* They look tattered and exhausted from their battle with the Nether.

Sam smiles, overjoyed at seeing his friends again. 'Gaia! Techna!' He cries, hearing a tiny, excited squeak in his voice.

'Hey Sam!' Techna replies, thumping his paw together with Sam's hand.

'I must admit, I doubted you could send the Nether back into the void.' Gaia says, in a satisfied tone. 'But I was wrong. I'm mightily impressed with how it's worked out; and with the Fleur de Vie revealed as a lily. But why a lily?'

'Because of Ma,' Sam explains, 'and on what happened inside the grove. The Nether vandalised *her* place, which helped me think of the Fleur de Vie as a lily. That experience made the Aether even stronger,' he sighs, recalling the peonies in the meadow and how soft they felt between his fingers. 'Ma loved lilies. She loved all flowers, as do I.'

'You're right! Lilies reminded you of your mother and so created a stronger connection with the Aether.' Gaia grins, spreading his wings in a proud panache. 'In fact, I, uh…' He blushes. 'I also think lilies are pretty.'

Sam and Techna chuckle at the white guardian's awkward honesty, and despite his embarrassment, Gaia is soon laughing. They fall quiet watching tiny particles of light zipping and sliding about them, the residue of the Aether's restoring power. Some fly right through their bodies.

'Has the Nether gone completely?' Sam asks.

'I believe so. It feels like it has.' Gaia replies. 'And it won't be returning now the Fleur de Vie is in full bloom.' His moth-feelers droop. 'But the energy used to recreate the Fleur de Vie and restore the Island has weakened the Aether. I fear it could be gone too.'

Sam shakes his head. 'I think you're wrong Gaia. It's still with me.'

Perplexed, the guardians exchange glances.

Techna says. 'You think so?'

'Yeah!' Sam smiles. 'Sure the Aether isn't a physical force, but it is powerful. It chose me and protected me against the gas-blast, and it remains ever-present inside me.'

'Ho-Ho! Insightful words, Sam!' Techna laughs. 'Perhaps you understand the Aether better than we do.' His expression saddens. 'Even if we should've never got you involved.'

'And I'm most guilty.' Gaia sighs. 'But you reminded me of Terra when you stood up against the Nether. It was my memory of her that triggered my aloof response. I should have trusted you and your friends. I was wrong and I am sorry.'

Sam starts. 'There's nothing to apologise for Gaia, and if I may speak for Terra, she would say the same. Wherever she is now, I'm sure she's happy you didn't give up on us.'

'Ha-Ha! He's right, Gaia.' Techna grins. 'See! You didn't give up on the humans after all.'

'Sam,' Gaia places a paw gently atop Sam's dishevelled hair, 'you're a curious fellow, that's for sure. But once again you're right. Thank pal!'

Sam laughs, fixing his hair. 'Hey, just because I'm smaller than you, doesn't mean you get to tease me.'

Gaia chuckles. 'Oh, can't I?'

They are interrupted by a brilliant golden light, beaming above their heads. It reveals a darkened space where there are countless numbers of stars: big clusters of them, all rotating in a gentle circle. The space is expanding, slowly filling the void with the night sky. Sam stares up in wonder. He turns towards the guardians, saddened by the expression he sees in their eyes.

'It is time for us to go.' Gaia sighs.

'Yep.' Techna nods.

'Wait!' Sam gasps. 'You're leaving *now*?'

'As I've told you Sam,' Techna explains, 'once our purpose here is fulfilled, we will leave to go someplace else. It is time for us to recover. We cannot stay here, not even in our bird forms.'

Gaia retorts, blowing a symbolic raspberry. 'Which means no more fur-ballers to roughen my feathers!'

Sam chuckles sadly, his eye pooling with tears. 'If that's what must happen then take care. You have guided us well and I've learned much about the Aether. Thanks to you and Sable, and the Flower of Knowledge too.' He pauses. 'But what if the Southern Island needs your help again?'

Techna rests his paw on Sam's shoulder and smiles. 'You know the stories. Keep reading them and perhaps we shall meet again. Who knows? It'll be good anticipating another rendezvous. Remember to look up, from time-to-time, and think of us Sam.'

'I hope I get to see you again.' Unable to contain his emotions any longer, Sam wraps his arms around Techna's neck. 'Thank you again, from all of us. You guys are amazing.'

Techna closes his eyes. 'As are you Sam.' Struggling to mask the tremor in his voice, he lifts his wings and envelopes them gently around Sam. 'Never forget that.'

Watching on, Gaia wipes a sneaky tear escaping his eye. It is another tearful farewell with another human, but this time it feels different. Despite the sadness, there is joy in this moment too. Ruffling his feathers, he regains his composure and steps forward and nuzzles his nose on the human's head. They share a final embrace; Sam runs his hand along the white guardian's back.

Gaia plants a reassuring paw on Techna's shoulder and whispers. 'Come Tech, it is time.'

The black guardian unfolds his wings from around Sam and steps away. 'Tell Addie that she's done good, alright Sam?'

'I will.'

The guardians prepare to leave. Studying the expanding night sky, they stretch their wings for their final flight. But they have one more task. They look at Sam.

'You need to return Sam,' Techna says, 'back home to where your friends are waiting for you.'

The guardians release a tender tune under their breaths. The gentle melody ripples through Sam's ears as the guardians soar skywards.

'*Thank you Sam!*' They cry, the sound of their voices diffusing from deep within the great expanse. Their bodies shrink from sight. '*And adieu!*'

Watching, Sam's vision blurs, thickening with patterns of mist. Black and white feathers start scattering around him, and he gasps, feeling his weight drop abruptly.

Home

Sandy gasps. 'Ah! *At last*. He's awake. Rise and shine, Sam!' Rousing, Sam gazes up at the sky, with its subtle mix of blue and pink hues. He sighs with relief at the absence of dark storm clouds. Sunlight streaks through the wispy-thin lavender-coloured clouds stretching out towards the horizon beyond the city skyline. Feeling groggy, he struggles to turn his head to take in his surroundings; listening to familiar sounds: the twittered birdsong emanating from nearby bushes and trees; the noise created by human busyness. Sounds he has not heard for a long time. A couple of finches, wings fluttering, dart across the sky. Another flies directly towards him and passes close enough for him to feel the touch of air on his cheek. Running his hands over the soft earth, he clutches at a handful of thick, luscious green grass. All seems well with the world.

People are shuffling impatiently beside him, causing him to turn and stare up at the figures of Sandy and Mandy.

'Hey you two.'

'Hi!' Mandy beams. 'Welcome back to solid ground!'

Sandy grins. 'You've had quite a fall.'

Sam rolls over and struggles to his knees. With Sandy's help he gets to his feet, rubbing his aching torso. The discomfort reminds him of his recent battle with the Nether. He glances over his shoulder. His wings have gone, replaced with two replicate designs embroidered on his jacket. Drawing his hand over his sleeve, he sighs: he is going to miss them, the wings that helped him through his adventures.

'Sam! Sam!'

Johnny and Mary hurry through the park gates, waving frantically, relieved to see Sam relatively unscathed. *They have been through this before.* Sam struggles to find the words to greet them, he tugs nervously at his hairlocks before stepping forward and embracing them. Mary covers his forehead with kisses, while Johnny steps aside, a broad grin stretched across his face.

'Nana! Gramps!' Sam cries instinctively, wrapping his arms around the couple; his fingers clinging to their shoulders.

Mary whispers. 'Welcome home, Sam.'

'Hello, lad.' Johnny tips his flat cap before uttering a pleasant and understated sigh. 'It's good to see you safe and sound.'

Sandy and Mandy smile at this heart-warming moment. They know how eager Sam has been to see Johnny and Mary again.

'Hey, I told you they were safe, Sammy! Even with those nasty critters trying to conquer our city,' Mandy grins smugly, hands on hips, 'and I know I was right: right from the beginning!'

Sam releases his grip and takes a step back. He turns his attention to the newly restored park, catching the sweet-smelling blossom of fresh flowers. The flower beds are back to their full glory, displaying a wide variety of vibrant colours: reds, yellows, pinks and violets. Natural colours mingling happily amongst the blues and greens of the sky and the earth. The trees are healthy and sturdy once more, covered in strong ripe bark and topped in shades of yellow and orange that blend with the vibrant, green-coloured leaves. *The park looks amazing.* There is water flowing freely again from the fountain. The statue stands proudly at the centre, an expression of triumph and joy. Its open mouth cascading fresh clean water into the pool. Finches and robins dance about its basin, bathing their feathers in the fine spray. A rook lands and joins the other birds inside the mist encompassing the edge of the fountain. It ruffles its feathers and twitches its beak. Beyond the park's perimeter the newly restored buildings stand tall and straight, their polished frames glistens in the sunlight. The surrounding streets reverberate with the reassuring sounds of motor vehicles accompanied by the rattle of a tram running on its tracks. The city is busy again.

Sam sniffs the fresh air. 'Is the city fully restored?'

'It sure is!' Mandy replies enthusiastically. 'Everything is back just the way it was before. I told you, didn't I? And there's none of those creepy metal critters anywhere.' She reaches for her phone, pulling it from inside her jacket pocket. It responds with a happy *ding*. Mandy is greeted with a colourful image of a group of her friends standing in front of a pair of brightly striped parasols on a beach. They are holding drinks aloft and grinning for the camera. 'And this thing is working again, which means I can call my friends!'

Sandy smiles, acknowledging Mandy's sense of priority. He stares towards the buildings beyond the park gates. The metal girders, the source of the eerie rumbling sounds that plagued Melsey for so long have crumpled to nothing. 'It's wonderful, now those dreadful metal girders are gone.'

Sam brushes the final flecks of gravel from his jacket, debris he collected during his fall from inside the void. He has safely returned, carried by Gaia and Techna's song. *The guardians, his friends.* He heaves a relieved sigh.

'That's good, but where is everyone?' He glances anxiously at the park gates, desperate to see his other friends again.

'*Sam*!'

And here they come: Frank, Mal and Addie, running into the park. They look fatigued, but happy at seeing their dear friend is safe. Feeling his heart rise Sam runs forward, raising his arms in greeting. Mal and Addie wave frantically, offering a chorus of cheers. Frank grabs Sam by the waist and lifts him off his feet, wrapping his arms tightly about his friend. He swings Sam around in a strong bear hug.

Sam chuckles. 'Hey guys!'

'You did good, Sammy!' Addie smiles, affectionately nudging his shoulder. 'You've shown the Nether who's the boss! When those storm-clouds burst, the nut-bolts just disappeared. We knew it was you who got the job done!'

'You sure did!' Mal chimes, watching Frank carefully lower Sam to the ground. She giggles. 'And my, wasn't that the cutest thing I've seen in a while!'

Sam and Frank exchange glances. Their cheeks turn tomato red. '*Mal!*' They gesture frantically, begging her to stop teasing.

Mal snickers, covering her mouth with her hand, but then offers an apologetic wave. 'I'm kidding! But it was cute.'

Addie laughs. 'You sure like teasing them, don't you Mal?'

'It's what I do best, Addie.'

They are distracted by Bonnie's soft bark as she bounds through the park gate. She bounces energetically past the fountain, causing the bathing birds to scatter for cover. Pushing herself into Sam, she throws him off his feet and licks him enthusiastically on his cheeks: yapping and squeaking excitedly.

Sam laughs aloud, trying to push the pup away. 'Hey, Bonnie. Are you okay?'

The pup nods her head vigorously and offers a joyful half-bark response.

Sam looks on disappointed, mindful that dogs cannot talk under normal conditions; in the same reality that humans do not have wings.

Bonnie snuggles closer to Sam. 'Actually Sam,' she whispers, 'I'm fighting fit!'

Relieved, Sam chuckles. 'That's good to hear.'

Mary muses. 'I'm amazed Bonnie made it out of the city and managed to find you.'

'Yeah.' Johnny nods, cocking an eyebrow. 'It's incredible she's followed you on your adventures.'

A tiny voice protests. 'Hey, don't forget us!' Dr Woodchuck hurries on all fours into the park. 'The dynamic duo is here!'

'*Yeah!*' Cedric perches on Mal's shoulder. 'It was a bit of a walk, or in my case fly, to get here from that airship of yours, Captain. What with all the people in the way,' he proclaims, 'but we are thankful that despite the dismal Nether weather, we remained ship-shaped throughout!'

Dr Woodchuck guffaws, noting the joke. 'Get it? *Ship-shaped?*'

'*Woody!*'

Everyone laughs. Addie falls to her knees and rolls over the grass in near full-blown hysterics. 'Oh gosh!' She shrieks. 'What a bird-brain!'

Mal giggles. 'Aw Cedric, you little joker!'

The eagle-owl pouts, pompously puffing up his feathers. He gazes at the others, his amber eyes sparkle as he shrugs his embarrassment away. 'Ah well!' He exclaims, with a muffled laugh. 'It's sure nice having a good laugh with everyone, now the calm has driven away the storm.'

'Yep!' Dr Woodchuck replies, absentmindedly stroking his whiskers. He is transfixed by the birds circling above their heads; flittering finches dancing and chirping merrily, chasing each other.

'And from the birds' happy songs, I believe Greystagg Forest has returned to its glorious best.'

'Ruffle my feathers! That means I get to go home and into my own bed! Now that's incredibly good news indeed, don't you think Mal?'

'It sure is.' Mal smiles, petting their heads.

Cedric and Dr Woodchuck responds affectionately, rubbing their faces against hers.

Mandy watches on, her eyes narrowing sceptically as she taps her fingers against her folded arms. 'Nope!' She shakes her head. 'I'm not convinced they're talking animals, even if I can hear them with my own ears. And nobody's gonna convince me otherwise.'

Sandy turns towards her, smirking. 'Are you sure Mandy?'

'Yep! I'm most *stubbornly* sure, Sandy.'

Mal is reminded of something. 'Sam!' She steps forward. 'Look what we found.'

She pulls out his red and yellow striped scarf from inside her poncho. It's ruffled and covered in grit.

'My scarf! Thank you.' Sam grabs hold of the scarf and runs his hand over the tattered fleece, overjoyed by its safe return. 'I'll soon have it cleaned and repaired and looking as good as new. Where did you find it?'

'I spotted it falling from the sky.'

'Hey!' Addie exclaims. 'Where are the guardians with their inflated egos? I want to thank them for their company, even *Mister Precious Pearl…*'

Sam sighs and lifts his gaze to the sky. 'They've gone.'

'What! For real?'

'I'm afraid so.'

'They did say they would leave, once the Nether was defeated.' Addie groans with disappointment. 'And now those nasty metal critters have been taken care of, thanks to those guys…' Her voice trails away and she sneakily wipes a tear from her cheek. 'But it would have been nice for them to stay around long enough for me to say goodbye properly.'

'I know Addie,' Sam rubs her shoulders, 'we all wanted that.'

'Ach! Damn it!' Addie claps her hands together. 'I wanted one of those pecky Nethmites as a souvenir. Stuffed, of course.'

Sandy cups a hand over his chin, eyeing the evening sky. 'Gaia and Techna, gone? That's a shame, although I did spot a raven and a dove together, just before we found you Sam. Such elusive creatures, aren't they? I wonder where they are now?'

'They've gone somewhere to rest up.' Sam smiles. 'But before they departed they said we should look out for them, and that maybe they'll return. *Look up and think of us, and we shall return one day.*'

'Well! That sound's promising!' Addie chimes, hands on hips. 'Then I'll be able to give them my sincere thanks. I for one am not ungrateful, even if I acted *gung-ho* at times.'

'Yeah, I suppose.' Mandy sighs doubtfully, shifting her eyes across the empty sky. Her eyes narrow and she furrows her brow. 'It's just I don't get the gist of this: *Aether magic and what-not.*'

'The power of the Aether is truly awesome Mandy. And starting out on my adventure, it's not what I expected at all. Certainly not the conflict with the Nether and its strange, beaky Nethmite hordes.' Sam laughs good-naturedly. 'But I got to visit enchanting places like Glen Bó, Greystagg, and Limehead. I even went to Farley to see dear Nina and Greg again. It was the positive energy of the Aether that set me out on my journey and brought me safely home.' He lifts his hands, hoping in vain to see the soft rose-coloured glow. 'But what made my adventure special, was sharing my wonderful and fulfilling experiences with my friends.'

Frank, Mal and Addie nod in agreement. Cedric and Dr Woodchuck share a knowing glance and offer a short shrug.

'And you are all amazing.' Sam smiles. 'Thank you for being there for me.'

Mal replies. 'And thank you Sam, for accepting us into your life.'

'Yep.' Addie nods.

Frank opens his arms. 'Group hug time!'

They step forward and embrace. No one wants to let go, not just yet. Bonnie, Cedric and Dr Woodchuck join in with this shared display of affection. All huddled together in a large, tight bundle.

Johnny pipes. 'Quite the fellowship they have.'

'Yep!' Mary chuckles. 'Most definitely.'

A trace of rose-coloured light spreads out from Sam engulfing his friends. It extends to embrace the watching Sandy and Mandy, and then Johnny and Mary. There is something reassuring in being bathed within this comforting energy.

Sandy confesses, pulling a pink handkerchief from his pocket. 'Oh! I do love heart-warming moments like this.'

'Sounds mushy to say it, but yeah, me too.' Mandy wipes away a tear. 'But I'm not crying! *You didn't see me cry!*'

The party separate and the rose-coloured light disperses.

Addie clears her throat. 'I'd love to say let's get this party started, but I shouldn't. I mean, doesn't that sound a bit selfish?'

'Oh no, certainly not!' Johnny counters. 'We insist on doing something to commemorate your brave adventure. I've asked Ted to make preparations to mark your return Sam, and your friends too. Just get to *The Root* this evening.'

Mary nudges Sam's shoulder. 'I bet you've missed *The Root*, while you've been away?'

Addie's mouth gapes open. 'Wait a minute, *The Root*? Isn't that the place you told us about Sam? Well then, let's get this party started for sure!' She makes a start, zipping through the park gates and leaving the others struggling in her wake.

'Hey!' Frank cries. 'Wait for us, Addie!'

They troop from the park, passing through the huge newly reformed iron gates and into the street outside. The street is filled with people, in contrast to the previous occasion they were here together. Now the Nethmites are gone, and everything is back to normal. Reaching Addie, who is dancing and squealing as a tram approaches, they pause to watch the marvellous machine rattling on its tracks as it passes by.

Sam remains inside the park, slowly progressing towards the park gates; his feet trudging on the soft ground. He turns and gazes fondly at the clusters of flowers growing in the beds around the fountain. Their colourful heads sway in the breeze: red dianthus and yellow pansies. There are also bunches of peach-coloured camellias too, grouped together in the beds. They remind him of the peonies he saw in the void. Distracted by a flutter of feathers beating against the wind, he glances skywards and catches a glimpse of a white dove and a black raven. They are climbing high into the darkening lavender sky. He follows their silhouettes as they cross the face of the waning moon. Daylight is failing and the early evening stars are already decorating the sky. With a gleam in his eye he spots a slowly moving point of light that blinks periodically as it crosses the heavens. *Is that the satellite? Has Noah has accomplish his mission?*

'Sam! C'mon, hurry!'

He hurries after the others, but he is forced to wait at the side of the road as a motorcycle zooms past. It is quickly followed by three more motorcycles. The riders faces are concealed inside helmets and Sam is unable to make out their features. They speed on, weaving between other vehicles before disappearing into the traffic beyond. *Curious.* Scratching the side of his head, Sam crosses the road and joins his friends on the opposite pavement.

He is reminded of something. 'Hey Addie! Gaia wanted me to give you a message.'

'He did?'

'He wanted me to tell you: *you've done good.*'

'You bet his ivory feelers I did good! Those Nethmites couldn't stop Silverhair's swift moves, even if they did chew down on my arrows! *The cheek!*'

'Well, you did good, my friend. No doubt about it.'

Addie stops and looks at her feet. Rubbing her shoulder, she feels her cheeks turning pink. 'Gee, I don't know what to say,' she gasps, 'but thanks Sam. You're a pal.'

*

Their progress is temporarily curtailed by Mary insisting they take a detour to the medical centre on Greenwing Avenue. She wants them to have their cuts and abrasions cleaned, and their blossoming bruises treated. As they wait in turn, they are treated to cups of sweet tea and crunchy biscuits. Johnny keeps the refreshments flowing by periodically pointing to his throat and forcing a sequence of dry coughs. By the time they step out of the surgery it is dark outside. There are more stars speckling the evening sky. A tram swings past them and the passengers peer through the windows at Sam and his friends. Recognising their heroes, they cheer and wave. Dr Woodchuck and Cedric then bid their friends goodnight and return to the Puppis, determined to avoid any unnecessary consternation from city folk hearing animals talking.

'I think we've had quite enough of their squared looks.' Dr Woodchuck reasons, as he and Cedric head for the seclusion of the airship.

'You said it!' Cedric agrees. 'Enough is enough, I say!'

Strolling through the bustling city, the rest of the party make for Hollandaise Street. It greets them with animated movement and colour, which pleases Sam. The last time he was here it was under the Nether's leaden sky. They tred the lively cobbled streets, filled with coloured lights and music. People standing in open doorways or leaning through open windows sing loudly, throwing their hands up before them. It feels like they are walking through a musical number, adding to the festiveness. People stop to shake Sam's hand and ask him about his next performance.

They reach *The Root*, with its restored green logo shining brightly above the entrance. The rustic-red-coloured walls are pasted with brand new colourful posters. The doors are open, inviting them inside. Sam is beaten through the entrance by Addie, who skips excitedly down the spiral stairwell. Music pounds through the walls, greeting them from below. It gets louder and louder as they descend into the subterranean club. Entering the main lounge, Sam is surprised by how few people are inside. Perhaps the doors have only just opened. At least it is easy to spot

Ted, who is busy cleaning glasses and arranging packets of crisps and nuts behind the bar. The small stage is blazoned by bright lights illuminating a drum-set, bass guitar and keyboard. Instruments pre-set and waiting for the next performance. *Is this for him?*

Sam is distracted by the sound of Louis playing in the other lounge. His emotive, brassy music vibrates through the adjourning wall.

'*Hoo-ee!* This place is awesome!' Addie bellows. 'Now I understand why you love it here Sam.'

Sam chuckles. 'I'm glad you like it.'

Hearing Sam's voice, Ted hurries around the bar. His cloth slips from his hands, and he almost drops the glass he is cleaning.

'Sam? Is it really you?' But before Sam can respond, he is pulled into a bear-hug. 'Nice to see you again buddy! You sure know how to have an adventure, don't you? There were times I doubted I'd ever serve you another shake with a cherry on top!'

Sam laughs, slapping Ted's back. 'It's great to see you too, Ted.' He nods towards the stage. 'How are the fellas?'

'They'll be here shortly,' Ted explains, 'they're just getting changed after the sound-checks.' He steps back, acknowledging Sam's friends. 'Hey! You're all here! What a party we're gonna have, huh! Let's get this celebration started.'

The club fills quickly as more customers pour downstairs, the clattering of their feet echoing off the walls. Some decide to enter the adjacent lounge to listen to Louis' performance, but most choose to remain in the main area. This is not just a celebration for Melsey, but for the whole of the Southern Island. They are here to meet their heroes. People crowd the bar, buying drinks and savoury snacks. A small audience gathers around Frank, who is sitting at a small table away from the bar. They watch as he pours flour, milk, eggs, sugar, and lemon curd into Old Faithful's funnel. There is growing anticipation as the blunderbuss chugs, and rumbles, and burps. Finally after a couple of firm shakes, Old Faithful blasts a perfect batch of lemon flavoured fondant fancies. These are quickly followed by a selection of strawberry and then chocolate fondant fancies. The audience gasp, puzzled by Old Faithful's creation of such perfect, pretty cakes. There is a muffled discussion on who wants to try one first.

Johnny volunteers, reaching out and grabbing one of the lemon fancies. He takes a bite, chewing slowly before swallowing. His eyes bulge. 'These are incredible!' He grasps Frank's hand. 'These would sell like hot-cakes in the café.'

The impressed audience applauds Frank's efforts, clapping enthusiastically, before trying out the fondant fancies for themselves. The lemon flavoured ones prove a huge hit and Johnny grabs another, to give to Mary, before they are all eaten. Frank takes a bow, watching proudly as his cake batches disappear as an increasing audience munch down on the sugary treats. Wearing a broad grin, he kisses Old Faithful's sticky funnel.

'Ah, Old Faithful,' he whispers, 'once again, you have served me well.'

Meanwhile, Ted is making a chocolate and cherry flavoured milkshake: mixing in cherry sauce, cocoa power with vanilla ice-cream in a blender. Pouring the finished concoction into a tall glass, he completes his creation by adding thick squirting cream before placing a small morello cherry on top. He slides the glass carefully across the counter, towards Mal, who is sitting on a stool at the bar.

'There you go, Mal!'

'Thank you, sir.'

Ted groans. 'Oh! Please call me Ted, *sir* sounds so pretentious.' He changes the subject. 'Sam told me you live in the forest.'

'Yes. I do now, but I used to live in Knapweed before I moved to Greystagg.'

'Knapweed?'

'Yeah. Do you know it?'

'Of course. It's on the western side of the Southern Island.'

'Yeah, but I haven't been there for a while.' She pauses, reflecting on Sam and Addie's reactions when they returned home. 'I'm overdue a visit.' She sucks hard at the straw, flinching slightly at the icy-cold concoction. 'This shake is pretty good. It's Sam's favourite, isn't it?'

Ted grins. 'Oh yes. He always orders one when he's here.'

'Heh, no wonder he loves morello cherries.'

Elsewhere, Addie is busy describing the Limehead swordfish to Mary, who has taken an immediate interest in the islet's culture and cuisine. *A fish that tastes better than tuna and cod.* Mary asks Addie about her poetry, prompting the ranger to retrieve a crumpled sheet of paper from inside her trouser pocket. She begins reciting a newly penned poem.

'Boom! Boom!
The storm-clouds have turned,
Till then, they dissolve, crying for their horde,
Now gone.
The sun is bright,
The wind is calm,
Thanks to the light that shone and shone!'

Mary claps her hands together as Addie bows. 'How charming! You must love doing this.'

'I do, especially when I get to shoot my arrows!'

'I meant writing poetry.' Mary laughs. 'You should keep writing, and share your poems too. Perhaps you should join a poetry club.'

'Thank you, ma'am.' Addie blushes. 'Maybe I will.'

'Call me Mary, my dear. Everyone calls me Mary. We're all friends here.'

Mandy is standing by herself studying the bustling lounge, watching everyone enjoying themselves as they wait for the performance to start. She sees her friends sitting at a corner table. They are waving for her to join them; their table appears weighed down with a large number of mocktails. Pleased to see her friends again, Mandy rushes over and sits down with them, grabbing the cream soda float offered to her.

'Whew! I didn't think this place could be crazy again!' She laughs. 'It's great seeing the city normal again. Do you gals know what happened?'

Her friends shrug. '*Do you?*'

'Well, it's kind of difficult to say.' Mandy replies.

She sits, soundlessly opening and closing her mouth as she tries finding the right words. Looking over to Sam and his companions: Mal and Addie are dancing together; Frank is sitting at a table piled high with the freshly made cakes. She smiles. A genuinely warm affectionate smile.

'As I was saying, it's special here, isn't it? To see it busy again, with everything back to normal. And it's all thanks to those guys: Sam's friends.'

'Huh? It sounds like you're daydreaming, Mandy!' Her friend Fran exclaims.

'Heh! Maybe I am.'

Sam is standing on the far side of the room refamiliarising himself with the many posters and framed photographs decorating the walls of the musicians who have performed here. He strokes his right cheek thoughtfully, spotting a photograph of him taken before the gas-blast. It is a picture of him sitting on a three-legged stool, holding Angie in his hands. *He is smiling: his right arm and left eye intact.* He flushes with embarrassment at the staged smile, recalling the occasion. It was taken just before he went on stage to perform for the first time. He runs his hand over his right arm, sensing the warm residue of the Aether lying deep inside him. Frank walks from the bar holding a drink with two ice-cubes sloshing around, a reward for his efforts with Old Faithful.

Frank asks. 'You okay?'

'Yeah, I've just been thinking. Reflecting on a different time.'

He studies Sam's photograph, exchanging glances between the Sam standing beside him and the Sam framed in the picture on the wall. 'You can always have a new one taken, to replace this one.'

'Maybe. But I like this one of me, even if it was taken before the blast.' Sam smiles. 'It's okay Frank, it doesn't make me feel awkward. Although I do *look* awkward in this picture.'

'If that's how you feel, then I won't push further. It's your call. But if you want it updated, like I've done with my leg, then just say the word.' Frank chuckles, downing the last of his drink. The ice-cubes chink inside the glass. He places the empty glass on a small polished wooden table. 'Whew! What would those four adventurers make of me now, having achieved a greater triumph than before? They'd probably make an even bigger wager!'

'Frank,' Sam fiddles with a lock of his fringe, 'you know the moment we met, for the first time?'

'Yeah, when I rescued your precious scarf.'

'A lot has happened since,' Sam nods, 'and we've become close: sticking together through thick and thin. All of us.'

'Yeah. They've been great, *even Addie.*'

Sam laughs. 'Even Addie.' He pauses, gazing across the lounge at the bustling numbers singing and dancing to the music. 'Frank?'

'Yeah?'

'Thanks for being there for me.'

Frank grins. 'No need for thanks, Sam. And we all did good, didn't we?' The sky-pirate removes his hat and places it on Sam's head. 'I'm glad you're my friend.'

'Me too, Frank.'

'And you better bake me that cherry pie soon, just like how your Ma made it.'

'Sure, I'll do that!'

They nudge knuckles, chuckling.

Addie is sitting with Mal at a small round table. 'Hey Sam!' She hollers, pounding the table top with the palm of her hand. 'They're ready for your performance. C'mon and get on stage! You promised.'

Sam sighs. 'I guess I did.' He returns Frank's hat. 'Coming!'

They head for the centre of the lounge and split up. Frank joins Mal and Addie at their table, while Sam proceeds to the stage. There is Angie, leaning against a large amp box, courtesy of Ted. He picks up his beloved guitar and strokes her curved body.

'Glad to see you again, girl.' He smiles, slinging the strap over his shoulders.

The bassist, the keyboard player and the drummer stride onto the stage. They spend a few minutes jamming, warming up, controlling the rising adrenaline the prospect of a live performance brings. The bassist begins playing a sequence of repeating notes. He is quickly accompanied by the keyboard player and the drummer, who bangs out the rhythm. Stopping abruptly, they nod at Sam.

'Okay Sam,' the drummer yells, 'let's play some sweet tunes!'

Sam grins and returns a *thumbs up*. 'Right on, Brandon!'

Turning towards the audience, Sam picks out Johnny, Mary and Bonnie, and there is Sandy and Mandy too, and Frank, Mal and Addie. They are all waiting expectantly. The companions he shared his great adventure with. Everyone begins cheering and chanting his name out loud, raising their hands and clapping to the beat. Sweeping his fringe from his face, the bassist steps up to the microphone.

'Alright dudes and dudettes, and any in between; please make some noise and welcome home our friend, our very own... *Sam McKenzie!*'

The audience cheer louder.

The bassist smiles at Sam. 'Sing it, dude.'

Sam grins shyly, feeling his cheeks turning pink. The noisy applause dissolves away as the crowd waits in rising anticipation. Stepping towards the microphone, he begins with a familiar series of notes on Angie, plucking with his yellow guitar pick in time with Brandon's clapping drumsticks.

He smiles at the audience, studying the many familiar faces, listening to them calling his name. Ready to strum the first chord, he announces:

'One… two… three… four…'

If you have enjoyed the story of Sam and his friends' adventures then please look out for future novels by Emmy Riley.

Included in this book is the opening chapter from Aether: The Jester of Chaos. The second novel in the Sam McKenzie series.

You can contact Emmy via the *Aether Page* on Facebook,

or by email: theentropiclibrary@gmail.com

Aether: The Jester of Chaos

Rrroar!

E vening gathers in Melsey as the streets empty of pedestrians. Some commuters are traveling home, sitting inside half-filled tram carriages racing along tracks with bells ringing. *The Melsey Clock* echoes over the city: chiming the third quarter of the fifth hour. The temperature is icy-cold and there are patches of settled snow scattered across the city. The sun has already set behind the buildings that provide the city landscape: impressive constructs that watch over the citizens on the streets. Inside the docks, beneath the shadows of large temporary constructs, otters swim in the River Melba. Their heads bob above the surface waters as they swim back and forth; keeping a safe distance from passing boats and prepared to prank surprised cormorants.

In Fry's Road, inside his florist shop, Sandy is completing his cleaning chores. He sweeps debris across the floor with a broom, having already mopped the puddles formed beneath dripping taps. After making one final sweep, he shoves the broom and mop into the cupboard; wincing at the clattering noise as he shuts the door. Pausing to the slide the sign from open to closed, he steps outside and turns to lock the door. *The Wooden Bridge* pub stands opposite and is bursting with patrons. Their silhouettes dance behind windows, in tune with the sounds emanating from inside. Sandy grins at the reddened sky as he makes his way to his red truck inside the car park. He is looking forward to taking a short break.

Rounding the corner from Cedar Avenue, Mandy is busily tapping the keys on her phone: writing text messages to her friends. Happy with what she has written, she stuffs her phone into her coat pocket and quickens her steps homeward. She hums a tune, pleased to have the pavement to herself. Pausing at the junction with Cherry Avenue, her hair slides across her shoulder. She pushes away the plait while muttering under her breath.

Hollandaise Street *looks* tranquil, but there is music blasting out from of *The Root*. The music is pulling people inside, via the spiral staircase en-route to the subterranean club. The main lounge is bursting with jive from a performance on the stage. Ted, the bartender, fills a large tankard to the brim of stout beer and hands it to a waiting customer. Stepping away to take a breather, he leans back into a stack of salty snack packets and then grumbles about his clumsiness. There is a clash of glass as a customer slams down an empty glass on the counter. They thank Ted before leaving, who picks up the glass and rinses it with water from the sink.

There is a large crowd attending the main lounge, listening to the musicians playing on the small stage: Sam and his three bandmates. They are known as *The Peachy Peonies*, and they are all wearing identical burgundy baker caps with a coral-coloured peony flower attached on one side. During an instrumental, Rhys, on keyboards, his fingers dancing over the keys, plays in perfect synchronisation with the bassist, Dylan. The latter bobs his knees and swings his long light brown hair over his face. The drummer, Brandon, holds up a tambourine and taps it gingerly, grinning from ear to ear. A chord change from Rhys is the signal for Brendon to grab his drumsticks and begin lightly beating the tom drum.

Sam, with his beloved Angie in his hands, plucks the strings of his guitar as he stares at the entranced crowd before him. Some wave glowsticks above their heads, swaying them from side to side. A bright spotlight bathes the stage, causing Sam to shield his face with his prosthetic arm. Fortunately the light dims, and he strums

Angie's strings with his pick shrouded in shadow. His bandmembers, in tune with the melody, sway to the rhythm.

'Hold my hand and I'll lead the way,
Through twists and turns of the night,
We'll laugh, we'll smile on the day we've had,
And chase off the troubling blues.'

Taking a step backwards, Sam strums his riff, fiddling Angie with sweeping major chords. His bangs fall over the left side of his face, dampened with sweat. He can feel the fingers of his right arm vibrate as he plucks the strings; they hum over the metal surface, tingling up to his shoulder. Turning his gaze to the encouraging expressions from his bandmates, he smiles. The audience continue to swing back and forth in tune with the music. At the bar, patrons stop sipping their drinks; a couple of fans take pictures of the band with the cameras on their phones. Sam lets out a loud gasp and continues singing:

'I'll tell you how much this day has been,
With words I'm gonna say.
We'll chase these clouds away,

And ride those hills and say goodbye to the stars,
When I'm with you!'

The song ends with Brandon rapping his drumsticks across a cymbal, as Rhys holds a long chord. Sam and Dylan stand still, grasping the necks of their guitars, their heads lowering to their instruments. The lights dim, cloaking the band in a hushed darkness. The silence is immediately broken by hands clapping and whistles from the audience. A faint light returns to cover the stage illuminating *The Peachy Peonies* once more. The band takes a second bow: their heads over their waists. Standing they wave, thanking the crowd.

Sam uses a red flannel to fan his face. He bends down and scribbles his name in a person's small book, followed by another.

'Alright, I think we can call it a night.' He announces to his bandmates as the audience starts easing away, heading for the other lounge. 'And I could do with sitting down.'

They jump from the stage, leaving their instruments behind. Pushing through the remaining patrons, they head for the bar. Ted has prepared post-performance drinks: Sam's black forest milkshake, Brandon's cherry soda, Rhys' cola and rum, and Dylan's fruit cider. To their surprise, there are four slices of vanilla cheesecakes drizzled with red fruit coulis and four forks lined up next to them. Sam's mouth gapes with surprise as he feels his hunger pangs winning. He picks up a fork and takes a bite of a piece... and then another, mixing the cheesecake with the fruity coulis.

'Excellent performance, fellers!' Ted grins, wiping a glass clean.

'Thanks Ted! I gotta admit, we've nailed it tonight!' Brandon yells, toasting his sparkling cherry drink: the floating ice chink. 'It's one of the best sets we've done! I've waited too long to make that epic solo!'

'You've already done solos, Brandon,' Rhys retorts, 'in more of our performances than I can actually count.'

'Have I? Oh!'

'It's not every day you've give us a dessert, Ted.' Rhys shakes his head and breaks off a piece of his cheesecake, humming at the pleasant taste. 'What happened to the usual salty snacks? Was this a special delivery?'

'You could say that.' Ted scratches his ear. 'I bought these on my way to work and kept them safe inside the fridge: for extra freshness; and to prevent Brandon from getting his greedy hands on them.'

'What!' Brandon shouts, his mouth full. 'I wouldn't do that!'

'And knowing you were performing tonight, I wanted to give you all a special treat.'

'And a delicious one too, although it does have an unusual texture.' Rhys compliments, nodding. 'It's quite lumpy.'

'Yeah! They're made using cottage cheese, instead of cream cheese. They told me it's new.'

'Huh. Interesting idea, using cottage cheese in things.'

Sam freezes, his fork hovering before his mouth. 'Cottage cheese?'

There is already a piece of the cheesecake inside Sam's mouth. His face pales, but he manages to swallow the dessert without gagging. Putting down his fork, he pushes away the plate with the half-eaten cheesecake.

'Excuse me for a second.'

Jumping from his seat, Sam hurries to the restroom on the other side of the lounge. The door swings open as he rushes through and slams against the wall with force. BAM! Nearby patrons jump with surprise, some frown at the restroom door.

Back at the bar Ted winces. 'Oops! I forgot Sam doesn't like cottage cheese. I should've asked the people in the patisserie to make a non-cottage cheese one. I didn't think.' Picking up Sam's plate he chuckles, 'Although I'm amazed how much he's eaten, before spilling the beans.'

Brandon asks. 'B-but why doesn't he like cottage cheese?'

The other bandmates shake their heads with feigned interest.

'I don't know.' Dylan replies, taking a sip of his cider. 'Has he ever said why?'

'Not to me.' Rhys replies.

Brandon stares at his cherry drink thoughtfully. 'I don't think he's ever explained why he doesn't like cottage cheese.'

'He told me he doesn't like the texture, but he's okay with the taste.' Ted shrugs. 'Perhaps he's had a bad experience with cottage cheese, and eating it acts as a trigger. Strange, huh?'

'I wouldn't say it's strange. I hate mayonnaise.'

'Mayo's not bad.' Rhys counters. 'It's great in chicken sandwiches.'

Dylan purses his lips. 'I don't like mayo either.'

'You too, Dylan? Man, you're unbelievable.' Rhys groans. 'Enough of this. Let's just stick to Sam not liking the texture of cottage cheese and agree not to delve any further into the matter.'

'Agreed.' Ted nods. 'It's an acquired taste for many, just not for Sam.'

Exiting the restroom, Sam returns to the lounge rubbing his forehead, ignoring the glare of patrons who had seen him charge inside. Back in his seat, he rips the skin of his cherry to eat it, dropping the stone to one side. Using a straw, he mixes the whipped cream in his shake; listening to the music from the other lounge:

another band is playing loud music with wailing guitars accompanying the vocals.

'Hey Sam,' Dylan's voice sounds thick after taking another swig of cider. 'How's the planning for tomorrow's ceremony going?'

'It's gone rather smoothly.' Sam replies, sounding confident. 'While I was walking around the docks earlier, I caught a glimpse of something large with a large cloth draped over it. Everything else was bordered up with a temporary wooden wall. I thought of taking a peek, but I didn't want to be too nosy.'

Brandon claps his hands, his eyes widen. 'OOH! Like a surprise? I like surprises!'

'Take it easy with the squeals, will you Brandon?' Rhys retorts, tweaking his ears.

'Sorry.'

Rhys continues. 'Anyway Sam, how did you feel when they've told you what was happening?'

'When I first heard the rumours I brushed them aside, thinking it's just silly talk. Then they confirmed to me that they're making a statue of me and my companions.' Sam pauses. 'It sounded a bit over the top,' he cannot help smiling with another thought, 'but on the other hand, I guess it's a nice gesture. And Addie will enjoy having the attention, given her proud nature.'

Brandon asks, 'Are you gonna do a speech?'

'Probably.' Sam sighs, stirring his milkshake. 'Although I'm not one to make big words for a lotta people.'

'Ey, don't let 'em force you. You should see how it goes.' Dylan ponders, wanting to get his words out in the correct order. 'That is if you want to, right? And don't think you'll botch it up. You botching up? Nah! Think about something that boasts your confidence.' He mindlessly taps his fingernails over the cold, wet glass, listening to its faint tings. 'Like, it could be about – I don't know – peaches swimming in rivers of yoghurt.'

Rhys winces. 'Dylan, you should lay off the smoothies for a while, spouting rubbish like that.'

'But this ain't a smoothie, it's a fruit cider: berry flavoured.'

'Okay. Then maybe lay off on the ciders too.' Rhys turns to Sam, smiling. 'But if I can translate Dylan's gobbledygook for you Sam, it's: just be kind to yourself.'

'That's what I've said!'

'Yeah, in your vernacular.'

'Vernacular?'

Pondering on the discussion, Sam's brow furrows. He puckers his lips. 'Sounds like a good idea,' he nods, 'and I do like peaches in yoghurt. Thanks for the suggestion, Dylan.' He watches the long-haired band member grinning from ear to ear. 'It can't be too difficult to come up with something short and sweet.'

'There you go!' Brandon chimes. 'Short and sweet, just like me!'

The Melsey Clock chimes the seventh hour, reminding Sam to head back home: to Johnny and Mary's house. Picking up Angie he heads to the stairs, pausing briefly to wave Ted farewell as he resumes working at the bar. Walking up the stairs, Sam leaves *The Root* with Dylan, Rhys, and Brandon following close behind. Outside, they stand together on the cobblestone surface of Hollandaise Street. The temperature has fallen even lower, to just a few degrees above zero. The sky has darkened to a deep blue-colour. There is a waning crescent moon and a handful of stars peeking through the wispy clouds to greet them. The nearby main road sounds busy, projecting the roar of vehicle engines accompanied by the *dinging-ring* of a passing tram. Sam sniffs at the mildly hydrocarbon scented air and glances at the sky. Closing his eye he runs his hand over his long fringe, feeling the pleasant aura around him. They take a step out from the protective shelter of Hollandaise Street...

A loud voice booms. 'Hey, there he is!'

Rhys looks over his shoulder and rolls his eyes. 'Oh no!' He groans. 'Not them again.'

A small gang of people run from the other side of the main street. Some are carrying microphones and notebooks in their hands; others are holding cameras. They charge with an almost perfect synchronisation. *It is another interaction with the media!*

A reporter shoves a microphone forward. 'Sam McKenzie, you contained the blast, stopped um, what was it? … The Nether? … And you restored the city after their attack. Tell us, what is your next adventure?'

'I'm not sure,' Sam replies, his voice shaking, 'it's been months since the battle with the Nether. And things are back to normal in Melsey.' He struggles for his next response. Shrugging his shoulders, he adds. 'So I feel like resting on my laurels, if that's okay.'

'And those weird creatures, the Neth… Neth…'

'Nethmites. It's Nether without the "er" and then "mites",' Sam explains, in what feels the thousandth time to him, 'and then combined into one word.'

'Right. Right. We better write that down.'

'Um, I don't think that's necessary—'

But the reporters are busy scribbling the word into their notebooks. Sam looks over to his bandmates. Brandon is fighting the urge to intervene, rolling his sleeves up to his elbows. Rhys's hand is resting on Brandon's shoulder, holding him back. Dylan puts his hands up into the air in exasperation. Sam knows Dylan is not one for physical altercations.

Another reporter lifts their microphone. 'Jim Phillips of MNN, Melsey News Network. You've said you had a power that did most of the work defeating the Nethmites and returning the city to normal. Like magic would you say? How did it work?'

'Well the Aether is a strong power, and unusual you would say—'

'And what about the dragon creatures?' A third reporter interjects. 'What purpose did they served to help the citizens of Melsey?'

'Well, I—'

Sam fiddles Angie's strap. He has not heard from Gaia and Techna since they left the Southern Island, having battled hard to defeat the Nether. The last time he saw the guardians was as they ascended from the strange white void buried deep inside the Nether's storm.

'Well?' The reporter asks. The other reporters nod almost simultaneously in agreement. 'Anything you want to add?'

Sam shakes his head. 'I don't like to speak on their behalf. They fought bravely to save us, I'd say. Now, please excuse me.'

He pushes through the media horde with a struggle, reuniting with his bandmates on the other side of the street. He puts a hand on Brandon and mutters some easing words to calm the drummer. They start walking down the street. The reporters groan, staggering to catch up. Some are forced to stop and gather up their equipment.

'C'mon, Sam!' Jim Phillips, pleads. 'Tell us!'

'Yeah, tell us!' Demands another.

VROOOOOM!

The reporters yelp, halted in their tracks by the edge of the road. The sound comes from a speeding motorcycle, but it's difficult making out any detail of the rider as it zooms past. A cloud of dust is blown over the pavement and into the reporters' faces. They cough and splutter trying to fan away the cloud; cursing whoever it was that has sped past them on the road.

Dylan chuckles at the reporters' suffering. 'Sorry everybody, interview's over.'

Sam sweeps back his fringe and coughs. For the moment the media gang have given up on getting any closer. Instead they turn away and disperse in the opposite direction. He gazes along the length of the road: there are a couple of cars approaching. He frowns. *Who was riding the motorcycle that had zoomed passed him at high speed?*

'I gotta tell you...' Sam huffs, 'I wish they would lay off the questions about my friends.'

'I agree.' Brandon replies. 'They just keep bugging you, and that irks me too.'

Dylan shakes his head. 'Media: you can't live with them; you can't live without them.'

'Tell me about it.' Sam sighs. 'They just poke their noses into my business, even more than Mandy and her friends.' Realising what he has said, he chuckles, adding. 'They're actually worse than Mandy.'

Continuing their walk along the high street, they carefully cross another road after waiting for a car to pass. Brandon leads the way, skipping ahead and humming a tune out aloud; much to Rhys' chagrin and Dylan's amusement. They reach Hunter's Road. It's quiet here. Most houses have lights on, behind tightly closed curtains. The trees lining Hunter's Road have lost most of their leaves. The fallen leaves are piled high against the pavement. There is an urgent flutter of wings and a screech, as a rook takes off from its resting place on an adjacent gate. The creeping shadow of a cat prowls beyond the fence.

Sam stops walking. Here comes another roaring sound. Another motorcycle is approaching. Its headlight is brightly lit, forcing them to shield their eyes. The motorcycle zooms past. They turn and catch the dark shape of the rider, formed from the illumination of the headlight. The motorcycle disappears from view, turning away at the junction. Sam has seen a motorcycle like this before. It was on the day he returned to Melsey and restored the city from the Nether's grasp. There had been four of them then, each with the same shaped forms riding them. The riders anonymous inside their helmets. He wonders if this motorcycle is one of the four he had seen before. Snapping away his thoughts, Sam hurries after his bandmates, who are approaching Johnny and Mary's house.

'It's not like you to be slacking.' Brandon muses, his eyebrow cocked. 'What's your interest in that motorcyclist, buddy?'

'I'm not sure.' Sam switches his gaze between his bandmates and the dark empty space the motorcycle disappeared into. He flinches from a snap of an icy-cold breeze. 'I couldn't see the rider's face, but I think I've seen them before. A while back. Except then there were four of them: banded together.'

He falls silent, glancing one final time along the road; just in case the motorcycle might return. He waits … but there's no sign, only the sound of the wind and the occasional rustling of birds in the trees.

Brandon breaks the silence. 'I just hope they aren't here to stir the peace, right fellers?'

Rhys nods. 'I agree.'

'Me too,' adds Dylan, 'although it looked a fine-looking steel horse.'

They reach Johnny and Mary's house. The hallway light is on, peeking through the tiny window in the front door. The garden gate swings in the wind, its hinges squeaking: demanding to be oiled. There are branches of ivy decorating the walls of the house. They almost reach the roof, their progress untouched.

'Here we are.' Sam makes his way to the gate and pushes it open. He winces at the squeak. 'I wonder what Nan is cooking tonight.'

He steps through onto the small, paved path leading to the front door; pausing he turns towards his bandmates.

Brandon pats his stomach and smacks his lips. 'Whatever it is… it smells good.'

Sam chuckles at the drummer's instinctive appreciation of good food. 'Nan's food always smells great, huh Brandon?' He smiles at the others waiting on the other side of the gate. 'Thanks for tonight's performance, and for accompanying me home.'

'No problem, bud.' Dylan smiles. 'We thought you'd like some company on the way home, especially after speaking to those media weirdoes.'

'We need to head home ourselves.' Rhys looks over his shoulder. He winces as a thought comes to him. 'I hope Brandon won't start singing again.'

'No sweat, Rhys!' Brandon yells with an echo. 'I won't be singing.'

'Case in point.' Rhys pats Sam's back, smiling at him. 'Goodnight, Sam.'

'See you, Rhys!'

After waving goodbye, Brandon starts humming as he catches up with a speedy Rhys. 'I'm only humming, Rhys!'

'I know. That's why I'm walking faster.'

Sam laughs as he watches his friends walk away, passing quiet houses. He is standing with Dylan, who is leaning over the gate. 'Brandon does love trying out his vocal cords, eh?'

'He does,' Dylan nods, 'but it's better for everyone when he sticks to the drums.' He chuckles, rubbing his cheek. He feels his foot tapping on the pavement, as if waiting for his next move. 'I'd better get going too. Say *hi* to Johnny and Mary for me.'

'Will you be coming to the Docks tomorrow?'

'Of course, we'll all be there. Why wouldn't we? Especially if there's refreshments going. That'll excite me, like it'll excite Brandon.'

Sam smiles, pushing the garden gate shut and securing the latch. There's another protesting squeak. 'See yah tomorrow, Dyl!'

'Later buddy!'

Dylan trots after Rhys and Brandon. Despite the increased distance, their voices remain distinct enough for Sam to hear Brandon arguing with Rhys, while humming to himself. As their voices fade away, he glances along the other side of Hunter's Road: something catches his eye. He focuses his gaze at a motorcycle idling, captured within the cone of light of a lamppost some distance away. Sam squints at its rider, who appears to be staring back at him. The helmet still conceals the rider's face. After a lingering moment of suspense, the rider revs the engine and drives away.

Sam keeps his gaze on the motorcycle as it passes. He shakes his head. *What interest does the motorcyclist have with him?* Trudging up the garden path, he approaches the front door; eager to be welcomed inside by Bonnie and his guardians. He reaches out for the door handle…

'*HHHROOOOOOOAAAAAAAAAAA!*'

Sam jumps in surprise as a thundering roar erupts through the air. It is so loud; he is forced to cover both ears with his hands. Yet despite the volume, the sound seems to originate somewhere far away: beyond the city limits. The ground shudders beneath his feet. The roar continues, loud and relentless. Sam sinks to his knees, wanting the silence to return.

'*HHHROOOOOOOAAAAAAAAAAA!*'

The thundering noise results in the neighbourhood awakening. Lights are turned on in the surrounding houses and front doors burst open. People rush outside to see what is causing this commotion. Many wear night gowns wrapped around their agitated bodies, others have hastily pulled on warmer coats or jackets. They look up and down the road: at different houses, up at the rooftops; seeking a cause for this deafening roar. Finally, after a minute or so, the roar fades to relative silence. All that remains is the wind brushing over treetops, until the neighbourhood fills with the sound of chattering voices. Most seem agitated and confused through Sam's muffled ears. Recovering from the trembling noise, Sam lowers his hands and watches as residents begin walking back into their homes: still muttering. Doors close and locks click, and hallway lights blink out.

He coughs, clutching his trembling knees. 'Golly! What a rush!'

The front door opens and Mary peers out. 'Sam? Are you alright? What in tarnation was that noise? It can't be thunder, surely. The weather is all wrong.'

Sam looks up at the calm sky. 'I'm sure it wasn't thunder, Nan.' He replies, his voice cracking from his previous fear. 'The clouds are not thick enough for lightning.'

'Well whatever it was, it caused us to jump with shock inside.' Mary chuckles nervously. She averts her gaze from Sam, who is looking at her with a pinched face. 'Sorry, that was a bad joke.' She beckons him to come inside. 'There's rice tea waiting for you inside.'

'That's what I like to hear!'

As Sam walks inside, Hunter's Road appears completely empty. Stepping through the hallway he heads for the stairs, while Mary returns to the kitchen. Entering his bedroom, he places Angie carefully down onto the floor and then removes his cap and tosses it onto his desk. He glances at his precious red and yellow striped scarf hanging at the end of his bed; and then at the photographs of his friends covering the corkboard on the wall. He smiles. Returning downstairs, Sam heads for the lounge. Inside her playpen, Bonnie is playing with her squeaky toy, rolling from side to side. She stops playing, hearing Sam's presence and grins.

Sam pets the pup's head. 'Hey Bon. What have you been up to while I was away?'

Bonnie barks and continues rolling around with her paws clutching the toy.

Johnny enters the lounge carrying a bowl of dog biscuits from the kitchen. 'She's had a lot of fun playing with Mary, while I was training the new baristas.' He chuckles, adding. 'They're very keen to benefit from my experience. Boy, I was busy!'

Sam covers a snort with a hand. 'As always.'

'Yep! Proud to be helpful.' Johnny lowers himself into his chair, groaning from his aching muscles, He quickly relaxes onto the soft cushions. 'How was your performance at *The Root*?'

'Pretty good.'

Sam sits in his armchair and reaches for his tea. Hot liquid touches his lips, causing him to flinch. He quickly blows over the steam.

'There wasn't much of a crowd, but it's been good. It's always nice to have a smaller audience.' He pauses briefly. 'The fellas escorted me home after I was waylaid by the media.'

Johnny shakes his head, smirking. 'They're still obsessed with you.' He turns to a nearby window and his brow furrows. 'I think they're hoping for more drama, some other disaster with you at the centre.' He pauses and looks at Sam. 'Perhaps they're right.'

'What is it, Gramps?'

'There's something odd out there, huh?'

'You mean that strange noise?'

'Yep! Heard it with clear ears; made me slop my tea.' Johnny nods at the wet cloth on the coffee table next to his half-filled cup of rice tea. 'It nearly made me fall out of my chair too. I wasn't thunder. It was loud, but it didn't sound close-by. It felt like an eruption or something.'

'Yeah, it made me jump too. And it awakened the whole neighbourhood.' Sam puckers his lips. 'Hm. The fellers will have heard it too, while they were walking home.'

'I'm sure they did.'

'It did sound strange, didn't it?'

Johnny smiles. 'Maybe the mountains are grumbling over a sore head.' He laughs, half-heartedly. 'Okay, I know it's not that. But if it does happen again, we've gotta have our ears trained so we can gauge where it's coming from. It could be anything: like something's been disturbed, or has arrived without introduction.'

'Maybe. Maybe I'll ask Rhys what he thinks.'

'Are they coming to the ceremony tomorrow?'

'Dylan said they are.'

'Good for them. I hope Brandon doesn't get too excited with the catering.'

'I'm sure Rhys will have him under control.' Sam laughs. 'The trouble with Brandon is his eyes are bigger than his stomach.'

'Okay, food's ready!' Mary calls out from the kitchen. 'Come and get it while it's hot!'

'Speaking of food,' Johnny remarks, patting his belly. 'We should be excited about our curry and rice. The only roar I'm hearing right now, is the sound of my stomach rumbling!'

Printed in Great Britain
by Amazon

28970812R00202